I0672198

Somewhere West of Roads

by

A. E. Poynor

Published by OMM Writing

Printed by CreateSpace, An Amazon.com Company

A. E. Poynor

Somewhere West of Roads

by

A. E. Poynor

OMM Writing, 47121 Wildberry Ct.
Kenai, AK 99611

ISBN: 0-9667915-4-1
ISBN-13: 978-0-9667915-4-9

Cover photo by M. Scott Moon
http://moon.photoshelter.com

I wanted the gold, and I sought it,
I scrambled and mucked like a slave.
Was it famine or scurvy - I fought it;
I hurled my youth into a grave.
I wanted the gold, and I got it.

From "The Spell of the Yukon"
by Robert Service

ACKNOWLEDGEMENTS

Although the author of a novel gets the credit, writing a book is never the work of just a single individual. Without the help of many other people, the author would not be able to pull everything together. With that in mind, I would like to thank the following people for helping *Somewhere West of Roads* become a novel.

Phil Nash, thank you for your guidance on the legal aspects of a complicated will.

No writer gets it right the first (or second, third, fourth, ad infinitum) time. Grammatical errors, spelling, skipped words and all manner of mistakes are missed by the bleary eye of the writer. I also owe a debt to my "cold readers" for not being afraid to tell me when certain passages plain sucked. Annie Kendall, Alyx McNeal, Holly Nunn, Virginia Walters and Marilyn Wheeless, thank you for your time, honesty, and most of all, sharp eyes.

While I have mined recreationally for over two decades, I want to thank Ken and Winona Lee of Cache Creek Cabins for explaining some of the ins and outs of running a recreational mining camp. And Eric Treider, I don't know whether to thank or curse you for getting me hooked on mining all those years ago. You did redeem yourself somewhat by helping me research smelting methods, so thanks.

CHAPTER 1

"My car's the gray Corolla, over there," the man said as the bouncer ushered him outside.

"No, your ride is the yellow one at the curb."

"But I'm not drunk," the man protested, "I barely got through the door when some guy sucker punched me."

"Oh, please," the bouncer replied sarcastically, tightening his grip on the man's arm as if expecting a struggle. "Take your pick, a private cab, or a public black and white one with flashing lights."

"What about the guy that decked me?"

"Not my problem."

The cabbie looked his passenger over critically as the bouncer stuffed the man into the back seat. The man gave the cabbie his address, and the bouncer stepped back to watch the cab pull away.

"If you're gonna fuckin' puke, tell me so I can pull over," the cabbie snapped as he jerked away from the curb. "I don't want no fuckin' puke in my office. Understand?"

"Yeah, no puking in your office."

The man looked down at the briefcase in his lap. Under a deeply embossed symbol of a globe at the top of the briefcase, "Occidental Investing" was printed in large gold lettering. Below that was a second line in much smaller gold lettering which read, "John C. Barstow, Investment Counselor."

John C. Barstow laughed to himself. *"Not much of an investment counselor. Don't have a penny to my name."*

Leaning against the door, John rolled down the window to let some air blow against his face. The wind felt cool on the throbbing spot under his right eye.

"Hang on! Hang on!" the cabbie shouted. "Let me pull off!"

"I am not going to puke!" John shouted back. "I'm just getting some cool air on my eye."

"Okay, okay. Just tell me if you're gonna puke. Don't want no fuckin' puke in my office."

John looked at the briefcase again and wondered why he was even dragging it around. It no longer served any purpose. After five years, Occidental had simply dumped him; no reason, no warning, no offer to help find another job, not even a sympathetic handshake. With a simple, "John, this is your last day with Occidental. Security will escort you off premises," his career as an investment counselor was over. The chickenshits waited until the last minute of the workday, just to make sure he couldn't let his co-workers know he was history.

"Just as well," John thought. *"Being an investment counselor is nothing more than being a sleazy, door to door insurance salesman dressed in a better suit."*

Still, John had to laugh to himself about the irony of the situation. He took the job with Occidental after sobering up. At the time he thought getting sober would get his wife back after she'd had enough of his drinking, and left him. For nearly two years he tried to convince her he'd changed. It didn't work. She had changed too.

"A new husband will do that to a girl," he thought, then cursed at his own stupidity.

John had stopped at the bar on a whim. Not a good choice for an alcoholic, but he didn't want to go home. Home should be someplace you want to be. Home should be someplace warm and inviting, with someone there who wants you there. That didn't describe where he was headed. He was headed to an empty apartment.

"At least it ought to be empty by now," John thought, *"Shelley's had all day to pack everything off. More irony. Wife leaves because I partied too much. Girlfriend leaves because I*

wouldn't party at all."

The cab pulled into the empty parking space which should have held John's car. John put the fare on his credit card. He signed the receipt and handed it back to the cabbie, who looked it over carefully.

"What! No fuckin' tip?" the cabbie snapped as John turned to leave.

"No fuckin' puke," John shot back over his shoulder.

John opened the door to the apartment and flipped on the light. Shelley had been efficient. There was nothing in the living room except his battered old recliner; a remnant from his marriage.

"Back to square one," John mumbled as he patted the back of the chair like an old friend, "at least until the end of the month."

The bedroom held his clothes stacked neatly in piles on the floor, or hanging on his end of the closet. The bathroom held his toothbrush and paste, one towel, one washcloth and a bar of soap. John picked up the washcloth and wandered to the kitchen, opened the freezer on the refrigerator and retrieved several ice cubes. Walking to the sink, he noticed an envelope on the counter. There was a note in Shelley's handwriting on the envelope, held in place by her key for the apartment. "This came for you today, certified. I signed for it."

He turned on the tap to soak the washcloth, and winced as he touched it to the swollen area just below his right eye. He scanned the envelope. It was addressed to his full name: Johnathon Calhoun Barstow. He flipped the envelope over and read the return address: Law Office of Wesley J. Bartholomew, Esq., 1545 L Street, Suite 201, Anchorage, Alaska.

That was curious. The only connection he had with Alaska was his uncle Hank, his mother's brother. John hadn't seen him since Hank had shown up unexpectedly at his sister's funeral. The last contact had been a sympathy card Hank sent following John's father's suicide, the year following his mom's death.

"That was what," John wondered aloud to himself, "almost nine years ago? Yeah, the same time I made a serious commitment to a social life with Mr. Cuervo. Mom, if you'd only known the course of events your cancer kicked off, you'd have at least given the chemo a try."

John distinctly remembered the note Hank had scrawled in the card. He could see the card as clearly as if he were holding it at the moment. It was one of those flowery ones that assures the remaining family things are better off for the departed, even though they suck for those left standing. Only in John's case, aside from Hank, he was the entire remaining family. Hank's handwriting had taken some deciphering, and was brief.

"I'm sorry to hear about your dad. We're the only family each of us has now. Don't be a stranger – Hank."

At the time, it struck John the note was more like an invitation to a backyard barbecue than one of condolence. He had thrown the card out with the first empty tequila bottle.

John tossed the envelope back on the counter and made his way to the living room. He felt completely used up. He was an orphan, two-time loser at love, and now, unemployed. Stretching out in the recliner, John mused that whoever decked him had actually done him a huge favor.

"*Shit, getting punched out was the best part of the day.*" John winced again as he rolled his head onto the hand holding the ice. "*Life sucks, and then you die,*" he thought as he drifted off to sleep.

A shaft of sunlight hit John's eyes, and he sat up quickly. His first thought was that he would be late for work, but then remembered getting to work was not an issue at the moment. His heart thumped in his chest. With every thump, he felt a throb under his right eye. Standing up slowly, John made his way to the bathroom. A quick look in the mirror showed he had a beauty of a mouse sitting high on his right cheek.

"*That will take a few days to go away,*" he thought. "*So much for running right out to line up job interviews. 'Hi my name is John, I'd like a job as a bouncer, or punching bag, whichever is available at the moment.'*"

He wandered into the kitchen to get more ice for his eye and saw the envelope from Wesley J. Bartholomew, Esquire. Carefully opening the envelope he pulled out the contents. The letter was bulky, and as John unfolded it another sealed envelope fell out. The second envelope was unmarked, so he set it aside for the moment and concentrated on the letter. Under the letterhead was the date of March first.

"Dear Mr. Barstow:

I regret to inform you that your uncle, Henry C. Grant, has passed away. First, I would like to offer my condolences at your loss.

"As Mr. Grant's lawyer, and following his directions, I have been named executor and trustee of his estate. You, as his only living relative, are named as a beneficiary of his estate. Per Mr. Grant's wishes, and specific directions, I am only allowed to explain the details of his estate with you in person.

"Enclosed with this letter is another envelope which contains a cashier's check made out to yourself for the sum of two-thousand dollars. The money will cover the cost of transportation to Anchorage, and lodging while in Anchorage. Once in Anchorage, please call my office, and an appointment will be arranged immediately for our meeting.

"I must point out, time is of the essence. Your rapid response to this summons is imperative. Per the instructions of Mr. Grant's trust, if you do not respond within two weeks of receipt of this letter his estate will be disbursed in a fashion that does not include yourself.

Sincerely,

Wesley J. Bartholomew, Esq."

"Okay," John thought, amused, *"this must be some sort of scam. I've got news for you, buddy, you couldn't get a fancy latte with the entire sum in my account."*

He set the letter down and opened the smaller envelope. It contained a cashier's check from the First National Bank in Anchorage, made out to Johnathon C. Barstow.

Suddenly, John's eye didn't hurt as much. He grabbed the letter and read it again, slowly. Questions about the legitimacy of the letter kept flowing in and out of John's mind. When he read the letter for a third time, the phone number for Wesley J. Bartholomew's office caught his eye.

"We'll just give old Wes a call," he thought. *"Nobody but a crackpot would expect someone to come running in response to just a letter."*

John returned to the living room and rummaged around in the briefcase to find his cell phone, then paused.

"What time is it in Alaska?" he wondered. *"It's eight-thirty here, but what time zone is Alaska? At least an hour behind LA, maybe two. It wouldn't hurt to give it an hour, at least. Maybe old Wes doesn't need the time to get his shit together, but I sure do."*

After a shower and a change of clothes, John walked down the street to a café. John sat quietly in the corner, studiously ignoring the stares of the other patrons as he sipped his coffee and nibbled on a roll. He felt as if his eye must be glowing fluorescent pink. Still, it was better sitting there to pass the time than to pace around in an empty apartment.

He tried hard to remember his uncle, but at his mother's funeral everything had seemed surreal, and John remembered very little of that entire period of time. The last time he could vividly remember seeing Hank was when he was a boy, almost thirty years ago. To a young boy, Hank was bigger than life and different from every other adult he had ever known; just the sort of man that would leave a boy in awe. Hank was considerably older than his sister. He had a face weathered and brown, covered mostly with a bushy beard and moustache. He was loud. He spoke in a booming voice that echoed like the vast wilderness from which he had come. He didn't dress like any grown up John had ever met. Even in the Southern California weather, Hank wore a flannel shirt, canvas pants and heavy boots.

"It's all I've got," Hank had explained when chastised by his sister for dressing so casually, "and I'm not wasting money on clothes I can't wear back home."

Hank had come for Thanksgiving at the insistence of his sister for the express purpose of seeing his parents for, as John's mom had put it, "what might be the last time." The visit devolved into a family argument. Hank's choice of lifestyle, and the location in which he chose to live it, were points of extreme disapproval.

"Gold prospector my eye!" Grandpa Grant had roared. "You're nothing but a bum! You scrape around in the dirt all summer, and lay up drunk all winter. You don't worry about your own family. Your own parents! You're worthless!"

This assessment of Hank's life and worth had come on the heels of Hank regaling tales of adventure in the Alaskan "bush" to young John. There had been encounters with moose, caribou, "salmon so thick you could walk across the river on 'em," and bears. Bears so big they could kill a man with one swipe of a huge paw. But it had been worth it, according to Hank, he'd finally hit pay dirt. He was now the owner of a patented claim. He might never be wealthy, he had told John, but he was beyond rich in the things that truly mattered.

To illustrate his point, Hank had produced a crumpled black and white photo of a group of ramshackle buildings. In the foreground of the picture, Hank was smiling broadly and shaking hands with another bearded man.

"See that, Johnny?" Hank had asked almost breathlessly, "That's mine. That's my life right there. That's the Last Chance. That's all the more any man could ever ask for."

His grandfather's statement hadn't changed John's opinion of his uncle, but it galvanized what was already a bad relationship between his uncle and his grandparents. Hank didn't attend either of his own parents' funerals.

John gave some thought to the picture. The buildings had looked like a bunch of old shacks straight out of a grade B western ghost town. If they looked bad thirty years ago, what kind of shape would they be in now? It didn't seem likely the old man could have left much of an estate. On the other hand, it was for certain a lawyer wasn't going to toss out two grand of his own money. Obviously, there was something worth looking into.

Checking his watch, John saw he'd managed to kill almost two hours. It was time to make a call.

"Hey, you ought to see the other guy," John said cheerily to a couple who had been staring at him, "he'll never play the piano again."

Back at the apartment, John picked up the letter from the counter and settled into the recliner to make the call. There was a long pause after John finished dialing before he heard the first ring. After the second ring, a lady's voice answered, "Bartholomew Law office, this is Doreen, may I help you?"

"Yes, my name is John Barstow. I received a letter from Mr. Bartholomew yesterday. May I speak to him, please?"

There was a pause as if Doreen had something to think over before she answered. "One moment, please, I'll see if Mr.

Bartholomew is available." There was a click, followed by canned music.

A veteran of countless sales calls, John knew the game. Bartholomew was nearby, and Doreen was going to see if he was willing to talk. If not, there would be some sort of excuse to put him off. John was not about to play that game.

"Mr. Barstow," Doreen said when she came back, "Mr. Bartholomew asked me to relay that he was *not* going to speak to you over the phone."

"Put Wesley J. Bartholomew, *Esquire* on the phone, lady. I don't have time to play games."

There was a click as Doreen tried to put John back on hold, but didn't quite get the button all the way down. John could hear the subsequent conversation clearly.

"Mr. Bartholomew, I don't think this guy is going to take no for an answer," Doreen said in almost a whine. She obviously knew what to expect.

"You tell that bone-headed, flat-land, city-slick, Californicator he needs to read that letter and get his ass up here by the twentieth, or someone else becomes beneficiary to Hardrock's estate!" Bartholomew roared. "I don't have the time, or the patience, to suffer fools."

"Yes, sir," Doreen replied sheepishly.

At that, John's end of the connection was cut back to canned music as Doreen pushed the button to take him off hold. There was a brief stretch of violins playing "Stairway to Heaven" before Doreen realized what was going on.

"Are you there, Mr. Barstow?"

"Indeed."

"I guess you heard Mr. Bartholomew's answer, then."

"Indeed. He's a bit of a cranky old fart, isn't he?"

"Let's just say, he is emphatic about the points laid out in the letter."

"Okay, I can spend your money. Just one question though. Who is Hardrock?"

There was an uncomfortable pause on Doreen's end. "Hardrock was Mr. Grant's nickname. I really must go now, Mr. Barstow. Good-bye."

John leaned back in his old comfortable friend. That had

been one of the most bizarre phone calls he'd ever made, and one of the most intriguing.

CHAPTER 2

It wasn't nearly as hard to get a flight to Anchorage as John had anticipated. He managed to get a reservation for an early, direct flight out of LA arriving in Anchorage at mid-day. March was obviously not a month with a great deal of draw to Alaska. With any luck, he'd line things out with old Wes and head home the next day, if he wanted. The ticket wasn't as expensive as he'd expected, so he upgraded to first class.

The flight to Anchorage was smooth until just before the plane started to descend. The seat belt light came on half an hour before they were to land with an announcement "some turbulence" was expected as they approached Anchorage for the landing.

"You ever been to Anchorage?" the man next to John asked.

"No, first time."

"Well, if they say *some* turbulence, you can bet there will be *plenty*. Just to let you know."

"Thanks, but flying isn't a fear of mine."

"Yeah, not yet." The man cinched his seat belt down tight and went back to reading his book.

The plane descended through a thin layer of spotty clouds and the mountains came into stark view. John thought to himself that he had never seen anything so bleak, and at the same time so beautiful, in his life. The mountain peaks were sharp. Some ridges looked as if they could split a man in two if he tried to stand on them. The snow covered everything except the steepest of angles, and the jagged outcroppings created dark, shadowy holes on the mountainsides where shafts of sunlight managed to make their way through the broken overcast. There wasn't a beach. The mountains ran straight to the water's edge, where a thin white line at the bottom of the mountains marked the beginning of the water. The water itself was choked with ice.

The plane banked steeply to the right and offered a nearly vertical look to the ground. A ribbon of road ran just above the white line at the base of the mountains. Vehicles teetered on the brink of the water's edge along the ribbon. The plane was recovering from the right-hand bank when the first sharp jolt hit.

"Whoa!" John found himself saying aloud.

"Told you," the cautionary man said. "There's no such thing as a smooth approach into Anchorage. Depending on the weather, this part of the flight can be anything from mildly bumpy, to outright violent."

"You fly in much?" John asked, more as a form of distraction than out of curiosity.

"Yeah. I'm a sloper."

"Sloper?"

"Yeah, I work on the North Slope in the oil fields. By five o'clock tonight, I'll be in Deadhorse, at Prudhoe Bay. I make this trip every two weeks."

John felt the plane shudder then slam down, only to bounce up violently. He felt nauseous, and could hear babies crying in the coach seating.

"They ever... you know... go down?" John asked nervously.

"The flights? Naw. These planes are built for worse than this. Say, you look a little pale. Might want to get your burpy bag out."

John was struggling to keep from throwing up. He swallowed hard, but his mouth was dry. However, he'd be damned if he was going to suffer the indignity of holding up a paper bag in the grim anticipation of parting with his breakfast. The plane continued to descend, running the gauntlet of Turnagain Arm. Anchorage was now visible out the window, and John concentrated on the layout of the city to try and take his mind off how sick he felt. He was making headway on the nausea when the lady across the aisle started to retch. John found himself clawing desperately at the magazine pocket in front of him. His seat mate calmly handed him the bag from his own magazine pocket.

"Keep it in the bag, man."

The plane continued past Anchorage, out over the Cook Inlet, and the turbulence subsided to an occasional bump. John had recovered from his bout of airsickness, and was dealing with only an occasional hiccup.

"Excuse me," John started to say, but was interrupted with a hiccup.

His seat mate cut him short, "Here, have a piece of gum. Hell, take the whole pack."

"Sorry," John replied, taking a piece of gum and putting it in his mouth. After chewing a few moments he continued to ask his question, "Didn't we just pass Anchorage? Is it too rough to land?"

The man laughed, "Naw, we'll swing around in just a moment for round two with the turbulence on the final approach. I'd keep that bag handy."

True to the man's prediction, the plane banked right all the way around and headed back in the direction it had come. The whine of the engines rose and fell as the pilot negotiated the turbulence with increased flaps. The plane felt as if were floating on the gusts of air. The result was more of a gentle side-to-side rocking motion which didn't create the stomach dropping sensation of the earlier turbulence. The descent rate increased as they approached the airport, and the turbulence all but stopped. John saw huge chunks of dirty, gray ice sitting in an expanse of mud, and then the plane was touching down.

As soon as the door opened, and the flight crew gave the nod, John practically sprinted down the jet way. As he passed the podium at the entrance to the jet way the ticket agent called to him.

"Sir?"

John stopped and turned to the lady, "Yes?"

"Unless you want to keep that as some sort of souvenir," she nodded at the burpy bag in his hand, "you can drop it in the trash can."

John felt his face go red. "Oh, yeah. Thanks."

John found navigating Ted Stevens International was simplicity itself compared to LAX. He walked down the stairs to the baggage claim area instead of riding the escalator, glad for the chance to stretch his legs. He found the carousel displaying his flight number and thought to himself that Alaskans were a trusting bunch, noting there were no barriers around the carousels, nor anyone to confirm luggage claim tickets. The wait was short. The light on the carousel started flashing and the carousel started turning just minutes after his arrival. In short order John had his single bag. He had packed light. He didn't plan on staying long.

He checked the time as he walked from the carousel following the signs toward the car rental counters. It was not even 1 pm. Hoping he could conclude business the same day, John set his bag down, pulled out his cell phone and the letter from Wesley J. Bartholomew. Doreen answered the phone immediately.

"Hello, Doreen, this is John Barstow. I have arrived in Anchorage."

"Mr. Barstow, how nice to hear from you, again," Doreen said as if she actually meant it. "Where are you staying?"

"Well, I don't know. I'm still at the airport, and was hoping..."

"Still at the airport? Perfect!" Doreen said excitedly. "Mr. Barstow, may I have your phone number? Mr. Bartholomew is out to lunch at the moment, and I'll have him call you immediately. Stay right where you are."

John gave Doreen his cell number and she hung up. John hadn't even taken ten steps toward the car rental counters when his phone rang. He stepped to one side of the corridor and set his bag down to answer it.

"Hello," he said, expecting to hear Doreen tell him she couldn't reach Mr. Bartholomew.

"Where are you?" a deep male voice demanded to know.

"Who is this?" John demanded back.

"Well, it isn't Time-Life Books, that's for damn sure," the male voice shot back. "This is Wes Bartholomew. Again, where are you?"

"I'm at the airport."

"I know that," Bartholomew snapped. "*Where* in the airport are you?"

John gave a moment's consideration to hanging up on the cantankerous lawyer, but thought better of it. "I'm just about to the car rental counters."

"You need to go back upstairs, outside, cross the drop-off lane and wait for me in the passenger pick-up lane," Bartholomew directed. "I'm less than five minutes away, and headed there right now."

"Right now?"

"Hardrock never mentioned you were slow. Yes, now. My afternoon is open. Be out at the curb, traffic can't stop to wait, and I don't like looping around. See you in less than five minutes."

"Wait!" John shouted into his phone, "How will I recognize you?"

"You don't need to, I'll recognize you."

With that, Bartholomew hung up. John pocketed his cell phone and wondered to himself how much more bizarre things could get. He picked up his bag and rode the escalator back to the main floor of the airport where he found an exit. Looking outside, across the drop off lane, John wished he'd worn his coat, instead of packing it at the bottom of his bag. The passenger pick-up zone was covered with broken patches of ice, and piles of snow were randomly situated in the middle of the uncovered area. John wondered if those five minutes were literal, or figurative. He decided it would be best not to second-guess the guy. Bartholomew didn't seem to be someone you would want to piss off.

The first blast of cold wind almost took John's breath away. He had expected it to be colder than LA, but hadn't anticipated just how cold it would be, and definitely hadn't considered wind-chill.

He walked down the curb, the wind biting into his face. Setting his bag down, he stuffed his hands deeply into his pockets. Fortunately, the wind was to his back as he looked down the pick-up lane. Another man walked up and stood next to him.

"Mister," the man, who was wearing a heavy work jacket and a thick knit cap, said to John, "I'm cold, so you have *got* to be freezing. Where's your coat?"

"All the way on the bottom of my bag," John said, through chattering teeth.

"You're not from around here, are you?"

John shook his head.

"Well, now you know where to pack your coat in the future," the man said and laughed.

John tried to smile, but found his face didn't want to

A. E. Poynor

respond. He hopped a little to try and keep his blood circulating and looked down the drive, trying to conjure up a vehicle he could seek refuge in.

"Come on, Bartholomew," he thought, *"if you don't get here pretty damn quick, you'll be handling my estate."*

He decided right there that as soon as things were finished up with Bartholomew, he was heading home. Any desire to explore Anchorage was completely gone. All he wanted now, was to take care of business and get back to the warmth of California.

John cursed himself silently for not insisting Bartholomew tell him what he was driving. He continued hopping lightly, first on one foot, then on the other. His ears burned from the cold wind, but he didn't want to sacrifice his hands to keep them warm. He kept his hands stuffed tightly in his pockets. John was about to go back into the terminal when a vehicle drove into view. John's hope fell when he saw it was an old pickup with a snowplow.

"Well, at least your ride made it," John said to the man in the work jacket.

"Not my ride," the man replied. "At least it better not be. When I left, my wife was driving a white Lexus."

The old pickup slowed down as it approached. It had definitely seen better days. It was brown, and had scattered rust patches intersecting the remnants of chromed trim clinging in broken sections down the sides. Dents had replaced the missing trim. On the front of the hood, just above the well worn snowplow, "olet" was all that remained of the original lettering. Rust had eaten away at the lower portions of the wheel wells. Through the cracked windshield, John could make out an older man with a neatly trimmed beard, wearing a red plaid coat over a shirt with a bolo tie. The truck stopped in front of John, and the driver leaned over to open the door.

"Just throw your bag in the bed and climb in," Wesley J.

Bartholomew instructed loudly. When John didn't move or reply, Bartholomew asked, "You froze to that spot?"

John stared into the truck. The interior was as thoroughly worn as the outside. Pieces of foam rubber protruded through cracks in the seat. The vinyl on the dash was split in several places. When he looked at the floor, John saw there were several holes where the bare metal had rusted entirely through. John looked back to Bartholomew. "Is this thing even street legal?"

"It's not like you've got a better offer at the moment," Bartholomew snapped. "Throw your bag in the bed and get in, quick. It's getting cold in here."

John looked into the bed of the pickup. It was full of snow on top of various odd shapes. He lifted the bag and placed it snugly against the cab of the truck, then slid into the cab. There was no handshake; no "nice to meet you."

"Slam the door hard," Bartholomew barked, "unless you want a surprise when it pops open. And buckle up, we've got a seatbelt law."

John did as he was told, and Bartholomew jammed the truck into gear to lurch away from the curb. "I really need to get the clutch replaced," Bartholomew muttered to himself as they picked up speed going down the ramp out of the airport. Once the truck was in motion, Bartholomew dispensed with the use of the clutch entirely, opting instead, to simply let up on the accelerator to yank the stick shift out of one gear and jam it into the next. A slight grinding noise occurred each time he shifted, but the process felt smooth. Bartholomew turned left onto a main artery and they headed in the general direction of the tall buildings indicating downtown Anchorage. There was no effort on either of the men's part to make conversation.

John stared out the window. Snow was piled high along the edges of the streets, and looked in spots as if had been shaved away to provide pedestrians a walkway, except there weren't any pedestrians. "*I wouldn't walk anywhere on a day like this, either,*" he thought.

The truck rattled as if it were going to fall apart at any moment, and after several minutes, John felt the need to make some conversation.

"Interesting truck you've got here, Mr. Bartholomew."

"Yeah, she's a bit rough," the older man grunted, "but runs good enough to pass the emissions test, and does a good job of plowing. I've had this truck for twenty years and two marriages. After the first marriage, it was the only thing I did have. I'm lucky she didn't want the truck."

They turned off the main road and pulled into a parking lot with piles of snow shoved to one end of the lot. John guessed it was some of Bartholomew's handiwork.

"We're here," the lawyer said flatly. "My office is on the second floor of the building. You can put your bag in the cab of the truck, unless you want to drag it in with you."

"I'd like to take it in, if it's not a problem," John replied. "I want to dig out my coat."

"I'll bet you do," Bartholomew chuckled. It was the first sign of anything other than a poor disposition the man had shown. "Follow me."

John followed Bartholomew into the building. The lobby wasn't large, but held several nicely upholstered chairs and tables with lamps. The floor appeared to be marble tile, and the walls were coated with a dark wood paneling which looked to be walnut. It reminded John of a hotel lobby, except there was no desk for check-in. There were several doors off the lobby. The two men proceeded to the far end of the lobby and started up a set of stairs.

"We could take the elevator," Bartholomew said, "but it's only one flight, and I enjoy the exercise."

John saw a directory for the building at the base of the stairs. The suites on the first floor were held by engineering, law and consultant groups. Only one suite was listed on the second floor, that of Bartholomew Law.

On the landing of the second floor, John looked out on another small lobby. The carpet looked expensive, a deep maroon color that accentuated a cluster of leather chairs. Overhead lighting cast a soft light on the entire room. The effect created an atmosphere of reserved elegance. Bartholomew led the way, down a hallway. On the left side of the hallway were three doors labeled as conference rooms. The right side of the hallway also had three doors. The first door was marked "No Admittance." Suite 201 was the second door. An engraved brass plate identified suite 201 as the Law Office of Wesley J. Bartholomew. Bartholomew opened the door and motioned John to follow him through it.

The space on the other side of the door was much different than the hallway and lobbies on the way in. The carpet changed to a lush green, the walls were covered with tan wallpaper, and the lighting was bright.

The room was long. Approximately half-way in the room was a large desk with a computer work station where a plump, middle-aged woman in a gray business suit sat. She was typing on the computer while carrying on a conversation on the phone, yet immediately looked up and smiled at the men. John guessed she was Doreen. Behind her desk were all the working components of a typical business office. Beyond that, a large window provided a commanding view of the Cook Inlet.

Bartholomew walked past the desk and opened a door on the far side of the reception room. "Come in, John, we've got a lot to talk about."

CHAPTER 3

Harley Pepperdine walked through the door, stepped up to the counter, and addressed the large man behind it, "I'm getting out, Mickey. I need to pick up my stuff."

The big man looked up from his paperwork and tapped the patch on his shoulder, "What's that say, Pepperdine?"

"Gee, let me sound it out... De... Depart... ment... of..."

"Department of Corrections, Pepperdine. You aren't out the door, yet. So, that would make me, what?"

Harley struggled to stifle his impulse to say "an asshole," but common sense prevailed. "Officer O'Neal. I have been released from custody, *Officer O'Neal*, and would like to pick up my personal belongings."

"That's the spirit, Pepperdine! It just so happens I have them right in this very envelope." As he called out the list, Officer O'Neal tossed the items on the counter. "Watch, wallet, pocket knife, assorted change, and a disgusting, bloody handkerchief, which has been hermetically sealed in a plastic bag for my protection. Sign there, and you're out of here."

Harley quickly scribbled his name on the line Officer O'Neal had indicated. He pocketed the wallet, knife and change, slipped on the wristwatch, and threw the plastic bag in a trashcan next to the counter. As Harley stepped toward the door, Officer O'Neal pressed a button under the counter. The door buzzed, and Harley opened it. He stood half-way through the door and turned back to look at Officer O'Neal, and a smile spread across his face.

"See you at the hockey game tonight, Mickey?"

"Yeah, Harley, I'll buy you a beer. Try and stay out of trouble, and for Pete's sake, stay away from Kells."

"It's a small community, Mickey. He'll probably be at the hockey game, too."

"Maybe, but he won't be with me."

Harley waved and stepped through the door. The bolt slammed behind him as the door closed. It felt good to be on the other side, in fresh air. The wind was blowing strong from the southwest, and had a bite. It was no more than fifteen degrees, and with the wind chill the cold cut through Harley's jacket. He looked up and saw a thick layer of cirrus clouds sweeping up from the direction of lower Cook Inlet.

"*Nasty weather is on the way*," Harley observed to himself. "*Just what we need in the middle of March, another foot of snow.*"

Harley walked down the fenced entrance to the gate at the end and waited for the officer behind the window of the building to hit the release. At the buzz, Harley walked through the gate to a black pickup waiting in the parking lot. He opened the door and climbed in.

"Welcome back into the world, Harley," the driver said with a broad smile. "Five days for a drunk on premises bust has to be a new record."

"Give it a rest, Trevor," Harley shot back.

"No, seriously, what took so long? I thought you were already out, until you called this morning."

"Apparently, there was a little trouble finding a judge. Winthrop is down in the Lower 48 on vacation, and Church was

snowed in on a spring caribou hunt. He was supposed to get back
Sunday, but didn't get in until last night."

"Really? Where'd he go?"

"I don't know, he didn't say, just somewhere west of
roads."

"Do any good?"

"Trevor, do I *look* like I give a shit? It was my
arraignment." Harley's tone let Trevor know the subject was
closed.

"Well, did you at least get a court date?"

"Yeah, April twenty-first. It's the earliest I could get. Where
are you headed?"

"I need to go to the Rainbow. Carole is working, and I'm
going to pick her up."

Harley sighed deeply. "What time does she get off?"

"About four."

"Trevor, it's not even two," Harley said flatly. "What the
hell are we going to do at the Rainbow for over two hours?"

Trevor winked at his passenger. "There's no restraining
order against you at the Rainbow, is there?"

"No."

"I'm thinking a beer and a munchy is in order. The judge
didn't say anything about not drinking, did he?"

"No."

"And I'm off for two days, so what's the problem?"

"Well, I guess the only problem is you aren't driving fast
enough."

Trevor punched the accelerator just enough to make the
wheels on the truck spin, causing the truck to fish-tail slightly on
the icy road, and both men laughed.

Close to a dozen customers were already scattered along the
bar when Harley and Trevor walked into the Rainbow. Each of
the regulars nodded to the newcomers and exchanged greetings.
Several good-natured comments about Harley's stint in jail were

made. Harley took it all and countered with a few verbal jabs of his own. The men sat down at a table in the middle of the room. A slender, attractive blonde in tight, black pants and white blouse walked up carrying a tray.

"Why, if it isn't Mr. Pepperdine!" the blonde said with mock surprise. She turned toward Trevor, "What are you doing hanging out with such trash?"

"The poor man needed a ride," Trevor replied, sliding his arm around the blonde's waist. "Can you ever forgive me?"

The waitress pushed Trevor's arm away. "What makes you think I was asking you?"

"Oh, that hurts."

"Sorry, Trevor," Harley said as the waitress sat down on his lap, "it's the bad boy image that draws them in." Harley lifted the waitress off his lap and looked at her, "How you doing, Carole?"

"Not bad. I got the slow shift, but things ought to pick up in short order. What can I get for you boys?"

"I'll have a beer," Trevor said immediately, "you, Harley?"

"Coffee, and I could use an order of poppers," Harley added with a smile, "I've been on what you might call a restricted diet for a few days."

Carole laughed and walked off. Harley sat back in his chair and threw one foot up on the empty chair next to him.

"I'm going to guess by the ribbing I took when we came in, my little social faux pas has been a popular subject of the gossip mill. Most of these codgers weren't even here that night."

"I don't know how you'd know who was here and who wasn't," Trevor shot back. "By the time I got here, you were completely wasted. And bleeding." Trevor leaned forward and continued in a very serious tone, "You know, Harley, there's a concept called moderate drinking you ought to check out. If moderation isn't in your vocabulary, maybe alcoholic will be."

Harley shrugged. "Trevor, I am not an alcoholic. I am a

drunk. There's a difference."

"Well I'll be damned if I know what it is."

"Well, strictly for your edification, alcoholics drink because they have to. A drunk, like me, drinks because they want to."

Carole came back to the table to drop off the drinks, interrupting the conversation. "I'll be back in a few with the poppers."

"I offer this as proof," Harley said holding up the coffee. "An alcoholic wouldn't order a cup of coffee after five dry days."

"And after the first couple coffees? Then what?" asked Trevor, his skepticism obvious.

"I don't know, Trev. Maybe I'll feel like having a beer. Maybe I'll feel like buying a shot to go with it. Maybe I'll get so wrecked I'll look Kells up and finish things."

Trevor leaned even farther into the table. "You listen to me, Harley: stay away from Kells, especially when you're drunk. On a good day, with all things even, you might get lucky and keep him from beating you senseless. The guy is bad news. Give it a little time, he'll give us enough reason to lock him up for a good long while."

"You're right," Harley said with a shrug, "but that day can't come soon enough to make me happy."

"And another thing," Trevor was on his soapbox and was going to clear a few things out of his system, "what the hell started things the other night? What were you doing picking a fight with Mark Kells? You know, if it had been any other Kenai cop taking that call, you'd still be in Wildwood, awaiting arraignment on felony assault, not looking at a drunk on premises."

"*Okay!*," Harley snapped, growing impatient with the lecture, "I owe you one, little brother. Let's drop it."

"No, you owe me an explanation." Trevor leaned back in his chair and tried to lighten things up, "Besides, we're only half-brothers. It's obvious I got the brains from my dad, not our mom."

Harley sighed and tossed the sugar packet he'd been playing with onto the table. He looked up at Trevor and said flatly, "Not that it's really any of your business, but it was about Maggie. I think that son of a bitch has been slapping her around."

"Maggie? Again? When are you going to quit meddling in her business? She's a big girl, she can take care of herself. Besides," Trevor chuckled, "I've seen her when she's pissed. Mark Kells just might come up a eunuch someday."

"I'm glad you think it's funny, Trev."

"I don't, Harley. Being a cop, I see that crap every day. It turns my stomach, but until Maggie asks for help, there's nothing anyone can do. And setting yourself up to get beat to a pulp doesn't help matters. Why do you insist in getting involved? It's obvious she doesn't want your help. In fact, she goes to great lengths to avoid you."

"She's embarrassed, Trev. You know her, you two dated for awhile."

"Harley, that was a long time ago, and only a few times. It was, shall we say, awkward at best."

"Well, my involvement goes a lot deeper than just a couple of high school dates."

"Do what you have to, brother, but you might want to make sure the girl wants your help before you go picking fights on her behalf."

Carole returned to the table carrying the poppers. "I see you boys are having a good time."

"Yeah," Harley said, "a regular family laugh riot. So, Carole, speaking of good times, how'd the rest of Hardrock's wake go after my premature departure the other night?"

"That was pretty much the grand finale. You know how it is, a good wake starts out sad, gets jovial while the stories are told, then everybody starts talking about missing the guy, and things get morose."

"Hardrock wouldn't have liked that."

"Yeah, that's why most folks decided to bag it. Things were wound down and back to normal by midnight."

"Normal, being?"

"Noisy, rowdy and no talk of the dearly departed."

Someone called from across the room about dying of thirst, and Carole walked off to save them.

Trevor and Harley sat and talked away the time until Carole finished her shift. As the afternoon faded, Harley switched from coffee to beer. By the time Carole got off, there were three empties sitting in front of him.

"That settles things for good, lady," Harley said in mock seriousness, "there will definitely be no tip for you. Don't you clear away the empties?"

"My good man," Carole replied in equal mock seriousness, "I am off shift now. You will need to take the subject up with your new waitress. Besides," she switched to a tone of genuine concern, "I want you to keep track. Don't overdo, all right?"

"You guys aren't staying?" Harley asked.

"The last thing I want to do," Carole replied, "after six hours of humping suds is to sit around this place."

"But I don't have any wheels," Harley argued. "I was going to the hockey game tonight. How about a lift out to Nikiski before we split up the party?"

Trevor shook his head. "No way, don't have the time. We're supposed to be in Soldotna in less than an hour. Here, take the key to my apartment and stay in town. No matter how much you drink, you can still stagger six blocks." Trevor dug around in his pocket and tossed a ring of keys on the table. "And for you, my dear," Trevor continued while reaching back into his pocket, "the key to my truck. I've had too many to drive."

The couple turned and walked to the door. As they did, Harley shouted, "Helluva jailer you are! Not a key to your name!"

Trevor flipped Harley off as he stepped through the door, but reappeared immediately. "Harley, you might want to take a cab when you leave, it's blowing a storm out here."

Harley waved him off, and Trevor shrugged then ducked back out. Harley waved to catch the attention of Carole's relief and ordered another beer.

CHAPTER 4

Bartholomew held back as John walked past him into the office. He turned to the desk in the reception room, "Doreen, would you please bring us some coffee?" He turned to John, "You take anything in yours?" John shook his head. "Just coffee, Doreen. Thanks."

John looked over Bartholomew's office. It was actually larger than the reception room, being much wider, and just as long. To the right was an oversized sofa and four chairs positioned around a large, circular table. Bookcases lined the other two walls on that end of the office. To the left of the door, more bookcases lined the wall behind a massive desk.

The wall opposite the desk was covered with numerous plaques and framed pictures. The pictures were predominantly photographs, some in black and white, and most looked to be personal in nature.

Bartholomew left the door behind him open and walked over to the massive desk. He swapped his red plaid coat for his suit jacket, then gestured at the wing chairs positioned between the desk and the wall covered with pictures.

"Have a seat, John. This may be a long conversation. We'll wait until Doreen brings in the coffee before we get to the details, but for now, do you have any basic questions?"

John looked the man over. He was fairly short, with a full head of silver hair. His beard still had shots of dark hair through it. He wore glasses, but his eyes were a steel gray, and piercing. John had the impression if Bartholomew wanted to know the truth, he could force it out with a very long, cold stare. He imagined Bartholomew to be very formidable, if not outright intimidating, when negotiating legal matters. John couldn't tell, yet, if he was a friend, or a foe. Judging by the looks of the man, John sincerely hoped for the former.

"I do have one thing bothering me," John replied with a smile, "how were you so certain you would recognize me? For all you knew there were going to be dozens of people waiting for rides."

Bartholomew leaned back in his chair and smiled back at John. "I may have been just counting to luck. However, I was betting most people waiting out on the curb, particularly on a day like today, would be picked up by local folks they knew. That would mean the passengers waiting on the curb were, more likely than not, locals themselves. It was a simple matter of looking for someone who was obviously not a local. It's March, and anyone with a deep tan, standing out in a wind chill of zero without a coat is not likely to be a local." He laughed at the last observation.

John couldn't help but grin. "Well I can tell you with absolute certainty, next time I'll know better than to pack my coat at the bottom of my bag."

"Next time, if there is one," Bartholomew said ominously, "I won't be guessing."

John felt Bartholomew's eyes boring into him. The old man was evaluating John's every reaction. John had played this game with customers, and had mastered the art of showing very little. He glanced around the room and noticed Bartholomew's window offered the same commanding view the reception room had, only on a larger scale.

"You have a phenomenal view from your office," he commented to break Bartholomew's stare.

Bartholomew broke his gaze and swiveled his chair toward the window. "Yeah, this part of town sits back from a bluff, so it doesn't take much height to offer a good view of the inlet. The bluff was made during the 1964 Good Friday earthquake, when the land on the lower side slid into the inlet. If the same sized quake happened today, the loss of life would be staggering."

There was a noise behind John as Doreen bustled in with a tray holding a carafe and two coffee mugs. She set the tray on the closest end of Bartholomew's massive desk and looked at Bartholomew, "Anything else?"

"Yes," Bartholomew responded immediately, "no interruptions, unless Kenai calls."

"Yes, sir," Doreen said and started for the door, then stopped. "It was nice to meet you Mr. Barstow," she said to John, then gave Bartholomew a little shot of stink-eye.

Bartholomew shrugged, "As much time as you two have spent chatting on the phone, I figured introductions were superfluous."

"Nice to meet you too, Doreen," John replied, "and please, call me John."

Doreen smiled as she closed the door behind her.

Bartholomew reached over and picked up the carafe, filling one mug and handing it to John. He filled the other mug, set it at his place, then opened a drawer in his desk.

"You still off the sauce?" Bartholomew asked.

John was taken aback by the direct question. "What do you mean by that?"

"Don't dance around on me, John, we don't have time for it. Are you still drinking heavily? Are you still a drunk?"

"I think the question you're fumbling for," John replied tersely, "is if I'm an alcoholic."

"Well?" Bartholomew demanded.

"Once an alcoholic, always an alcoholic, Mr. Bartholomew. The real question is, do I stay sober? The answer to that, is yes."

"I'm glad to hear it. You have a problem if other people imbibe?"

"Not at all, some of my best friends are drinkers," John answered sarcastically.

With John's answer, Bartholomew reached into the drawer and pulled out a bottle of Irish Cream. "That's also good to hear," he said while adding a dollop of the creamy liquor to his coffee, "I enjoy a coffee with a little Irish Cream in the afternoons, if my schedule permits."

"Whatever floats your boat," John replied flatly. He always hated it when people were obvious about testing his sobriety. "So, do you have any other intensely personal questions you'd like to ask, Mr. Bartholomew?"

"Why don't you call me Wes, it would make things much less formal, and perhaps less intimidating."

John's face reddened. His customer face was completely blown, and he was running out of patience. "All right, *Wes*, what else would you like to pry into?"

"I don't mean to offend," Bartholomew explained, "but I am under an obligation to learn certain things about you before the final disposition of your uncle's estate can take place. I'm doing my job, so please just bear with me." Bartholomew could see he had put the younger man in a defensive position, and decided the situation needed to be defused. "I hope this isn't too personal, and it's just curiosity on my part, but what happened to your eye?"

John held his hand up to his right eye, where the bruise was barely visible from his run-in at the bar the previous week.

"Oh, that..." he was thinking as fast as he could, but Bartholomew's eyes were boring into him, and decided it was no use continuing with the lie. "Okay, you can take this anyway you want, Wes, but I got punched out in a bar last week."

Bartholomew showed no visible reaction whatsoever. John found it unnerving. After a moment's thought, Bartholomew leaned back in his chair and chose his words carefully. "How long were you drunk?"

"What makes you think I was drunk?"

"Alcoholics don't go into bars and get into fights recruiting for AA, John. Let me rephrase the question." Bartholomew continued, as if he were deposing a witness on the stand. "How long had you been intoxicated prior to being struck, and how long after the incident did you continue to drink?"

"I wasn't drunk. I didn't even drink. I admit, I went there to toss away five years of sobriety, but luckily fate stepped in to prevent it. And if you knew the entire situation, you wouldn't be so quick to judge."

"Again, John, I'm not judging, I'm not prying, there are certain..."

"Yeah, yeah, I know, you just have a job to do. It's nothing personal, you just like messing with people."

Silence descended on the room as uncomfortable as a cold mist. John reached out to take his first sip of coffee and found his hand was shaking. He held the mug in both hands to control the trembling as he brought the mug up to his lips and sipped gently.

After a few moments of staring at the wall behind John, Bartholomew turned his attention back to John. "I'd like you to turn around and look at the pictures on the wall behind you. Let me know if anything about any of them looks familiar."

Eager for a chance to escape the old man's gaze, John got up and looked the wall over. His eyes settled on a black and white picture of two men, perhaps slightly older than himself, smiling broadly, shaking hands. It could be any two friends, in any picture in the world, were it not for the collection of ramshackle buildings in the background.

John quickly turned toward Bartholomew, "Is that Uncle

Hank? I saw that picture about thirty years ago! He showed one to me just like it the first time I ever met him, only it was much smaller. How did you get this?"

"Hardrock, I mean Hank, had just taken possession of the mine when the picture was taken. You can take it down and look at it more closely, if you'd like."

John carefully lifted the picture off the hook on the wall. He held the picture and ran his hand over the glass. It was Hank, all right, plaid shirt, canvas pants, bushy beard and all. This man had been his only living relative for almost ten years, until a few weeks ago, and John had never even bothered to contact him. Now, here was his ghost to remind John of one more failed chance at a relationship.

"You okay?" Wes asked quietly.

"I'm fine. I didn't know the man, really. It was just a surprise, is all. How did you get it?"

"You wouldn't know it to look at me now, but I'm the fellow Hank is shaking hands with. By the way, everybody friendly with your uncle called him Hardrock, or Hardrock Hank."

"Were you his partner? I mean you look as happy as he does."

"His partner? No. I was then, as I am today, acting as his lawyer. I represented him in getting the patent on his mine finalized. There was stiff opposition to it, and some dirty tricks to boot. It was a lawsuit everyone said we could never win. It was a major triumph for both of us. Because of your uncle and his case, the success of my career was assured."

John looked up from the picture and saw Wes looking directly at him with those piercing eyes.

"When I tell you I need questions answered, it's not out of some morbid curiosity. I am acting as Hardrock's lawyer, but my involvement goes much deeper than simple professional duty. Hardrock was also a good friend. Now, are you ready to answer my questions?"

John put the picture back on its hook. He had his doubts about Wesley J. Bartholomew, but decided at some point he'd have to give in, if for no other reason than to finish things up. He nodded and sat back down.

The first thing Wes asked was for John to clarify the circumstances around the fading black eye he was sporting. John related the events in the bar, omitting the reasons he went there. He didn't think they were important. All he told Wes was that he'd had an exceptionally bad day, the worst he could recall in years, and had succumbed to the temptation of seeking solace in an old friend. "In a way," John explained finally, "I view it as a lesson learned. I'm probably the only guy you'll ever meet that was grateful for a black eye."

Wes sat through John's explanation without interrupting him, and without exhibiting any facial expressions which might have given away what he was thinking. When John was finished, there was a pause in the conversation while Wes gathered his thoughts.

"Well, it's damn sure it must have been one fine shiner," Wes finally said to break the silence. "What was so bad about that particular day?"

"Do we really need to talk about it? What are you, a part-time shrink, too?"

"I couldn't afford the pay cut," Wes answered, laughing. "I'm asking because it may prove to be important to the final disbursal of the estate. What almost tripped you up?"

John sighed. Where to begin? He started out explaining how Shelley left him, when Wes interrupted.

"You and this Shelley married?"

"No, not that I hadn't considered it."

"You were married at one time, right?" Wes continued to pry.

John felt himself getting irritated again. "Not that it matters a bit, but yes. It ended over my drinking."

"Any legal issues hanging over the divorce? You owe her... Lilly, wasn't it? You owe Lilly anything?"

It was the second time Wes had thrown an absolute ringer from out of nowhere. Obviously, he knew more about John than he was letting on. John decided it was time for Wes to answer a few questions himself.

"Hold on right there," John demanded as he stood up. "How is it you know so much about me? Even my uncle wouldn't have had that information." John leaned into the expanse of Bartholomew's desk. "You need to get on the level with me, and I mean now."

"Fair enough," Wes replied slowly. "Sit down and cool off. Please. Your uncle was fully aware of your marriage, and your drinking. You may not have been in contact, but Hardrock kept track of you from time to time. Whether you knew it, or not, Hardrock considered family important. He maintained regular correspondence with your mother until her death. How do you suppose Hardrock showed up unexpectedly at her funeral? He probably knew she was dying before you did, and asked her to make sure someone contacted him when she died. I can't say why he didn't go south to see her before she passed away, but I can say with certainty your father and Hardrock did not get along, and your father did not contact Hardrock about your mother's passing."

John had never really given much thought to the how, or why, his uncle showed up at his mother's funeral. He assumed his father had sent word to his uncle.

"And how do you suppose," Wes continued, "Hardrock knew your father had committed suicide? It wouldn't have exactly been an item for front page news up here."

John was stunned. Even more, in some peculiar way he felt as though the years of his private hell had been thrown open for public display. He was torn between being incensed at the violation of his privacy, and saddened by the fact he never knew someone, beyond his parents, had actually cared enough to show an interest in his life.

"But why? Why keep track of me? And why didn't he ever contact me?"

Wes shrugged when he answered, "I don't know why he never actually contacted you. We were good friends, but there were some things Hardrock didn't discuss in detail with anybody, not even me. Perhaps he felt it was too late to foster a relationship. Maybe he thought the rancor between himself and your father was transferred to you. Who knows? As far as keeping tabs on you goes, you were his sister's son, and his only family. Basically, you were his legal heir. When you seemed to have turned your life around, after your divorce, he just kept tabs on you enough to keep up-to-date with your current address."

"Were you involved?"

"In the actual research? No."

"*Research?* Is that what you call it?" John snorted. "More like surveillance, I'd say."

"Okay, I wasn't involved in the *surveillance*, if that's what you want to call it. Hardrock asked me to arrange for him to contact people who do that kind of work. It was no different than running a missing person down, or doing some leg work for a background check, or even a divorce investigation. By the way, if it makes you feel any better, your drinking didn't drive Lilly away. It just made an easy excuse for her to run off with the guy she ended up leaving for the guy she left for the guy she married."

John threw his head back against the chair. "*Damn!* It certainly *does not* make me feel any better. What say we agree to just keep those extra little details about my life, of which I am blissfully ignorant, a secret?"

Wes smiled. "It's a deal. I'll ask the questions, and you tell me what *you* know about your life."

Wes continued on with his questions, and John found it almost a relief to answer them honestly. Did John owe Lilly anything? No, and there was nothing in the divorce which would give her any claim to anything he might accumulate, or be entitled to. Was there any kind of arrangement, or promises made, with Shelley? No, not even a chance of a palimony claim. Any children, of any sort? An emphatic no. What about his current employer, Occidental Investing, was he happy working there? Did he ever think about leaving?

"Well," John answered the last question slowly, "I wasn't totally miserable, but the correct term would be previous employer. That was the other part of the equation that led me to the bar. They fired me the day Shelley moved out. They simply sauntered into my office and announced I was no longer needed. There had been talk of cutbacks, but you know, you never *really* think it's going to be you that gets the axe."

Wes allowed as to how such a double whammy could definitely tempt a guy to drink, then abruptly changed the subject.

"You seem to be fairly fit for a guy your age. Do you have any sort of physical ailments, or limitations?"

Before John could answer, Doreen called on the intercom, "Mr. Bartholomew, your call from Kenai is on the line."

Wes apologized for the interruption, and asked John if he would mind stepping out into the reception room, explaining the call was privileged. John closed the door behind him before Wes picked up the phone.

Doreen sat behind her desk typing on her computer, but looked up and smiled when John walked out of the office. "You need anything, John?"

John asked if there was a restroom he could use, and Doreen directed him to a door on the opposite side of Wes's office. When John stepped back into the reception room, Wes and Doreen were just finishing up a conversation.

"Okay, it's two-thirty now," Wes said, "contact Era and find out about the five-thirty. If there's room, make the reservation. If not, get the next available. And make the transfer to activate the account."

Wes turned toward John and gestured toward the open door of his office. He held a thick file in his hand. Even though Doreen had been given her marching orders, she waited to make her call, sitting and smiling sweetly. John felt slightly paranoid, as if he were the subject of a private joke. He nodded to Doreen and entered the office. Wes followed him and closed the door again.

John went back to his chair in front of Wes's desk and sat down, but Wes remained standing, pacing slightly. He held the folder in one hand, and was rubbing his beard with the other, while looking down preoccupied.

"Where were we when Doreen interrupted?"

"You were asking about my health. It's good to excellent, so if you're selling life insurance, I'm not a candidate."

"Good to hear. Are you averse to hard work? By that I mean do you mind physical work?"

"I don't mind working up a good sweat, if that's what you mean. The physical inactivity was one of the things I disliked most about working for Occidental. On the other hand, I wouldn't want to spend my life digging ditches by hand, either."

Wes actually seemed a little relieved to hear the response. He sat down, laying the folder in front of him. "You like the outdoors?"

"Are you serious?"

"It's important. Yes."

"I haven't spent much time outdoors lately, but I was a Boy Scout, and we went camping as a family quite a bit while growing up. In fact, some of the best memories of my folks are from those camping trips, so I'd have to say I do like the outdoors. But I don't see ..."

"Well, I hope you do," Wes interrupted, "because it's about to become a big part of your life, if you agree to the proposition."

Before John could say anything, Wes opened the mysterious folder on the desk and began laying out the details of Hardrock's estate.

"The Last Chance Number 3 was Hardrock's life," Wes explained, "and in the end, it was most of what he had."

"Last Chance Number 3?" John asked, interrupting. "That sounds a little conflicted."

"Not really," Wes said in a matter-of-fact tone. "Claims are restricted in size. In the territorial days of Alaska, miners staked entire lengths of creeks using multiple claims. They would often use the same name with a number to show the association with the registered owner. Hardrock's claim was the third in a string of other claims in the Gold Creek Valley, so it's legal description is Last Chance Number 3. Since the other claims no longer exist, the mine is now referred to simply as Last Chance."

John nodded his understanding, and Wes continued, "The questions I've been asking were based upon what Hardrock wanted to know about his heir, before arrangements were made to transfer ownership. Hardrock wanted the mine to stay in the family, but wasn't willing to pass it along to someone who wouldn't, or couldn't, put an honest effort into keeping it. It seems Hardrock had some questions about your ability to live up to his expectations. He left his estate in trust with specific instructions for me to decide if the Last Chance stayed in the family, or went to an alternate beneficiary."

Wes went on to describe the current state of Last Chance. The mine had changed considerably since the picture John was familiar with had been taken. There was now a main lodge and cabins on the site. The original buildings had been maintained, and somewhat restored, to preserve the historic value of the property, but the place didn't look at all the same. Wes produced several pictures from the folder to show John. It was, indeed, different. There were established paths between the cabins and the lodge, and even patches of what looked to be a lawn of sorts. The lodge was picturesque with its tall prow front, peeled logs, large front windows and a deck littered with chairs which looked to be crafted from logs.

Hardrock didn't run it as a mine, per se," Wes explained. "He turned it into a tourist destination, a pay-to-mine operation. As currently set up, the mine offers an opportunity for people with a spirit of adventure and an appreciation for Alaskan gold mining history to actually give mining a try on a recreational basis. The facilities on the claim have been updated to accommodate up to twelve people at a time. A trip to Last Chance provides a comfortable, although rustic, experience. Quarters are log cabins, meals are provided, as is small scale mining equipment. To sum it up, Hardrock figured out the best way to get the gold, and that was to mine the miners."

"Sounds like one of those fantasy camps rabid baseball fans go to," John quipped, "only with good scenery, fresh air, and bears."

Wes nodded and explained that as beneficiary, John would take over the operation of Last Chance, and all property Hardrock had owned. By the time Wes had finished listing everything to which he was entitled, John's head felt light.

"You mean to tell me all that's mine?" John asked. "I'm now the owner of a gold mine, and everything that goes with it?"

"Well," Wes said hesitantly, "it's not exactly that simple. You have to earn Last Chance."

"Earn?" John was even more confused. "You mean I have to pay for it? Hell, I can't even afford to lay out two month's rent in advance to get an apartment!"

"No, John, you don't understand at all. By earn, I mean you have to satisfy certain conditions Hardrock laid out before the patent will be signed over."

Wes pulled out a copy of an agreement from the folder. He explained the agreement was a legally binding document between John and Hardrock's estate, with Wes representing the estate. Wes went down the list of conditions and explained each one of them to John. Among other things, John would immediately take possession of Hardrock's home in Nikiski, a small town north of Kenai.

John nodded, and Wes continued. John would assume responsibility for the operation of Last Chance Adventures, which was the name of the pay-to-mine business, for a period of one season. If, at the end of that period, Last Chance Adventures showed a profit, transfer of ownership to John would be completed, along with all associated properties and chattel. However, if Last Chance Adventures failed to show a profit, the mine and the business would go to a secondary beneficiary.

"So, in a nutshell," John summarized, "if I make the operation pay, it's mine. If I don't, I get squat."

"Not entirely," Wes replied. "If you fail to show a profit you lose the mine and the business, but you get to keep the house and will receive fifty thousand dollars."

"That's some consolation prize. What's the mine worth?"

Wes explained the ownership stipulation in the agreement. If John received ownership of the mine, he was not obligated to continue operation of Last Chance Adventures, but could neither sell, nor lease out, the mine for a period of ten years from the date of transfer. If John failed to pay the property taxes on the mine, should he decide to abandon it, the estate would step in to pay the taxes, take ownership of the mine and sign it over to the secondary beneficiary. In other words, John would be locked into owning the mine for ten years, even if he wanted to be shed of it, unless he wanted it to go back to the estate and then on to the secondary beneficiary.

"Who is this secondary beneficiary that keeps cropping up?" John asked.

Wes flipped through the agreement and found the paragraph outlining John's relationship with the secondary. Simply put, there wouldn't be one. John would not learn the identity of the secondary beneficiary unless he defaulted on the agreement, or failed to make the business succeed.

"I'm going to guess this agreement," John said, pointing at the folder, "is some of your handiwork."

"You would be correct," Wes answered with a sly smile, "and it is ironclad. You might be able to beat it with a team of lawyers as good as myself, but you would just end up giving the mine to them to pay for it."

"What if I don't want to take up the agreement?" John asked slowly. "Do I just walk away with nothing?"

"Not at all. Should you choose to decline the agreement, you still get Hardrock's house, and twenty-five thousand dollars."

"Do I have to decide right now?"

"No. It's a big decision, and Hardrock's instructions were that you would have exactly forty-eight hours, from the time I explained the agreement, to make the decision."

John mulled the proposition over in his mind. He weighed how much of the travel money he still had left, and whether it would pay for two nights of high living in the big city of Los Anchorage.

"So I need to come back here day after tomorrow and let you know if I want to sign, or if I want to pick up the money."

"No, I will bring the agreement to you."

John looked confused. "So, I need to call to set up a place to meet?"

"No, I already know where you're going to be. You will be in Nikiski, at a place called the Shuffle Inn, waiting to give me your answer."

John sat totally dumbfounded at how well Wes, or was it Hardrock, had orchestrated the conditions and events. He felt as if he had no control over his own life at the moment, just like when Mr. Cuervo had been calling the shots.

Wes spoke quickly as he laid out the planned course of events. Doreen had made arrangements for John to be on a flight to Kenai that evening. Once in Kenai, John would rent a car and drive to the Shuffle Inn, in Nikiski. From there he would meet with a man named Harley Pepperdine, the maintenance man for the Last Chance; a man named Reeder, the only man Hardrock trusted to fly him in and out of the Last Chance; a man named Billy McCrane, who provided groceries and supplies for the mine; and Cynthia Smythe, who kept books and ran the office for Last Chance Adventures.

"Time is short, John," Wes said wrapping up his description of what John was to do. "You have an opportunity to start over. You have a last chance, to play on words."

"But I only have six hundred dollars on me. I can't just start running a business with less than even a month's rent at a flop house!"

"You have a credit card?" John nodded yes. "Then you have a rental car, which is all you need. You'll find Hardrock was not only well known in Nikiski, but also highly regarded by most. Just being his nephew will provide certain 'courtesies' shall we say. A line of credit would be one of them. I need to mention one other thing. Should you decide to sign the agreement, there will be an account in a Kenai bank with one-hundred thousand dollars in it for the purpose of one year's operating expenses of Last Chance Adventures. That sum of money will determine whether there has been a profit. At the end of a year's time, there must be more than one-hundred thousand in the account."

John looked directly at Wes and asked, "How do you know I won't just empty the account and run?"

"If I thought there was any chance of that, my boy, you'd be leaving here right now with a house in Nikiski, and twenty-five grand. We need to get you back to the airport. Doreen will give you a list of the names of people you need to contact while making your decision. She will also call you a cab for the ride back to the airport. Beyond that, you are on your own for the next two days."

Wes hustled John out of his office and turned him over to Doreen. Wes quickly shook John's hand and retreated back into his office, closing the door behind him. Doreen was ready with the information John needed on who to contact in Nikiski. She hadn't been able to get John on the five-thirty flight, but had managed to get him on the next flight, at seven. She explained to John it was a quick flight to Kenai, usually less than twenty-five minutes. The drive would be easy, since there was only one major road between the two towns, and he should still get to Nikiski well before nine. As she explained all this to John, she glanced out the window, and shook her head.

"It's too bad you're going to be driving in the dark. Looks like there's a storm blowing up the inlet. It could be pretty nasty in Kenai, so take your time."

John had been rummaging through his bag to dig out his coat while listening to Doreen. At her last comment, he stood up to look out the window. The sky was dark and overcast, and the gray water of the inlet disappeared into an indistinct veil of white on the horizon. The white wall hid the mountains that had been visible when he first arrived. He thought of the flight into Anchorage, and winced at the prospect of flying into something which might be even worse.

"Will they fly in weather like that?" he asked nodding out the window.

"Oh, sure," Doreen replied casually, "as long as they can see to land and take off, the flights continue. But if I were you, I wouldn't eat too much before the flight. There's a reason the flight to Kenai is called the Vomit Comet."

It was an uneventful ride to the airport. The wind had not abated, and the gray skies were starting to shed light snow. The snow swirled out from underneath the cars in thin bands, sliding like so many white snakes along the streets. John thought to himself the image couldn't be much more bleak. He couldn't envision what the small town he was headed to must be like. The cabby asked what airline John was flying on, then drove past the curb check-ins for the major airlines and dropped him off at the far end of the terminal. There was no activity along that section of curb. Glancing at his watch, John noted he wouldn't have made the five-thirty flight anyway, as it was a little past five already.

Walking in the door, John saw the Era Aviation counter to the left. He walked up to the single attendant at the counter and gave his name. As she typed his name into the computer, she told him there could be a slight delay in his flight due to the weather in Kenai. The storm just making its presence known in Anchorage was raging in Kenai, limiting visibility and requiring the ground crews to plow the runway between flights. In answer to John's question about the possibility of the flight being cancelled, she assured him the situation was not completely out of the ordinary. "We deal with weather like this all the time," she said in a bored, almost dismissive tone.

John thought to himself as he headed to the gate that the ticket agent could afford to be blasé about the situation. She wasn't the one about to be bouncing around in a storm.

There were over a dozen people sitting in the waiting area. Four men, all dressed in dark blue uniforms with the name "Schlumberger" embossed across the backs, were standing in front of the check-in station, talking to the attendant. John couldn't help but overhear the conversation.

"Well, how long will it be delayed?" asked one of the men, "My crew is supposed to be in Kenai at six."

"I don't know, sir," the attendant replied in a tired tone. She had heard it all before. Oil field service hands were always in a big hurry, even when there wasn't anything to be in a hurry about. "The conditions in Kenai could change at any moment, and the flight could leave only slightly behind schedule."

"Or they could get worse, and we sit here all night," the man snapped back.

"Relax, Boss," one of the other men said, "it's not like the job will get done without us."

"That's exactly the problem, Billy, the job won't get done, and we'll be stuck in Kenai when we should be heading home. God, I hate Kenai jobs."

The men wandered off, grumbling amongst themselves about how they hated getting pulled off the North Slope for "pissant" jobs in Kenai, particularly just before they were scheduled to finish up their stints and head home to the Lower 48.

John stepped up to the counter and asked the tired looking attendant if he was waiting at the right place. She nodded, and repeated the warning about a possible delay. The attendant seemed surprised and smiled when John didn't debate the issue with her, actually thanking her for the information.

John looked out the window in the waiting area. There, sitting on the flight line, was the smallest plane he'd ever seen. He remembered seeing a little snack stand on the way to the gate, and with his coat under his arm, headed in that direction. A light snack and something to drink sounded good. He had at least ninety minutes to kill. The prospect of sitting at the gate, watching the snow swirl around the tiny plane as it rocked in the wind was unappealing. What would it be like when they were off the ground?

Mindful of Doreen's warning about not eating too much, John picked out a small sandwich and a bottle of water. He threw his coat across the back of one chair, and sat down on another at a table on the edge of the little snack area. The table offered a limited view of the waiting area for the gate; one without the unnerving sight of the tiny plane. Nibbling on the sandwich,

John pulled out the list Doreen had given him.

The list had several names on it, and a note about what role each would play in the next two days. At the top of the list was the name Gary Fisk, the owner of the Shuffle Inn, a bar/hotel combination, where John would stay. At the bottom of the list were the directions to Nikiski from Kenai.

The directions were simple: right turn out of the airport, right turn at the highway, then drive twenty miles. There were a few landmarks along the way, but basically, the directions were to drive until John saw the Shuffle Inn on the left side of the road. John shook his head. He wouldn't need the navigational skills of Magellan to find the Shuffle Inn. Directions so simple could only mean there wasn't much of interest in the area. He toyed with the idea of just blowing off going to Nikiski, dumping the unseen house, and collecting the twenty-five grand. It seemed he would just be wasting his time by going, but curiosity had the upper hand. And really, what else did he have demanding his time at the moment? The trip might be worth the effort just to see Hank's turf.

John was still having a hard time wrapping his mind around the idea Hank had secretly kept tabs on him all those years. It appeared Hank had harbored some regard for family, contrary to everything he'd heard from his grandparents and his father. His mother's comparative silence on the matter, which he'd never really given much thought to, was now clear. She had known the truth, and had kept in touch with Hank via mail, but said nothing to keep peace in the family. No telling what kind of beef there had been John finally thought, and put the matter to rest. He settled back into his chair to wait as the time passed slowly.

Eventually, passengers began to stir in the waiting area. John checked his watch and noted it was quarter to seven. He grabbed his coat and walked toward the counter in the waiting area, where a new attendant was speaking into the microphone.

"Ladies and gentlemen, conditions have improved enough

in Kenai for our departure" the attendant said cheerfully. "Due to the delay, we will be combining passengers from the five-thirty flight with the seven o'clock flight. We will begin boarding immediately. We apologize to our five-thirty passengers for the delay." With that, she set the microphone down, and walked over to a podium at the door to the flight line.

People immediately started lining up at the podium. John made his way in that direction, and saw a larger airplane was now on the ramp. It was still much smaller than anything he'd ever been on. John pulled on his coat and got out his boarding pass and driver's license. The attendant took them, gave them a cursory glance and handed them back with a thank you. Snow fell steadily, but there was less bite in the wind. The temperature had climbed a little with the arrival of the snow.

Being last in line, John found there wasn't much choice in seating to be had. He slid into the first available seat and found himself sitting next to one of the men from the Schlumberger crew. On the other side of the aisle, two more Schlumberger hands were sitting together. The one in the aisle seat leaned over to John and held out a pair of ear plugs.

"You want a pair?"

John looked at the plugs and asked, "Are the engines that loud?"

"They're not for the engine noise," the hand explained, "they're for Billy's screaming." At the comment, he and his partner roared with laughter.

John turned and looked at his seat mate. Billy did appear to be a little pale.

"Don't pay any attention to those guys. I'm not quite that bad," Billy said softly, "I just don't like to fly... even in good weather."

At the front of the plane, the flight attendant closed and locked the hatch to the plane. The turbines on the engines whined as each of the engines was started. While the plane rolled slowly forward, rocking with the wind, the flight attendant came on the intercom and gave the same pre-flight spiel John had heard on every flight he'd ever been on, until the very end.

"Ladies and gentlemen, we are expecting some moderately heavy turbulence on the way to Kenai. For that reason, the captain has requested I stay in my seat for the duration of the flight, and I will not be offering any in-flight service. Thank you."

Billy moaned, and John searched frantically through the pouch in front of him to find the burpy bag. The assholes across the aisle emitted gales of laughter.

The plane taxied out, turned to the left, and followed the taxiway along the main runway to the end. The cabin lights dimmed as the aircraft made a hard right onto the runway, straightened out, paused briefly and then lurched forward as the pilot gave the engines throttle. John looked out the window as best he could, and saw the snow become a white blur in the landing lights as the plane gathered speed. Billy pressed his head back against the leather of his seat and squeezed his eyes shut as the plane rapidly gathered speed. John could feel the plane lift slightly, then angle upward sharply. The pitch in the engines changed, and the plane banked to the left as it continued to climb. The turbulence promised by the flight attendant was not lacking. The plane bounced and rocked sharply as the pilot completed the left-hand bank and continued over the Cook Inlet. With every jolt of turbulence, John could hear the aircraft flex. At one particularly sharp drop that left John's stomach in his throat, Billy's hand shot up to brace against the overhead luggage compartment. His eyes were still clenched shut.

"Don't worry mister," Billy mumbled, "I don't get sick."

"*Good thing,*" John thought to himself, "*we don't want no puke in the office.*"

The violence of the turbulence decreased after several minutes and the plane settled into an almost rhythmic rocking, with the occasional dip that made John feel lightheaded. Just as the knot in his stomach would loosen a little, another bounce would tighten it back up. He was glad he'd taken Doreen's advice about avoiding a large meal.

The Schlumberger hand across the aisle leaned over and spoke to John in a serious tone. "How's Billy doing?"

"Well, he hasn't screamed, anyway," John replied. "He really doesn't like to fly, does he?"

"Scares him half to death. Every time we get into weather, Billy has a serious come-to-Jesus meeting. Never gets sick, though." The man laughed and added, "I guess when you're honestly, completely paralyzed with fear, nothing works, not even your gag reflex."

John tried to look out the window, but there was absolutely nothing to see. He couldn't tell if that was because of the dark, or if there was truly nothing there. He thought about asking the guy across the aisle, but he and his buddy were busy yukking it up over something.

The plane started to descend. The engines changed pitch frequently, and it felt as if brakes were being applied to their forward motion. The landing lights came on, and the landing gear dropped out, locking into place. John thought he could make out lights in the distance through the interference of the snow. Eventually, the plane's descent rate stopped and John saw runway below the plane. There was a long glide just above the runway, then the plane thumped down hard, followed immediately by a roar from the engines as the pilot reversed pitch in the props to act as an air brake. The plane wobbled slightly on the slick runway as it slowed down and then turned to the left toward a spread out, well-lit building. The attendant got on the intercom and announced the obvious. Once the pilot had shut down the engines and the props had been secured by the ground crew, the hatch was opened and the passengers began filing off the aircraft.

"Thank you, amen," Billy muttered aloud then lowered his arm and opened his eyes.

"I don't know about you," John said as he stood up, "but it seems to me a prudent, thoughtful man would give serious consideration to finding another line of work. Maybe one that requires no flying."

"You can't beat the pay," Billy said with a shrug.

Stepping off the plane John looked at the Kenai terminal through the blowing snow. There wasn't much to it. People made their way toward a door on the right-hand side of a large window where people could be seen watching for expected arrivals.

Inside the building, John walked down a glass enclosed hallway to the waiting area. The welcome parties milled around, mixing with the arrivals to create a knot of humanity expressing the simple joy of seeing someone who had been gone and missed. The scene made John feel truly alone.

To the right of the waiting area was a looping conveyor belt for luggage claim. Beyond the throng, John could make out two car rental counters, but only one looked to be open for business. Winding his way through the people, he walked over to counter and found a note saying, "Back in 10 minutes."

"The way Alaskans keep time," John thought, *"I could be waiting until midnight."*

He turned around and walked toward the conveyor belt. When the belt started moving, people stepped up to grab their bags and wander off. Again, nobody checked claim tickets. After retrieving his bag, John returned to the rental counter.

At the counter, John studied two glass display cases located on opposite ends of the waiting area. One contained a collection of mounted fish. There were several species on display, including a rainbow trout bigger than John thought they could possibly grow, and several kinds of salmon. Across from the display of fish was another glass case in which a stuffed bear stood on its hind paws, a snarl was frozen permanently on its lips, its front paws reached out with claws that had to be at least six inches long. The bear was enormous, at least eight feet tall. John thought back to his uncle's description of the unbelievable fishing and the animals in Alaska he had encountered. If what was on display in the cases was any indication, the old man hadn't been exaggerating.

"May I help you, sir?"

John jumped at the voice. A young man had slipped behind the counter, unseen. "Yes, I need to rent a car for two days."

"We can do that. Just two days?"

"Yeah," John replied, "at the very most."

CHAPTER 5

Harley Pepperdine viewed his handiwork spread out on the table at the Rainbow. There were five empty beer bottles, and three empty shot glasses. He was feeling pretty good, and finishing up on the sixth beer. Since Trevor and Carole had deserted him, the Rainbow had started to gather a crowd. Harley visited with the people who stopped by his table on their way in. Most wanted to know what had happened after his run-in with Mark Kells. His response to each inquiry was the same. There wasn't much to tell. He'd spent a few days as a guest of Kenai, at Wildwood, and had a court date for the charge of "drunk on premises." That drew a laugh every time. What else could be expected in the Rainbow on a Saturday night, if not a drunk on premises? All parties expressed the same opinion: Harley was lucky Trevor had made the arrest. Harley grew tired of hearing he owed his younger half-brother, big time.

He picked at the label on his bottle for a few moments and mulled over the same question that had been bouncing around in his head all night: what was life after Hardrock going to hold? He had worked for the old timer for almost eight years. It was the only reliable job he'd ever had. He owed the old miner for keeping him on, and for overlooking his obvious flaws. Steady work for a jack-of-all-trades kind of guy was spotty, at best. Temporary summer work was the best he had been able to find before Hardrock took him on.

Before Hardrock's wake started, Wes Bartholomew had pulled him aside and told Harley he'd still have a job, no matter what, but wouldn't go into any details. Wes told him things would shake out no later than the twentieth of the month. Wes, it seemed to Harley, was being more than just a little cryptic. Harley liked Wes, but sometimes he didn't like the lawyer that was Wes.

Harley held up his bottle and shook it lightly it at Ginger, the waitress who had relieved Carole. Ginger walked over to Harley's table. She was a stout woman, in her forties. One look at her, and it was obvious she'd seen more than her share of years dealing with all the trials serving drinks could provide.

"How about a cup of coffee, instead?" she asked Harley in a raspy voice.

"Coffee? Bleah! There is absolutely nothing worse than a wide awake drunk. No, I think another beer is in order."

"Can't do it," Ginger said firmly. "Mel told me you've had enough. Look what's on your table."

"Oh, those. See, that's not my fault. Carole started it. And for that very reason," Harley said with mock satisfaction, "she left without receiving a gratuity."

"You are one tough customer, Harley. But the boss says no more alcohol."

Harley leaned to one side and looked past Ginger at the bar, where Mel was holding up a pot of coffee. Harley waved him off, then looked back at Ginger.

"No, my dear," he said as he stood up unsteadily, "since this establishment seems to have run out of hospitality, I think it is time for me to take my leave. Can my tab stand?"

"Better than you. You want a cab? It's too ugly out there to be walking around."

"No, I'm good. Got Trevor's key right here. Just a slip, stagger and fall away." Harley held up the key to Trevor's apartment then slid it into his pocket.

Ginger glanced toward the bar, at Mel. Mel simply shrugged and turned to pour another drink for a customer at the bar.

Harley slipped on his coat and gloves, pulled his hat down over his ears, and headed for the door. The cold air served to clear his head slightly as he stepped out into the snow. He walked with an unsteady gate. Once out of the Rainbow, he walked toward the Spur Highway. Trevor lived in an apartment complex off the Spur, slightly less than a mile away. Harley wanted to walk, hoping it would sober him up a little. Besides, he was in no hurry, and comparatively speaking, it wasn't very cold. The temperature was in the upper twenties, and while it was still snowing, the wind had laid down.

At the highway, Harley checked his watch and saw it was just a few minutes before eight o'clock. In Harley's drunken logic, it seemed fairly early in the evening. There would be, no doubt, plenty of traffic between Kenai and Nikiski for the next few hours. Undoubtedly, some of that traffic would recognize him. After all, he reasoned, someone doesn't grow up and live somewhere for over thirty years, without a good number of people knowing you by sight. In short order, Harley had convinced himself in the soundness of hitchhiking home, and was on the other side of the highway, sticking his thumb out for a ride, making his way along the road in the new snow.

His reasoning was borne out when a large red truck with a snow plow on it slowed down and pulled over.

"Harley! What the hell are you doing walking around in this weather?" the driver shouted out through the passenger window.

"Hey, Pete, haven't seen you for months. A better question would be, what the hell are you doing *driving* around in this weather?"

Pete Waller made his living as a commercial fisherman, working set nets in the summer with his brother, Don, off the beaches near a community called Ninilchik, forty miles south of where he lived in Kenai. Since salmon prices and numbers can often be disappointing, he ran a snowplowing business for a steady income in the winter. Contracted out to various businesses, when the snow fell Pete was expected to respond.

"Plow rounds. This stuff is supposed to play out completely before midnight, so it's time to get started. You need a ride?"

"Yeah. How far north are you going? I'm trying to get back to the Shuffle."

"I can get you as far as the fire station at Lower Salamatof. That will get you a good portion of the way."

Harley nodded in agreement and climbed into the truck. The two men caught up with each other as the lights of Kenai faded behind them.

"Say, Pete, I know a man of your occupation, being as it entails hours spent in inclement weather, would never venture forth inadequately supplied to survive the arctic rigors. Do you, by chance, have some anti-freeze you could share with a poor, half-frozen wayfarer, such as myself?"

"Pepperdine," Pete snorted, "you are so full of bullshit, someone ought to spread you out on a field. Check the glove box."

Harley popped the glove box open and pulled out a bottle of apricot brandy. "Don't worry," he said to Pete as he unscrewed the cap and took a large swig, "I'm sure the doctor was completely wrong, and it's just a cold sore."

Pete laughed loudly and waved Harley off when he offered him the bottle. "Cold sore, or not, it's a little early in the rounds for me to get started. Mostly, that bottle is for when Don and me go ice fishing."

"A prudent man, you are," Harley said as he took another deep pull on the bottle. He screwed the cap back on and put the bottle back into the glove box. The brandy was thick and almost too sweet. Harley felt it's warmth as it hit bottom. He felt a glow spread across his face.

Several miles outside of Kenai, Pete slowed down and pulled off to the edge of the road where a car sat with its rear end stuck on a snow berm. Tracks in the snow indicated the car must have spun around on the slippery road before getting stuck.

When the truck stopped, the driver's door on the car opened, and a man stepped out. He waved excitedly. Pete stepped out to talk with him. Harley, feeling the double whammy of the brandy on top of his previous drinks stayed in the truck.

"I never even saw it until it was right in my headlights. It was *huge!*" the driver exclaimed. "I swerved to miss it, and spun around into the snow bank. I've never seen anything like that! One second the road was clear and the next, it was all I could see!"

"Yup. Moose are like that," Pete said calmly. "You okay? Anyone hurt?"

"I'm fine, and nobody is with me. I think the car is just stuck. I can't seem to get enough traction to get out of the snow bank."

"That's a rental, isn't it?" Pete asked in a disgusted tone.

"Yeah, I just picked it up at the airport not twenty minutes ago," John Barstow replied.

"I'm also going to guess you're not used to driving in snow."

"Not at all. It all just happened so fast! I just can't believe it. First time I see a moose and it almost kills me!"

"Damn car rental agencies," Pete spit out, "they don't even put good snow tires on their cars, let alone studs, and then rent them to people from Outside with no experience driving in the snow. It's practically criminal!"

Pete walked over to the car and examined the situation. There was no visible damage to the car. The problem, it appeared, was the rear axle was simply hung up on the hard packed snow. It was a simple fix. He went to the back of his truck for a shovel he kept there.

"You wan' help?" Harley slurred.

"The best help you can offer is to stay out of the way," Pete replied.

After Pete and John dug out around the back end of the car, Pete gently eased it off the berm with a tow strap.

"Hey, thanks a lot," John offered from inside the rental. "I'm sure I'd have been here for quite some time if you hadn't stopped."

"Not really," Pete replied as he unhooked the tow strap, "people around here are pretty good about checking out cars off the side of the road. Where are you headed?"

"I'm trying to find a place in Nikiski called the Shuffle Inn. You have any idea where it is?"

"Just so happens my friend is headed there. It would save me a bunch of trouble and worry if he could hitch a ride with you. I really need to get on with my plow rounds."

"It's the least I could offer."

"I'll level with you, he's drunk as hell."

"But he's a congenial drunk," John finished. "I'm very familiar with the condition."

Pete laughed again, "Exactly. In fact, he'll probably sleep all the way there."

"Since he's not going to be any help navigating," John said, handing Doreen's list and directions out the window, "would you look at the instructions on the bottom of the page, and fill in anything that's missing?"

Pete looked at the paper John handed him and scanned the instructions. He also noticed Harley's name on the list at the top of the paper. He was familiar with most of the other names as well, and was immediately suspicious. "That will get you there just fine," Pete said handing the paper back. "What are you doing in Nikiski?"

"It's a long story, but my uncle recently died and I'm supposed to look some things over for his estate. Maybe you knew him, Hank Grant. I guess most people called him Hardrock."

"Sure, I knew Hardrock, but I didn't know he had any family. I was sorry to hear about his passing. Helluva guy, Hardrock."

"Wha' 'bout Har'ock?" Harley called from the truck as clearly as his spinning head would allow.

Pete excused himself and stepped quickly to the passenger side of his truck and whispered sharply, "Shut up. This guy says he's Hardrock's nephew. You understand me, Harley?"

"Everything okay?" John called out.

"Everything's good," Pete shouted back, "I'm just telling my buddy you'll give him a ride." He turned back to Harley and continued his whispering. "Harley, this guy has a list with your name on it. He's here about Hardrocks's estate. Hardrock must have left Last Chance to him. He might be your new boss. Don't tell him who you are until you get a chance to sober up, okay? *Okay?*" Pete thought he saw a flicker of comprehension in Harley's drunken gaze.

"You need any help getting him in the car?" John called out.

"No, we're good," Pete answered.

Pete jerked the door of the truck open, and Harley pitched himself out, made a grab at Pete and landed spread-eagle on his face. Pete could hear the man in the car laugh. He grabbed Harley's collar and hoisted him up.

"Tha's a tall truck ya got, Pete," Harley mumbled as Pete slung Harley's arm over his shoulders and dragged him toward the car. "An' tha' brandy? Better stay 'way from it."

Pete assured Harley he'd leave the brandy alone as he dumped him into the seat of John's rental. He shut the door and walked around to John's side of the car as Harley fumbled with the seat belt. "I've got to get going. He'll be fine. You need to drive slower than you're used to on these roads, but I guess I don't need to tell you that, now."

"Definitely not," John answered emphatically. "By the way, my name's John." He stuck out his hand toward Pete.

Pete shook it, "I'm Pete, good to meet you." With that, he returned to his truck, hoping Harley had actually understood what he had been saying. He waved to John and continued on down the highway to the first of many parking lots the night held in store.

Harley had a hard time doing it, but finally managed to get his seat belt fastened. John watched him with a combination of humor and sad recollection.

"We got seat belt laws here," Harley said very deliberately.

John shook his head, and pulled slowly out onto the highway to turn north. He focused all of his attention on the road, certain the first moose had a suicidal friend lurking about. He kept the speed under forty-five and drove on in silence.

Harley's head was spinning. The snowflakes flashing in the headlights of the car weren't helping the situation. The sweet brandy he'd gulped down wasn't sitting well on his stomach, either. He understood fully what Pete had said. He glanced occasionally at John, and tried to focus on the man. His eyes weren't cooperating in the effort. He felt hot, and needed some fresh air. "Mind if I roll the win'ow down some?" Harley finally asked. "I'm not feelin' so good."

"Go ahead," John replied, "we don't want no fuckin' puke in the office." He laughed to himself.

"Huh?"

"Nothing. Go ahead and roll the window down. Let me know if you need to puke, and I'll pull over."

Harley rolled the window down half-way, and put his face where the wind would blow directly on it. It helped push away the nausea.

Thinking maybe the drunk needed some conversation to preoccupy him, John tried striking up a conversation. "Looks like you've been out celebrating."

"Didn' start out tha' way," Harley said and started laughing hard.

Even though he was clueless as to what the drunk meant, John couldn't help but laugh along with him. "Well, what did you end up celebrating?" he asked in an effort to keep the conversation rolling.

Harley caught his breath. "Foun' out I didn' lose my job, I got a new boss." Harley laughed even harder.

John shook his head. He wondered how many conversations like this one he'd had in years past that he didn't remember.

Wind in his face, or not, Harley was feeling sick. Before he could get his lips to form the words to stop the car, he was throwing up.

"Oh, *shit!*" John shouted as he pulled the car over and slid to a stop.

Harley pushed the door open, leaned out and finished retching on the side of the road. He sat up and slammed the door closed, then wiped his mouth with the back of his hand. "S'okay, s'okay. Mostly on the floor mat. No prob. Jus' some poppers, anyhow."

"You done?" John asked curtly.

"Yup. Feel much better. Clean 'er up when we get to the Shuffle."

John toyed briefly with the idea of pulling the mat out, but decided it would best wait until they got somewhere he could see what he was doing, and after he got rid of the drunk. He pulled back onto the highway to continue on down the road.

Harley felt much better after puking. With the cold air whistling through the car, his head was clearing up. What Pete had told him about the man driving flashed back into his consciousness. That man could possibly be his new boss, and he had just thrown up in his rental car.

"*I'll bet after tonight,*" Harley thought, "*he's gonna want to see references.*"

That struck Harley as the funniest thing he'd ever thought up, and he broke out into another round of hysterical laughter. John didn't want to know what was so funny this time. He just wanted his day from hell to come to an end. The snow had all but stopped falling, and he drove on, pushing the car along as fast as he dared. Finally, John caught sight of the sign for the Shuffle Inn.

John pulled off the highway and up to the building. There was only one other vehicle in the parking lot, an old, battered truck. Immediately to the left of the Shuffle Inn, stood a two-story building which looked like a small, rundown apartment building. However, the painted wooden sign on top of it proclaimed it to be a hotel.

Harley fumbled with his seat belt latch and started to climb out of the car, hanging onto the door for support. John stepped out of his side of the car and started around to help Harley to the entrance of the bar, when he saw a large wolf-like dog approach from the front of the parked truck. The animal lowered its head as the hackles on its back raised slightly. It approached Harley, bared its teeth and growled ominously.

"Git!" Harley shouted at the animal. "Scram, ya mutt." The dog snarled at Harley menacingly in response. "I mean it, sombitch!"

John stood frozen, unsure of what to do. He didn't want to see the drunk get mauled, but wasn't at all willing to face a dog that large himself. When the dog turned its attention to John, its demeanor changed immediately. His tail wagged, his lips relaxed and his tongue lolled out. He trotted up to John, sniffed him gently, then nuzzled John's gloved hand.

John heaved a sigh of relief. He looked toward Harley to see how he was doing. Harley was hanging onto the door for stability.

"Damn, wuthless, flea-bag, sombitch. Somebody oughta shoot it," Harley grumbled.

John patted the dog's head, and the dog responded to the affection by wagging its entire body. "He seems fine, now," John said, continuing to pat the dog's head. "Do you know whose dog is it?"

"Yeah," Harley replied in a disgusted tone, "it's mine. Sombitch never has liked me."

At the sound of Harley's voice, the dog curled its lip one more time, then slunk off in the direction of the hotel building.

"You okay?" John asked Harley.

"Yeah. I'm feeling better. Hey, sorry 'bout your car. It's mostly..."

"Yeah, I know, on the floor mat. You already said. You need help getting in?"

"No, I'm good. Gonna get some fresh air first. Go 'head."

Stepping into the Shuffle Inn, John noticed the conversation between the only two patrons in the bar stopped. Their heads swiveled to look him over. It made John feel as if he was being sized up for trouble. After a moment the men went back to their conversation. Judging from their nods in his direction, he was now the topic of discussion.

John looked toward the bar and saw an enormous man standing behind it, wiping it down with a towel. The man was one of the most intimidating people John had ever seen. His shaved head was accentuated with a dark, bushy beard. His massive forearms were covered in tattoos. Some looked to be professional work, but others looked to be amateur work, like something a person would get while serving time in prison. John guessed, just by looking at him, few people who entered the building would be a match for this giant. John swallowed hard and walked toward the bar.

"Excuse me, I'm looking for Gary Fisk," he said softly.

The huge man looked John over carefully, and then extended a hand the size of a country ham and offered a smile. "You must be John Barstow," he said in a deep voice, "Wes called and told me to expect you. I'm Gary Fisk, but most folks call me Doorway."

John made an effort to shake the man's hand, but found he couldn't completely wrap his fingers around it. The giant's paw engulfed his hand, his grip was firm but not crushing, and he seemed totally unaware of how awkward John's grip was. It was probably a normal event for a man of that size.

"Doorway?" John asked.

"Yeah," one of the men at the table, who had obviously been listening in, replied, "because he fills one when he walks through it."

Fisk smiled broadly, and both the men at the table laughed, which immediately put John's concerns to rest.

"Wes said you just flew in today. I'll bet you could use something to drink," Doorway said as he withdrew his hand. "What can I get you?"

"To be honest, I don't drink," John said, waiting for the usual comments, but Doorway's response was quick and surprising.

"Me either, at least not anymore. How about a cup of coffee? I've even got decaf if you want it."

"No, a cup of the high octane stuff would be better. I'm feeling a little bleary-eyed. It's been a helluva day."

John slid up on a stool at the bar as the big man set a mug down on it. Doorway looked past John toward the door and saw Harley walk in and studiously shut it.

When Doorway started to call out, Harley shook his head vigorously and held a finger up to his lips to cut him off. He also shot a quick look at the two men at the table, then nodded toward John. The men both nodded, and went back to their conversation. They knew the rule of the "North Road," as the folks in Nikiski often referred to their community, was not to ask questions. If someone didn't want their name known by a stranger, there was probably good reason for it.

John put down the mug and looked at Harley sourly. He was irritated at the prospect of having to clean up the mess in his rental. At the same time, John wasn't hypocrite enough to condemn the guy, as he was sure it was a karma thing coming back to haunt him from his own similar transgressions.

Doorway sensed something was going on, and tried the waters. "You two met?"

"In a manner of fashion," John mumbled into his mug as he took another sip. "I drove him here after his buddy pulled me out of a snow bank alongside the road. I figured it was a good way to pay back his buddy's kindness. However, my new friend here, barfed in my car about ten miles back."

"So, you haven't actually been introduced?" The bartender let out a loud laugh.

"Name's Bob," Harley said, holding onto the bar with his left hand to steady himself while extended his right hand toward John.

John looked at the hand, and the vision of it wiping away the remnants of vomit from the drunk's mouth less than half an hour earlier played largely in his mind.

"Bob, I'm John. I mean no offense," John replied slowly, "and it's nice to meet you, but let's shake hands later, since I know where that hand has been."

"No 'fense taken," Harley answered. Wobbling a little, Harley turned to the bartender. "Doorway, you got my key?"

"I do," Doorway replied as he turned around to pull a key ring off a peg on the wall behind the bar, "been keeping it safe for you. Been feeding your dog, too."

"Ha! Shoulda let that fur bag sombitch starve."

Doorway held out the key, and on the second try, Harley managed to focus enough to grab it. With key in hand, Harley picked his way back through the challenging maze of chairs, opened the door, gave a quick wave to all, and disappeared for the night.

"Looks to me like Bob's been giving your competition quite a bit of business," John commented to Doorway. "Does he have a drinking problem?"

"Nah," came the quick reply, "he rarely goes on a bender like that. He's had some personal problems recently, is all. I'm sure he'll be a completely different person when you see him tomorrow." Doorway chuckled a little, then changed the subject, "I understand from Wes, I'm supposed to put you in touch with some people?"

"Yeah, Wes gave me this list," John said, pulling the paper from his shirt pocket, "I guess the first person I need to talk with is a fellow named Pepperdine, Harley Pepperdine." There was an outburst of laughter from the two men at the table. John glanced in their direction, then continued on, "I understand he lives in your hotel? You must keep at least two of your rooms filled most of the time, between Pepperdine and Bob."

"I only rent a few of them out steady during the winter months," Doorway answered quickly. "In the summer, my winter renters have jobs away from here, and it's more like a regular hotel then."

"I see. So, this Harley Pepperdine, suppose he's around?"

With North Road etiquette in effect, Doorway decided to tackle the question head-on, and called out to the men at the table. "Hey! Either of you guys seen Harley?"

"I can't say that I've seen him, Doorway."

"I can't say, either," the second man echoed, then both men hunkered back down to their private conversation and beers.

John sighed deeply. He felt like things were simply not going to be as smooth as Wes had led him to believe.

"I'm sure you'll connect tomorrow," Doorway offered, "I know for a fact he'll be here tomorrow. Wes told me to expect him to show up no later than the morning, and Wes seems to have a knack for knowing such things."

John laughed, then commented, "Wes is a piece of work, isn't he?"

"That he is," Doorway agreed. "By the way, I'm sorry about Hardrock, he's going to be missed. He had more friends than most."

"Yeah, so I understand," John said quietly. He suddenly felt an emptiness. It wasn't a feeling of mourning at the loss of his uncle so much as it was a sadness brought on by not having had the chance to truly know what he had lost. It was time to talk about something else.

"Doorway, what do you know about getting puke out of a car?"

"Ah, that little problem. Is it on the seat?"

"No, it's on the floor, and according to Bob, it's 'mostly on the mat,' but I didn't look to see."

"Well, he was close enough to the subject to know. If it was me, I'd let it sit the night out and freeze. It'll be easier to clean up frozen, and you'll be able to see better in the morning light."

"That's sound advice. Besides," John said in a tired voice, "I've had about all I can handle for one day. I'm beat. Wes said you had a room for me?"

Doorway turned around and pulled another key off a peg on the wall behind the bar. This one had a regular hotel style key ring attached to it bearing the number four.

"Here you go. It's the middle room on the second floor. Sorry about the climb, but I figured since you aren't used to the colder weather, you'd want the warmest room in the place."

John took the key and asked what he owed for the room.

"It's paid for. Wes took care of it."

John was surprised. "I need to sign anything? Fill anything out?"

"What for? You plan on stealing my fine quality linens? Speaking of which," the big barkeep continued with a wink, "the stylized 'S' embossed on the towels and washcloth stands for Shuffle Inn, unless they have a green 'H' on them. In that case, it stands for Hotel."

John laughed. He liked the big man's easy-going manner. Hank had told the truth those thirty years ago, when he said people in Alaska were a different breed.

After retrieving his bag from the car, John made his way over to the hotel. The stairs on the side of the building led up to the second floor in one stretch. They were welded from heavy steel and had treads made of expanded metal with serrated edges on the walking surface. They seemed industrial to John, but upon feeling what a solid surface they provided, it made sense. In a climate where snow and ice were the norm for half the year, stairs that didn't hold snow or water were entirely logical.

Icicles hung at a slight angle from the edge of the overhang protecting the walkway. They were pushed in one direction from a prevailing wind. The temperature was cold enough they weren't dripping. John guessed they grew when the sun shone, melting the snow on the edge of the overhang. He turned the key in the lock and pushed his way in with the bag, and felt for a light switch with his left hand. Finding it, he flipped it up and a lamp in the far corner lit up the room.

To the left was a living area with a recliner on the far wall, a sofa with an end table on the left hand wall, and a television in the corner at the end of the sofa. The front wall of the room had a window looking out onto the front porch. On the right side of the entrance was a little kitchen, complete with small refrigerator, stove, coffee pot, microwave, sink and dinette. The back wall of the kitchen served as a divider to the sleeping area.

The sleeping area, open to the main room, had a bed neatly made up with a cover in a mottled tan. Extra blankets were laid across the foot of the bed, although John doubted they would be needed as the room was warm. Next to the bed was a chest of drawers, and in the middle of the back wall was another window. Built into the back side of the kitchen wall, was a large closet. Opposite the bed was the door to a small bathroom with a shower stall.

It certainly wasn't the finest place he'd ever stayed, but it was apparent to John the long-term residents of the Shuffle Inn Motel could get by comfortably.

John threw his bag and coat on the bed. He pulled out his shaving kit and the shirts he would hang up, but the rest of his clothes could stay in the bag. He wasn't going to be here long enough to worry about unpacking.

After putting his shaving kit in the bathroom, and hanging up his shirts, he walked over to the sofa. Arranging the pillows in the corners of the sofa, he sat down and kicked back. The events of the day rolled through his mind. Had he really left LA less than a day ago? It seemed like a week. All the information Wes had thrown at him seemed fuzzy, at best. Most of all, there seemed to be more questions than answers. What little information he had on the people he would meet in the next two days was contained in the list Doreen had given him. He pulled it out to read it again to see if there was anything he'd missed the first dozen times through. Each name on the list was underlined, as if it was important for John to memorize them.

John didn't know if Doreen had written the list in any particular order, but at the top was Gary Fisk.

"Gary Fisk is the owner and principle bartender at the Shuffle Inn. He will provide you with lodging in the hotel associated with his bar while you stay in Nikiski. He will also serve as your contact to reach the remainder of the people on this list."

At that, John thought, *"If Doreen knows him so well, I wonder why she didn't just call him Doorway, like everybody else? And it sure would have been a help to get a physical description, just as a warning."*

The list continued with Harley Pepperdine. "<u>Harley Pepperdine</u> has worked for your uncle at Last Chance over eight years. He is an easy-going man, with many friends in the area. If there is someone you want information about, Harley can probably provide it. He was born and raised in the Nikiski/Kenai area. Hardrock took him in when nobody else would give him a job, due to his reputation for drinking heavily. However, drinking has never been an issue, and his reliability is without question. Hardrock had complete faith in him. Wes believes he will be critical to your success, should you chose to accept the agreement to operate Last Chance Adventures."

John thought the part about Pepperdine having so many friends somewhat humorous. *"Well, for a guy with a lot of friends, people sure have trouble keeping track of his ass. Even his landlord didn't have a clue where he was tonight."*

Mr. Reeder was the third person on the list. "<u>Mr. Reeder</u> owns an air taxi and freight service in Nikiski. He has served as the principle transport service for both your uncle and the guests staying with Last Chance Adventures since its inception. Mr. Reeder is the only pilot your uncle trusted completely."

John looked at the name again. *"Being a pilot must command a lot of respect in Alaska,"* he thought, *"he's the only person on the list with a title. Maybe it's because Hank thought so highly of him. Or maybe Doreen just doesn't know his first name."*

The only female name on the list was fourth in line. "<u>Cynthia Smythe</u> is the booking agent for Last Chance Adventures, maintains a web presence for the business, takes care of advertising, and handles the correspondence with potential clients. She also keeps the books. You will want to review the financial records with her."

"Sounds as if she's the person I'll spend the most time with." John re-read Cynthia's description, and noticed

something. *"Funny, though, she's the only person that doesn't have some sort of personal comment. I wonder how long she's been running the show."*

For a reason he couldn't quite identify, the last name on the list seemed familiar to John this time through the list. "Billy McCrane owns the store next to the Shuffle Inn that bears his name- McCrane Mercantile. He also supplies bush orders. There is little in the way of supplies Billy can't provide, from food and fuel to hardware and lumber. He works with Mr. Reeder to get things out to the Last Chance."

John laughed. *"The store! That's where I saw the name. This Billy McCrane sounds like a one man Costco operation in a cracker box storefront. Well, Mr. McCrane, I hate to break it to you, but your business days with Last Chance may have come to an end."*

John thought about the people on the list. He had already met Doorway, who was sure John would meet with Pepperdine tomorrow. After reviewing the list again, John wasn't so sure meeting with Pepperdine was all that critical anymore, nor was meeting McCrane. *"What's the point?"* he thought. *"Unless lightning strikes, and I take up the offer to try my hand at being a tourist trap operator, it would be time wasted. And it's not too likely I'll be running Last Chance Adventures, since I don't know squat about mining."*

John did, however, want to meet the pilot and the bookkeeper. The pilot he'd like to meet just for the opportunity to fly over and have a firsthand look at Last Chance. It was unlikely, but maybe there was something out there that would make giving up a year of his life worthwhile. The meeting with Smythe would be able to answer the question about being worthwhile. Who could tell, maybe mining the miners was more profitable than he imagined. If Doorway was the point of contact for these people, John decided he would ask him to arrange for an early meeting with Reeder, followed by one with Smythe. The others weren't really a critical part of the equation.

A quick glance at his watch told John there was a reason he was ready for some sleep, it was eleven o'clock, LA time. He thought about taking a shower, but didn't want to run the risk of waking himself up. He settled for just washing his face.

CHAPTER 6

A faint glow spread out from behind the insulated curtains on the window when John woke up. The alarm clock on top of the dresser by the bed showed quarter after seven. The last time he had looked at the clock it was showing two in the morning. He wanted to blame that last coffee, but the truth was he simply couldn't shut his mind off after he laid down. He would just start to drift off to sleep, and another question about the bizarre situation he found himself in would spring up in his mind.

He felt an urgency to get things rolling, but figured he would have to wait at least a couple of hours before he would see Doorway. John cursed when he thought of how he should have made some sort of arrangements for a meeting time with Doorway. The clock was ticking and he had to tread water. He should have at least gotten Doorway's phone number, and asked how late the bar stayed open. He decided to look Gary Fisk up in the phone book and give him a call. John hoped Doorway didn't stay open too late at the bar, and calling so early wouldn't cause a problem. Doorway was way too big to piss off.

The number listed to Gary Fisk provided no answer, voice mail, or even an answering machine. John decided he would try again after taking a shower. He set up the coffee maker to run its two cups, then went into the bathroom to take a shower.

After the shower and a few sips of coffee, John tried Doorway's number again, with the same result as before. It seemed obvious to John that Doorway was used to working late, and sleeping late. He probably turned the ringer off on his phones to keep from being disturbed. But even with that, any sort of answering device should still work. He found it unbelievable, given this age of electronic communication, the man didn't have any sort of way to record phone calls. As far as communication went, Doorway's phone was truly the "Last Frontier."

John mulled over what to do. There was always the car to clean up, but the prospect of doing that, even before he had breakfast, made him feel queasy. Breakfast had to be the first order of business. Perhaps the store next door opened early. He would walk next door to McCrane Mercantile and buy something to eat. While there, maybe he could find out what time Doorway usually showed up at the Shuffle Inn. He wouldn't try to look up Billy McCrane. Of all the people on the list, John considered McCrane to be the least important. He grabbed his coat from the closet and headed out.

There were just a few clouds in the sky when John stepped out onto the porch. The wind had shifted, now coming out of the north. Although the wind was light, the ambient temperature was much colder than it had been when he walked to his room the night before. He looked at the icicles on the edge of the overhang and noticed their pronounced lean was lined up with the current flow of the wind. John pulled the collar of his coat up around his neck against the cold air.

"I doubt if they'll be growing much today," he thought as he looked at the weak sunlight glinting off the icicles.

Looking in the direction of the Shuffle Inn, John noted most of the parking spaces in front of the building were taken. The majority were obviously working vehicles, pickups bearing the names of businesses, from private contractors to major oil field service companies. His curiosity piqued, he walked over to see what was going on.

The door of the Shuffle Inn opened just as John reached for it. Four men stepped out, leaving the door open for John in their passing, and walked around him on their way to a crew-cab pickup. They wore familiar blue coats. John recognized them as the Schlumberger crew he'd flown with from Anchorage to Kenai. He marveled at what a small world this part of the world actually was. They climbed in their truck, still bitching about how much they hated going to Kenai.

When John stepped through the door he saw most of the ten tables were occupied by at least two people, and several people sat at the bar. There were women as well as men in the crowd. All the patrons were dressed in a similar fashion, work boots, canvas coveralls and heavyweight shirts. Coats were slung over the backs of chairs, or left hanging on the rack by the door. Some of the coats had business logos and names on them, but most were the plain canvas type made by the likes of Carhartt. This was a working stiff's breakfast gathering. A steady hum of conversation, punctuated with an occasional exclaimed profanity, filled the air. The individual conversations were indistinct, but taken as a whole, it felt they were all one long, uninterrupted chatter.

"I told the boss we didn't have enough welding rod... and then when he lifted the load... he said the tranny has to be rebuilt... you know the guy, he's the... sonofabitch if he didn't get the rig... yeah, damn cold... it wouldn't even turn over..."

John looked the crowd over. This was a group picture of the community, a snapshot of the people who were the collective organism called the population of Nikiski. They looked to be rough enough to make it in a place that could be as harsh as Alaska; even the women, dressed no differently than their male counterparts. In fact, they looked as if they would thrive on the challenge such a harsh place could serve up. It sure as hell wasn't a scene from an LA bistro.

Unlike the previous night, the customers sitting at the tables took no notice of the outsider coming through the door. It was time to get on the job, and the tables were being vacated quickly. There were no new patrons coming in to fill the emptied seats. As each of the diners stood up, they tossed cash on top of the check that had been placed next to them as they ate. It was a practice everyone was well versed in: order, eat, pay, leave. It was only after they got up from their tables and walked past John that any of the people took notice of him. Some simply smiled, others looked him over critically, and shook their heads. None were curious enough to ask what a guy in Dockers, an L.L. Bean polyester blend coat and loafers was doing in their turf.

A younger woman with long, light brown hair, tied back in a ponytail and covered with a bandana, was hustling the tables clean. She was dressed in jeans and a red T-shirt. Even though the T-shirt was loose, John could tell she had an admirable figure. She buzzed past him without a glance, focused on gathering dishes and setting them along the length of one arm. With the other hand she was collecting the bills and cash left on the table. She moved with a liquidity and grace that indicated she was not only accustomed to the work pace, but fit beyond the need of her occupation. John almost turned a full circle in an effort to keep watching her. His focus on the woman was broken only when a booming voice called his name.

"John! There you are, *finally!*" Doorway roared from behind the bar. "I was beginning to think you skipped out on your bill." He laughed loudly at his own joke. "C'mon up to the bar, I've got a mug of coffee with your name on it."

John pulled his gaze from the woman, and continued on up to the bar. His surprise at seeing Doorway must have been legible on his face.

"What's with the face? Who else did you expect to see

behind the bar?" Doorway asked as he set a fresh mug of coffee down in front of John.

"Well, certainly not you. Don't you have a home? Better question yet, don't you sleep?"

"There will be more than plenty of time for sleeping when I'm dead," the big man shot back. "Besides, I own the place, this *is* home. Why would I want to be anywhere else? I get to see my friends from first thing in the morning, clear through to the last thing at night."

John shook his head. He would give just about anything to feel that way about a job.

"So, your place is also a restaurant?"

"Just in the mornings. Nothing but slap-dash breakfasts for working people. You hungry?"

John's answer was cut off by the woman bussing tables as she squeezed past Doorway, shooting a remark in his direction about how hard it was to find good employers nowadays. John watched her intently until she disappeared through a door at the far end of the bar. There was a clatter of dishes, and she reappeared to pick up another load.

"Doorway, damn it, I'm trying to work here. Why don't you go loaf somewhere else?"

Her boss took it all in stride. "Maggie," he said to the woman, "this is Hardrock's nephew, John. John, this soon-to-be unemployed smart-ass is Maggie Peters."

At the mention of Hardrock's name, Maggie stopped abruptly and turned toward John. "I was sorry to hear about your uncle," she said, "he was someone very dear to me. I'll miss him very much."

Her blue eyes glistened as she spoke, giving irrefutable testimony to the truth of her statement. She quickly turned and slid lithely between the scattered chairs to the next table in need of cleaning. John watched her closely until Doorway spoke.

"She and Hardrock were close. She had a tough childhood,

and Hardrock kept her out of trouble. At times, he was her best friend, and sometimes he was the father she needed."

John was stunned. He had never given any thought to the depth of his uncle, and the possibility he might have had a life encompassing something more than Last Chance. Maybe Hank had found family somewhere outside the blood relations he'd left behind in California.

"You want something to eat?" Doorway asked again, interrupting John's thoughts.

"Now that you mention it, I would."

"Maggie!" Doorway called out across the room. "Could you whip up something for John here?"

The woman turned and walked toward the bar, both arms loaded with the last of the dishes. She nodded at the Miller Gold Draft beer clock on the wall behind the bar. "The grill's down, Doorway. It's after eight. I've got to get this mess cleaned up and get to the heliport to pick up Mark. He's due in at nine, and he doesn't like to be left waiting."

Maggie slid behind Doorway again. John blushed when she smiled at him with a shrug as she disappeared through the door at the end of the bar. There was another clatter of dishes, but Maggie didn't reappear.

Doorway looked disgusted as he watched her pass through the door. "Don't want to leave Mark waiting," he repeated. "She ought not just leave Mark Kells waiting, she ought to leave his ass. Period."

John could tell by the tone in his voice Doorway and Maggie had already covered the subject more than just one time. It wasn't any of his business.

"Guess you'll have donuts," Doorway said, pointing to a bakery box on the bar to John's left. "Help yourself. Don't know how many are left, but eat your fill. They aren't much good after sitting around for a day, and I hate to throw things out. I need to duck into the back and help Maggie square things away. I'll be back in a couple of minutes."

Doorway turned and walked to the door Maggie had gone through. As he passed through it, John observed first hand that the big man's nickname definitely fit.

John looked around the bar and realized he was the only person remaining. He grabbed the mug of coffee, slid off his stool, and repositioned himself in front of the bakery box at the very end of the bar. In the silence of the empty bar, he could hear the activity in the kitchen. Between the clanging pans and rattling dishes, there was a heated discussion going on. John couldn't hear the entire conversation, but it quickly became apparent Doorway was letting Maggie know his opinion about what she should do with Mark Kells. Again, John reminded himself it was none of his concern, and he turned his attention back to the donuts.

He lifted the box lid and looked in. There were three donuts left. John picked one up, broke it in half and dipped it into his coffee. He wondered if it tasted so good because he felt half starved, or if it really was the best donut he'd ever eaten. The remainder of the donut disappeared quickly. He reached back into the box and grabbed another. He had just dipped it into his coffee when Maggie burst out of the kitchen. She was hurriedly pulling on her coat, and shouting over her shoulder.

"I don't have time for this crap, Doorway! We've been over all this time and time again. It's my call, and I'm in no mood to listen to you ramble on about it anymore. The tables are cleared, the dishwasher is loaded, and I am gone." John watched her as she stomped to the door and snatched it open. Just before she stepped outside, she turned and looked at John directly. Her bearing completely changed as she addressed him in an almost angelic voice. "It was nice to meet you, John. And I *am* sorry about Hardrock."

She turned and continued out the door, slamming it behind her. John sat for a moment and stared at the closed door. Pretty, or not, his opinion was that she needed some sort of medication to control one, or both, of her personalities. He turned back to the bar and saw Doorway was standing there with his back to him, pouring a cup of coffee. He turned around and held up the coffee pot, John nodded, and Doorway topped off John's mug.

"She's a spitfire," Doorway commented as he put the coffee back on the burner.

"I was tending more toward thinking she was unbalanced. Does she always go off like that?"

"Not unless you tell her something she doesn't want to hear, like her boyfriend is a total asshole."

John laughed at Doorway's observation, but could tell the situation actually dug at his new friend deeper than he let on. "Tell me something, Doorway," he said in an effort to change the subject, "how is it you can close the bar at midnight, and be back here to serve breakfast? Either you are superhuman, or there's more in your coffee than just a little caffeine."

"It's a simple matter of having somebody else open up shop and get things ready," Doorway explained. "I don't get here until a little before six, just in time to let the first of the customers in. Maggie comes in at three-thirty to get the place going. By the time the first customers show up, she's already got several breakfasts almost ready to serve. We have about the same number of people every morning, around fifty, so if there's a few extra, it doesn't require much effort to respond. Most are regulars, so they usually want the same thing every day."

"And people who just want a donut and coffee aren't a problem at all as far as prep time is concerned," John added.

"Exactly. I'll be right back," Doorway said suddenly. "I need to make sure the dishwasher isn't flooding out the kitchen. It's been leaking lately. When I get back, we'll figure out who on your list you want to get ahold of first."

Doorway went back into the kitchen, and John continued to sip on his coffee. In his estimation, there wasn't any figuring out to be done. He had decided the night before the pilot and the bookkeeper were the two most important people on the list. It was unlikely he'd be seeking out the others.

John heard the door to the bar open. He turned around to see who was coming in, and saw a familiar face.

"You're looking a little rough this morning, Bob."

Harley just grunted in return. He approached the bar slowly, with his head lowered. John recognized the gait and stance. If he was feeling anything like John thought he should, conversation would be limited, and less than interesting. Still, John thought he might have a little fun.

"Want a donut?" John asked with a straight face, reaching for the box.

Harley cast a glance at the box with blood-shot eyes. "Knock yourself out," Harley replied softly, "I'll just have coffee."

Harley walked around the end of the bar to the coffee pot, pulled a mug off the shelf, and filled it. He took a small sip and let out a low moan. Shuffling slowly, he came back around the bar and sat on the second stool to the right of John. After setting the mug on the bar, he hung his head over it and allowed the steam to rise up into his face. He sat that way, motionless and silent, for several moments, then spoke in a low voice.

"Sorry about the car. I'll take care of it."

"You going to live long enough to do it?"

"Dying isn't a problem, I woke up dead."

"Yeah," John said with a sigh, "been there and done that, more times than I care to recall."

John went back to sipping his coffee while Harley continued his coffee steam facial. They sat in silence for several minutes before Doorway returned from the kitchen. The bar owner paused for a moment, to assess the situation. Unsure of whether Harley had told John who he really was, Doorway decided it would be best to avoid using his name.

"Hey! You survived!" he exclaimed. Harley simply raised a hand up in response and continued soaking up the smell of the coffee. Doorway winked at John, and continued to badger Harley. "You're too late for breakfast, but there's some donuts left."

"I already offered," John said, joining in the game, "he's not in a donut mood."

Harley moaned and looked up at Doorway. "Let's have a little respect for the dearly departing, please."

The big man turned to John, "So, do you know who you want to talk to first?"

"I think I ought to talk to Mr. Reeder first, and make arrangements to fly out to Last Chance, if possible. I'd like to see it."

"I'm sure he can accommodate you. I'll call him right now."

"By the way," John added, "does he have a first name? Doreen's list just has 'Mr. Reeder' on it."

"He does, but everyone around here just calls him by his last name. We aren't a formal bunch here," he added with a wink, "so we drop the mister part."

Doorway stepped away from the bar and picked up a phone handset from its cradle on the wall behind the bar. While Doorway was dialing Reeder's number, John glanced to his right and saw the recovering drunk was staring at him in an appraising manner. It fell just short of a glare.

"What?" John said sharply, expecting the man to simply go back to hanging his head.

"What are you going to do with Last Chance?"

The blunt question took John aback. "What makes you think it's mine to do anything with?"

"You're Hardrock's nephew. I figure he left it to you out of some familial obligation. So, what are you going to do with it?"

"I don't see where it's any of your business," John answered curtly, then turned away to look at Doorway.

"Reeder has a couple of things to do first," Doorway said, placing the handset on the bar, "but said he would be here around noon. Anybody else you want to see between now and then?"

"Cynthia Smythe is next on my priority list."

Doorway paused for a moment before he picked the handset back up to call Smythe, then turned away from the bar. John glanced back to his right. There was no chance of mistaking the look he was receiving for anything other than a glare.

"I'm not the only one around here that would be interested in what your plans are for Last Chance," Harley said flatly.

John was tired of not only the man's persistence in pursuing his question, but the impertinence of the questioning itself. He decided to put the matter to rest.

"Look buddy, the situation is complicated. And more than that, it's private. I'm not going to discuss what I did, or did not, inherit from my uncle with a drunk I picked up alongside the road just last night."

"*Whoa!*" Doorway interrupted, "Let's just settle down a bit. What's going on?"

"I just asked the man a question is all," Harley said with a shrug. He looked back at John. "I'd like to know what your plans are for Last Chance."

"And I told you, the first time you asked: *it's none of your business,*" John shot back in a loud voice.

"I think you're wrong," Harley persisted, raising his own voice. "Hardrock was more a part of our lives than yours. He was the same as family to a lot of us. We've got more interest in Last Chance than just some passing curiosity, or greedy plans on turning it into a lump of cash."

John was off his stool now, clenching his fists. The last comment, although it may have been close to the mark, was definitely out of line. He could feel his face burning. Harley slid off his stool to stand his ground. Doorway moved more quickly than most people would think possible for a man his size, and was around the end of the bar, between the men before they even realized he had taken a step.

"That's enough!"

The big man stood solidly between the two smaller men. His sheer size alone created an effective barrier, but the cold tone of his voice let both men know he was prepared to do more than just act as a wall.

Harley looked at the big man and asked, "Are you taking his side, Doorway?"

"I don't see any sides to take. Barstow is right, it's a lot more complicated than a simple inheritance, you're out of line."

"Bullshit!" Harley spit out then turned away from the bar and made a straight line for the door, kicking a couple of chairs out his way as he left. The door slammed loudly on his departure.

"Between Maggie and him, I'm going to need a new door," Doorway sighed. "They're wearing that one out!"

His comment had the intended effect, and John laughed. "Thanks, Doorway, things were definitely getting a little tense."

A big hand slapped John roughly on the back as Doorway went back around the end of the bar.

"I didn't do it for you. I promised Wes I wouldn't let anything happen to prevent you from checking things out. I figure getting your ass beat to a pulp falls neatly into that category."

"And what makes you think I'd be the one to get thumped?" John asked indignantly.

"Just guessing by the look of your right eye," Doorway answered, pointing to the remnant of the shiner on John's cheek. "Looks to me like you beat the hell out of somebody's fist with your face."

John blushed and felt chastised, but knew further defense of his actions would be a waste of time. Time was running out. He needed to stay focused on meeting the people on the list. "You're probably right. Thanks. So what did Cynthia Smythe have to say?"

"I got her voice mail, and left a message for her to call me. I told her you were here."

"Well, I wasn't really planning on it," John said slowly, "but I guess since we've still got some time to kill before Reeder shows up, maybe I ought to meet Harley Pepperdine."

Doorway took a deep breath and let out a long sigh. "You already have. He just left."

John was confused for a moment, then the exact meaning of Doorway's reply struck home. John climbed back up on his barstool and stared at the big man. Doorway placed his hands on the bar and leaned against it, and hung his head. The two men remained silent, fixed in their positions for several minutes.

John's first thought was that he'd been betrayed. The events of the previous night played through his mind. He thought about how Pete, or whatever *his* real name was, must have seen Pepperdine's name on the sheet of paper, which explained the little pow-wow at the truck before he poured Pepperdine in John's car. It also explained what Pepperdine thought was so funny on the drive to the Shuffle Inn. It was all quite a little gag on the outsider when everybody went along with the "Bob" thing. They certainly made a fool out of him.

"*Man, these north woods hicks are thicker than thieves,*" John thought. "*No, thieves aren't that close,*" he corrected himself, "*they're more like family.*"

His last thought struck a chord. Pepperdine had said as much, but John had taken it as hyperbole at the time. Apparently, that was what he walked into. The "family" was protecting one of its own against a stranger. At least he was now fully aware of where he stood.

John rolled things around in his mind, and it occurred to him that he couldn't really blame them for stepping up for someone they knew, someone who was an integral part of their lives, over a total stranger. He also realized how arrogant his approach to the people on the list must have appeared to Doorway. Those were people important to him. John's simple prioritization of them- important to me, not important to me- must have fully justified any misgivings about John the big man might have had in his mind. Maybe there was still time to correct the situation. All he knew was it was time to move forward.

"Doorway?"

"What?" the big man said, not so much as a question, but a demand. He lifted his head and looked John over.

"I need you to be straight with me, here. Do you know the stipulations of my uncle's will? Has Wes told you what my visit is all about?"

Doorway stood up fully, his normally smiling face was somber. "No, he has not. Besides, you said it yourself, it's none of my business."

John could tell by the expression on the man's face, and the tone in his voice, John's comment to Pepperdine had cut Doorway, too. It was time for some fence-mending.

"Well, that might not be exactly true in your case," John replied slowly. "Since you are supposed to be my contact with these people, you should know why it's important for me to see them. The first thing you should know is Hank did not leave me Last Chance, directly. In fact, it could very well never be mine."

Doorway shifted uneasily on his feet in response to John's last statement. "Whose would it be, then?"

"I really can't tell you. Hank stipulated that I not know, unless the ownership passes to the secondary beneficiary."

"And how could that happen?"

John explained the stipulations of the agreement. After laying out the details of the decision he had to make, John explained the reasoning behind his prioritizations of the list. He hoped it would smooth things over with the big man, and put him back in John's corner. He needed a friend, and Doorway was the only one he had at the moment.

"So, let me get this straight," Doorway said after John had finished, "if you do nothing, you get twenty-five thousand and Hardrock's house, but if you take on the agreement to try running the mine for a year, and fail, you get twice the money. If you succeed, you get the mine and tour business. That cover it?"

"Yeah, that's about it in a nutshell."

"Have you seen a picture of Hardrock's house, or did Wes describe it?"

"No, I didn't even think to ask about it. I just assumed it would be an average home, maybe two or three bedrooms, basic yard. You know, the usual house."

"You have no idea what passes for a 'house' around here!" The big man slapped the bar and roared with laughter. "Hardrock's 'house' is actually an old, ten by fifty-foot mobile home set on a foundation, with a lean-to attached to it. Next to it is an old Quonset hut. And you mentioned yard?" More laughter interrupted the big man's description. "It's got plenty of land around it, sure, but there isn't anything that could be mistaken for a yard about it. Other than where the house and shop sit, the entire five acres are either spruce woods, or alder."

The description of the house left John reeling. His plan of selling it for enough to set himself up back in LA was not going to be a reality. In spite of the bad news, John had to smile to himself. It was becoming all too apparent his uncle was making his wishes known from the grave.

For the first time since Wes had laid out the details of the agreement, John could actually see how there might be a benefit to taking it on. After all, it was not as if he had grand prospects waiting for him back in LA.

"That bit of information certainly puts things in a different light," John said after thinking about the house he now owned. He looked at Doorway, "I'd sure like to hear your opinion about my options."

"Oh, no," Doorway said quickly, "I'm not giving you any advice about this. This is your decision to make. But I'll tell you what I'd do for starters."

John looked up at the only friend he had at the moment, hopeful there would be some sound advice coming his way.

"The first thing I'd do, even before I started to make the decision, is make damn sure I was on good speaking terms with a certain Harley Pepperdine. You've got some time before Reeder gets here."

When the door slammed shut behind him upon storming out of the Shuffle Inn, Harley started swearing under his breath. With every step he took away from the bar on the way back to his room, a new invective directed at John Barstow poured out. In Harley's estimation, there wasn't a phrase, name, or curse foul enough to lay upon the man. He was no longer employed by Last Chance Adventures, of that he was certain. It didn't matter anyway. He wouldn't want to work for someone so arrogant, no matter that he was Hardrock's nephew. In fact, he *couldn't* work for an asshole like that.

Harley's room was the farthest from the Shuffle Inn, on the bottom floor. As he approached the door, the large wolf-like dog stuck its head out of a doghouse on the side of the building, it curled its lips and emitted a low growl as Harley approached.

"Piss off, Dawg," Harley snapped, "I'm in no mood."

The dog stepped out of its doghouse and sniffed at an empty steel bowl in front of it. Again, he growled at his owner. Harley continued to mutter curses as he stepped up to the porch and opened a small trash can sitting next to his door. He reached into the can and pulled out a plastic cup filled with dog food, walked over to the doghouse and pitched the food into the steel bowl.

"There, you worthless feed-bag, happy now?"

The dog looked at Harley with an expression of total detachment, then went to work on the contents of the bowl.

Harley pitched the plastic cup back into the trash can, put the lid back in place and stepped through the door.

His head was throbbing, but Harley wasn't sure if it was from the hangover, or because he was about to explode in anger. After kicking off his boots, he walked over to the little refrigerator in the kitchenette just inside the door of his efficiency apartment. He opened the refrigerator and stared at the contents. He evaluated the choices carefully: beer or soda. A little hair of the dog might be just what he needed at the moment, but he opted for the soda, hoping it would settle his stomach. He popped the top on the can and took a big drink. The drink had the desired effect, and Harley belched loudly, feeling better for it.

He walked over to the recliner occupying the space in front of the television and flopped down. Having run out of things foul enough to throw out about John Barstow, he began assessing his situation. Things looked bleak, at best. After eight years of working for Hardrock, he would be hard-pressed to line up any sort of reliable work for the summer. He could probably hit up Pete, or any one of the other dozen set netters he knew, for work picking nets during the salmon season, but salmon season was over three months away. In the mean time, he might be able to find some temporary work at Ocean Beauty, if they were processing anything, which was iffy. Besides, the thought of going back on the slime line with its grueling working conditions, unreliable and weird hours and low pay was less than appealing. Processing work would be his last option.

Harley had never imagined he'd be in this position. He had never even considered what would happen if Hardrock died. For that matter, he had never imagined Hardrock could die. To Harley, Hardrock had always been an immortal, no different than what any kid thinks about a parent. Those prominent figures in your life aren't expected to go away. He suddenly felt a mantle of sadness lay heavily over him. It wasn't the prospect of being jobless and broke again, he'd been there before and came through it okay. It was the prospect of not seeing Hardrock ever again. That old man had been there for him for as long as he could remember; even before Harley had the good fortune to work for him.

Harley took another big slug of his soda and belched again. He laid his head back on the recliner and thought about the past six days. *"Hardrock,"* he thought, *"I'm sorry, but I've really screwed the pooch this time. You always told me I was my own worst enemy. Now, I don't even have you to remind me just how bad I've messed up."*

Visions of life out at Last Chance wandered through Harley's mind. It was so simple there. Life had predictable patterns, it had a routine set by the clock of living in the bush. As routine as every day was, every day could offer up something different. The weather set the pace, and the needs of everyday living set the work schedule.

Sitting in the quiet of the room, Harley reflected on Hardrock. He had been demanding, but never without cause. There had always been a solid reason for everything Hardrock demanded. Harley chuckled to himself when he thought back to the first year he worked for the old man. Time after time, Hardrock admonished Harley for not carefully collecting the black sands the guests left behind in the panning tubs. According to Hardrock, the black sands were just as valuable as the gold flake and nuggets the guests kept. Once, after Hardrock saw Harley pitch a tub of black sands on the ground, he made Harley carefully shovel up all the dirt in the area and pan it all out to reclaim them. He wouldn't let Harley use a sluice, he insisted it all be panned by hand. All the while, Hardrock had stood over him, critiquing the job. That was the last time Harley ever threw out any black sands.

Harley's reverie was interrupted by a knock at the door. "It's open," he called out, and sat up.

The door opened and John Barstow stood there, gently scratching the large dog's head. The dog looked lovingly at Barstow, then glanced at Harley and walked away.

"What the hell do you want?" Harley demanded.

"We need to talk," John answered calmly. "May I come in?"

Harley paused in answering, giving some thought to blasting the man with a few of the worst things he had been muttering on the way over from the Shuffle, but thought better of it. "If you've got the nerve to come over, I guess you can. Take off your shoes."

John stepped through the door and did as Harley instructed. He stepped into the little living room and looked around. It was the mirror image of his own suite, only decorated with a few obviously personal items which were set out on the tables, and photographs hung on the wall. One item on the wall caught his eye. It was a large photo of Hank and Harley standing on either side of an attractive woman. A stream was running through the background. The picture bore an inscription, "Thanks for the wonderful time, Myrna." John looked closer at the picture, and recognized the woman.

"Is that Myrna Filmore, the movie star?" he asked incredulously.

"Yeah," Harley replied coolly. "She and her husband stayed with us. They caught some salmon, panned some gold and left a large tip. But I'm sure you didn't come over here to check out my pictures. What do you want?"

"You mind if I sit down?"

"I doubt if you're going to be here long enough to make yourself comfortable."

John's face flushed. He didn't expect this to be easy, but wasn't willing to tolerate too much guff, either. In his opinion, Harley was more responsible for the earlier argument than himself. If Harley had been honest to begin with, there wouldn't have been as great a chance for things to get unpleasant. Nevertheless, Doorway had been right, he needed to get on at least civil speaking terms with Pepperdine.

"Look," John said, "Doorway told me who you are. Had I known that, our earlier conversation would probably have gone much better. I'll admit I was dismissive, but you have to admit, you didn't really put me in a position where I would feel obligated to explain things."

Harley stared at John thought about what he's said for a few moments. He didn't feel like *admitting* anything, but Barstow made a good point. Besides, if Doorway sent the guy over to talk to him, there must be a good reason for him standing there.

"Well, let's just say there was a definite misunderstanding," Harley finally answered. "Have a seat. You know what my first question will be."

John sighed and sat down on the couch on the far end from Harley. He was beginning to feel like a broken record, running through the details of Hank's will and the agreement, but repeated it again for Harley's benefit. Just like Doorway, Harley wanted to know who the secondary beneficiary would be. Unlike Doorway, Harley seemed skeptical about John's denial he knew who the secondary would be.

"Why is it so important?" John asked in frustration. "Why would it matter at all? *Somebody* will end up in possession of Last Chance. If it's not me, then why should you care who it is?"

"Because," Harley said emphatically, "Last Chance is a huge part of my life, and the lives of several other people in this area. If it's going to end up in the hands of some tour conglomerate planning to tear it down just to throw up a resort for city slickers, I want to know, because I'll fight them with everything I can throw at them! You have no idea how many offers Hardrock got from developers. Hell, Filmore's old man wanted to buy it!"

Harley's reply took John aback. He hadn't given that

prospect any thought. He couldn't imagine his uncle, or Wes for that matter, allowing such a thing to even be remotely possible.

"I can't guarantee it isn't a possibility," John responded, "but I honestly don't have a clue who, or what, the secondary may be. The trust simply says I have to give it a go to keep it from the secondary. And if I fail, it goes to the secondary, with no recourse."

Harley, at last, decided the man was telling the truth. In Harley's mind, looking at John, the odds were better than not Last Chance would end up in the secondary's hands. To Harley, John didn't look like he could handle a week as a guest, let alone a year as the owner.

"So, what are you going to do?" Harley asked, while inside he was thinking, "*I am so screwed.*"

"I'm not sure. I'm going to fly out with Reeder this afternoon to look at the place, and then I need to talk to Cynthia Smythe to review the financials and what is lined up for this coming season. After that, I need to make the decision, Wes will be here tomorrow afternoon to hear my decision."

Harley laughed out loud. "Hardrock never was one to let things sit around undone. Full speed ahead, we'll handle the consequences as they come up."

John joined in the laughter, while inside he was thinking, "*I am so screwed.*"

The shared laughter helped to ease the tension between the two men.

"So, what do you need from me?" Harley asked.

"Hank obviously..."

"Okay," Harley interrupted, "the first thing you need to learn is *nobody* called your uncle, 'Hank.' At least not without saying 'Hardrock' first. If you keep calling him Hank, people aren't going to know who you're talking about, or worse yet, figure out you really didn't know the man."

"Fair enough, I'll try, but that reminds me of something I'm curious about. How did my uncle get that name?"

"It has something to do with his younger years working in a placer mine," Harley answered, "I never heard the whole story. He just shrugged when I asked him. So, you were saying?"

"*Hardrock* obviously put a great deal of faith in you," John picked up where Harley had interrupted. "You worked with him for eight years. I'm hoping you can explain how the operation runs to me. And if I decide to sign the agreement, I'm hoping you will consider working with me."

Harley listened to John, looked him over and decided he was sincere. He also noted how he had used the term "work with" instead of "work for." That was exactly how Hardrock had always put it.

"Can you cook?" Harley asked suddenly.

"What?"

"I asked if you can cook. Hardrock did all the cooking out at Last Chance."

"Most of my cooking involves frozen dinners."

"*I am so screwed,*" passed through Harley's mind again. "Well, unless you're really fond of beans straight out of a can, you don't want me to cook, and I don't think a menu like that would garner any recommendations from the clients. What do you know about mining? Ever done any?"

"*I am so screwed,*" passed through John's mind when he thought about trying to cook for a mining camp. "I did some panning once as a kid on vacation," John replied to Harley's second question.

"This certainly isn't going to be easy. Can you say, 'massive learning curve?'"

Both men laughed out loud and said simultaneously, "We are so screwed."

Their laughter was interrupted when Harley's phone rang. He picked the phone up and answered it, listened for a moment and said something John couldn't make out, then turned to John.

"That was Doorway. Reeder is at the Shuffle, and ready to go."
He paused for a moment, then asked hesitantly, "You want me to
go along with you?"

John suggested Harley go back to the bar with him, and they
could decide after he had met Reeder.

When the two men stepped out of Harley's apartment, the
large dog fell in step beside John, nipping playfully at his hand.
It shot furtive glances at Harley, who ignored it completely.

"What's this dog got against you?" John asked, patting the
large head as the dog trotted alongside him.

"I don't know. It's not like I've ever been mean to him.
He's just never been real affectionate, at least not to me."

"He got a name?"

"Yeah, Dawg," Harley replied, "but I've got a lot of other
choice names for him, depending on the occasion."

"*Dawg*? No wonder he doesn't like you. You couldn't give
him a better name?"

"Hey, I named him after a movie star hero. Remember the
John Wayne movie, 'Big Jake?' Where his dog saves the day
before a bad guy can kill the grandson? Now *that*, my friend,
was a hero."

"Maybe you ought to explain it to him."

"I tried," Harley replied with mock sadness, "he just won't
listen."

John laughed all the way to the Shuffle Inn, where Harley
entered first. Dawg dutifully sat down outside the door.

CHAPTER 7

Doorway was at his station, talking animatedly with a man in an old military style parka who stood with his back to the door. The gray-green hood on the parka was edged with tatters of what had been at one time, a fur ruff of some sort. The man in the parka turned around when Harley and John approached. He was not a tall man, and looked to be almost as old as Wes. The silver hair poking out from under a dark blue watch cap, matched the silver moustache extending well over his upper lip. What struck John the most about the man's appearance, however, was the glasses he wore. John could not recall ever seeing a pair of glasses so thick. The thick lenses magnified the man's eyes to the point he looked owl-like. The man extended a gnarled hand toward John.

"So, you're Hardrock's nephew. Don't see much of a family resemblance. Good to meet you." He glanced toward Harley and acknowledged him with a nod.

In spite of how gnarled the man's hand looked, his grip was firm and strong.

"And you are Mr. Reeder," John replied, "good to meet you, too."

"You can drop the mister, it's just Reeder. I wouldn't want anyone to think I was getting important." Reeder took a moment to look John over from head to toe in a manner that made John feel uncomfortable. Finally, Reeder asked, "Those the only clothes you got?"

Taken by surprise with the question, John stammered, "Well, no. I've got a couple more shirts and pants in my room. Why?"

"What Reeder means," Doorway injected, "is do you have anything more suited for the outdoors. You know, boots, not loafers, heavy pants, not slacks, and so forth."

"Exactly," Reeder pitched in, "once we get west of roads and start stomping around in the snow, you're going to get awfully uncomfortable dressed like that."

John suddenly felt foolish, which seemed to be a frequent condition he'd found himself in for the past day and a half. "To be honest, I had no idea what I'd be doing when I came up. I thought I'd just have a meeting with Wes Bartholomew, and be staying in Anchorage. This is as good as I've got."

"Well, it won't do," Reeder said sharply. "I won't take you to Last Chance unless you're dressed properly. If we ran into trouble, you'd freeze to death right away. Harley!"

Harley, who had been staring down at his feet, almost as if Reeder were chastising him, jumped when Reeder barked his name.

"Harley, you and John here," Reeder continued, "look to be about the same size. Loan him some proper clothes so he can go have a look at his mine."

John started to go into his spiel about how the mine wasn't really his, but Reeder waved him off.

"We're burning daylight, boys," Reeder snapped, "the weather isn't going to get any better than this. Get a move on!"

Harley and John hustled back to Harley's apartment where Harley handed John a pair of huge rubber boots, and a set of insulated coveralls. The boots fit loosely, but were workable, and the coveralls were a perfect fit.

When Harley handed John a heavy parka he said, "Well, that settles whether, or not, I'm going. That's the only heavy coat I've got."

John thought about how gruff Reeder was, and wished sincerely Harley had two coats. Something else was bothering him. "Is it safe to fly with Reeder?" he asked seriously.

"Why wouldn't it be?"

"I don't know if you've noticed, but the guy has crystal balls for lenses in his glasses. Is he even legal to fly?"

Harley laughed as he answered. "You noticed, huh? I've been around him so much I don't even notice how thick they are anymore. As long as a pilot's vision can be corrected to 20/30, he's legal to fly. Being a licensed air taxi operator, Reeder has to pass a physical." Harley explained. "Of course," he added, "the fact he flies the doctor out each year for a moose hunt probably weighs heavy on the final numbers the doc comes up with."

Harley took an almost perverse delight in how pale John suddenly appeared, but took pity on him and relieved his fears by admitting he was just jerking John's chain. "Besides," he continued, "once you're off the ground, it's more about feeling the aircraft than seeing."

"Maybe so, but coming down could hurt if the guy can't see the ground until he feels it."

When they got back to the Shuffle Inn, Reeder was standing outside, next to an old, rusty Bronco, patting Dawg on the head.

"That's a fine dog you've got there, Harley," Reeder said just to irritate him. The dog wagged its tail at the compliment, and Harley scowled.

Reeder climbed into the driver's side of the Bronco as John climbed in the other side. He rolled down his window and told Harley to expect them back before dark. Reeder started the Bronco, which emitted a dark cloud of exhaust as it rumbled to life.

It was a quick drive to the airstrip, which was visible off the highway. Reeder turned left down another paved road, then another left less than a quarter-mile from the highway. He pulled the Bronco up to a small shack with a sign that said, "Reeder Air" in bold red letters. Several airplanes were tied down in front of the shack, and an elevated tank with a gas hose on one end was located a short distance toward the airstrip.

Reeder didn't waste any time. "I've already filed a flight plan, and the plane is always fueled up, so let's go. We're taking the one-eighty-five."

John wasn't at all familiar with airplanes, so stood where he had stepped out of the Bronco.

"Get in the little red and white one with skis," Reeder said impatiently.

Reeder walked over to a small plane sitting closest to the shack and threw the latch on the right hand door. He then walked around the plane, examining all the surfaces, struts and the cabling on the skis carefully, and kicked both ends of each ski lightly to break them loose from the ice on the ground. Satisfied everything was ready to go, he climbed in on the left side of the aircraft. He motioned for John to get in the right-hand seat.

"Pull the door closed, and push the latch down and forward," he ordered brusquely. "Now, clip that harness down around your lap and shoulder. Wouldn't want you to fall out."

John, already nervous about being alone with the gruff old pilot, swallowed hard. It didn't go unnoticed. "You aren't a puker, are you?" Reeder demanded to know.

"Not so far," John replied as well as his dry mouth would let him. In response, Reeder handed him a large, sealable plastic bag.

Next, the old pilot handed John a pair of ear muffs with a cable and microphone sticking out from one side. The cable was plugged into a jack above and behind John's seat. "We can talk better with these," Reeder explained. "Just don't talk if I'm on the radio with anyone else."

John nodded, and slid the muffs on. He wondered how effective the microphone was going to be over the engine noise.

As John adjusted the fit of his muffs, Reeder busied himself turning on various instruments, adjusted the choke and pressed a switch. The prop in front of John turned jerkily a couple of times, then the engine caught and roared to life, spinning the prop into a barely visible film. Reeder ran the engine up a bit, and John could feel the plane strain to move forward. After a few moments of watching the gauges carefully, Reeder increased the throttle until the plane edged forward. The plane bumped lightly across the frozen ground. As Reeder guided it to the runway, he worked the control surfaces and kicked the rudder from side to side, making the aircraft fishtail slightly. Once out on the runway, Reeder glanced at the windsock on top of the shack and steadily increased the throttle.

The plane picked up speed as it traveled down the runway. At the higher speed, the light bumps John had felt disappeared.

Eventually, John felt the tail of the plane lift slightly, then the entire aircraft lifted from the ground. The sound of the prop was distinct through the muffs, and John wondered how loud it would have been without them. Climbing rapidly, Reeder banked the plane to the left, and headed west. When he straightened back out, John looked down at Nikiski. There was more to it than he had guessed from what he'd seen driving in. Aside from the mall, where McCrane Mercantile and the Shuffle Inn were located, there were clearings visible in the woods throughout the area where houses of various sizes stood.

In short order, they passed the bluff at the edge of the Cook Inlet. John looked down at the water's edge. What had looked like a white ribbon from twenty thousand feet in the air the day before, was a line of huge, jagged pieces of ice stacked up on the beach from one thousand feet. The water looked to be flowing, pushing more flat, hunks of ice down the inlet.

"We've got a pretty good tide going out right now," Reeder said over the intercom, "really makes the ice scoot."

John looked at the roiling water below. It looked cold, even though the sun was shining on it. He wondered how long a man could last in water like that, if he was lucky enough to survive the crash.

As if Reeder had read John's mind, his voice came in over John's headset, "A man would be dead from cold in less than fifteen minutes in that water. In the summer, you might make it for forty-five."

John looked out at the horizon. "Is that an oil platform?"

"Yeah. This is the birthplace of the oil industry in Alaska. Oil was found in the Swanson River drainage, east of Nikiski, back in 1954. The platforms mostly date from the sixties. The oil's about done, and several platforms are idle now. There's still plenty of natural gas left to find though, so it wouldn't surprise me if they never go away."

Contrary to what John had feared, the flight over the inlet was smooth. There was an occasional gentle bump, but nothing like he anticipated after the previous day's flight into Kenai. The view was even more spectacular than from higher up on the commercial flight. The mountains off to the west, on the other shore of the inlet rose up from what seemed to be the inlet itself.

The most visible had a trail of clouds drifting off its peak.

"What's with the clouds on the mountain top?" John asked.

"That's not clouds, that's steam. It's a live volcano called Mount Redoubt. It sputters around from time to time, and every now and then, erupts. Spreads ash from hither to yon. That's a major pain in the ass. When the ash flies, the planes don't."

Reeder angled the plane in a more southerly direction and continued until they approached a ridge of hills stretching out from the mountains. Reeder banked the plane to the right and started descending. As the plane came out of the bank, Reeder pointed up a small valley.

"See the flat area up ahead? Look at the far end, and you can see Last Chance."

John felt an odd excitement knot up in his stomach. Looking at the rugged terrain, the wide expanse and the incredible, rough beauty of the spruce forest stretching out in all directions made him realize what a special place Last Chance had to be. He hadn't been able to imagine what the place would look like, but nothing he could have imagined would have compared to what he was actually seeing.

Reeder continued on up the valley, and John could see the individual buildings making up Last Chance. The most prominent of the buildings looked out over the flat area Reeder had pointed out. John recognized it as the lodge from the picture in Wes' office. From the vantage of the plane, it didn't seem as large as it had in the photo. Reeder flew over the buildings to one side, and banked the plane slightly so John could have a better view. Next to the lodge were four smaller cabins. Behind them, farther from the flat expanse, were three very small roofs, barely peering out from the snow. The one closest to the lodge had what looked like a trail between it and the lodge.

Reeder increased the plane's bank to the right, and began to descend rapidly. Having performed a one-eighty turn, he straightened out and descended toward the flat area in front of the lodge. He cut back on throttle, slowed down and the plane settled on the expanse, spewing snow out from under the wings. Other than the deceleration of the plane and the tail settling down, John had felt nothing. It had been like slowly sliding out into a quiet pool of water. Reeder increased throttle to turn around and taxi toward the lodge. John was stunned. The snow glistened in the sunlight as if a dusting of diamond chips had been scattered thickly across the surface.

When the plane was almost to a rise in front of the lodge, Reeder throttled up the engine one more time to spin it around, then shut the engine down. The following silence was as pronounced as the roar of the prop. John removed his muffs and the only sound he heard was the ticking of the plane's engine exhaust as it cooled down.

"Welcome to Last Chance," Reeder said with a smile. "Okay, here's the drill. When you step down out of the plane, expect to find fairly deep snow, so hang onto the wing strut for balance. I'll hand you a pair of snowshoes to put on. They make walking a lot less tiring."

Following Reeder's instructions, John unlatched his door, and leaned out to grasp the wing strut. When he stepped from the plane with his right foot, he immediately sank up to his knee in the white stuff. He hung from the strut, his right leg buried, and his left foot caught on the edge of the plane. Trying to reach his left leg with his left hand to pull the leg free, he lost his grip on the strut and tumbled into the snow.

Reeder watched the acrobatics from his seat. "That happens a lot," he observed dryly. "Getting out is sort of a learned technique."

John floundered around in the snow. Each time he tried to push himself up, his arm went deep into the snow, filling his sleeve with the cold powder. Finally, he found the ski on the landing gear and righted himself. Snow melted on his face and dripped down his collar. He felt cold and foolish. Pushing himself up, he slapped his hands to get the snow off his gloves and wiped the melted snow from his face.

"Now, *that* was refreshing," he commented.

Reeder held out a pair of snowshoes from the plane. With a very firm grip on the wing strut John reached out and grabbed them. They were much lighter than he expected, made of an aluminum tubing frame and a solid layer of plastic material spanning the frame. In the middle of each snowshoe was a harness with a loop to slide the toe of his boot into, and a strap with a buckle to secure the boot across the back and over the top.

"It's not a complicated process," Reeder instructed, "but you need to make sure everything is cinched down as tight as you can make it. If you don't, that puppy will pop off and trip you up for sure."

John heeded the advice, sliding his toe into the first snowshoe and pulling everything as tight as he could. When he placed his full weight on the secured snowshoe, his foot barely sank into the snow. As he was cinching down the second snowshoe, Reeder shuffled up to him. John looked up, surprised.

"I've been doing this a year, or two," Reeder said dryly. "You ready to have a look at your mine?"

John only nodded. The silence surrounding them put a feeling of awe in him. Each time they spoke, the words seemed to drift off, lost in the vastness. He marveled at the ground view. Behind him, the flat, white expanse they had landed on stretched for at least half a mile, and was easily a quarter mile in width.

"Is this a landing strip?" John asked.

"Of sorts, at least that's what we use it for. It's actually a lake. In the summer, we land on floats, in the winter, it's skis. Pretty good fishing, too."

Reeder turned and stepped out with a wide, steady gait. John tried to follow suit and tripped slightly when the edges of his snowshoes hung up on each other. Reeder turned around at the clacking sound.

"You've got to walk deliberately, with an extra wide stance. It takes some getting used to, and you're going to feel it in your hips." He turned back to his path toward the rise leading to the lodge.

It wasn't long before John realized Reeder wasn't wrong about feeling his hips. Making his way up the slope of the rise, he could feel the muscles in his hips tighten and complain about the awkward motion. Progressing up the slope, he noticed they were walking in a slight trough in the snow.

"Are we on a path?" he asked, stopping to stand straight and stretch his hips a little.

"Yeah, this gets tromped down pretty good over the course of the winter."

"People come out here in the winter?"

"Mostly just Hardrock," Reeder said, turning around to look

at his charge, "but sometimes Harley comes out, and of course, me. Too far to walk from Nikiski," he added with a wink. "Hardrock came out to keep an eye on the place, do some maintenance, and just get away from civilization. He loved this place."

Looking around at the entire valley, John saw how the desire to get away from civilization would be easily satisfied. He could also understand his uncle's passion for the place. Even in the dead of this winter expanse, there was a beauty and serenity he'd never experienced.

Reeder turned back toward the lodge and continued on. John stepped in behind him. They crested the rise and John had his first close-up look at the lodge. It was as tall as it appeared in the picture at Wes's office, much higher than a single story house, but not as large overall. The building was no more than twenty-five feet wide, but looked to be much deeper. The roof line was very steep. Windows stretched from just above the level of the first floor, to just below the log beams supporting the roof. The peeled logs were shiny and light brown. A wooden porch stretched the width of the building, and was partially covered by an overhang. Snow lay piled in a line along the porch from where it had slid off the roof. Reeder walked up to the stairs leading onto the porch, and stopped.

"He was right up there," Reeder said, pointing generally to the porch.

"Who?"

"Hardrock. When he died. I came out to check on him, since nobody had heard from him for a couple of days."

"You found him?"

"That's what I said, wasn't it? He was sitting in a chair, just looking out over the valley. Except for the color of his skin, he could have been asleep."

John didn't know what to say, he hadn't given any thought to *where* his uncle had died. Wes had simply said he'd died of a massive stroke.

"It was a shocker, I can tell you," Reeder continued, "nobody expected it. Other than the usual problems of getting older, Hardrock seemed to be in good health."

"He stayed out here all by himself?" John asked in disbelief.

"Yeah, all the time," Reeder said nonchalantly. "He had everything he needed. It must have hit him fast, his coffee cup was sitting on the porch right next to him."

A macabre picture formed in John's mind of his uncle sitting in the chair, blue as ice, staring out across the frozen landscape.

"It's exactly how he would've wanted to go," Reeder sighed, "although it was a bitch for the rest of us."

"How so?"

"Well, not to put too fine a point on it," Reeder answered flatly, "lugging a frozen, one-hundred sixty pound man around isn't easy."

The mental image John had been working on instantly became an order of magnitude more macabre.

"The good news," Reeder continued in a totally factual tone, "is he froze in a sitting position. Once I got some help, we could pick him up, chair and all, and tote him down to the plane, sort of throne-style."

The image in John's mind shifted from macabre to outright bizarre. "Who helped?" he asked absent-mindedly.

"I called the State Troopers," Reeder answered, his tone strictly conversational, as if such things happened all the time. "They came out just to confirm no obvious foul play was involved. We tag-teamed the effort to get him from the porch to the plane. The real fun started when we got to the plane. He was pretty well froze to the chair, so we had to break it up to get him out. I guess, really, it was fortunate he died sitting up. Sure made it easier to strap him into the seat."

The image of three men in snowshoes carrying a frozen dead man like a king in a throne, then lashing him into a plane seat was just too much for John. He started laughing. "I'm sorry," he gasped, "I don't mean to laugh, but that just seems..." he cut himself off another bout of uncontrollable laughter.

John's laughter was so intense, almost hysterical, that he doubled over. Reeder stood looking at him with a blank face, wondering if John had snapped. After a moment of thought, a grin spread across his face, too.

"Yeah, I guess that must have been quite a sight. Hardrock would have really appreciated it."

When John regained his composure, they removed their snowshoes and went up the stairs onto the porch. The entrance door to the lodge was flanked by large windows, over which, sheets of plywood were hung. The large door itself was a golden colored wood, with deep relief carving depicting various Alaskan animals and scenery. The door obviously pulled open, but had a bar dropped across the front of it. Reeder lifted the bar and laid it aside.

"Expecting somebody to try and break out?" John asked.

"Bears," came the terse reply. "If you don't cover up your windows, and bar the doors, no matter which way they swing, they'll get into a place and completely wreck it."

"I thought bears hibernated."

"They do, but brownies, or what you'd call a grizzly, often get up and roam around a little bit during the winter, and now that spring is about here, they could start scrounging around any day. You haven't seen a mess, until you've seen what a bear can do to the inside of a cabin. What they don't try to eat, which usually isn't much, they tear up. What's left, they crap all over."

Reeder pulled the large door open and John looked inside the lodge. The light was poor, but the size of the room was unmistakable. It went the full width of the building, and was almost as deep. As John's eyes adapted to the diminished light, he could make out details of the room. The front half of the room held several upholstered chairs and a sofa, with end tables fitted in among them. A large wood stove sat in the front left corner of the room. In front of the wood stove were two smaller chairs.

Beyond the sitting area, a large rectangular table was surrounded with dining chairs. The table was made from thick slabs of wood, and the chairs were fashioned from bent limbs. The feeling was entirely rustic, yet even in the limited light and cold, John could see that the place would be warm and inviting.

There was a rattling behind John as Reeder, who had stayed just outside the door, removed the plywood panels from a window. The increased light immediately made it possible for John to look farther back into the room. The back wall had a door situated just to the right of the middle. To the right of the door, another wood stove stood in the corner of the room. On the left side of the door, a counter ran along the wall, and above the counter, a window passed into another room. The counter held dishes and a number of containers with flatware. John couldn't see through the dark window, but guessed it passed through to the kitchen.

"Homey place," Reeder said, stepping into the lodge. "Hardrock loved it when the place was full. As much as your uncle enjoyed time here alone, there was nothing he enjoyed more than being hospitable. He thrived on showing people his version of Alaska."

Reeder produced a flashlight and motioned John to follow him through the door into the room behind. The beam pierced the darkness as Reeder flashed it around. It wasn't nearly as big as John had expected.

"This is the kitchen to the left. There's a stove and oven, sinks, work counter, and an island for more work space. The refrigerator and freezer are over there."

As the light moved along the wall above the sink area, John saw all the cooking utensils necessary to prepare meals for a dozen people at a time.

Something struck John as he looked over the appliances, and he asked, "There's electricity out here?"

"There's a generator, sure, but most everything runs off propane, to include the lights. I'd get some light in here for you, but we'd have to go out back to turn it on. We aren't going to be here long enough to make it worth the effort."

The two men stepped out of the kitchen, and Reeder pointed the beam of light to the right, at a door, "That's the door to the pantry, there." He opened another door and shined the light down a short hallway at a door on the left. "And that's the lodge staff shower. All the other showers open up to the outside of the lodge. At the end of the hall, is Hardrock's room."

Reeder started down the hallway. John hesitated, he felt as if he were prying into a stranger's private life. He was debating if he should go any farther, when Reeder urged him to keep up.

Reeder opened the door to the room and flashed the light around quickly for John to see. John evaluated the room. It was spartan, to say the least, containing just a bed, a woodstove, a desk piled with paperwork, a dresser and a rack, from which hung several items of clothing. It looked like a cut-rate version

of a cheap hotel room to John. On the back wall there was a
door, which Reeder explained led to an outside lean-to used for
the laundry area. The door was barred from the inside.

"Not much to it," Reeder commented, as if he'd been
reading John's thoughts, "but Hardrock wasn't one waste much
time laying around. He was the kind of man who wanted to be
doing something whenever possible."

Reeder turned and walked out of the room, leaving John in
the dark to close the door behind them. They walked out of the
lodge, and John helped Reeder replace the plywood over the
window. Once the bar over the door was back in place, and the
lodge was secured, Reeder walked to the left side of the porch to
point out the other four cabins in the complex.

"The one closest to the lodge is where Harley stays during
the summer. In the winter he sleeps on the sofa in the lodge. The
other three cabins can each sleep up to four people."

John looked at the cabins, the closest didn't look to be much
more than ten feet square. The others were a little larger. He
noticed each of the cabins had a stove pipe rising up from the
roof.

"What are those other buildings?" John asked, pointing to
another set of rooflines in the distance, barely visible above the
snow.

"Those are the original buildings for the mine. There were
living quarters, a workshop, and a chow hall. Hardrock restored
them as much as possible, at least to the point where they won't
collapse. The workshop is where the equipment is stored."

"And those?" John pointed to the three very small roofs
rising above the snow, lined up behind the cabins. The two
farthest were situated between the guest cabins, while the third
was between Harley's cabin and the lodge.

"Those are the outhouses," Reeder replied. "The ones
behind the guest cabins are incinerator toilets. The other one,
between Harley's cabin and the lodge, is a regular outhouse. You
want to take a look at the cabins? If so, we need to get busy.
We'll have to dig out the doors."

John considered it for a moment, then thought of trying to
shovel snow while standing on snowshoes. He glanced at his
watch and saw it was already late in the afternoon. The only

question that would be answered by looking at the cabins first-hand was a simple, but important, one. He decided Reeder was blunt enough that he could rely on him for an honest answer.

"I don't think so," John said, "if you can tell me what kind of shape the cabins and lodge are in, structurally speaking."

"Excellent," came the quick reply. "Hardrock spent any spare time he had looking for things to fix, and Harley did the work."

John swept his eyes over the collection of buildings. There were things about running such an operation that were so far removed from his experience and comfort zone he had serious misgivings about even entertaining the idea of taking on the agreement. There was little doubt now, why Wes had asked about his physical condition and interest in the outdoors. This was pioneer living, albeit with plenty of modern twists. He took in a deep breath of the cold air and let out a long sigh.

"I've got more questions about the operation than answers at this point."

"Well, the only one I can answer is about getting to and from," Reeder said. "For the nitty-gritty on operations, you need to talk to Harley. Hardrock would have been the first one to tell you he couldn't have run this place without him."

The statement, so matter of fact, made John wince. With the way he and Harley had started out, he wasn't sure there was going to be any future in the operation of Last Chance. They seemed to have smoothed things over enough to get along before John left with Reeder, but getting along for an hour was one thing; getting along for months was another. Another problem would be John assuming the role of boss. How would Harley accept him as his employer when he knew nothing about even the most basic operations? From his own experiences with Occidental, where young MBA's without so much as a month of sales experience supervised him, he knew the potential resentment that could exist.

John's admiration for his uncle was growing. Given the way he had set things up for John to inherit the mine, he knew as much about human nature as he did mining, maybe more. John also found himself with a growing respect for Harley as he considered all the work and ingenuity it must take to keep a

place like Last Chance running. He realized how wrong he had
been in his prioritization of who to meet first. Finances were
important, but without the wherewithal to put them to use there
was no point in having them. It was time to have a long, serious
talk with Mr. Pepperdine.

"You ready to go?" asked Reeder, interrupting John's
thoughts.

"I guess so," John answered, looking around at the place for
perhaps the last time. "It sure isn't hard to see why my uncle
loved this place."

John's hips complained loudly as he strapped the
snowshoes back on. He was glad they weren't going to walk any
farther than the plane. He let Reeder extend the lead on the way,
stopping every now and then to take in the view and imagine
what it would be like to call this home for half the year. *We'll
see,"* he thought, *"but this is likely to be the last time I set foot
here."*

At the plane, Reeder was busy stomping out a path in front
of each of the plane's skis. "Need to pack it down a bit, so we
can gain enough momentum for the skis to float on the loose
snow," he explained.

John joined in, trying to judge the width of the path he
needed to pack down. When they were done, Reeder told John to
leave his snowshoes outside the aircraft, and climb in. Reeder
then went through the same routine he had before they took off
from Nikiski. Before climbing in, he loaded up John's
snowshoes and pulled his own off. Watching Reeder climb in,
John couldn't help but think how easy the pilot made it look,
which further reminded him of how little he knew about the
basics of life in such a place.

Taking off the lake and rising up from the valley, John
marveled again at the beauty of the location. He looked ahead
and saw the far side of the inlet was almost out of view. It
reminded him just how remote Last Chance was.

It was nearly five when they touched down in Nikiski. John
knew he wouldn't get around to meeting Cynthia Smythe until
the next day. That wasn't a problem. Setting things right with
Harley had become the number one priority.

John felt the exercise on the snowshoes as he stepped out of

Reeder's Bronco at the Shuffle Inn. His first few steps toward the bar were stiff and awkward.

"A little stiff from the snowshoes?" Reeder asked, noticing John's awkward gait.

"Yeah. Oh man, that would take some getting used to."

"I go through it every year the first couple of times. Seems like it takes me longer to shake off the stiffness each year as time goes by."

John was struck by the comment. He was probably thirty years junior to the pilot, and yet he'd had a tough time keeping up with him.

Doorway greeted both men from his station behind the bar when they entered. John wondered if there was ever a day the big man didn't spend every waking moment walking back and forth along the same twenty foot path. It was Friday night, and the bar was already filled with customers. Harley was not among them. John and Reeder took the only two open barstools next to each other. Doorway stood across the bar from them. He handed John a mug of coffee, and Reeder a beer.

"Good trip?" Doorway asked as he set Reeder's beer down in front of him.

Reeder just nodded and took a sip of the beer. John was more vocal as he peeled off the insulated coveralls Harley had lent him. "I didn't think there could be a place on earth so spectacular," he gushed. "My uncle told me it was like no other place on earth, and he wasn't exaggerating. You truly have to see it to appreciate it."

Doorway smiled. He'd heard essentially the same words from every cheechako he'd ever met. It was one thing to look at pictures and hear Alaska described, but it truly couldn't be appreciated without firsthand experience.

"Cynthia called back shortly after you left. I told her where you were, and she said to stop by about nine tomorrow. I'll give you the directions after you've had breakfast."

The mention of food made John realize he was very hungry. A couple of cake donuts weren't much to get a guy through the day.

"What can I do for dinner?" he asked Doorway.

"You've got two choices within walking distance,

depending on what you want. One place offers up good pizza and Italian food, the other has good pizza and burgers."

"How far is walking distance?"

"Half-way down the mall, and at the far end," Doorway replied, then he laughed. "I'll bet you have snowshoe hips."

"Indeed he does," Reeder pitched in. "And for a minute there, I thought he was going to drown in snow."

The scene of rolling around in the deep snow played through John's mind. "I'm glad I had those insulated coveralls, or I'd have been wet and miserable. Speaking of the coveralls, where is the owner?"

"I think he's at his apartment. He hung around for most of the afternoon, but left when the place started getting busy. To tell the truth, I think he's still suffering from last night's consumption. You want me to call him?"

"No, I'll just swing by his place on the way to the closest restaurant. I can always leave them in my room if he's not there. But if he's not there," John added, "and you see him before I do, please ask him to get ahold of me. I don't care what time it is."

Doorway assured John he would pass along the request. While John finished his coffee the three men talked about the flight in to Last Chance. Reeder answered a number of questions about his air taxi services. Not only did he ferry Hardrock to and from the operation, he was the primary air taxi for the clients staying with Last Chance Adventures. He owned another, larger airplane than the Cessna 185 John had flown in, called a DeHaviland Beaver. He used the Beaver when there were large groups of people headed into the claim, or when there were large loads to be ferried. Reeder's air taxi service also serviced other remote operations and he flew bush orders in for McCrane Mercantile; primarily orders placed by remote fish camps, mining camps and various government survey teams. It kept him busy, particularly in the summer.

When John asked how much he owed for the day's flight, Reeder shrugged and told him he'd make the money up from the clients staying at "his" mine. John thought about explaining to him that taking on the mine wasn't a certain thing, but decided to let it go. He did, however, insist on paying for Reeder's beer, which Reeder accepted without hesitation.

When Reeder finished up his beer, he explained it was Bingo night at the American Legion Hall in Kenai, and his wife wouldn't take kindly to missing it. He shook John's hand and waved to Doorway, who was pouring drinks at the other end of the bar, and left. Doorway came back to where John was seated, finishing up his coffee.

"Reeder's a piece of work, isn't he?" John commented.

"He sure is. He can be as blunt as a well-worn maul, but you won't find a better bush pilot."

"Why does everyone call him by just his last name?"

"His full name doesn't really fit the bush pilot persona," Doorway explained. "Most people don't even know it. Even his wife calls him Reeder."

"Do you know it?"

"I do. Hardrock told me Reeder's full name is Oliver Wendell Holmes Reeder. But don't ever tell Reeder I mentioned it."

After a moment's consideration John said, "That's a mouthful of name. Is there a story behind it?"

"I don't know, but I'm certainly not going to ask Reeder."

John agreed that, given Reeder's temperament, he wouldn't think it prudent to pry into the circumstances, either.

John finished up his coffee and headed out to Harley's apartment. When he stepped out of the Shuffle Inn, the last light of the day was fading. A brilliant orange glow from the other side of the inlet was all that remained. John held Harley's coveralls draped over one arm, and without the insulation they provided, he distinctly felt the cold. He clumped across the parking lot in the huge rubber boots Harley had lent him, eager to get them off. They may have been warm, but his feet felt damp from being confined in boots that let no moisture escape. John couldn't imagine wearing them for extended periods of time and wondered if, just like so many other things in Alaska, there was a secret to making them comfortable.

Dawg came out of his house to greet John with a wagging tail as he approached Harley's door. John scratched the big mutt's ears, and the dog licked at his hand in appreciation. Harley answered the knock on his door with an invitation to come in, and the big dog returned to his post in his doghouse.

"Welcome back," Harley greeted John when he stepped through the door and took off the rubber boots. "I see you survived both the trip and the pilot."

"Indeed. It was..." John struggled for words adequate to describe his impression, "simply incredible."

"Just toss those on my bed," Harley said, nodding at the coveralls. "I'll put them up later. I want to hear what you thought of Last Chance."

"I really need to get something to eat. Doorway said there's two places right here that have good pizza, you want some?"

"Sure. Personally, I prefer the pizza at Tuscan Villa because I like it spicy with lots of meat."

"Sounds good to me. That the closest place? I'm a little stiff from the trip."

"Sounds like someone had their first go at snowshoes."

On the way to the Tuscan Villa, Harley repeated his question about John's impression of Last Chance. John could only repeat what he told Doorway. Following a long list of superlatives to describe his impression, John said he had serious reservations about trying to run Last Chance Adventures. He wanted to have a long, serious discussion with Harley. John had questions, and Harley had the answers. Harley replied he had questions of his own, for John.

The walk to the restaurant was mercifully short. A waitress greeted Harley by name when they entered and told the men to pick any open booth they wanted. Desiring as much privacy as possible, Harley led John to the first booth on the right side. It was farthest from the kitchen, and less likely to fill up quickly.

"I'm probably wasting my time giving you a menu," the waitress said to Harley with a smile. "Who's your friend?"

Harley introduced John by his name, not mentioning he was Hardrock's nephew, for which John was grateful. John was tired of hearing about taking over Last Chance. He and the waitress exchanged greetings, then she took their order for drinks. Much to John's surprise Harley ordered a root beer, just as he had, instead of a real beer. When the waitress left them to look over the menus John asked about it.

"I figured you for a true beer and pizza kind of guy."

Harley shifted uncomfortably in his seat a little, apparently embarrassed. "I figured I might want to keep my head about me while we discuss things. Besides, last night wasn't exactly a normal occurrence, and I'm still not fully recovered." He looked at John with an appraising eye and asked, "You don't drink?"

"I'm a recovering alcoholic," John said flatly.

Harley wasn't sure exactly how to handle such blunt honesty, and all he could come up with was, "Oh."

"I've found being completely honest is the best way to let people know. Now, for your next question: no, it doesn't bother me to be around people who are drinking, at least not anymore. That life is in my past, but the problem is part of who I am."

The waitress interrupted any further discussion of the subject when she returned with the drinks. After a quick discussion about what to order, John went with Harley's suggestion to get a large version of the pizza he always ordered. The waitress didn't bother to write it down, and left.

"So, tell me," Harley said as soon as the waitress was safely out of earshot, "what are you going to do?"

"I still don't know," John said as he leaned back, "I've got so many questions, most of which can be answered by you."

Harley evaluated John from across the table, trying to determine if he was the kind of man to lay out flattery. He decided John was not. He was tempted to tell John that his own livelihood hung in the balance, but didn't want to appear as though he was prepared to grovel. Although, after thinking about it all day, he was. Harley had grown to love the life working for Hardrock had offered. He saw a purpose to it, and it was gratifying work. True enough, working with some of the more demanding clients was difficult at times, but those only stood out because they were so infrequent. The majority of clients were eager to learn about Alaska, mining, fishing and what life was like where you were more likely to run across a bear than another human. More than that, he'd helped Hardrock build the place into something Harley himself couldn't wait to go back to every chance he had.

Harley assured John he would answer any questions to the best of his ability, and that he had a few of his own to ask. He suggested the serious discussion wait for the pizza so they wouldn't be disturbed. John agreed, and the conversation returned to his flight out to the mine.

When the waitress brought the pizza to the table, John asked her to bring a pitcher of root beer in an effort to keep interruptions to a minimum. While she was gone, John tried a slice of the pizza and told Harley his recommendation was an excellent choice. With the pitcher delivered, and the waitress gone, John decided to get right down to business.

"What kind of business relationship did you have with my uncle?"

"I was his employee," Harley replied as if stating the obvious. "I worked for him steady from April through at least September, sometimes October. During the winter months I worked off and on, as he needed me."

"That's, at most, only seven months of work," John stated, doing a quick calculation in his head. "You could hardly call it full-time employment."

"I never really kept track of the time, but we flew over to work on the cabins during the winter. It's hard to do any work on them when clients are there. Almost all of the inside maintenance has to take place during the winter," Harley explained.

"So, what did he base your pay on? I mean, did he pay you hourly wages, or what?"

"No, he paid me a salary, Plus, I kept the tips people left behind. At the end of the year, he usually gave me a bonus."

"At the end of the year?" John asked. "The end of December? That's what, three months after you closed up for the season?"

"Yeah. I figured it was probably a tax thing."

John gave that piece of information some thought, and decided Cynthia Smythe would be able to shed more light on the financial reasons for such a pay arrangement. To John, it sounded more like a retainer than a bonus. Perhaps it was a way to keep Harley from looking for more steady work. John decided to switch subjects.

"Reeder tells me you kept the place running. He said Hardrock couldn't have done it without you."

"I wouldn't say that. Anyone handy with basic carpentry and a knack with mechanics could do it."

"Obviously there's more to it," John countered. "If all he needed was a maintenance man he could have put an ad in the paper."

"Look," Harley said firmly, looking John squarely in the eyes, "I don't know why Hardrock kept me on. He never said, and I never asked. But like I told you last night, Hardrock was a part of my life from childhood. He was as close to me as family. Who knows? Maybe he considered me a substitute for the real family that ignored him."

As soon as the words were out, Harley regretted them. John's face grew red, then he stared down at the plate in front of him. An awkward silence hung over the table. John slowly raised his head to look directly at Harley.

"You don't know a damn thing about my family's relationships, good, bad, or indifferent, so don't sit there and judge me," John shot back. "I'm just beginning to piece a few of the things about those relationships together myself."

Harley swallowed hard. "I didn't mean that the way it came out. Truly. All I meant was that people up here leave their roots behind, sometimes, and develop surrogate families. Reeder and Doorway are examples. For whatever reason, they left a life behind and made a new one here. Hell, more than half the people you meet up here are either running from, or running to, something. Hardrock fell into that category is all I meant. No offense was intended."

John studied the man, and realized he had just heard about as close to an apology as he was ever likely to experience from Harley Pepperdine.

"Fair enough," he finally said, then moved on. "I don't have to tell you how little I know about mining, let alone the actual operation of a remote lodge. I'm hoping you can fill me in on the basics. For instance, when do you go out to set up for the coming season? And how do you communicate with people while you're over there? How do you get the building materials you need? And what's the deal with propane appliances? And for that matter..."

With the tension broken, Harley laughed and held up his hands. "Hold on, hold on! One question at a time. First, we usually fly in supplies and start getting ready before the snow disappears and the ice breaks up on the lake. We go out to stay full-time near the end of April. Reeder can put down on the lake, or up the valley, as long as the ice and snow hold out. Once the ice clears off the lake, usually by the third week of May, he can start flying in on floats."

"So you're stuck out there, with no chance of leaving, for roughly three weeks?" John asked incredulously.

"I wouldn't call it stuck. If there was a true emergency, a chopper could come in. It would be expensive, but definitely an option."

John thought about the time frame for a moment. Three weeks from solid ice to open water suddenly seemed to be a very short period of time. He said so to Harley.

"We call it 'breakup.' When things finally start to thaw, it happens in a hurry," Harley explained. "One week, everything is white and frozen, and seemingly the next, the leaves are out and everything is green. We literally go from winter to summer in a course of roughly four weeks. When old man winter lets go his death grip, nature moves fast."

John thought to himself breakup was just another facet to the cut of Alaska that had to be experienced to fully comprehend.

"You asked about communication," Harley continued, "it's much simpler now than when Hardrock first started building Last Chance. Back then, sideband radios were the only communication. Now, there's cell phone reception. In fact, that's what prompted Reeder to check on Hardrock when he found him. When he hadn't heard from Hardrock for a couple of days, he thought there might be a problem."

John thought a moment about his sourdough uncle and Reeder yakking to each other on cell phones. The incongruity of the image struck him as very funny, and he chuckled to himself.

"There's a generator for electrical power," Harley continued, "but we only run it when we have to. Mainly it's for clients who can't live without charging up their laptops to check in with the outside world via satellite internet service."

"Whoa," John interrupted, "there's internet out at the lodge?"

"Such as it is. It's slow as hell compared to most everywhere else in the world, but it will get the job done. By the way, the internet service is something you ought to think about, upgrading. We get more bitching about how slow our internet is than any other single item."

The way Harley glibly threw out, "you ought to think about," gave John a start. He was already acting as though John was going to be making decisions on running Last Chance Adventures, as if he knew John would be taking on the agreement. How could he know that, when John himself didn't? The surprise of the statement quickly wore off, and John suddenly felt a strange feeling of ownership, and even a bit of pride, that Harley would give him such an indirect statement of confidence.

It was a turning point for how John looked at the prospect of running Last Chance Adventures. As Harley explained more of the details, John's confidence in the feasibility of the idea grew. So did his confidence in the man his uncle had trusted to keep the place running. When the pizza was done, John had only one more question to ask.

"If I take on the agreement, and that's still a big if, depending on what Cynthia Smythe shows me tomorrow, would you consider working with me for the same salary and conditions you did with Hardrock?"

Inside, Harley's stomach was doing flips, but he didn't want to show it. John wasn't the only one with misgivings. John's total inexperience in all aspects of an operation like Last Chance Adventures had Harley concerned. He didn't want to end up babysitting clients *and* his boss.

"Before I give you an answer," Harley said slowly, "I've got a couple of questions myself. The first is, just how committed are you to making this work? I mean, you're some kind of highfalutin investment counselor. If things don't work out, you can just run back to California, pick up where you left off, and live happily ever after. Seems to me you're in a pretty good position to bag it, if things get tough."

Harley half expected for his blunt statement to raise John's ire, so when he laughed out loud in response, Harley was surprised.

"Boy, gossip runs fast in a small community," John said. "I imagine the term 'investment counselor' conjures up images of me having a portfolio of sound investments. Truth is, that was a title Occidental gave to *all* of its employees in sales. The only investments I worked with were life insurance policies. You know the sort. Buy a policy, and after paying on it for a lifetime, there will be X-amount when you're too old to spend it on anything but prune juice and denture cream."

Harley smiled at the description. He had not only heard of such policies, but had actually bought into one a few years earlier. It originally sounded like a sound savings plan to him, until he realized there wasn't anyone he really wanted to name as a beneficiary for the life insurance, and the savings portion was as John described.

"Truth is," John continued, "my *investment counselor career* was nothing more than a job I didn't care for and didn't pay very well. To add insult to injury, they canned me just before I came up here. I'm in the same boat you are, Harley. Hell, I'd be willing to bet your bank account is bigger than my own. I never even made enough to invest in my own company's products!"

That piece of information shook Harley. He never thought John might be in a position even less advantageous than his own. It started to make sense to him why a successful business man would just drop everything, fly up to Alaska and show so much interest in something so obviously out of his comfort zone.

"That explains quite a bit," Harley replied. "The other thing I'm curious about is just what active part in the operation you expect to play. I mean, I know what my job is, I know what Hardrock's portion of the load was, but what do you plan on doing? No offense here, but you don't know anything about the business, mining, or living in the bush. I can't do it all."

John sat for a moment to ponder Harley's question. It was the same one he'd been asking himself since Wesley J. Bartholomew had first explained the agreement. He had very little to bring to the operation, other than a desire to make it work.

"I'm not entirely without some skills," John started, "I may not be as experienced as you, but I've done some carpentry." He left out the part about how it had been temporary work, while bouncing from job to job during his drinking days. "I've got exceptional people skills. You can't get people to spend money on something as mundane as life insurance without being able to put them at ease. But the main things I could bring to the operation are a willingness to try, and the fact I'm a fast learner."

"That sounds good," Harley replied skeptically, "but how's it going to work when you're the boss, and I'm telling you what to do? You don't think it will create some friction?"

"That's a good question. Fortunately, we both know exactly what I don't know, which is everything. I can't guarantee there won't be times we don't get along, but I'll bet it wasn't always happy camper time with Hardrock, either."

Harley smiled. There had been many times when he and Hardrock had gotten into shouting matches over one small item, or another.

"The important thing we'll both need to remember," John continued, "is to keep those disagreements away from the clients. As long as we *appear* to get along in front of the clients any disagreements we might have won't hurt the operation. I'll say it again: I'm a quick student, and I want to learn."

Harley took it all in. The man seemed sincere in everything he said. If John really was willing to make it work, and he really would listen without bowing up at an employee giving him directions, things might just go smoothly.

"Well the first thing you need to learn," Harley finally said with a chuckle, "is how to cook because I'm a lost cause on that front."

John nodded, wondering exactly how clients would take to frozen dinners warmed over a wood stove. "Fair enough, but that takes us back to my question. Would you be willing to work with me for the same salary Hardrock paid, even though you're going to be teaching me everything?"

Harley sat for a moment, as if giving it some serious thought. What choice did he have, really? At this point, anything looked better than the prospect of a season on the slime line. "I'll agree to giving it a try for one season," he answered slowly, "and we'll see where it goes from there."

"One season is all we have," John replied solemnly.

John picked up the tab for the pizza, joking that he'd keep the receipt for a business write-off, and the two men headed back to the Shuffle Inn. It was busy and crowded with customers. A layer of smoke hung over the patrons, who were loudly enjoying themselves. When Harley stepped into the crowd, several people greeted him with everything from friendly hellos, to good-natured insults. Nobody mentioned his release from Wildwood. That had become old news in the span of a day.

Doorway had help behind the bar, a middle-aged woman who looked like a hefty version of Dolly Parton. Doorway looked up and gave a shout to both Harley and John. While Harley hung back to chat with a group at a table, John picked his way through the crowd toward the bar, but there wasn't an open spot to be found. Doorway nodded toward the end where he normally stood by the coffee pot and John worked his way over there to wait.

"You and Harley get things hashed out?" Doorway asked when he'd finally caught up with the orders.

"Yeah, it was a good discussion. I think we came to an understanding. He's agreed to continue on with me, if I decide to take up the agreement."

Doorway nodded his approval. "I'm glad to hear that, John. I didn't say anything before, but I don't think you'd be able to make it fly without him."

"I'm certain I couldn't. In fact, I have my doubts about it even with him. But I won't know if I'm even going to give it a shot until I talk to Cynthia Smythe."

Doorway looked at John. If there was anything Doorway was good at, it was judging people, and he judged he'd be seeing Hardrock's nephew for quite some time to come.

"Speaking of tomorrow," John continued, "you want me to come here? What time do you open?"

"Same as usual," Doorway said in a matter of fact tone.

"What? It's Saturday," John said amazed, "you're going to be here late."

"No later than normal. Sheila closes up on Fridays and Saturdays," Doorway said, nodding at the woman at the far end of the bar. "Maggie comes in at her usual time on Saturdays to fix breakfast."

"You have enough business on Saturday morning to serve breakfast?"

"John, you saw who was at breakfast this morning. Most of

them are independent, small business owners. They can't afford to turn work away. Most will work at least half the day, and oil field support companies work seven days a week."

"Okay, I'll be here for breakfast, and see Smythe at nine. What about Billy McCrane?"

"You'll see him at breakfast," Doorway stated with certainty. "He comes in Saturday mornings, before he opens up the store at nine. Again, he's an independent businessman."

"That will give me a clean sweep of all the people on my list before Wes gets here in the afternoon," John said. He thought how ironic it was the last person he would meet with, was the first one he'd intended to.

John turned down Doorway's offer of a mug of coffee, explaining he was completely worn out, and just wanted to get some sleep. Inside, he laughed to himself; like he was going to sleep with everything going on in his mind. In truth, he needed to get somewhere quiet to sort things out. He said good night to Doorway and waved to Harley as he left the bar.

CHAPTER 8

John woke with a start from the sound of the alarm at six-thirty. His neck hurt from spending the night in the chair, where he'd drifted off. It hadn't been a restful night, filled with dreams of drowning in snow, as dead men sat in rocking chairs, watching him from a high porch.

"Pizza is like that," he thought, *"guaranteed to give you bad dreams while it bubbles and ferments in your guts."*

He deliberately set the alarm early to give himself plenty of time to get ready. John wanted to wake up slowly, take a hot shower and ease into what he anticipated to be a very intense day. He stood up, tipping his head from side to side in and effort to work out the stiffness. The first steps toward the bathroom reminded him of his time on snowshoes the day before. It was not a particularly auspicious beginning to what could ultimately prove to be the most important day of his life.

He felt better after taking a shower. The hot water flowing down his neck helped to loosen it up. Walking around the room worked out the stiffness in his hips. He sat at the small table in front of the window, sipping on a cup of coffee, and looked out at the glow in the horizon as it moved toward sunrise.

A layer of clouds lay just above the horizon. The rising sun reflected off them, and from the bottom up the colors changed. The edges of the clouds closest to the horizon were a brilliant yellow that graduated into a bright orange, then morphed into a brilliant pink that was topped off with a deep lavender at the top of the clouds. They seemed to drift upward as the sun rose, until they were entirely pink, then white when the sun finally lifted above the horizon.

"*If one could judge by initial appearances,*" John thought to himself, "*it is going to be a beautiful day. But the weather doesn't seem to be something you can count on around here.*"

At seven-thirty John stepped onto the porch. Dawg wandered over from the far end of the building to greet him at the bottom of the stairs, happy as always to see somebody other than Harley. John wondered what Harley did with Dawg when he went to Last Chance.

At the Shuffle Inn, Doorway was busy shuttling plates of breakfast, and told John to help himself to the coffee. John poured a mug and sat down on the barstool at the end. On his way past John, Doorway asked what he wanted for breakfast. John asked for a bowl of oatmeal, and Doorway disappeared into the kitchen, reappeared quickly, and set down a large bowl of oatmeal with a small pitcher of milk. He then returned to the kitchen and came back out with a plate heaped with fried eggs, bacon and four pieces of toast, which he set before a man three barstools down from John. The man looked to be in his early thirties. He was small, with red hair. John couldn't help but wonder if a guy that small could pack all those groceries away.

Turning away from the small man with the mound of eggs, John looked around the room and noted there weren't quite as many people in the place as the day before, but there were faces he recognized. It was obvious many of the customers made this a routine, and had tables they preferred. Many of the faces he recognized sat in the exact locations as the last time John saw them. The atmosphere hummed with the same kind of conversations from the day before. Doorway bussed tables as he brought out orders, but as the population dwindled he became less diligent in clearing the tables. While John worked on his oatmeal, Doorway positioned himself on the other side of the bar.

"How is it?" he asked, nodding at the bowl in front of John.

"I was going to ask for some brown sugar, but it doesn't need any. This is the best oatmeal I've ever had. What's in it?"

"That's Maggie's secret, but part of it is maple syrup. She puts something else in it, but won't tell me. Says she'd have to kill me if she did."

"Well, I can't afford to lose a friend, so I'll try and figure it out myself," John replied with a smile. "By the way, you said I'd see Billy McCrane here this morning. When does he usually come in?"

Doorway nodded toward the little man with the big pile of breakfast before him. John looked down the bar and noted more than half the pile of food was missing, and the little man seemed to be picking up speed as he ate his way through it.

"I'll introduce you when he comes up for air," Doorway said. "Just keep your arms and legs clear of his plate, and you'll be safe."

Doorway moved down the bar toward Billy McCrane just as Billy piled an unbroken egg yolk on a piece of toast and stuffed it into his maw. He listened and looked toward John as Doorway said something to him. Then, after a quick nod to John, he dove back into his plate. Doorway walked back to John.

"He'll be done in a just a minute. Billy doesn't converse much when there's better things for his jaws to be doing."

When Doorway wandered off to clear more tables, John continued working on his oatmeal. He watched Billy out of the corner of his eye. He'd never seen anybody eat a pile of food as aggressively as that man. When Billy had finished using the last piece of toast to wipe up what little remained on his plate, he wiped his mouth, grabbed his coffee and stood up. In actual fact, there was no "up" to the standing. Billy McCrane was about as tall standing up, as he was sitting on the high bar stool. He was barely five feet tall, and had a lean, wiry build. John was even more impressed with what he had just seen the little man put down.

"Pleased to meet you, Mr. Barstow," Billy said with a broad smile while extending his hand, "I'm Billy McCrane. I understand you will be taking over Last Chance."

John pushed aside his empty bowl and grasped the extended hand. McCrane's stature may have been small, but John could feel his energy in the way he enthusiastically shook hands.

"Possibly," John replied when the little redhead finally let go, "the final decision hasn't been made. I understand your store provided the supplies for my uncle's operation."

"We did, indeed, and would be more than willing to provide the same service to you. In fact, we could be of tremendous help to you in preparing for the upcoming season."

"How so?"

"Do you know what you need in the way of supplies?"

The question rocked John. He hadn't given any real thought to what he would need, vaguely assuming Harley would be able to tell him. Billy McCrane's smile grew even larger when he saw John pause, obviously stumped for an answer.

"You don't need to know. I can tell you exactly what you'll need. McCrane Mercantile, started by my father, has been supplying the Last Chance for more than twenty years, and we have the invoices for each purchase. Aside from incidentals and building materials you may want as the season goes on, a duplication of the past two or three year's invoices would set you up just fine. Based on previous season's deliveries, we can schedule resupply shipments, so you don't have to worry about the staples. Sure, we cost a little more than if you went to a big box store in Anchorage, or even Kenai, but using us eliminates additional transportation charges, not to mention the city sales tax in Kenai. Consequently, costs are pretty much a wash. And there is always the advantage that if you're not happy with something, you'll deal directly with me, not some assistant manager, or assistant-to-the-assistant."

It was perfectly clear to John that Billy McCrane had come to breakfast prepared not to take no for an answer. It struck him as ironic that he would be on the receiving side of a well planned sales pitch, similar to those he had delivered.

"You make a very convincing case for continuing to use McCrane Mercantile," John interrupted. "If I decide to make a go of operating Last Chance, I'll be in contact with you."

John offered his hand to Billy who grabbed it and again pumped it enthusiastically before saying good-bye and bustling off to his store.

"That boy's going to blow a gasket some day. He's like a

humming bird on speed," Doorway commented upon Billy's departure.

"Seems to be likeable, though."

"Oh, he is. He just wears me out watching him bounce around is all. He'd do anything for you, and he and his wife are involved in almost every youth organization in the area. If you do business with Billy, you'll get a fair shake."

John glanced at his watch, and changed the subject. "It's almost eight-thirty, Doorway, I should probably head out to see Cynthia Smythe. How do I find her?"

"I'll show you," came Harley's voice from behind. "She's just down the road, we've got time for me to have a cup of coffee before we go, though."

Doorway poured a cup of coffee for him as Harley sat on the stool next to John. Just a few stragglers remained from breakfast, and Doorway stood at the bar with the two younger men since there wasn't any rush to clear the tables. In a few minutes Maggie appeared from out of the kitchen and started clearing the remaining dishes from the tables. John watched her as she gracefully moved around the room. He thought again how attractive she was.

"You're a helluva lot of help," she shot at Doorway on her way to the kitchen with a load of empty dishes.

"Good morning," John said to her as she squeezed behind her oversized boss, "you make a mean bowl of oatmeal."

Maggie smiled and winked in return, and John could feel himself blush.

"No doubt about it," Harley agreed, smiling broadly at her, "Maggie makes the best oatmeal in the world."

"Piss off, Harley," Maggie snapped, then disappeared into the kitchen.

Doorway and John laughed as Harley just hung his head.

"Guess we better go," Harley grumbled, "or she's likely to take off my arm to get my coffee cup next trip, just for fun. C'mon, John, you've got an important appointment."

Walking in the direction of John's rental, Harley asked, "You don't mind if I come along, do you? I mean, I don't want to seem nosey."

"No, I don't mind at all. Why would I? You've probably

seen the books on this operation many times before."

"Actually, I haven't. It was never anything I was curious about, and Hardrock never suggested that I might want to know the business end of the operation."

John thought about it for a moment. It struck him as odd that as integral as Harley was to the operation of Last Chance Adventures, he would be totally ignorant of the financials. "Well, I'd have to say that maybe it's time you learned about that aspect. Besides, if the news isn't good, you won't be surprised with the decision it will lead me to."

When they got to John's car, he paused. "You sure you want to take my ride? I forgot to clean it up yesterday."

"It's clean," Harley replied softly. "I took care of it while you were at Last Chance yesterday. I don't expect anyone to clean up my messes."

The drive to Cynthia Smythe's office took them farther up the North Road, past the fire station, in the opposite direction Reeder had taken the day before. A mile down the road Harley directed John to turn right, off the highway. The road was narrow, made even more so by the berms of snow that had been pushed to the sides over the course of the winter. Spruce trees formed thick borders on both sides of the road, broken only occasionally by driveways wandering off into the trees. The road was rutted from traffic driving on the snow-packed surface during the relative warmth of the previous day, when the temperatures had eked above freezing. John's low-slung rental occasionally made scraping noises as it bounced down the road.

Harley directed John to turn into a driveway with a small sign which read "Smythe Bookkeeping." Other than the sign, the driveway looked no different than the others they had passed. It was narrow enough that only one vehicle at a time would be able to drive down it, and was defined sharply by dense, barren bushes along either side. Like the main road, snow was piled up on either side of the driveway. Between the bushes and snow pressing in on either side, the impression was almost that of driving in a tunnel.

The drive curved hard to the right and ended in a plowed opening where a trailer house sat at an angle to the drive. The trailer house looked to be typical of the kind popular in the late

1970's, being predominantly beige, with a faded green trim overhang at the front end. On one side, running the full length of the trailer, was an attached lean-to which effectively doubled the size of the entire structure. The lean-to, obviously newer than the trailer itself, had a door at the end closest to the drive and served as the main entry for both the lean-to and the trailer house. On the door hung a sign identical to the one at the end of the drive.

Parked in front of the trailer were a battered, black pickup truck and, to the left of the pickup, a newer silver Subaru station wagon. The pickup wore a snowplow and a sign that said, "Smythe Handyman and Plowing."

John parked his rental next to the truck. He turned to Harley and said, "Cynthia's into a little bit of everything, isn't she?"

"That's her brother's rig," Harley said laughing, "but you're right, they're a family of entrepreneurs just like lots of folks in the area. When there isn't much of an industrial employer base, you do what you can to earn a living. Derrick is about as diversified as any one man can get. Hell, a sign listing everything he does to earn a living would cover the entire truck!"

The door on the lean-to opened as John and Harley approached it, and a tall, young man dressed in insulated coveralls stepped out.

"Hey, Harley," he said cheerfully, "didn't expect to see you here." The young man turned to John and extended his hand, "I'm Derrick Smythe, Cynthia's brother. I'd guess you're John Barstow, Cynthia's new boss."

John shook Derrick's hand. His grip was strong, and his hand calloused, an indication to John that this was a man familiar with hard, physical work.

"Good to meet you, but I'm not the boss yet."

"Well, let's just say," Derrick countered with a laugh, "she's nervous enough about impressing you that she's run me off. Didn't want to make any bad impressions."

"Hell, that's not nerves," Harley quipped, "just sound judgment."

Derrick laughed, flipped Harley off and continued onto his truck. Harley continued on to the door of the lean-to, and John followed. Entering the lean-to John noted the first section was an enclosed entryway. Directly across the entryway was a coat rack and a door with a full-length window allowing an unobstructed view of a desk, where a brassy blonde was sitting behind a computer screen. After hanging their coats on the rack, Harley opened the inner door, and the blonde jumped up and started around the desk.

John immediately noticed the young woman's extremely tight-fitting blouse and ample figure, enhanced by the similarly constrictive pants she wore. Her bare midriff sported a silver navel ring that sparkled in the shaft of sunlight streaming through the window to their left. As she shimmied across the room, the bangle bracelets on her left wrist chimed lightly with each step.

"Hello, Harley," she practically cooed as she stepped closely to him, "it's been so long, I need a hug."

Harley let the young woman envelope his neck in a generous squeeze. John thought he could see Harley's ears redden as he mumbled something unintelligible into the woman's ear. Whatever it was, it had an effect. Cynthia slowly released her tight grasp of Harley, cleared her throat slightly and turned to John. "I'm sorry, I was totally rude. I'm Cynthia Smythe, Mr. Barstow."

She started to step toward John, who, not wishing the embarrassment of a greeting similar to Harley's, immediately extended his hand and looked directly into her eyes. Cynthia leaned forward and shook it eagerly. As he introduced himself, asking Cynthia to use his first name, John looked closely at her face for the first time and noted she looked to be barely out of her teens. A deeper look revealed eyes with a depth of experience, if not age. She seemed determined to keep his hand, even though he had loosened his grip. In an attempt to draw her attention to her grip, he glanced down. Two things stood out. First, Cynthia had, perhaps, the longest fingernails, and painted in the brightest shade of pink, John had ever seen. Second, the inside of her forearm bore a striking tattoo of a stylized bee with big eyes and long, flirty lashes. It looked like a cross between Betty Boop and a killer bee. The letters "N. R." were inscribed just above the bee in a gothic script.

"That's some unique art," John said, nodding at her arm.

Cynthia immediately let go of John's hand and slid her left

hand over the bee as she crossed her arms in front of herself. "Oh, that. I hope you don't find it offensive."

"Not at all. I like to admire tats, some are real works of art. I'm just too chicken to get one myself," John said trying to ease awkward moment. "Mind if I ask if there's a story behind it?"

A blush rose in Cynthia's cheeks. "It's from when I was a kid. My dad would tease me and my friends about being 'North Road Honey Bees.' So when we graduated from high school, we all got them as a joke. Our folks found it totally unfunny at the time."

"Well, as I remember, everybody else got it," Harley said. "Maybe we ought to get on with business."

Cynthia nodded and stepped back behind her desk to turn the computer screen so the two men could see it with her. John glanced at Harley with a quizzical look. It was obvious to John there was something between Cynthia and Harley, but he received only a noncommittal shrug in response.

As he rearranged his seat to better see the screen, John looked at the wall behind Cynthia. Two certificates of completion from an online university were contained in ornate presentation frames and hung prominently in the center of the wall, above a row of file cabinets. One certificate was for accounting, and the other was for web design. They were surrounded by personal pictures, all of which were in plain, considerably less expensive frames.

"So, before we start looking at the books," John said as he sat down, "I'd like to know a little about your business, and your working relationship with my uncle. I'm just curious. No offense, but you don't fit the stereotypical image of a bookkeeper."

The red glow returned to Cynthia's face as she glanced briefly at Harley and shifted in her seat. "Okay, what do you want to know, precisely?"

"Again, I don't want to offend," John said slowly, "but you don't look old enough to be the primary accountant for a business."

"I'm twenty-seven, Mr. Barstow," came the cool response, "and have a daughter who is eight. I have had this business since I was twenty-two. Your uncle told me to quit pissing my life away and get a skill. He encouraged me to get some accounting skills and then hired me to do his books. After that, he pushed me to learn about web design so I could handle online advertising and booking for him. From there, he suggested I open my own business and take on other clients, which I've done. I don't give a damn if I fit your 'image.' I'm good at what I do, and Hardrock would've been the first to tell you that."

It was John's turn to shift uncomfortably in his seat. It was obvious this North Road Honey Bee had a sting. Harley covered his mouth and looked away to keep from laughing out loud.

"Alright," John replied, "I guess that just about covers the first question, and would be a solid recommendation from my uncle, were he here. Let's look at what you do, and see how things look in the books."

Cynthia loaded the previous five year's financial ledgers for Last Chance Adventures for John to review on the screen. Starting with the first year, she explained the various expenditures as she worked on through the records. John found it interesting that most of the major expenditures were repetitive annually, generally within a week's timeframe. There were a few exceptions, primarily purchases of equipment, but there were also some sizable payments made to Cynthia's brother, Derrick.

"I see your brother's business has received some big payments over the years."

"He does, or did, carpentry work for Hardrock. I can find receipts, I'm sure, if you are curious about the nature of the work."

"He's a helluva finish carpenter," Harley interjected, "and there are some things neither Hardrock, or me, are good with, and finish carpentry is right on top of the list. Whenever Hardrock wanted to spruce the place up a little, he called in Derrick. Hardrock always wanted the place to look as fresh as possible for the clients. It was a point of pride for him."

John glanced at Cynthia for confirmation, but she was preoccupied staring at Harley, hanging onto his every word. The image reminded John of a lovesick schoolgirl.

"No, I don't need any receipts," John said, suddenly realizing how his comment must have sounded more like an accusation of impropriety than the simple observation it was.

On the whole, it looked to John as if Last Chance Adventures was, on average, just slightly better than self-sustaining, considering his uncle had to live on what was left after all the bills were paid. The balance for the last year's operation was noticeably the worst of the lot, showing a meager annual profit of less than thirty-thousand dollars. It seemed like very little for a place as famously expensive to live as Alaska.

"What's the story about last year?" John asked. "Why are last year's profits down so significantly over the previous?"

"It was a poor year for tourism," Cynthia replied. "It's been a general trend throughout the industry. We have fewer tourists. That's the bad news. The good news, for upper end destinations at least, is the tourists who do come up are wealthier, and willing to spend more. Unfortunately, Last Chance Adventures isn't a destination that would attract people who want luxury."

John sat in thought for a moment before continuing. "I can tell you from personal perspective the economic situation hasn't improved much over last year. How are things looking for this year, so far?"

The young bookkeeper pulled up a schedule of the bookings from the previous year and the current reservations for comparison. "We're down almost thirty percent from last year," she said softly.

A low whistle escaped John's lips as he leaned back in his chair and looked at the ceiling. Separated from the euphoria of the previous day's trip, and faced with the fiscal realities of the books, thoughts of birds in hand flitted through his mind. Twenty-five thousand and an unseen trailer house were starting to sound pretty attractive.

"Something to consider," Harley said breaking the silence, "is that it's still early in the year. I'll bet lots of people wait before making their minds up. The numbers might not be as bad as they look. Right?"

"It's true, we could make some of it up, but it's a big gap, and I think the final bookings will fall short."

Her response was disappointing, and it was Harley's turn to lean back and examine the ceiling. Separated from the previous day's euphoria of the promise of an enjoyable job and faced with the reality of losing it, thoughts of salmon in hand flitted through his mind.

John sat up. "Well, it's food for thought, anyway. Let's move on. Cynthia, tell me about the web site and the booking process."

With a few clicks Cynthia closed the ledger and booking records, and called up the web site for Last Chance Adventures. A picture of the lodge and cabins, taken from out in the lake, filled the page immediately. The water was glass-smooth and reflected the mountains in the distance. The picture was obviously from the middle of the summer, and John was struck by how green and lush the vegetation in the picture looked. At the edge of the lake a small dock extended from the shore, and at the end of the dock stood his uncle, dressed in a plaid shirt, waving. John tried to recall if he'd seen a dock, and finally decided he hadn't. It didn't matter, the image did an effective job of capturing the beauty of the place.

After a brief moment, text started to appear across the screen. The text, a style suggestive of newspaper type used at the turn of the century, was red and stood out starkly against the background of the lodge. "Somewhere west of roads..." it started, "there is a place so special you have to go there to believe it. Come visit us, it may be your last chance to experience the true Alaskan frontier." The first lines of text disappeared to be replaced by an arc of text stretching above the lodge reading "Last Chance Adventures." A navigation bar displayed along the bottom of the page.

Cynthia walked John through the various navigation buttons, explaining what each opened up. She had individual buttons that addressed every conceivable question a visitor to the site might conjure up: history of the claim, Alaskan facts, activities at the lodge, amenities, transportation, wildlife, even a link to videos of people mining at the camp and fishing in the creek. The largest button, located at the bottom of the navigation bar, was labeled "Book a visit."

With Cynthia clicking on the buttons, John took a tour of the entire web site, taking note of details he had not been able to see during his brief visit with Reeder. The guest cabins were much nicer than he had imagined from the porch at the lodge. Each video segment was dubbed over with narrative provided by a professional studio. John thought to himself that had he wandered across the site by accident, he would want to visit the place himself. On the booking button, Cynthia walked him through the process, how the deposits were collected, and explained how she was the chief contact for the operation.

Although she was explaining things to John, Cynthia kept looking at Harley and smiling. It was obvious to John she was trying to show Harley what an integral part of the team she was.

John was pleased with what he saw. Any initial reservations about the competence of the young bookkeeper were relieved.

"That's an effective page," he said, "it's certainly not the web presence driving down the bookings."

Cynthia took the compliment with a nod and finally a smile for John, instead of Harley.

"I researched the demographics on the kind of tourists most likely to be interested in a place like Last Chance, and built it with that information in mind. The most likely visitors are late middle-aged people with an appreciation for the outdoors, or those with an interest in the gold rush era. Other demographic groups included people from the big cities who want to 'rough it' in the wilderness, those simply looking for some peace and quiet, and fishermen looking for uncrowded conditions. So with that information, I went for a homey, tranquil feel, like friends inviting you to share a personal experience, while showing off the wilderness."

Her brief explanation of what went into the development of the web site left John staring at Cynthia and chastising himself for his quick judgment. She was much more of a professional than her outward appearance might suggest. Looking at his watch, John was startled to see more than two hours had elapsed since they had arrived.

"Well, Ms. Smythe," John said as he lifted himself from his chair, "you have been most... surprising. I can see why my uncle put his trust in you. I need to get going, but I'm sure Wes Bartholomew will be in touch with you no later than tomorrow." He shook hands with Cynthia and noticed Harley was still seated. "You coming?"

"Yeah, I'll be right behind you."

John closed the door to the office behind him and put on his coat. As he stepped out of the entryway into the bright sun he glanced back through the window into the office. Cynthia had her arms wrapped around Harley's neck, again. John chuckled all the way to the car.

"*Maybe she's the bee,*" he thought, "*but Harley is definitely the honey.*"

John only had a moment in the car to himself to think over the financial condition of Last Chance Adventures before Harley came out the door and trotted toward the car. He got in and John looked at him for a moment.

"You've got a little lipstick on your cheek, chief."

Harley wiped his cheek with the back of a gloved hand, then rubbed it hard. John backed the car up and turned down the drive in silence.

The two men drove down the road toward the highway in an uneasy lack of conversation. Half-way to the highway Harley asked John to stop the car.

"Tell me what you're thinking."

With a slight smirk John replied, "I was thinking maybe you two ought to get a room."

"No, goddamn it! About Last Chance."

John let out a long sigh. "I don't know, Harley. Honestly, I don't. It sure doesn't look good. As intrigued as I am with the prospect of owning it, becoming a part of it, the chances of success look grim."

"Oh, hell. That's what I thought you'd say. Okay, you've met me, and now Cynthia. Do you realize... understand... what kind of impact, what kind of devastating hole not having Last Chance in our lives would be?"

"Does it occur to you that's something I'm taking into consideration?" John asked quietly in reply. "If I take it on, and don't make a go of it, it may postpone operation by someone who could. In the long run, you will both be in the same positions you're in right now. Only, it may be with someone who has the capital to ride out the rough times."

"That is *such* bullshit! You walk away with twenty-five grand, go back to California to restart your life, and we get left out in the cold, unemployed, to watch some conglomerate wreck another piece of Alaska, not to mention our lives."

John didn't reply, he put the car back in gear and started back toward the highway. At the highway, John paused before pulling out. "I'd like to see my uncle's place. Which way do I turn?"

"It's on the right, half-way back to the Shuffle. No street sign, but there's a cluster of three mailboxes, one with 'Grant' on it. Hardrock's place is at the end of the road." Harley's tone was dispassionate, but there was a simmering anger in his eyes. "Do me a favor though, drop me off at the Shuffle. I don't want to go to Hardrock's."

John turned toward the Shuffle Inn, and Harley pointed out where John needed to turn to get to Hardrock's place. There was no other conversation during the ride. At the Shuffle Inn, John parked and started to get out of the car with Harley.

"What are you doing?" Harley asked coolly.

"I need the keys to the trailer."

"No you don't. I don't think Hardrock even had keys for it." Then added as a parting shot, "And you won't have any trouble getting into the place, Derrick always kept it plowed out for Hardrock."

Harley slammed the door on the car as John got back in. He turned away from the car and stepped into the Shuffle Inn to announce the tragic loss of an institution.

John drove to the end of the road Harley had pointed out, where there was a turnaround with one narrow passage similar to the drive into Cynthia's. At the end of the passage was a large, open plowed area. A large Quonset building was situated directly across the plowed area, perpendicular to the drive. A trailer house with a small lean-to enclosing the front door sat to the left at a ninety-degree angle to the Quonset. The two buildings were just barely far enough apart for Derrick's plow truck to push the snow away between them.

John pulled up in front of the trailer and turned off the ignition. He sat for a moment wishing he had a friend to talk to.

"Just who the hell does Harley Pepperdine think he is?" John ranted to himself. *"Who is he to pass judgment on me? Asshole. I don't want to be the guy that lost the Last Chance. It's not like anybody around here wouldn't blame me when it folds. It would be a year later, and the result would be the same. I can't*

change that."

Deciding he needed to go inside, if for no other reason than to satisfy a nagging feeling of obligation, John climbed out of the car and headed to the entry of the trailer. Almost to the door, he heard a loud bark and turned. Running toward him was a large dog with its hackles raised.

"Dawg? Is that you?"

The animal instantly slowed to a loping trot and wagged its tail. It approached panting, tongue lolling out to display his usual good-natured manner. John reached out to pat him on the head.

"You really get around. Got a lady friend in the neighborhood?"

The big dog leaned heavily against John and accepted the attention.

"You're the only one who would give two shits for me right now, boy."

The dog nuzzled up against John's gloved hand, trying to get some more attention.

"Don't get used to it, buddy. I'm pulling the plug. Just want to look this place over before I meet with Wes."

The dog continued his display of affection unabated, totally unconcerned about the dramas of humankind. After rubbing the dog's ears, John pushed him away and turned to enter the trailer. Dawg laid down between the car and trailer.

Harley had been right, the outer door was unlocked. It opened up to a small entryway where various coats and jackets were hung from a bar on the left side. A line of boots and shoes were lined up on the floor underneath. A chest freezer occupied the opposite wall. The entry was neither heated, nor finished on the inside. Exposed electrical wiring ran along the bare studs to an overhead light fixture, but a single window above the freezer provided enough light to see clearly. A worn strip of green indoor/outdoor carpet stretched between the exterior door of the entry and the door into the trailer. Taking in the austere entryway, John found himself thinking that if the home itself wasn't a vast improvement over the entryway, there was little wonder his uncle spent as much time at the mine as possible.

The door into the trailer was also unlocked, and John stepped through it slowly. It was dim inside, but he could see it was laid out in common trailer house fashion: kitchen and dining area to the right, living room to the left, with a hallway leading to the back of the trailer.

Finding a light switch on the wall next to the door, John turned on an overhead light in the middle of the living room to see more clearly. Like Hardrock's room at Last Chance, the trailer's décor was best described as Spartan. The carpet looked to be the same as what was in his room at the Shuffle Inn. The furniture was a simple arrangement of a couch on the far wall, a coffee table in front of the couch, and two recliners angled toward the couch. A large window over the couch was closed off with heavy curtains.

"If this was my place," John mumbled to himself, "I'd spend all my waking hours someplace else, too. This is depressing."

The original walls on either end of the living room were hidden with built-in bookshelves, obviously made by the owner. Harley was right: Hardrock had been no finish carpenter. The bookshelves were made of unfinished lumber, built for purpose, not looks. With the exception of an occasional knickknack taking up space, the shelves were laden with volumes of classic literature, some of which looked to be quite old. Overall, there was a glaring lack of female influence in the room. This was obviously the home of a single, tidy man.

John started slowly down the hallway. Just as he had at the lodge, he was overcome with a feeling that he was prying. Relation, or not, this was the home of a stranger, and he was intruding. He had to question, were his uncle still alive, if he would be welcome to walk so freely about his home, looking where he wanted. He half expected someone to storm into the trailer demanding he leave.

The first door down the hall was for what had originally been a second bedroom, but was currently set up to be an office. It was small. A large desk with a computer was situated at the far side, under a window. Stacks of paperwork were set neatly on either side of the computer. John wondered if someone had come in after his uncle's death and straightened the place up, or if he had truly been that meticulous.

The second door opened up to a bathroom which also

contained a washer and dryer. A basket, half-full of shirts and pants, sat on top of the dryer The avocado color of the tub and sink placed the age of the trailer firmly in the early seventies. White towels hung neatly folded on the racks, again indicating the occupant was a single man.

John turned from the bathroom, looked toward the bedroom door and paused. He stood wondering exactly what he was doing, prowling through the trailer. He had seen nothing which meant anything to him, he was walking through a stranger's home. There was nothing he wanted, and judging from what he had seen, there was little likelihood the trailer contained anything which might hold any special meaning to him. The best thing to do, it seemed to him, would be to give the place to Harley. At least the guy would have a place of his own to live in if Last Chance Adventures folded.

Deciding he might as well see everything, John stepped into the bedroom. It was also darkened by heavy curtains on the windows. When he turned on the light, John saw his uncle's penchant for simple furnishings followed through to the bedroom. It contained a neatly made bed and a small dresser. However, this room was strikingly different as framed pictures covered every possible space on the walls. What had been lacking in any sort of personal effects throughout the rest of the trailer were assembled in this one room. John started around the room to examine the pictures more closely.

There was no order, no reason, to the pictures. Old, yellowed, black and white photographs were mingled with newer, colored prints. There were old and new pictures of Last Chance, but most of the photographs captured people and times that must have been important to their owner. John stopped at a faded color picture of his uncle and young boy standing next to a red bicycle. It was hard to tell who had the larger grin. The same boy was in the next picture, along with a young girl and his uncle. All three were holding fishing poles. John wondered who the boy was, and what kind of relationship he had enjoyed with his uncle. He felt almost jealous of the boy in the picture. He took the picture of his uncle and the boy down from the wall and slid it into his coat pocket.

Some of the subjects in the pictures he recognized. There

was one of his mother and himself camping when he was young. But what caught him completely by surprise were the pictures of himself; his Little League picture, high-school graduation, college graduation, even a picture of he and his ex-wife on their wedding day. Wes's statement about John's mother and his uncle keeping in touch over the years, and his uncle monitoring his life came back to him.

Standing at the foot of the bed, in the middle of the room, John looked around at the collection of pictures. It dawned on him they were actually a grand collage of his uncle. They were his history, his family. John swept his eyes around the room again, and had a revelation: of all the pictures, those of himself were displayed most prominently. The note scribbled in the condolence card from his uncle, when John's father died, rolled like thunder through his mind. *"We're the only family each of us has now. Don't be a stranger - Hank."*

"Damn," John said softly to himself, "I blew it. I never thought... never even tried." He hung his head. His eyes burned.

He turned off the lights and closed the doors firmly on his way out. When Dawg saw John emerge from the entry way, he jumped up and trotted over to him. After receiving a pat on the head, the animal bounded toward the Quonset hut, as if leading the way, and stopped halfway to glance back. John checked his watch; it was a few minutes past one.

"I've got time," he said to the dog, "I guess I better look at everything."

With that, Dawg trotted over to the door on the Quonset hut. It was actually much larger than the trailer, and John guessed it pre-dated the trailer considerably. He walked up to the door, which was flanked by two large stacks of split firewood. An overhang protected the door and the wood from the elements. This door was also unlocked, and when John opened it, Dawg pushed past him into the building, and settled comfortably onto the end of a heavily worn couch. John could almost hear the dog sigh as he curled up, as if he had been anticipating the luxury for quite some time.

"No, really, make yourself to home," John quipped. Dawg thumped his tail on the couch in response.

The first impression, on entering the building, was that of

walking into a well-lit cavern. Two large windows on either side of the entry allowed light to fill the room. The arc of the building made the ceiling higher than ten feet. The room was very large, even though short walls were brought down on both sides. John had expected to walk into a workshop, but the room was laid out for comfortable occupation. In addition to the couch Dawg was on, there were two equally worn leather chairs and tables covered with a collection of outdoor and mining magazines. A patchwork of rag rugs covered most of the cement floor, except in the left-hand corner, where a large, cast-iron wood stove stood. John wished the wood stove was in operation. Even though the temperature was cold, the room itself felt like a place you would want to spend time.

To the right of the door behind a broad desk, stood another crudely constructed bookshelf, similar to the ones in the trailer. This one was filled entirely with books, all of which were technical in nature: chemistry, mining, Alaskan history. John wondered if the man had, indeed, read all the texts, and marveled at what must have been the breadth of his uncle's knowledge, if he had. The desk was scattered with topographic maps and aerial photographs. Scrawled annotations dotted all of them. The room's appearance started to make sense to John.

"So, you weren't a compulsive neat-freak after all," John thought aloud to himself. "I'm guessing this is where you spent most of your time when you weren't at Last Chance."

The back wall of the room was solid, and paneled. More photographs were hung on this wall, along with a moose head and four skulls, which John guessed to be from bears. He took his time to look closely at the pictures, hoping to gain further insight into his uncle. Unlike those in the trailer, these were all from Last Chance. A signed duplicate of Harley's picture of Myrna Filmore hung among them, leading John to the conclusion they were mainly pictures of clients past, but several were older pictures of miners working along a huge trough. The back wall made the room about fifteen feet deep. By John's estimate, this would have been less than a third the length of the entire building.

Curious about what the remainder of the building held, he walked over to the door leading to the other side of the wall.

Looking more closely, John noted the door was made of solid metal plate painted a dark brown. He rapped on it and could immediately tell the plate was very heavy. Where a knob or latch for the door should have been, there was a stout, welded box, open on the underside. Looking up into the box, John could make out a latch secured in place by an impressive padlock. He stepped back and looked at the hinges for the door. They were a security type, welded in place.

Staring at the door, mulling over the incongruity of the only locked door he had encountered, John noticed a button to the left of the door. Curious, he pushed the button. A loud horn immediately blared on the other side of the wall, and Dawg launched himself from his comfortable spot on the couch to bark at the noise. The sound was loud where John stood, and he imagined it must have been practically deafening on the other side.

"Well, Dawg," John said after a few moments, "whatever is behind that door is where Hardrock really wanted it to stay. That's enough fooling around, I need to go see a man about a trust."

It was slightly past two when John pulled into the Shuffle Inn. He had to park near his room because all of the parking in front of the bar was taken. Even though it was a Saturday, it seemed early to John for the place to be so busy. The uneasy quiet that fell over the room when he stepped into the bar gave an indication of what might have contributed to the increased number of patrons.

Making his way between the tables toward the bar, the smiles and nods John extended in greeting were received with blank looks, or faces that turned away. It was definitely not his natural charisma that had drawn a crowd. He settled onto a stool at the end of the bar, next to Harley, who was sipping on a beer. The people in the bar returned to private conversations after John turned his back to them.

"Looks to be a tough crowd," John observed as Doorway handed him a cup of coffee. "I wonder why." He looked directly at Harley.

"Might be they've had some bad news recently," Harley replied. "You find anything of interest at Hardrock's?"

John gave brief thought to asking what Harley had said in the bar after being dropped off, but decided it was better just to move on. Retrieving the picture he'd taken from Hardrock's bedroom, he handed it to Doorway. "You know who that kid is?"

The big bartender looked the picture over and smiled. "I have an idea," he said, extending his arm. John reached for the picture, but Doorway's arm stretched past him. "Harley, you got an idea who the kid is?"

Harley took the picture and glanced at it. "Oh, hell. That's me when I was nine." He couldn't stop a small smile from appearing. "It was at Nikiski Days, and I won that bike in a drawing. First bike I ever had. I think Hardrock was more tickled about it than me. Who would've thought he'd keep something like that?"

John didn't reply. He also didn't mention the other picture of Harley hanging on the wall. He did, however, suddenly realize he knew the answer to his question about the relationship between the boy in the picture and his uncle. It was, after all, a family gallery.

Harley continued to stare at the picture a few moments, his expression a conflicting mixture of emotions. "Here," he said handing it back to John, "thanks for showing it to me."

"You keep it. It's a picture of you, not me."

Harley only nodded as he carefully set the picture on the bar.

"Wes ought to be here any minute," Doorway said to John. "Reeder flew up to Anchorage to get him right after you dropped Harley off. He was going to pick him up at Lake Hood and come right back."

As if on cue, the door opened and Reeder stepped through, followed by the lawyer. At least John thought it was Wes, he looked completely different out of a suit. Dressed as he was, fur hat, plaid shirt, canvas coat and jeans, he looked like a local, except he was carrying a leather satchel. John watched him as he returned greetings with some of the patrons; shaking hands and exchanging comments. Watching him, it occurred to John the old lawyer didn't just *look* like a local, he *was* one. Eventually Wes made his way up to the bar, where Doorway extended a mug to him.

"Here, Wes," the big man offered, "coffee and Bailey's."

"Just what I need! Damn pilot tried to freeze me to death!" He turned to Reeder and asked, "When are you going to get that heater fixed?"

"It is. I just didn't turn it on. I like to watch you shiver, ya damn sissy!"

"Sissy? Really? A real sissy wouldn't face death by voluntarily getting in a plane with you."

Reeder shook his head and turned back toward the door. He knew from years of experience, exchanging banter with Wes was a losing proposition. "I'll be at home. Call me when you need a lift... if you've got the nerve."

Wes turned back to Doorway. "You have a place John and I can talk?"

Doorway nodded in the direction of an empty table at the farthest corner of the bar. "That ought to do. I set one all the way in the corner, and moved the others a little away from it, but you might have to remind folks to keep their distance when they creep up to listen in."

"No problem there," Wes said, and then turned without another word to walk over to the table.

John continued to sit at the bar, watching Wes set up at the table. Since his arrival, Wes had not so much as looked at him. He felt as though he was being pointedly, and publicly, snubbed. He turned to Harley. "I'm guessing you made everybody within earshot privy to our last conversation."

"Yeah," Harley answered, staring at the framed picture on the bar, "bad news travels fast."

"It does, indeed," John agreed, and then laughed. He set his mug of coffee on the bar and turned to leave, and then turned back to Harley. "But, I guess it all depends on your personal definition of bad." He didn't wait for a reply and walked over to join Wes at the table.

"Come here often?" John said in an effort to lighten the lawyer's mood.

"Quit screwing around, and just sit down," Wes snapped without looking up from the satchel he was digging through. "Let's get this over with."

John sat down opposite the lawyer. "Wes, I'd like to ask

146

you for your opinion."

"What?" It was more of a demand than a question. Wes still didn't look up from the satchel.

"Tell me what you think my uncle wanted me to do."

Wes stopped rummaging and looked up with a piercing glare. "Son, you've been here two days, talked to people who knew him well, and have been through his home. If you haven't figured it out, you are, and please pardon the legalese, dumber than a fucking stump."

There was a round of chuckling from the previously unoccupied table next to them. Wes turned on the occupants of the table. "You kids just go back to where you were before you got so curious. *Now!*"

Without protest or comment, the men got up immediately and left to reclaim their previous seats.

"You honestly can't tell me who the secondary beneficiary is?" John asked.

"No."

"I was afraid of that," John said with a sigh. "Wes, I've reviewed the books. The business isn't looking good."

A loud laugh erupted from the lawyer. "Kid, business *never* looks good. That's the nature of business. The only guarantee is that there is no guarantee involved."

"I'll take your word for it."

John glanced back to the bar. The only person not taking at least furtive glances in his direction was Harley, who sat staring down at the bar, slowly turning a beer bottle. Wes had finally pulled out everything he had been looking for, and set the small stack of papers on the table in front of John.

"Okay, I'll need you to sign on the lines I've indicated with tabs, and initial the highlighted spots. We will have to meet in Anchorage on Monday for you to get the check for twenty-five grand and title to Hardrock's home. With your signatures, you relinquish all further claim to anything else in the estate. Do you understand?"

"Yeah, I understand," John said, pushing the stack back toward the lawyer. "I understand you got the wrong papers out. Now, if *you* will quit screwing around and get out the right papers, I'd like to get this over with."

It felt good to see the crotchety old lawyer slightly befuddled.

"I thought you told Harley less than three hours ago you didn't want Last Chance," he said, digging back into the satchel. "Why the change?"

"It's a family thing."

"I don't think so. Hardrock didn't waffle on making decisions. Not even big ones."

"Well, that might be because my uncle knew who his family was. I'm just beginning to figure it out."

A small smile appeared on Wes's face as he pulled out a different, and much thicker, stack of papers from the satchel. "Don't get intimidated," he said as he set it in front of John, "these contain the details we discussed in my office. I'll show you where to sign, and answer anything that isn't clear to you."

After a few minutes of watching Wes guide John through the documents, the crowd's interest in their activity waned. By the time the last signature was on the agreement, conversations in the bar had returned to normal. However, when the two men stood up, the conversations quieted down.

As they shook hands, Wes leaned over and asked John, "You want to say anything to the curious?"

"Not until I have a word with Harley."

"Going to dish out a little dirt?"

"I owe it to him, but no. I just want him to be the first to know."

Wes held his mug up to Doorway to indicate he needed a refill, and headed toward the bar. He shook his head and deflected the questions from people who stopped him on the way. John walked directly back to the empty stool next to Harley and sat down. To his surprise, Harley turned toward him immediately.

"Listen, I'm not happy with the way things turned out," Harley said, "but I guess I understand your position. Anyway, I wish things had turned out differently, and that's why I went off on you earlier. Just wanted you to know."

"Is that an apology?"

"No, just an explanation."

"Okay. I want you to know it really pisses me off you told

148

everyone I'd decided to turn down Last Chance. It wasn't yours to do."

Harley's cheeks flushed as he looked down and nodded.

"Really," John continued, "did you see the way people treated me when I walked in? Did you see how Wes treated me? Jesus, Harley! If there had been a rope in the room, I'd be hanged by now."

"All right! I'm sorry! Happy now?"

"Not really," John replied, truly enjoying the moment and trying hard not to show it. "I only think it's fair you make it right."

"What? You've got to be kidding! And exactly what do you think *I'm* supposed to do?"

"Well, for starters, you could publicly explain to all these good people you were wrong."

It took a moment for John's meaning to sink in, then Harley's jaw dropped.

"You didn't!"

"Oh, yeah."

"You *asshole!*" Harley shouted, and all conversations ceased throughout the bar. Nobody wanted to miss the brewing fight.

"Pepperdine," John said evenly, and loud enough for all in the bar to hear, "you need to learn that is probably not the best way to address your new boss."

CHAPTER 9

John was relieved the next day was Sunday, a day of rest. For the first time in almost two weeks he had the luxury of not worrying about his next immediate move. Wes had left the bar after a couple of hours of celebration, citing the need to get back to Anchorage, and his desire for Reeder to make the flight in the daylight. John had stayed long after Wes left, with Harley introducing him to one person after another until even John, with his salesman's ability to remember names and faces, was overwhelmed. Eventually, Harley reached a point at which his speech was slurred and introductions became laughable. John called it a night at that point, seeking some peace and quiet in his room.

Sitting in the recliner in his room, enjoying the quietude of Sunday morning, John was jarred from his thoughts by the phone ringing. He answered it, and was greeted by Reeder's gruff voice.

"You need to pick up your permanent set of wheels. Hardrock left his rig at the strip when I took him over the last time. It's yours now."

"What time do you want me to meet you there?" John asked, hoping it would be later in the day.

"No need, unless you want a ride to turn in your rental. I cleared it off yesterday, and the keys are in the ignition. Pick it up whenever you want."

"I could use some help making the swap. But was hoping to do it later."

"Well, the wife and I are headed into Kenai in a couple of minutes. I'll take your rig and park it at the airport. The keys will be under the floor mat on the passenger side."

John tamped down a laugh at Reeder's clever security. "Sounds good to me. What am I looking for?"

"A dark blue Chevy Suburban. You can't miss it."

After hanging up, John allowed himself a good chuckle at Reeder's anti-theft practices. *"Hell,"* he thought, *"in LA you keep the keys in your pocket, your car is set to blare an alarm if someone so much as farts on it, and still it gets stolen. In Nikiski, you keep the keys in the ignition. In Kenai, which must be a hotbed of car theft, you hide the keys under the mat on the passenger side."*

Following another cup of coffee, and making sure everything personal was cleaned out of the rental car, John drove into Kenai. It was a completely different drive in the bright sunshine, and seemed to go much more quickly than when he drove to Nikiski in the dark. Once in Kenai, he drove by the bank Wes had instructed him to visit on Monday to establish his signature on the account for Last Chance Adventures. He also noted the location of several restaurants. There was obviously more to Kenai than he had seen on the night of his arrival.

The rental desk was closed. A lock box with directions for returning rentals sat on the counter. He dropped the keys and a copy of his rental agreement in the box, and headed back out into the sunshine. Reeder had been right about finding the vehicle, it was impossible to miss. It was huge. The dark blue paint was coated with a brown road grime, but a decal with "Last Chance Adventures, Inc." above a gold nugget was easily visible on both of the front doors. John felt like he was standing next to a bus when he walked up to the vehicle. It certainly wasn't a vehicle where the term "climb in" was merely figurative. He winced at the thought of the mileage the beast must get.

On the drive back to Nikiski John decided to grab something to eat at the Tuscan Villa, then go to the trailer to check things out more closely. His initial inspection of the place had been revealing, but not thorough. At the time, he hadn't given any thought to actually living there. Now, it was his home. It was an odd feeling, the thought of actually owning a home. It was something he'd given up on a long time ago.

After lunch John decided to stop off at the bar to see Doorway. He found him talking to Billy McCrane. They made a mismatched pair: the big, bald man sporting a collection of tattoos, wearing a Grateful Dead tee-shirt, and the diminutive, red-headed storekeeper neatly dressed in a suit and tie.

"I was hoping I'd see you," Billy said as he grabbed John's hand and pumped it heartily. "When would be a good time for us to get together to discuss what I need to order for you?"

"Well, I'm not sure, Billy. How long will it take?"

"Oh, no more than a couple of hours, for sure. Just long enough to review your uncle's past orders so you can see what he started out with. I could just order it, but it would be better if you had a chance to okay everything. You might have questions. How's tomorrow?"

"I don't know, Billy, I've got to..."

"Well, you don't want to wait too long. Season's coming up and one of the ways I keep costs down is by ordering well in advance, and in bulk."

"Okay, *not* tomorrow," John said firmly, "I'll come by the store first thing on Tuesday."

"Great! Hey, I've got to run. Youth group at the church starts at two." Again, the little dynamo grabbed John's hand and cranked it rapidly, "See you first thing Tuesday. Later, Doorway." With that, Billy McCrane quickly buzzed out the door.

"That guy wears me out," John said.

"Yeah, and today is his day off. He's in his relaxed mode. Good luck on Tuesday, trying to keep up with him."

"It should be a challenge."

"And one more thing you might want to be aware of," Doorway added, "he's going to hit you up for a donation to the Grilling for God contest."

"The *what*?"

"The Grilling for God contest. It's really a fund raiser for Billy's church youth group. It's how they get money to pay for the kids to go out and do missionary work."

"You are kidding me."

"No, seriously. It's a barbecue contest. People pay an entry fee to compete for the title of best barbecue on the North Road. The youth group sells tickets to taste the entries, and each ticket exchanged is a vote for that entry. It's an annual community event. I host it every year, and everybody shows up for it."

"I've heard it all now, a Baptist church, sponsoring a barbecue contest, hosted by a bar!" John laughed loudly and slapped his knee.

"You laugh now, but you wouldn't believe how much dough the kids raise. Besides, it's a helluva lot of fun." John rocked on his stool gasping for air as Doorway continued, "Just so you know, Hardrock donated a lot of money to support it and Billy is going to press hard, hoping you'll do the same. Be prepared."

John regained a little of his composure, and wiped tears from his eyes. "Oh, I'm in! I'm in for sure! When is the big event?"

"We try to hold it on the weekend as close to the solstice as possible. And this year, the solstice is on a Saturday. Ought to be a great turnout."

The image of a mixed crowd of drunken roughnecks and pious Baptists, all gathered around a bar, eating barbecue in the midnight sun was more than John could handle. He was racked with another spasm of uncontrollable laughter. When he finally got himself back under control, he noticed Harley standing behind him. He looked better than John had expected.

"What's so funny?"

"I just told him about Grilling for God," Doorway explained. His face and voice were sincere and devoid of any humor.

"Is he really serious?" John asked skeptically.

"Hell yes, it's a big deal. Raises a lot of money for the youth group. Hardrock was a big supporter. Every year he flew back from Last Chance just to go to it. He wouldn't have missed it for anything."

John looked at the two men and could tell they were, in fact, not pulling his leg. "All right, when Billy McCrane hits me up, I'll match what my uncle used to donate. And I'm not going to miss it, either. That is something I have *got* to see."

"Before you ask, *boss*," Harley said, settling on the stool next to John, "I'm doing fine. However, if you had some aspirin, Doorway, I could use a couple to go with a glass of water."

The bartender produced two sealed packets of aspirin from behind the bar and set a glass of water in front of Harley. He then nodded at a couple settling down at a table, and walked off in their direction carrying two beers.

"I'm guessing I missed quite a celebration by leaving early."

"Yeah, people kept buying me drinks and congratulating me."

"Congratulating *you*? For *what*?" John asked incredulously.

"I don't know. Maybe for keeping my job, or maybe they thought I goaded you into taking on Last Chance. Who knows? I'm not one to question a free beer."

"I noticed. Look, I know we touched on this before, but I need to know if drinking is going to be a problem at Last Chance."

Harley bristled slightly. "I told you. It was, and will be, a hard and fast rule that staff doesn't drink."

"I know, but what if a client offers that 'free beer' to you?"

"Did I ever mention to you that my religion forbids drinking?" Harley replied with a wink. "That shuts down the offers, and prevents any hard feelings. Besides, it's different when I'm west of roads. People are depending on me to have a clear head. Including you, now."

"Fair enough. I won't bring it up again."

Doorway stepped back behind the bar. "What'd I miss?"

"Nothing, just some ground rules," John answered quickly, then changed the subject. "By the way, I was wondering if I could keep my room for a few more days. I'm not too sure I'm ready to move into Hardrock's place just yet."

"Not a problem. I figured as much. Besides, it's not like I'm being forced to hang out a no vacancy sign."

"I appreciate it. Speaking of which, I'm going to head over there right now. Harley, you want to come along? There's some things there I think Hardrock would want you to have." Harley hesitated in answering, and John continued. "Seriously, there's some things I think you *should* have. Plus, you might be able to explain something to me."

"Sure, I guess," Harley mumbled.

Harley said nothing about John having the Suburban when they climbed in, and the silence continued as they drove to the trailer.

"Have you been here since Hardrock died?" John asked as they pulled into the drive.

"Nope, no reason to."

"Well, you were right, Derrick kept the place plowed out."

"Yeah."

John parked the Suburban in front of the trailer lean-to, climbed out of it and walked to the door. He turned around and saw Harley take a deep breath before he slowly climbed out of the rig. John guessed this was the first time Harley had really faced the fact his old friend was gone. This was not going to be easy for either of them.

"I didn't look in the freezer when I was here yesterday," John said in an effort to perhaps lighten the mood. "What do you suppose is in it?"

"Salmon, halibut, moose meat, and maybe some caribou. Hardrock always had friends dropping stuff off to him." Harley's reply was monotone.

John led the way into the trailer, and flipped on the overhead light. "I'm sure you're familiar with the place."

"Yeah. But if Hardrock wasn't already out in the hut, it's where we headed. I don't think he did much in the trailer except eat, sleep and read."

"I noticed there's quite a collection of classics here."

"Yeah," Harley agreed. "He just about wore this one out." He pulled a book from a shelf and handed it to John.

"Robert Service, 'Bar Room Ballads.' It figures."

Harley swallowed hard. "He had lots of Service's poems memorized. He'd keep the clients entertained at night reciting them. When he'd recite 'Bessie's Boil' people would practically be rolling on the ground."

"Did you ever have reason to go into Hardrock's bedroom?" John asked as he slid the volume back into its place.

"No. Why?"

"Well, there are pictures hanging in there, and I think you ought to have some of them." John led the way down the hall and opened the door to the bedroom. "Over there, on the left."

Harley stepped tentatively to where John had pointed. A small gasp followed by, "Oh, hell," escaped as he gently touched the frame containing the picture of his younger self, Hardrock and the little girl. His voice was tight as he continued, "That's one of me and Maggie with Hardrock."

John could see Harley's eyes welling up. He told Harley to take his time, that any of the pictures he wanted he could have, and that he was going to look things over in the kitchen. He slipped out of the bedroom, closing the door on the sound of stifled sobs.

The kitchen was small, but efficiently laid out. John took stock of what was there. His uncle must have been a pretty good cook. The cabinets and drawers held a wide assortment of utensils, pots and pans, all of which looked to be well-used. The man must have had some culinary skills. John wondered if he worked out potential meals at home before serving them to the clients. At any rate, the kitchen held more cooking gear than John would require for his simple cooking needs.

John was poking through the refrigerator, noting what had expired, when Harley reappeared from the back of the trailer.

"I'd like to keep these," Harley said, holding out four pictures. Three of the pictures Harley held were more recent ones of Hardrock and himself at Last Chance, and the fourth was the picture of Harley, Maggie and Hardrock. "I'm going to give the old one of us to Maggie. I'm sure she'd want it. Most of the pictures are of people I don't know."

"There's a lot of my relatives hanging on the walls in there, but some must be old friends from years past. I'll pass those along to Wes, maybe he'd want them."

"So, you said you wanted me to explain something to you," Harley said to change the subject.

"Yeah, let's go out to the Quonset hut."

John led the way out of the trailer to the other building, stepped inside and pointed to the steel door on the far side of the room. "This is weird: the trailer is unlocked, the front door to this building is unlocked, but when you step inside, you run into the front gate to Fort Knox. What's so important behind this door?"

"Beats me."

"You've never been in there?"

"No. I don't think Hardrock let anyone in there. He even bolted the door from the inside when he was doing whatever he did in there."

"That's why there's a buzzer," John mused, "so people could get his attention when he was in there."

"Yeah, that sucker is loud. But it needs to be, with all the racket he made."

"What the hell was he doing that was so secret?"

"I don't have a clue. All he ever said was that he was working on projects. It's not so strange. I know lots of guys who don't like people nosing around in their shops."

"You have any idea where the key for the lock is?"

"No, but Wes might."

"Well, it's not going anywhere, so it can wait."

John walked over to the desk and asked Harley about the topographic maps and aerial photographs. Harley explained they were how Hardrock planned out the season's digs. The annotations were the results of tests he and Hardrock made. The aerial photographs showed the rows and piles of tailings on the claim.

"That's Gold Creek running up the valley," Harley explained. "When the mine was in operation, up until World War II, they used hydraulic mining. All those lines and mounds are the tailings."

"Hydraulic mining?"

"Yeah, water was run down from this creek," Harley pointed to another creek on the topographic map, "using piping from a coffer dam up on the top of this ridge. The pressure created from the water source being so high was enough to supply huge nozzles to wash dirt from the valley walls on Gold Creek. Believe it, or not, there was enough pressure off the nozzles that the miners could literally push boulders around with it. The dirt washed off the walls was run through a channel sluice where the gold would settle out. Anything too big to go through the sluice, and all the material that washed through, was piled up

in those tailings. There are some pictures on the wall over there
of the mine in operation during the twenties."

The two men walked over to the pictures and Harley
described the operation in more detail, explaining that a
significant amount of gold passed through the sluice to collect in
the tailings. He also explained how all the equipment had been
sledged in during the winter months, taking advantage of the
frozen ground and snow. John marveled at how much work it
must have been to get everything to the mine.

"Those old timers were tough as hell," Harley said with
obvious admiration. "They earned every ounce they found.
That's also why practically everything they dragged in is still out
there. It wasn't worth the expense of dragging it out. The clients
love to look at that stuff, although it drives the guys with metal
detectors nuts."

John found the thought of being a continuation in such a
colorful history appealing. He grilled Harley with questions for
quite some time, until Harley finally ran out of answers and told
him to look through Hardrock's collection of reference books.
Inside, Harley was not only pleased, but relieved, to see his new
boss was getting caught up in the spirit of Last Chance
Adventures.

The last two weeks of March passed in a blur of activity.
Following the directions he received from Wes, John made all
the administrative changes necessary to get himself on the
various accounts for Last Chance Adventures. Every day for a
week, Harley took John around the area to meet people who
were peripheral, but necessary, to the operation of the business.
By the end of the week, John's head was swimming with
information. He eventually resorted to making notes in a binder
to keep all the contacts straight. Making the rounds had also
shown John that Harley was not only good at dealing with
people, he enjoyed it.

The meeting with Billy McCrane had been the most
interesting. Before John even settled into a chair, Billy presented
a list of everything the first shipment of dry goods would contain
on his computer screen. While Billy quickly went down the list,
Harley made comments on the quantities based on his
recollection of previous needs. John found himself to be mainly

a spectator in the discussion.

Having settled the dry goods shipment, Billy immediately pulled up an example of a typical grocery list. He was well down the list before realizing neither of his clients had made a comment. He looked up to see two blank faces staring at him. "You're okay with this list, right?"

"I don't know," John said. "Harley, does that sound right to you?"

"I don't know. I told you Hardrock did all the cooking."

"Well, what did he cook?"

"I guess the stuff on that list. Look, I just dealt with the finished products. We had stew, we had noodle stuff, and sometimes steaks. Breakfasts were always good."

"Well, thank you mister details man."

"Wait a minute," Billy broke in, "who's going to do the cooking?"

"We're looking for a camp cook right now," John answered. "If we don't find one, I drew the short straw for that chore."

"Really. You have any experience cooking?"

"I'm a wizard with frozen dinners."

Billy closed the window on the monitor. "Okay, until you get your cook, I'll hold off on setting up the grocery orders. Before you go though, John, I'd like to talk to you about Last Chance Adventures' donation to the Grilling for God contest. You got a minute?"

"Sure. Doorway told me about it. I'd be glad to match whatever my uncle used to give."

"Oh, great! So, I'll put you down for one thousand dollars."

John froze. "One thousand dollars? I thought I was donating, I don't know, like a bike or something."

"Oh, no! Hardrock always bought the meat for all the contestants."

"That's a lot of hamburger!"

"There's no hamburger to it," Billy replied seriously. "It's brisket, pork ribs, pork shoulder, chicken and beef ribs."

"Each contestant cooks all that?"

"Oh, no. Each contestant draws for what they'll barbecue. That way, nobody is at an advantage every year. They never know what they'll be cooking until a couple of days before the

event. I'd like to see some steaks in there, but it would require a
bigger donation."

"The menu sounds fine as it is," John said quickly.

Billy hid his disappointment poorly. "Okay. You can write a
check to the youth group anytime before June."

Billy jumped up from his chair and pumped John and
Harley's hands vigorously before walking them out of the store.

"Wow. That's some support," John said once clear of the
store.

"Yeah, but Doorway gives at least as much. He buys all the
stuff for the side dishes."

"I suppose so, but Doorway has a steady clientele to rely on.
We don't."

With all the business arrangements made, John flew back to
LA for the last week of March. He packed up, or threw out, what
little Shelley had left behind in the apartment. With no small
amount of sentiment, he dragged his old recliner out to the curb
and pinned a sign on it saying, "Free to good home." It had
found a good home the first time he checked back on it. He felt
he should have done the same with his car by the time a dealer
agreed to "take it in the shorts" for him the day before he left
LA.

The few friends John called all expressed disbelief when he
told them he was leaving. Everyone wanted him to call, or write,
now and then to let them know how he was doing. He promised
he would, but knew it really wouldn't happen. On the way to the
airport he reflected on how simple it had been to wipe out his life
in LA, and condense it all into two large suitcases. There had
been nothing to keep him there, and he surprised himself when
he realized there was nothing regrettable, or even mildly
nostalgic, in his departure. He smiled to himself as the plane rose
up from LAX: it was April first.

"*That's fitting*," he thought as he settled back in his seat for
the long flight.

While waiting for the connecting puddle-jumper from
Anchorage to Kenai, John tried to call Wes. He wanted to know
if Wes wanted any of Hardrock's pictures, and he was curious if
Wes had any idea where the key to the back of the Quonset hut
might be. Wes was in court and wouldn't be available for the rest

of the day, according to Doreen. She promised to pass along John's questions when Wes came into the office.

Harley was waiting for John at the Kenai airport. "Welcome back. Ready to haul ass?" Harley asked as he grabbed one of John's bags and headed for the loading zone.

"Indeed. I guess the first order of business is to get moved into the trailer."

"Only if you can do it tonight. The 'haul' part of that question is literal. We need to start hauling things out to Last Chance. Starting now. You don't have time to be playing Johnny homemaker."

"So much for being the boss," John said sarcastically. "You mean to tell me I don't even have time to get settled into the trailer?"

"That's exactly what I'm saying. Because from now, until the end of the season, you're going to be out at Last Chance, for all practical purposes. We'll be shuttling stuff out every day until Reeder drops us off to stay at the end of the month."

John thought about what Harley said for a moment. "But we'll be back in the evenings until the end of April."

"Not always, it depends on what we're doing. If we're in the middle of setting something up in the camp, we'd be wasting time and money for Reeder to make a trip just to bring us out for the night. It would be better for you to just stay at the Shuffle."

The drive from Kenai was spent with Harley describing everything he had done at the Last Chance in the past week, and all that needed to be done before the Last Chance would be ready to receive clients. The list seemed endless, and John realized it would make sense to keep his room. In addition to spending so much time at the camp, the work sounded very physical. It was now clear to John why Wes had asked about his health and any aversion to physical work. He suspected his evenings for the next few weeks would be spent collapsed in exhaustion.

"It's about time," Reeder greeted the two men as they entered the Shuffle Inn, "we've got work to do if we're going to take a load out tomorrow."

"Good to see you, too, Reeder," John shot back, "but let's not get sentimental. Do I have time to put my stuff up?"

"Sure, sure. Just as soon as we get things loaded for

tomorrow." Reeder slid off his perch at the bar, grabbed his coat and headed toward the door. "See you at the strip in five minutes."

"Have fun boys," Doorway called to John and Harley as they followed Reeder out the door, "don't stay out too late." His laughter was cut off as the door closed behind them.

"Told you," Harley said to John as they climbed into the Suburban. Reeder's truck was already disappearing down the highway.

"Damn. What's the big hurry?"

"It's the start of the season for Reeder, too. He flies supplies for more than just us. He's undoubtedly got other flights besides us tomorrow. Everyone is getting ready for the summer. Fish camps, lodges, other mines, everyone who has a seasonal operation is getting set up. The season is too short to waste any time."

At the strip, Harley parked the Suburban next to a larger plane than the one Reeder had piloted on John's first trip to Last Chance.

"We use the Beaver to haul large loads," Harley explained, "it is the quintessential bush plane: lots of capacity, and short take-offs. Noisy as hell, but reliable. We're going to be hauling propane cylinders out tomorrow."

Harley headed immediately to the aircraft, followed by John, and looked inside. Reeder was already inside the Beaver, checking the tie-downs for racks on the floor of the plane. Following Reeder's directions, the two younger men went to a shed at the edge of the strip and retrieved a large cylinder strapped to a dolly. John immediately wished he was wearing something more suitable for work than slacks and an oxford shirt.

"Don't worry," Harley said as if he'd read John's mind, "you won't get dirty, just sweaty." He tossed a heavy pair of leather gloves to John. "Wear those to protect your hands. These cylinders weigh about 170 pounds apiece, and you don't want any pinched fingers. I'll lift from inside the door of the plane, and you lift from the ground."

It was a simple process to load the cylinders, but time-consuming. Each cylinder was wheeled to the side of the plane with the dolly, where Harley and John would grunt the cylinder into the aircraft. Harley and Reeder then moved the cylinder into position, and Reeder would meticulously secure it in place as another cylinder was retrieved from the shed. John was surprised at how late it was when the sixth, and final, cylinder was secured. Most of the time had been spent waiting for Reeder to get the cylinders secured to his satisfaction.

"It'd be a bad day for all parties concerned if one of these cylinders broke loose and started bouncing around," Reeder growled when Harley complained about how long he took.

With that image in mind, John was grateful for the old pilot's extra caution.

"What time tomorrow?" John asked when Reeder finished closing up the Beaver.

"Be here at seven. I'll drop you boys off, then come back later. I'm running some supplies out to Port Alsworth after your load, and will pick you up on the way home. We'll load the other six cylinders when we get back, and take them out the next day."

"Long day tomorrow," Harley observed.

"More for you than for me," Reeder said with a chuckle as he walked toward the flight shack.

On the way back to the Shuffle Inn Harley explained why their day would be longer than Reeder's. Once they arrived at Last Chance, he and John would have to move the cylinders up from the lake to the storage points at the lodge. They would use snowmachines and sleds to move them around, but would have to physically wrestle them into their storage points.

"It's going to be hard work, with lots of it done using your favorite mode of transportation, snowshoes." He laughed when John groaned.

Doorway told John keeping his room wasn't a problem, as long as he was cleared out at the end of the month, when John left for Last Chance. The room would be needed for travelers and tourists by late May.

Over dinner, Harley told John what to pack for the next day's adventure. In the week before going down to LA, Harley had taken John shopping to get an adequate Alaskan wardrobe. Along with the clothing, Harley had insisted John get a backpack, which he said would serve as John's suitcase when traveling to and from Last Chance. The list of everything Harley instructed John to pack was a long one.

"Seems a bit excessive, doesn't it?" John asked, reviewing the list.

"There's always a chance we could be staying for more than just the afternoon. If the weather turns nasty, or Reeder gets delayed, we may be staying at Last Chance overnight, or even a couple of days. It's happened before."

"But two sets of clothes?"

"By the time you get done humping those cylinders around, you're going to be soaked in sweat, and will want to change. Trust me, there's nothing worse than sitting around and soaking in your own sweat when it's cold. And if something happened, and we ended up staying, you'd definitely want a change."

"Yeah, but Reeder said he'd be back in the afternoon to pick us up."

Harley waved him off and replied in a serious tone, "You need to adjust your thinking. When you leave the road system, you have to start thinking in terms of days ahead, just in case. If Reeder couldn't get to us, because of a sudden change in weather, for instance, nobody else could, either. He might not admit it, but even Reeder can't control the weather. West of roads, you're on your own. Expect the best, but prepare for the worst."

Harley's words made John's stomach flip. He had never been anywhere help wasn't just moments away. He found the prospect of being truly isolated both exciting and frightening at the same time.

After agreeing to meet for breakfast at six, the two men said good-night, and John went up to his room to pack. Maybe Harley was just being melodramatic with his lecture, but John hadn't seen anything yet to indicate that was in the man's nature. He decided to follow Harley's list to the letter.

CHAPTER 10

The alarm wasn't due to go off for another half hour when John awoke. He lay in bed for a few moments thinking about what the day might bring. The knot of anticipation he felt in his stomach made the decision to get up easy. He decided to put the extra time to good use by going through his backpack one more time to be absolutely certain he'd packed everything on the list Harley had given him. In an odd way, he almost wished they would have to spend the night out at Last Chance. He found the possibility, no matter how remote in reality, exciting. It would be a chance to face a challenge; a true adventure. He laughed at himself for letting his own melodramatic fantasy run away on him.

A few minutes before six, John stopped at the Suburban to toss his backpack into it. Another backpack, much more weathered and worn than his, was already on the back seat. Obviously, Harley was ahead of him. John patted Dawg on the head as he stepped into the bar. The four people sitting at a table near the door were staring at the bar, where Doorway and Harley were arguing loudly. The big man had a firm grip on Harley's left arm.

"I said *sit down!*" Doorway pressed down on Harley's arm, effectively pinning it to the bar top, forcing him back onto his stool. "She said she doesn't want to talk to you. She doesn't want to see you! Let it be."

"Let go, Doorway," Harley squirmed under the big man's solid grip, but couldn't shake it. "I need to see her."

John hurried over to the bar and put his hand on Harley's other shoulder. Harley reacted immediately, swinging his right arm up to knock John's hand off and then drew back his fist ready to strike. John stepped back quickly and held his own hands up. As soon as he recognized John, Harley relaxed a little and lowered his fist to the counter. He turned back to Doorway. "Goddamn it, Doorway! *Let go!*"

"No fucking way, Pepperdine," Doorway hissed back, leaning even more forcefully on Harley's arm, "not until you settle down and stay put. She'll be okay. They had a fight is all."

"It's not okay. The sorry bastard hit her." Harley turned toward the table behind him as best he could under Doorway's grip and shouted over his shoulder, "You hear that, Sherman? Tell your buddy Kells I'm going to find him and turn his sorry ass inside out!"

John didn't know which of the men was Sherman, but all four of the men suddenly decided breakfast somewhere else sounded better and left quickly.

"I mean it," Doorway continued, "settle down. Maggie said she doesn't want to talk to you, so let her alone."

"Okay. I'm fine. Let go."

"Not until you promise to cool off." Doorway's grip hadn't loosened a bit.

"I promise! Jesus Christ, Doorway! You're cutting off the circulation to my hand! I'll just sit here, I promise."

"Good. And stop scaring off my customers, you're killing me." Doorway slowly let go of Harley's arm. "I'm going to go get you boys some breakfast. John, keep an eye on him."

Doorway stepped into the kitchen, and John sat on the stool next to Harley.

"Just what the hell was that all about?"

"That worthless piece of shit beat Maggie up."

"Who? That Kells fella?"

"Yeah." Harley rubbed his arm where Doorway had been squeezing it.

"What happened? What set him off?"

"Does it matter?"

166

John wasn't sure how to proceed from that point. He didn't know Maggie nearly as well as he'd like to, and had never felt comfortable enough to ask Harley about the history between her and him.

"Let's eat breakfast and get over to the strip."

Harley shot John a disgusted glance. "I'm not hungry."

"Not now, but you will be in awhile."

The kitchen door opened up and Doorway walked through carrying a bag. "I slapped some eggs and bacon between pieces of toast for each of you. Why don't you guys eat them at the strip? I don't need any more trouble."

Harley slid off his stool without a word and started for the door. John took the bag from Doorway and thanked him before quickly following Harley. At the Suburban Harley told John to eat on the way over to the strip as he climbed into the driver's seat. It was the only conversation that passed between them, and John was glad to concentrate on his sandwich, rather than risk getting Harley fired up again. When they pulled up to the flight shack at the strip, Reeder opened the door.

"You boys are early. I haven't even started the Beaver to warm it up."

"We just grabbed something to eat and headed over," John said.

Harley didn't reply, or even acknowledge Reeder. He slipped past the pilot and flopped down on a chair on the wall opposite the door. Reeder's face expressed how he felt about being ignored.

"What's your problem?"

"There needs to be one less asshole in the world."

Reeder turned to John. "You two having words?"

"No. There's been some sort of incident involving Maggie and her boyfriend."

"I wouldn't call Kells smacking her around just an incident," Harley said flatly.

Reeder let out a sigh. "How bad?"

"I don't know," John said, "I didn't see her."

"That's right, you didn't see her," Harley interrupted. "The whole right side of her face is bruised!" He stood up suddenly, "I ought to go find that son of a bitch and kick his ass."

Reeder stepped in front of the door to block it. "No, you need to stay out of it. It's Maggie's call. You just need to tend to the business at hand. I need to go warm up the Beaver. There's coffee in the pot to go with your breakfast."

"You need any help?" John asked. He hoped to escape the confines of the flight shack.

"No, it's just a matter of starting the engine and making sure there's adequate oil circulation. It's a radial engine thing. I need about fifteen minutes before we can take off. Stay here and keep Mary Sunshine company."

When Reeder stepped out the door John threw the bag containing Harley's sandwich to him. Harley sat back in the chair, pulled out his breakfast and nibbled at it. John watched from the window as Reeder walked around the plane, making his pre-flight check. Apparently satisfied, the pilot climbed into the cockpit and busied himself with the control panel. After a few minutes the plane's engine coughed, then caught, issuing a cloud of smoke from the exhaust. The throaty rumble of the radial engine replaced the silence of the flight shack.

John glanced at his watch and became painfully aware at least another ten minutes would pass before they would climb into the plane. His curiosity got the better of him, and he decided to broach the subject of Maggie.

"So, what's the deal between you and Maggie?"

The question interrupted Harley's brooding stare into space. "What do you mean?"

"Well, with the way you're acting, there's obviously something between the two of you. I've seen you try and talk to her, and she doesn't want anything to do with you."

"We've got a long history, and it's complicated. I don't want to talk about it."

"Your call."

"Yes, it is." Harley stood up and pitched the major portion of his sandwich into a trash basket. "I'm going to grab the bags and load up."

John watched Harley stow the bags behind a cargo net in the tail of the aircraft. Reeder turned around, saw who it was, and signaled for Harley to take the co-pilot seat. Harley shook his head, and Reeder responded by emphatically pointing to the co-pilot seat. Harley complied and put on the headphones the pilot handed him. A few minutes later, Reeder waved to John, indicating he needed to get on board. John latched the door and buckled into the only passenger seat that hadn't been removed to make room for the propane cylinders. He put on the earmuffs hanging next to the seat. Unlike the headphones for the co-pilot's seat they weren't wired for communication.

Reeder taxied to the far end of the strip, spun the plane around and increased throttle. John was surprised at how quickly the plane was airborne, given the load it was carrying. He looked out the window, marveling again at how many buildings were tucked away in the surrounding trees until the plane was out over the water. There wasn't much to look at once over the Cook Inlet, so he turned his attention toward the front of the plane. Judging from Harley's animated gestures there was a heated discussion going on, and John realized why Reeder had insisted on Harley sitting up front. He hoped the old pilot could talk some sense into Harley, but knew a man in love was rarely sensible.

Reeder set the Beaver down without circling the claim. Unlike the last time he had landed on the lake, this landing didn't feel like floating in on a cushion to John. Once they touched down it felt bumpy. The snow was flat and wind-blown, and the surface showed depressions in places.

"The overflow is getting bad," Reeder commented after shutting down the engine, "if it stays this warm, I may be dropping you off in the valley."

"Overflow? Valley?" John asked.

"Overflow is water on top of the ice, under the snow," Reeder explained. "It's forced up through cracks in the ice by the weight of the snow during the winter, and as melting occurs it collects on the surface this time of year. The ice is perfectly safe, but the water turns the snow to slush. If it gets too bad, I'll use a flat in the valley, up Gold Creek."

"That's a pain in the ass," Harley added, "because it's about a mile from here, and we have to sled everything in."

"You mean to tell me we would have to drag the cylinders a *mile*?"

"We don't actually pull the sleds. That's what snow

machines are for."

John's relief was visible, and the other two men shared a laugh at his expense before the work began. Just walking on snowshoes had been a challenge for John on the previous trip. Unloading the propane cylinders while burdened with them proved to be a monumental task. John suspected Harley was slacking off in the effort for the sheer entertainment value it provided in watching him stumble around. Reeder grew impatient, and switched from urging them to hurry the process, to barking orders. Once the cylinders were unloaded, Reeder quickly left the two younger men standing on the edge of the lake.

"What now?" John asked.

"A lot of sweat. I came out while you were gone and got things ready. The machines and sleds are at the lodge. I also rode around to make some trails."

At the lodge, Harley had John put on a lighter jacket to prevent overheating and soaking his clothes while they worked. Since John had never ridden a snowmachine, Harley gave him a brief lecture on starting and riding. Staying on the trails was a point he kept emphasizing.

"Follow me. If you get off the trail, you could bog down, and then we'd have to dig you out. It's a lot of work, and a waste of time."

Each man's snowmachine had a sled hitched to it, and each man would pull three cylinders up from the lake, Harley explained. Harley walked John through starting his machine, then started his own and quickly sped down the trail to the lake. John followed at a much slower rate of speed.

"My grandma was slow," Harley said when John pulled up next to him, "but she was old and gray."

"Give me a break, arctic boy."

"It's not just a matter of going fast, these are two-cycle engines. If you run them at low rpm's all the time, it will foul the plugs. I want you to run around on the lake a few minutes. Practice throttle control and turning like we talked about."

On the flat of the lake, riding the snowmachine was fun. John practiced the techniques Harley had explained and felt much more comfortable on the machine after a few minutes. He was just starting to really enjoy playing when Harley waved him in.

By the time all six cylinders were loaded up and secured to the sleds, both men were sweating and in need of a rest.

"You seem to be doing better than you were when we left this morning," John said as he sat on his machine to pull off his snowshoes.

"Yeah, over here, troubles don't seem so big."

"So, you want to talk about it?"

"No, I don't, touchy-feely boy," Harley replied. "And I don't need you on my ass about it along with Doorway and Reeder."

"I just don't want you to do anything stupid. If for no other reason than I need you."

"From what Reeder told me on the way out, I won't need to. Sounds like Kells may be tying a noose in his own rope. Apparently, he's become quite the little pharmaceutical entrepreneur. Only a matter of time before he's busted. My brother, who's a cop in Kenai, sort of alluded to that a few weeks ago."

"Sounds like your gal, Maggie, really knows how to pick 'em."

"First off, she's not my gal. Second, you don't know the whole story, so stay out of it."

Harley's sharp tone told John it was time to drop the conversation, and perhaps best not to bring it up again. Following a stretch of silence, Harley told John to follow him up to the lodge.

They set the first two cylinders in a covered area along the lodge where John estimated the kitchen was located. The next two were dropped off at the far end of the lodge, in a similar protective covering. At both locations, Harley connected the cylinders to a common header. The final two cylinders were split between two incinerator toilets behind the guest cabins.

"We won't hook these up until the snow melts away," Harley explained.

"What's the deal with incinerator toilets, anyway?"

"They're more pleasant for the guests, since there's no outhouse odor. They also don't require a septic system. They actually work quite well. By the way, staff uses the real outhouse by the lodge."

"Lucky us."

After setting the last cylinder the two men went to the lodge. As John pulled the plywood from the front windows to let in the light, Harley started a fire in the smaller of the two woodstoves. The heat thrown off the stove wasn't enough to warm the room, but it felt warm sitting next to it.

"This is lunch," Harley said, producing two foil wrapped packages from his backpack and setting them on the top of the woodstove. "Give those a few minutes on each side, and we'll have toasted ham and cheese sandwiches. And for the perfect compliment, I have a thermos of tomato soup."

"Well, I guess that settles that."

"Settles what?"

"Who's doing the cooking this summer."

"No way," Harley laughed, "we're hiring a real cook."

"Doorway says we need to get someone lined up right away."

"Only if you want somebody worth a damn, not a drunk, or somebody who can't cook any better than you and me. Call Cynthia and have her put the word out, and get an ad in the paper."

John considered suggesting Harley go see Cynthia himself, just to give him a ribbing, but decided female relationships were a topic best avoided at the moment. Instead, he asked what needed to be done before Reeder picked them up. Harley ran down a list of things that could be done, but suggested they go out to the workshop and check out the equipment. John liked the idea, seeing it as a good opportunity for some basic education on the equipment he was supposed to be an expert in operating.

The workshop was much bigger than John had expected. The building was easily the biggest of those remaining from the original mining operation by at least twice, and was filled with equipment. In addition to the sluices and header boxes for the highbankers, were hoses coiled and hung from the walls, ATV's and even a towable backhoe.

"Hardrock told me this was originally the blacksmith shop," Harley said, "which was a critical operation at any hydraulic operation. Way in the back is an old forge and anvil, and a bunch of other junk."

"They used that many horses?"

"The blacksmith wasn't for horses, he fabricated and maintained pipe, mostly. All the hydraulic pipe they used came as flat iron sheets, and the smith rounded and riveted them into the pipe. There wasn't any such thing as seamless pipe, like today. When the snow melts you'll see all the pipe laying around, and just how busy the smith was."

"There's a helluva lot of stuff in here," John observed, "but it looks organized."

"Yeah, Hardrock was kind of a neat-freak. He expected things to be right where they were supposed to be. If they weren't, he wasn't afraid to let me know about it. And let me tell you, your uncle knew how to make a point when he was pissed. When he ran out of the conventional profanity, he made up new." Harley laughed when he added, "I think 'turgid turd' was my favorite."

John was still laughing as Harley began walking through the shop, pointing out the various gold recovery equipment, explaining how it was used.

"This is a highbanker," Harley said. "This is what the clients use to initially process the dirt."

Harley stood next to a stand holding an aluminum trough at a slight angle. The trough had a black plastic box mounted on the high end. John stepped closer for a better look. The trough had what looked to be a metal ladder laid over a matting material on the bottom. The box was wider than the trough and was angled in the opposite direction. The bottom half of the sides on the box were angled inward to match the width of the trough. Harley stood at the box end.

"Highbankers make it possible to sluice material at locations away from flowing water," Harley explained. "A pump draws water from a source, sends it up the hose to the header box, where it is funneled into the top of the sluice." Harley ran his hand along plastic pipe fastened to the top edges of the header box. "The water is fed into the header through this spray pipe. The pressure of the water helps to break up the dirt fed into the header box before it washes into the sluice."

John looked into the header and saw the side of the box was open to the high end of the sluice. A series of bars were suspended above the bottom of the box. The bars extended lengthwise beyond the end of the sluice. They were obviously designed to allow water and smaller material to wash into the sluice, while blocking larger rocks and providing an exit for them out of the header.

"Once the dirt has been broken up by the water spray," Harley continued, "it flows into the top of the sluice. The heavier stuff, like black sand and gold, settles behind the riffles. Fine gold gets trapped in the mat."

"Seems pretty simple," John observed.

"In theory, it is. The real trick to optimizing a highbanker's operation is to get it level horizontally, then adjust the incline of the sluice to match the amount of water pumped into it. The incline is set by adjusting the legs on the stand. Getting the right combination of sluice drop and water flow takes some experience, along with some trial and error."

The time passed quickly as Harley coached John through setting up a highbanker and adjusting the drop. After John's crash course in recreational mining, Harley took stock of what yet needed to be done in the way of maintenance. When the distinctive sound of the Beaver's engine sounded overhead, John checked his watch and saw almost four hours had elapsed in the shop.

Reeder was waiting in the Beaver when the two men walked down from the lodge, where they had left the snowmachines. He was impatient, as always, to get underway. Arriving back at the air strip the three men repeated the loading process on the last six propane cylinders. It would be another early flight out the next morning, Reeder told them. Remaining in the Shuffle Inn had been a good decision. All John wanted was something to eat, followed by a hot shower and bed.

The next morning John hurt in places he didn't even know existed. Over the next several days, however, he became more accustomed to the physical labor involved in preparing the mine for the upcoming season. Even snowshoeing, which he never thought he'd enjoy, didn't bother him anymore. Every day held something to accomplish, and John hadn't known such satisfaction in years, if ever.

All the dry goods and supplies were shuttled over and stored by the middle of April. The guest cabins had been dug out and inspected. All propane systems had been purged, and all the appliances were set up for use. Several nights had been spent out at the lodge in order not to interrupt the progress. On those nights the idea he almost passed on Last Chance seemed totally ludicrous to John. His only regret was that he hadn't done it years earlier, when he could have shared the experience with his uncle.

Harley's court appearance for his arrest in March was set for April twenty-first, a Monday. John decided to take advantage of Harley's need to be in Kenai and check in with Cynthia. He hoped there had been an unexpected increase in bookings. He also wanted to look at the books a little closer. He had not talked to Cynthia since asking her to find a camp cook. Since he hadn't heard back from her, it meant there had either been no interest in the position, or no qualified applicants. She had agreed to keep the entire day of the twenty-first open for him.

With the routine of early flights out to Last Chance, John and Harley had developed the habit of meeting at the bar for breakfast every morning. The twenty-first was no different, except Harley was dressed in a shirt, tie and slacks.

"Ain't he pretty?" Doorway called out, pointing at Harley, when John stepped through the door.

"Wow," John said in mock admiration, "somebody's been on a shopping spree at Armani's."

"Like hell! I stole this getup off a missionary that stopped by last night. Don't sit too close, you might get me dirty."

"I'll try not to splatter any of Maggie's oatmeal in your direction."

Doorway set a mug of coffee down in front of John, then stuck his head through the door to the kitchen to let Maggie know about the oatmeal. He barely had time to get back to the bar when Maggie came out of the kitchen carrying John's bowl. The bruise on the right side of her face from the blow Kells had dealt her was gone. John looked at her and found himself wondering why such an attractive woman would pick such an obvious loser for a boyfriend. It was obvious to him why Harley was so persistent in pursuing her.

"Ah, you are an angel, Maggie!" John said. "So what do you think of the winner of the North Road fashion show?"

Maggie looked Harley up and down with a critical eye for a moment, and then looked at John. "You can dress a pig in a pink tutu, and it's still a pig."

Gales of laughter from Doorway and John followed her back into the kitchen. Harley blew a kiss at the door as it closed.

"Your court time isn't until one, right?" John asked.

"Yeah, but I need to meet with my lawyer at noon. I don't know what there is to talk about, since I'm pleading guilty. I guess she wants to coach me in how to appear appropriately contrite."

"Well, I'm going to Cynthia's at eight, and that leaves you time to go with me."

"What for?"

"Primarily because," John said with a wink, "it should be very entertaining."

Harley skipped over John's last remark and asked again, "Why do you need me?"

"I need an extra set of eyes, and your memory. I didn't do much besides look at the final figures and the recurring charges last time. If bookings are down, we may need to look at ways to trim costs, and you know the actual business better than me."

Harley thought about it for a moment before replying. "I'll go, but have to get out of there by eleven. Besides, looking at the bookings will give me an idea when to do my community service, if I don't get off completely."

John's eyebrows shot up. "Community service? How long? When?"

"I might get community service as a sentence. My lawyer couldn't say how long, but she did say I would probably be offered a chance to choose the time frame."

"I thought you'd just get a fine. But being gone from the claim, that's another matter."

"It may not happen, but we ought to be prepared, just in case."

John hadn't considered the prospect of being at the mine alone for any length of time. The idea he might be left with clients, particularly experienced ones, was more than just intimidating. He ate in silence, thinking about the possibility. When he was finished he signaled to Harley, who was still carefully picking his way around his own breakfast, that he was leaving. Harley said he'd follow in a few minutes.

On the way to Cynthia's John marveled at the change in the snow levels that had taken place in just three weeks. Even though there had been a couple of light snowfalls, the sides of the highway were clear to the ground. Brown grass was visible stretching out two feet on either side of the pavement. Remnants of the berms along the road were now ragged, and looked dirty and worn. The road off the highway, which had been covered with rutted ice on his first trip out, now had stretches of slimy mud for a surface. It was no wonder every vehicle John saw was encased in a brown crust.

Cynthia was standing on the steps to her office, smoking a cigarette and enjoying the bright sunshine, when John pulled up. She looked decidedly disappointed when she saw he was alone.

"You're early. Where's Harley?"

"He'll be along shortly," John replied, and the pretty blonde's face lit up.

"That's good. While we're waiting, I'll show you what I've done to the web site."

John followed Cynthia inside, thinking to himself that Harley might be missing a good thing by pining away for Maggie instead of being more receptive to the attractive bookkeeper. After hanging up his coat, he walked into the office and stood at her desk as she quickly pulled up the cabins page.

"Hardrock got me some different pictures of the cabin interiors, something with a little higher resolution so the details would show better."

Harley stepped through the door to the office just as John was about to comment on the new pictures. Cynthia immediately sprang from her chair.

"Harley! Don't *you* look nice," Cynthia cooed as she walked up to him.

Before he could defend himself, Cynthia gently grabbed Harley's tie and straightened it, then smoothed the fabric on his shoulders, sliding her fingers down his upper arms more slowly than necessary. Harley's face reddened appreciably. He quickly side-stepped around Cynthia and walked toward John.

"Have you seen anything interesting?" Harley asked.

"Just in the past few seconds."

"In the books, John."

"We were looking at the changes to the web site," Cynthia said as she stepped up beside Harley, who crossed his arms over his chest when he felt Cynthia's hand reach for his. "I was telling John about the new pictures. You want to see?"

"I don't have time right now. I have to leave at nine."

"I thought you said eleven," John said. Harley's discomfort was palpable, and John suspected an early exit strategy.

"Originally, but my lawyer, Lucy, called and..."

"Lucy Dittweiller?" Cynthia interrupted. "What does that slut want?"

"It's Lucy Holmes, now," Harley corrected, "and she wants me early."

"I'll bet she wants you early. And often," Cynthia sniped, obviously jealous of the lawyer.

"Coffee!" John said suddenly. "God, I would love a cup of coffee, wouldn't you Harley? Cynthia, do you have any coffee? You'd be a real lifesaver."

The bookkeeper, taken by surprise at the sudden request, stammered she could step into her kitchen and make a pot. She turned and disappeared through the door separating the office and attached trailer, closing the door quietly.

"Okay, you've had your fun," Harley growled at his boss, "but I mean it, I'm out of here at nine."

John laughed softly. "Did your lawyer really call?"

"Yes. End of discussion. We need to look at the bookings first."

While Cynthia was out of the office, John and Harley looked over the new cabin pictures. Harley offered the opinion the newer images were definitely better. When Cynthia came back into the office with the coffee, John asked to look at the bookings first.

The first clients of the season arrived on Memorial Day weekend. Harley recognized the name. They were repeat clients from Anchorage.

"Nice folks, the Johnsons," he commented, "parents with two, very active, twin boys. I think this will be their fourth year out. They're low-maintenance types, and know their way around." He looked at John, "Watch them, and you'll pick up some tricks I may forget to teach you."

"I called them after Hardrock died, by the way," Cynthia said, "just to let them know."

"Good idea. The boys just loved Hardrock. It could have put a damper on their visit if they hadn't known."

With the exception of the third week, when a group of four was scheduled to come in, June's bookings were all two people per week. The number of clients for June was about normal, Cynthia explained, July and August were the bread and butter months.

Harley's eyes lit up when he looked at the last booking in June. "Sam and Polly Burlington are coming out on the twenty-eighth. That would be a perfect time for me to be away."

"Sam and Polly Burlington?" John asked, "I take it they are repeats."

"Even better than that," Harley said with a smile, "they're old. They come out mostly to sit and visit. They're long time friends of Hardrock's." Harley's expression changed to one of concern, and he quickly looked to Cynthia, "They are still coming?"

"Definitely. They called right after they heard Hardrock had died, wanting to know if Last Chance was going to operate this summer. I told them yes, since Wes had told me not to turn down any bookings, and they confirmed."

"Perfect! Since they knew Hardrock, we won't need to bullshit them about John's experience. If I have to do community service, that's the week for it."

"And if someone else books for that week?"

"Not likely," Cynthia said, "Fourth of July week is always slow. I don't know why. That's probably the reason Burlingtons are coming out. By the way, Hardrock never charged them in the past, they came as his personal guests."

"Actually, this is a good deal for you, John," Harley said. "Sam has forgotten more about finding gold than I'll ever know. Hell, you ought to pay him for lessons."

John raised an eyebrow at Harley. "Let's not get carried away."

The number of bookings increased with the first full week in July. There were four clients in the camp most weeks through the first week of September, and three of those weeks showed six clients. September showed no bookings at all after the first week. Cynthia pulled up records from previous years, so John could easily compare the number of bookings. In previous seasons there were never fewer than six clients in the camp, usually eight, through the third week in August. Septembers past had consistently hosted at least two clients per week. Cynthia pulled up spreadsheets with the projected revenue from the confirmed bookings and the previous year's costs. The bottom line was sobering.

"If we don't get more clients," John said, "or everyone wants to work for free, I don't see any way we'll show a profit this year."

"There's always people who might book during the season," Cynthia said hopefully. "Maybe we could attract more from that market."

"How so?"

"We've never advertised during the season. We've always counted on pre-season bookings. Lots of people come up here and are disappointed to discover how crowded the Kenai is at the height of tourist season. We could run a local advertising campaign offering a chance to see the Alaska they envisioned."

"Yeah, that could work," Harley chimed in, "particularly if the salmon runs are weak. We could even offer shorter stays to make it more attractive, say three-day packages in the middle of the week. That way, people could fit a visit in, even if their time was limited."

"What about Reeder," John asked, "would he be willing to adjust his schedule for the extra trips?"

"I don't see why not. It's more business for him."

Cynthia laid out ideas for local advertising, using her contacts in the area. She quickly estimated a cost for the impromptu advertising campaign, based on what their current brochures had run, and her understanding of the local advertising rates in other media. John was impressed with both how connected the young bookkeeper-cum-webmaster was in the area's business community, and her marketing acumen. Before getting too involved, however, John asked her to let him clear the transportation with Reeder. Cynthia said she would work up some examples of what she wanted to use to advertise the shorter bookings, and call John when she had something to show him. All agreed it was a good plan, and offered a ray of hope.

Harley let out a gasp when he noticed it was nine-thirty. He quickly jumped up, deflected Cynthia's offer of a good-bye hug, and bolted from the office. Cynthia remained standing at her desk and stared at the door Harley had just slammed. She looked deflated.

"If you don't mind me asking," John said, "what is there between you two?"

"Not a damn thing, unfortunately," came the soft reply.

"Ever been anything?"

"Nothing that hasn't been entirely one-sided." The pretty blonde looked at John, her eyes looked tired and much older than they should have. "I've been in love with Harley Pepperdine since I was seven and he was thirteen. He babysat Derrick and me to earn pocket money."

"He was your *babysitter*?"

"Yeah, until he got old enough to pull set nets and earn some real money. Truth is, most of the stupid stunts I did in high school were to impress Harley. I got knocked up trying to make him jealous."

John felt embarrassed. "I'm sorry, I didn't mean to pry."

"No biggie," Cynthia shrugged and smiled, "it's common knowledge."

"You ever think about maybe trying on someone else?"

Cynthia cocked her head to one side, put a hand on her hip, and flashed a coy smile. "Mr. Barstow! Is that an inappropriate offer?"

John put his hands up quickly. "Absolutely not!"

"Yeah, I know," Cynthia winked at him, "damaged goods with a kid."

"Not at all," John said firmly, desperate to extricate himself from the conversation. "I'm the master of bad relationships. I want a break from any relationships. Good, or bad."

An awkward silence settled in as they each stared at the other for a moment, until Cynthia sat down in front of the computer. "Let me pull up the ledgers, and we'll get started."

They went over numbers and entries until John's head ached. Cynthia could explain almost all of the entries. The exceptions were significant credits to the account made in the last two months of each year.

"Where are these deposits coming from?" John asked.

"Hardrock made them."

"Are they deposits for reservations?"

"No, I make all of those. I don't know where Hardrock's deposits came from, he would just give me the deposit receipt and I would enter them into the books."

"They couldn't be tips," John thought aloud, "much too large and too far after the season."

"Besides," Cynthia replied, "Hardrock had Harley keep any gratuities."

"Another thing bothering me," John said, pointing to the line of deposits and then a large debit, "is that every year, a large debit brings the ledger value to exactly one-hundred thousand dollars just before January. What the hell is that debit?"

"That's what Hardrock called his 'bribery money.' He split it between Harley, Reeder and me. It was really a bonus, but your uncle used to say it was the only way he could keep us around. By the way, don't believe it."

John smiled. "I'd also imagine there were tax advantages to that."

"I suppose so, but I don't do taxes. Wes has somebody in Anchorage do the taxes for Last Chance Adventures."

The numbers showed the business had been run with fiscal efficiency, and there was no room for significant reductions in the operating costs. Unless John could figure out the source of the mystery deposits, or the new advertising campaign paid off more spectacularly than seemed possible, it was a certainty the business would not show a profit in a year. Perhaps Harley had an explanation for the deposits. It didn't really matter, John was committed to moving forward and making the best of the situation, no matter how it turned out.

"How are we doing on getting a cook?" John asked.

"Not good. I've had a number of people contact me in response to the ad, but none have panned out. The only one that had any promise couldn't commit to working remote. She has a young family."

"Why did she even apply?"

"She was hoping I might be able to give her a lead on a job at a local lodge."

"And?"

"I kept her number and told her I'd call if I heard of anything."

"Maybe you ought to add 'head-hunter' to your business cards," John said with a chuckle. "None of the rest had any potential?"

"All the others were either totally inexperienced, wanted more money than we're offering, or looked like someone I wouldn't want touching my food."

John laughed again. "Yeah, it wouldn't do to give the clients food poisoning. And we can't offer more money, it simply isn't there."

"Lots of seasonal workers don't come up until May, so we've still got a chance of finding someone. I'll keep the ad going. But just in case," she added with a wink, "you and Harley ought to brush up on your kitchen skills."

John called Reeder before leaving to ask about meeting with him. Reeder seemed anxious to talk to John, and asked him to come by as soon as possible. As both Harley and Cynthia had predicted, Reeder welcomed the opportunity for more business. John explained all the details of the shorter visits weren't worked out yet, but would be before the season began.

"That's something else we need to talk about," Reeder said, "the beginning of the season. It's going to start earlier for you than planned."

"How so?"

"I know you weren't planning on going out to stay until the end of next week, but I don't think we can wait that long. I flew over Last Chance today, coming back from Port Alsworth. The ice on the lake is covered with water, and the snow in the valley is fading fast. By the end of this week, I may not be able to put down either place."

Harley had mentioned the possibility of an early departure because of the unusually pleasant weather. John mentally went through the preparation checklist Harley had given him to see if there was anything major left yet to do.

"How soon are you thinking we need to fly out?"

"First thing tomorrow morning would be best. Absolutely no later than the next morning. Once the melt starts, the difference between one day and the next can mean the difference between having a place to land, and not."

John had been around Reeder enough to know he wasn't prone to hyperbole. If the old pilot said time was essential, it was gospel. "Okay. What time tomorrow?"

"We need to go early in the morning, before the snow softens up too much. Sunrise is at six-thirty, so be here at six, ready to load up."

The knot in John's stomach grew as he drove back to the Shuffle Inn. He had known this moment would arrive, he just hadn't expected it to drop into his lap so suddenly. Being dropped off in the middle of nowhere, with no readily available means of getting out, seemed more frightening than exciting now that it was a reality. John parked next to Harley's battered pickup and walked directly inside. Harley was sitting at the bar, drinking a beer, chatting with Doorway.

"We need to talk," John said quickly as he sat next to Harley, "we need to leave. Now."

Harley finished a sip of beer and turned toward John. "We need to leave and have a talk?"

"No, we need to talk about leaving."

Harley looked at his boss carefully. He looked distraught. "Doorway, don't give this man anything caffeinated, he's wound tight enough already. Calm down, John."

John took a deep breath to steady himself. "I just came from Reeder's. He says we need to leave first thing tomorrow morning."

"Okay."

"We weren't, I mean we aren't, ready that is. Are we?"

Harley looked up thoughtfully, then gasped, "Oh, sweet Jesus! No, we're not!"

"Damn! I knew it! I just knew it!" John slapped the bar.

Harley pulled out his cell phone and punched in a number. "Hey, Billy, it's Harley. Can you get the perishables we talked about for the first trip ready? Cool. We'll pick them up in about half an hour. Thanks." Harley folded his cell phone up, dropped it back into his pocket with a little flourish, and smiled at John. "Now, we're ready. By the way, Reeder came by earlier and told Doorway he was hoping to take us out tomorrow."

Harley winked at Doorway, and the big man laughed loudly. John hung his head. His ears burned with embarrassment at his overreaction. Harley slapped him on the shoulder.

"Hell yes we're ready, John. What do you think we've been doing for the last month? Doorway, can we keep the groceries here overnight, and pick them up on the way to the airstrip tomorrow?"

"Works for me," Doorway said while shoving a mug of coffee under John's nose. "Here you go. It's decaf."

John picked the mug up and looked over the rim at the two widely grinning faces. "Oh, fuck you both."

When he was done laughing, Harley told John about his court appearance. In spite of his lawyer's excellent argument for leniency, the judge decided on a sentence of community service. However, since Harley had already spent five days in pre-trial confinement, the judge reduced the amount of time to sixty hours.

"Sixty hours," John gasped, "that's a week and a half of work!"

"Only if I work eight hours a day," Harley replied, "I can do it in five twelve-hour days."

"Will they let you do that?"

"Sure. I'll be working for the city maintenance department, and I know the supervisor. They'll be getting ready for the Fourth of July festivities, and more than happy to give me extra hours. I'll leave June twenty-eighth and be back on July fifth."

The knot in John's stomach had completely disappeared by the time he and Harley picked up the groceries from McCrane Mercantile and stored them in Doorway's kitchen. Afterward, the two men split up for the evening, agreeing to meet at five-thirty the next morning. Harley stayed at the bar, and John went to the Tuscan Villa. After dinner, John spent the remainder of the evening moving what little he was leaving behind into the trailer. When he left for Last Chance in the morning, his room would be empty and ready for Doorway to rent out. When he came back, his home would be the trailer.

CHAPTER 11

Reeder shouted over the intercom the landing would be ugly. Jagged rocks reached up from the snow, ready to snag the plane out of the air. Alarms were ringing just before they crashed. John opened his eyes to the darkness of his room at the Shuffle Inn and realized he was safe, but the ringing continued. He looked at the clock next to his bed. The illuminated display showed a few minutes past three. The phone rang again, and John picked it up.

"John, it's Doorway."

"Kind of early for a wake-up, isn't it?"

"Listen, we've got a problem here."

"Please don't tell me Harley got drunk and in trouble," John moaned.

"No, that's not it. I need you at the bar right now. Don't call Harley."

"This better not be a gag, Doorway."

"It's not," Doorway said seriously, and hung up.

John pulled on his clothes and slipped out into the cold night air. Doorway was waiting at the door to let John in immediately. Doorway closed and bolted the door behind them.

"So what's the big emergency?" John demanded.

Doorway nodded in the direction of a table near the end of the bar. A woman sat at the table, her back to the men. A huge jacket was draped over her shoulders, which were shaking

187

slightly. Her head was bowed down, her light brown hair just brushed the surface of the table.

John looked at Doorway and whispered, "Maggie?"

"Yeah. Kells slapped her around and threw her out of their place. Didn't even give her a coat. She walked over here, let herself in, and called me."

"Did you call the police?"

"No. Says she won't talk to them. She won't even confirm it was Kells. Go figure."

Doorway slipped behind the bar and loaded some ice into a bar towel. John walked slowly toward the shaking figure, and around to the other side of the table. Maggie slowly raised her head, and John controlled his urge to recoil at the sight. A trembling hand held a bloody rag to the left side of her forehead, her left eye was almost swollen shut, and her lower lip was discolored and bleeding. Dried blood ringed the one visible nostril. The sight made John nauseous. He sat down across the table from the young woman.

"Who did this? Kells?"

A large tear escaped the swollen eye and trailed down the outside of her cheek as she shrugged.

"C'mon, Maggie, who else would it be? You need to stop this. He could have killed you. Let's call the cops."

"No. Please." Her reply was more like a squeak than a verbal reply, and she pulled her arms in tighter to herself.

"Well, what do you want to do?"

Maggie shrugged again and lowered her head. Doorway sat in a chair facing Maggie and coaxed her hand away from her forehead. A small, but obviously deep, cut at her hairline was exposed.

"That looks better," Doorway observed, "at least it's not gushing anymore. Head cuts bleed to beat hell. I don't think you need stitches, but we ought to take you to the hospital just to make sure."

Maggie pushed Doorway's hand away. "No. They'll call cops. Have to." Her words were slow and deliberate; a result of her swollen lip.

"Well then, if you're going to be stupid about it, you're stuck with me patching you up," Doorway replied. "Good thing for you, I've had plenty of practice. Hold this to your eye and lip while I get a couple of butterflies."

Maggie took the bar towel containing the ice and gingerly applied it to her face. Doorway got up and disappeared into the kitchen.

John leaned back in his chair and let out a long, deep sigh. It was perfectly clear why Doorway had told him not to wake Harley. He looked at Maggie and had to struggle to control his own rage.

Maggie's good eye opened. "Don't tell Harley. Promise."

"I won't have to," John replied coolly, "one look at you will tell the story."

Maggie stared through him with her good eye and made no reply.

Doorway returned from the kitchen with more towels, a bowl of water and first aid supplies. He quickly went to work, and John was amazed a man so large could be so gentle. After cleaning the cut on her forehead, and applying a butterfly with a small amount of alum to stop the bleeding, he very cautiously checked Maggie's nose. It wasn't broken.

"I've got an idea," Doorway said as he finished wiping dried blood from under Maggie's nose, "which is why I called you, John. You still need a camp cook, and Maggie here needs a place to go."

"Not good," Maggie grunted, "Harley."

"Shut up," Doorway ordered as he leaned back to admire his handiwork. "You don't have a say in the matter, since you won't let us call the cops." He turned to John. "What do you say?"

"I'd say that if Maggie doesn't want to go, it would be a helluva lot like kidnapping." John turned toward the woman, "Doorway has a point, Maggie. Would you be willing to go?"

Maggie lowered the towel from her face. She fixed a steady gaze on John. "You'll make Harley behave?"

John met Maggie's gaze, even though it made him queasy to stare at her damaged face. "Yes."

"Okay," Maggie agreed in a soft voice, "but I need clothes."

"That's a minor problem," Doorway replied. "How do we get you out to Last Chance without Harley seeing you and going ballistic?"

That exact question was making laps in John's head before Doorway even verbalized it. Harley's reaction the last time Kells hit Maggie told John this situation wasn't simply volatile, it was explosive. Harley couldn't see Maggie until they were all out of Nikiski, or it would be impossible to contain him.

"Here's what we're going to do," John said. "First, we call Cynthia, and take Maggie over there. While I do that, you call Reeder to see if he can make two trips into Last Chance this morning."

"Two trips?" Doorway asked.

"Yeah, the first to take out Harley, and the second to get Maggie and me. I'll tell Harley I got a late call from Cynthia about a possible camp cook, and am hoping to bring them out with me."

"I don't know," Doorway said slowly, "sounds pretty weak, to me."

"If you've got a better idea, I want to hear it."

"I don't, but you better be a really good liar."

"My good man," John said, puffing up to feign offense, "I used to sell life insurance for a living."

A little snort escaped from behind the towel Maggie held to her face, followed quickly by a low moan.

John felt some trepidation about calling Cynthia, given her reaction to Harley's lawyer and the past relationship between Harley and Maggie. He wondered how cordial the interaction might be between the two women. However, Maggie wasn't hesitant about going to the other woman's home, and Cynthia's irritation at being called so early quickly dissipated when John explained the circumstances.

On the ride to Cynthia's, John resisted the urge to ask what set Kells off. Maggie was in no shape to carry on a conversation anyway, and sat silently. The lights were on at the trailer when they pulled up, and Cynthia opened the door to let them in.

"Oh, shit!" the blonde said immediately upon seeing Maggie's face. "Girlfriend, my ex was a real asshole, but your boy is a true rat-bastard!"

"Looks worse than it is," Maggie replied.

"Liar."

Cynthia led them into the trailer kitchen where they sat at a
dinette. John explained his plan fully. He also asked Cynthia if
she had any spare clothes.

"I'll loan you anything you need. Things may be a little big
for you in certain areas, but they'll work."

"Bras are out," Maggie said, then winced as she giggled.

"Oh, honey, be free!" Cynthia replied with a laugh.

John reddened and shifted uncomfortably in his chair. "You
two just stay here and laugh it up. I'm going back to set things
up with Harley."

On the way back, John wondered just how deep the pile of
shit he'd just stepped into was going to be. He and Harley were
supposed to meet Doorway at the bar at five-thirty to pick up the
groceries, and it was a few minutes after five when he parked in
front of the bar. To his relief, Harley was not there when John
stepped in. Doorway poured him a cup of coffee as he
approached the bar.

"Did you reach Reeder?"

"Yeah. It was not pleasant. If you think he's gruff during
the day, try waking him out of his beauty sleep. He says we're
all nuts, we should call the cops, but he'll go along with it.
How'd it go at your end?"

"Good. Cynthia has clothes she can loan Maggie."

Doorway chuckled to himself. "Gonna be loose in places."

"They touched on that very subject, much to my discomfort.
Anyway, I'll go back and pick her up after Harley leaves. What
are you going to do about breakfast?"

"There's a nasty flu bug going around," Doorway said with
a wink, "and I don't cook. So the real question is, what is
everyone else going to do for breakfast."

"If you call Cynthia today, she might have a number for
someone who could replace Maggie."

Doorway raised an eyebrow but didn't inquire.

While waiting for Harley, the two men discussed Mark
Kells. John wanted to know how someone like Maggie could be
involved with such a low-life. Doorway explained Kells had
always tended towards being wild, but he was also handsome,
and his "bad boy" image seemed to attract women. Doorway
confessed he never had liked Kells much, but it wasn't until the

last few months that he had gotten mean. Doorway started to offer his speculation for the change when the door opened up, and Harley stepped in.

"Somebody is raring to go. I had to hump my duffel and backpack all the way across the lot."

John put on a smile and faced Harley. "My bad. Didn't stop to think I might wear you out so early."

"I'll just have to take a nap this afternoon." Harley took a mug of coffee from Doorway and nodded. "Thanks. Any chance for breakfast?"

"No," Doorway said quickly, "Maggie isn't here, she called me a couple of hours ago."

Harley's face darkened. "Anything wrong?"

"No, just a touch of the flu."

"Damn. Tired *and* hungry."

"I do have some good news, though," John said. "I talked to Cynthia after I left last night, and we may have a cook."

"Really? Who?"

John felt a twinge of panic rising as he tried to think of a name. "A guy named Bob."

"And does this Bob have a last name? Maybe I know him."

"I'm sure not," John replied casually, "he's not from around here. But Cynthia recommends him highly."

"He's a friend of Roberta's," Doorway interjected.

"Cynthia's cousin in Portland?" Harley looked confused.

"That's right," John replied, "Cynthia's cousin, Rebecca..."

"Roberta," Doorway and Harley corrected together.

"Her, too," John continued somewhat flustered, "she has a friend named Bob, who wants to spend a summer in Alaska for the adventure." John took a deep breath to calm down and continued, "Turns out the guy is a short order cook, and a pretty damn good one at that."

"So, where is this Bob with no last name?"

"He's not here yet. Doesn't get into Kenai until later this morning."

"So we're not going out today?"

"Oh, absolutely! You're going to fly out at six, then Reeder is going to take me out later in the day. After I pick up Bob."

"Why don't we just wait for Bob, and all go out together?"

"His flight might be late," John explained, struggling to appear casual, "and Reeder says we might not be able to go in the afternoon because the snow would be too slushy."

"Reeder could fly us out today, and Bob out tomorrow," Harley countered.

"I guess, but I want to meet him before he gets to the camp. Just in case. You know."

"No, I really don't."

"Well, in case I decide not to hire him. What if he's weird, or something?"

"Christ," Harley shook his head, "he couldn't be any weirder than the boss."

Barring anymore probing questions, John felt confident the ruse had been pulled off. He took another deep breath and concentrated on his coffee.

"Well, we better get started loading up," Harley said, and set his mug down on the bar.

"What's the hurry? It's barely five-thirty, and we only have to load six boxes."

"And Dawg," Harley added.

"You're going to love this, John," Doorway said with a large grin.

Once the groceries were loaded, Doorway handed Harley a pepperoni stick from behind the bar. Harley unwrapped the snack, broke it in half, and stepped out the door of the bar, where Dawg lay dutifully. John and Doorway followed. Harley showed his large dog the pepperoni stick, then started breaking little pieces off and tossing them to the dog. Dawg responded by snatching the treats from the air with increasing fervor. Harley made his way to the Suburban and opened the back door. After throwing the last piece from the first half of the pepperoni stick to Dawg, Harley waved the second half in front of the big animal, then threw it into the back of the Suburban. Dawg followed the treat without hesitation, and Harley slammed the door behind him. Harley bowed in Doorway's direction in response to his applause.

"Someday he's going to wise up," Doorway said, "and then where will you be?"

"I'll be at Last Chance," Harley replied, "and you'll be here, stuck feeding that worthless flea-bag."

Harley and John shook hands with Doorway, then climbed into the Suburban. On the way to the airstrip, Harley produced a leash for his animal. Dawg bared his teeth and snarled viciously while Harley groped around to find the ring on the dog's collar to clip on the leash.

"How many times has he bitten you?" John asked.

"Funny thing is, he never has. But if he was half as mean as he sounds, I'd be scared to death of him."

John shook his head and wondered to himself if Harley Pepperdine had ever had any kind of normal relationship.

Reeder directed the two younger men as they loaded up their gear and groceries. He then lashed the cargo down tightly with a net. They were going in the Cessna 185 and one of the passenger seats had been removed. An open space was left immediately behind the co-pilot's seat for Dawg. John noticed a tarp was laid out on the floor in that area.

"Okay, Harley," Reeder growled, "get your dog loaded."

Reeder stepped back and folded his arms over his chest, looking as if he was anticipating a show. Harley opened the back door to the Suburban and grabbed Dawg's leash to pull him out. The big animal jumped to the ground and immediately laid down, going completely limp.

"Passive resistance," Harley said to John, "the big sissy is scared to death of flying."

Following several failed attempts at coaxing Dawg along, Harley dragged him over to the plane. Snarling punctuated every step of the trip. Harley asked John to help him hoist the beast into position.

"You grab his hind end," Harley directed.

"Watch yourself," Reeder said dryly, "he usually pisses himself about now."

As if on cue, a strong stream of urine sprang from the dog's underside. John started to let go of his end.

"Hold him up! Hold him up!" Harley shouted. "Otherwise he'll lay down in it and stink all the way over."

When the stream stopped, Harley counted to three, and with a grunt the limp dog was dumped unceremoniously into the plane. John was laughing so hard he almost dropped his end at the last moment.

"I think I know why your dog doesn't like you, Harley. That's quite an effort."

"You can laugh," Reeder grumbled, "he gets airsick, too. You give him pepperoni?"

Harley nodded to the affirmative.

"Great," Reeder groused, "gonna smell like an Italian pukefest, again."

Harley and Reeder climbed into the airplane. As they taxied down the strip, John saw Dawg sit up behind Harley. His muzzle was pointed skyward, howling.

John climbed into the Suburban and sat for a moment to collect his thoughts. From the second his eyes opened, the entire morning had felt surreal. For a brief moment he wondered if he had simply changed bad dreams. He pushed the mental images of what might take place with Harley, when he and Maggie arrived at Last Chance, out of his mind. It was certain to be unpleasant, but worrying about it wouldn't make things any better.

Cynthia stepped out of the trailer before John even shut off the engine. She walked over to the Suburban and spoke to him in a quiet tone.

"Listen, it's more than just her face. She's got some bruises on her body, too. That..." Cynthia's voice choked off in anger.

"How bad? C'mon Cynthia, pull it together," John coaxed.

Cynthia cleared her throat and let out a deep breath. "Nothing that won't heal quickly, but John, that wasn't just about being jealous, or losing control, that was a deliberate beating." The young woman stepped closer to John and quickly whispered, "I'm not even sure it was Kells who did it."

John felt light-headed and sick. "Who, then? Why?"

"I don't know, but Derrick told me a couple months ago he thought Kells was dealing crystal meth. Maybe Maggie got into the middle of something, somehow."

"She's not using, is she?"

"Maggie? Oh, hell no. She watched her real dad kill himself with drugs and booze. She rarely even drinks a beer."

John weighed the new information. Not calling the authorities went against everything that seemed to make sense.

He had one question, "Who do you think Maggie is protecting?"

"Maggie," came the quick response. "If she called the troopers, they'd just take a report and leave. What then? Where would she go? She's scared, John. Do you blame her?"

"No, I don't."

John paced back and forth the length of the Suburban a few times. This was turning into a mess, one he wasn't sure he wanted to deal with. On the other hand, he couldn't just leave Maggie behind to face whatever might follow. He was committed to helping her, but deep inside he knew there was more to it than just helping someone. He stopped pacing in front of Cynthia.

"Fine, goddamn it, we'll stick to the plan. Let's get her loaded up."

They drove to the airstrip in silence. John parked the Suburban on the back side of the flight shack to hide it from the view of anyone that might drive onto the strip, or pass by in the distant highway. He glanced over at his passenger. Cynthia had given Maggie a pair of large sunglasses to hide the swollen eye. She was sitting straight up and John couldn't tell if her eyes were open. The ice had reduced the swelling in her lip, and she didn't seem to be in obvious pain, but John still had reservations.

"I really am okay," Maggie said as if she were reading John's thoughts, "just a little sore. I'll be fine tomorrow."

"Shit, lady," John laughed derisively, "you won't be able to move, tomorrow. Cynthia told me about the bruises."

"She's got a big mouth."

"Yeah, maybe, but you've got a bad attitude."

"Guess I'm having a bad day."

"I'd say so. And that makes two of us."

The time ticked away in a long stretch of silence until Reeder arrived. John pulled around from behind the flight shack and parked near the plane after Reeder shut down the engine. He told Maggie to stay in the vehicle as he climbed out and hauled Maggie's bags over to the plane. When everything was set, Maggie stepped out of the Suburban and walked over to the plane. Reeder started to open his mouth, and was swiftly cut short.

"Don't say a goddamned word, Reeder!" Maggie snapped.

Whatever remark the pilot may have had in mind died before it passed his lips. He simply pointed to the rear of the plane and helped Maggie step up into the plane. John climbed into the co-pilot's seat.

The flight over the inlet was bumpy, a result of a weather front moving into the area, Reeder explained. He told John there might be significant rain mixed with snow associated with the weather system. If there was more rain than snow, Reeder warned, it would surely mean he couldn't land in the valley again. It sounded ominous to John, but he was grateful to have something else to think about, aside from the other passenger.

John was relieved to see Harley wasn't waiting in the valley for them. His presence would have made getting everything unloaded more complicated. Reeder speculated the turnaround time had been quicker than Harley expected. He asked John if he should wait until Harley showed up, but John said it would be best if Reeder left. That way, there would be no way Harley could insist on flying back to exact justice. Without anything further to discuss, Reeder climbed back into his plane and took off.

John pulled the tarp off the snowmachine and sled, tossed Maggie's bags into the sled, and tucked the tarp back over the bags. There was no sign of Harley.

"You ready for the fireworks to start?" John asked in an effort to lighten the moment.

"It won't be the first time we've had words," Maggie said calmly. "How about if you just stay clear, keep your mouth shut, and let me do the yelling?"

"You know what?" John snapped back, irritated at Maggie's dismissive tone. "If I ever meet an Alaskan woman who isn't ready to kick somebody's ass, and full of attitude, I'm going to marry her."

For the first time that day, Maggie smiled without wincing. "You find a woman like that, mister, and she won't be an Alaskan."

Harley was inside the lodge. He had just finished putting away the gear and groceries that came out with him. Fireworks started the moment Harley saw Maggie. In short order it was obvious to John his presence was neither required, nor wanted.

He left the lodge and closed the door behind him. As he stepped off the porch, loud accusations and rebuttals flew back and forth between the combatants. John decided to bide his time at the workshop while things were aired out. About half an hour later, John heard the other snowmachine fire up. He looked out from the workshop in time to see Harley flying down the valley at full throttle.

John rode his machine back to the lodge and found Maggie sitting in one of the large easy chairs next to the woodstove. Dawg was stretched out at her feet. Her head was laid back and her eyes were closed. She didn't move when John walked in.

"Where'd Harley go?"

"He's off sulking. It's what he does best. He'll cool off."

"Things okay between you?"

"John, things haven't been okay between us for years. There isn't a thing you can say, or do, to make that better. Just stay out of it."

"I already got that lecture from Harley. My concern is how it will affect the operation. You two can't be blowing up at each other in front of the clients."

"We'll be civil with each other, eventually," Maggie sighed and lifted her head. "Listen, I feel like shit. Where am I staying? I'd like to lay down, if you don't mind."

"Yeah, sure. You're going to stay in the lodge, in Hardrock's room. That way," John said with a wink "you won't wake me up too early, rattling around in the kitchen."

His effort at levity was wasted.

John spent the rest of the day setting up the farthest guest cabin for his own quarters. He made frequent trips to the lodge to add fuel to the woodstove and check on Maggie. She was poor company the few times John actually saw her. Early in the evening Harley came back to the lodge, just as the rain and snow Reeder had predicted started to fall. Without a word, he walked into the lodge, grabbed a loaf of bread and a can of Spam from the pantry and disappeared into his cabin. John stayed at the lodge until it was dark, then walked to his cabin and fell into bed, exhausted. It had not been a promising beginning to the season.

Throughout the night, sheets of rain frequently interrupted

the thick, heavy snowfall brought by the storm front. The combination of wet snow and rain laid down a thick layer of slush that compressed the existing snow. The snow level was visibly lower the next morning. By mid-day the temperatures had risen enough to change the precipitation entirely to a steady drizzle. The warmer air created a fog that hung a just few feet above the lake. Nothing moved. The winds from the leading edge of the front had passed, and the drizzle fell straight down. John looked out the window of the lodge and thought how bleak and surreal the view was.

"Is this normal?" he asked Maggie.

"It's breakup. Anything is normal," came the reply. "It could be sunny in fifteen minutes, or switch back to heavy snow."

Maggie grabbed a stack of plates from under the serving counter and headed back to the kitchen. She wanted to start cleaning the place, more out of a desire to do something, anything, than an actual need.

John continued staring out the window and listened to Maggie rattle around in the kitchen. He wondered where Harley was. Harley hadn't answered when John knocked on his cabin door earlier, but both snowmachines were still parked in front of the lodge. He decided to check the workshop, announcing his departure to Maggie as he left.

Harley stood at the workbench when John stepped through the door. He had a sluice box set on the bench and didn't look up from his work.

"I thought we were going to check out the generator today," John said. Harley shrugged noncommittally and continued his work without comment. John's patience was wearing thin. "All right, what the hell are you mad at me for?"

"You and Doorway lied to me." Harley turned to face John. "How do you think I should take it?"

"Okay, *Bob*," John said, referencing the first night the two men had met.

"That was different."

"If you think you can explain how, I'm ready to hear it." Harley shifted uncomfortably, but offered no rebuttal. "Look," John continued, "if we had told you the truth, things would have flown out of control. Where would that have gotten us?"

Harley leaned back against the bench and hung his head. John was right, and Harley knew it. Still, the only thing he felt like doing at the moment was throttling Kells. He wanted to make that bastard pay with blood.

"We're here now," John continued calmly. "Maggie will be fine in a few of days. We all need to just move forward, get along and work together."

Harley looked up at his boss and nodded. Given the state of the weather, he knew there was no chance he'd be able to get back to Nikiski until the lake was ice free. He would have to bide his time, maybe look Kells up while he was back doing community service. He forced a smile.

"Did you give Maggie your 'one big, happy family' speech?"

"No way! That's going to be your job." John said, and both men laughed.

"Fine. The hired hand always gets stuck with the dirty work."

While the friction between Harley and John was eased with a blunt conversation, it was another four days before a truce in the cold war between Harley and Maggie was established. On their fifth night at the claim, Harley asked if he could join John and Maggie at the table for dinner.

"Had enough Spam?" Maggie asked.

"Yeah," Harley replied, "but I don't need to swap it for vinegar." He turned to leave.

"Sit down, shut up, and eat," John ordered. "Both of you. I mean it."

Harley complied, and much to John's surprise, so did Maggie. It was, perhaps, the quietest meal John had ever experienced, but it was a start. The next morning, when Harley showed up for breakfast, there was a palpable decrease in the tension between the staff.

John wasn't sure if it was the improved relations between she and Harley, or that Maggie's wounds were healing, but her demeanor had improved. She laughed more readily, and her sharp tongue came out only on occasion, and then only directed at Harley. John found himself enjoying her company. At her suggestion, she taught John how to play dominoes, and even invited Harley to join in. It became part of the daily routine for the three of them to play a game after dinner. It was during one of those games John realized he wasn't looking at the tiles being laid, but was staring at Maggie. He quickly glanced at Harley to see if he had noticed. Fortunately, Harley was concentrating on his own dominoes.

"Not a good idea at all," John chided himself silently, *"don't even think about it."*

The first week of May brought the end to most of the snow in places with southern exposure, but the lake was still completely iced over. With the snow either gone, or fading quickly, the final outside preparations were completed, and John's education in mining began in earnest. Using the maps and aerial photographs from Hardrock's place, Harley took John around the claim to show him where Hardrock had marked to initially set up clients. Each marked point on the map had notes. The notes were simple, indicating what had been found at the sites. Those locations Hardrock thought showed the most promise were marked with stars.

"We'll suggest the clients work those locations first," Harley explained. "Although, returning clients, like Bill Johnson and his family, usually have an idea where they want to go."

"Why would this spot get a star?" John asked, pointing to the map he was holding. "The notes only say, 'fines with heavy black sand.' This spot here, with no star, produced small nuggets."

"Black sands usually indicate gold. Hardrock always said it was better to put clients on top of black sand with certain gold, than to have them chasing nuggets which might not exist. For most of our clients, people who have never mined, just finding some gold, even if it is small, is a thrill."

Every day Harley showed John another aspect of the business. From working a highbanker and panning the concentrates, to running the small, towable backhoe used to rake down the tailings. With each new item, Harley first showed John how it was done, then walked him through it. Operating the backhoe was a challenge for John, but he couldn't keep the smile off his face the entire time he was on the controls.

Harley was not only good at what he did, he obviously enjoyed sharing his knowledge. He was a patient, thorough teacher. John's skills and confidence grew daily under Harley's tutelage, as did his admiration and respect for his tutor. Any reservations John may have initially had about working with Harley Pepperdine were completely allayed. And more, John realized a true friendship was developing between them.

From the first day they had flown into Last Chance, there had been calls to, or from, the other side of the inlet. Cynthia kept John apprised of her progress toward launching a local ad campaign. Maggie, using John's cell phone since hers had been left behind, called Billy McCrane to order groceries and supplies. Doorway called occasionally to keep tabs on them. On the nineteenth of May, Harley told John to call Reeder and let him know the lake was clear enough of ice to land. Reeder, being Reeder, simply said that unless they were all starving and had resorted to cannibalism, he would see them with their first clients, on the twenty-fourth.

A light rain was falling when the Johnsons arrived. Reeder made a pass over the claim before setting down to let everyone know of their arrival. John and Harley drove down to the lake on ATV's, towing trailers behind them. They walked out on the floating dock they had just recently put out and waited as the Beaver taxied up. Reeder cut the engine and the plane drifted up to the side of the dock, where Harley directed John to grab the wing strut while he tied the plane off to the dock. The plane was no sooner secured than the door opened and a boy scrambled out and onto the dock.

"Hi, Harley!" the boy shouted enthusiastically.

"Hi, Marc!" Harley shouted, mimicking the boy's enthusiasm.

"I'm Erik."

Another boy burst out of the Beaver onto the dock. "I'm Marc. Hi, Harley." Other than the clothes he wore, it could have been the same child.

"I can see you guys haven't slowed down any. Boys, this is John Barstow. He owns the mine, now."

The boys gave John a cursory wave and turned back to Harley. "Is Hardrock buried here?"

"No, he's not," John said, trying to break the ice, "but his spirit is here, and I'll bet if you listen, you'll hear him laughing in the wind."

Both boys turned blank expressions on John. "That's just weird," Marc said.

"Totally," his sibling agreed.

"Boys," a female voice said from the plane, "that's not appropriate." A person to associate with the voice emerged from the plane. "Why don't you run up to the lodge while we unload?"

"Can we take a four-wheeler?"

"Absolutely not! Go on."

The boys took off like they'd been launched in the direction of the lodge, and the woman stepped onto the dock, followed closely by her husband. By appearances, John judged the couple to be active and into outdoor pursuits. They were both fit and trim, although the husband looked to be several years older than his wife. Harley made the introductions, then told Bill and Kayla in which cabin they would be staying. He also explained that since they really didn't want to eat anything he, or John, might cook, the new camp cook's name was Maggie. The couple laughed in response and started out toward the lodge.

"C'mon," Reeder called from the Beaver impatiently, "I've got more to do than sit on this lake."

"Good to see you, too, Reeder," Harley shot back. "By the way, don't think I'm not pissed at you for being a co-conspirator."

"Big deal," Reeder replied, and threw a duffle bag onto the dock to emphasize his lack of concern.

With the Johnson's gear and the groceries off the plane and loaded onto the ATV trailers, the three men gathered on the dock.

"Either of you talked to Doorway recently?" Reeder asked.

"Not for a couple of days. Why?" John responded.

"Well, he told me last night the scuttlebutt going around is that one Mr. Kells is missing. Seems there was a big drug bust off English Court about a week ago, and Kells hasn't been seen since."

"Maybe he's just out on the platform," Harley offered.

"That's not it. He pissed hot, and they ran his ass off the platform right after you left. No, rumor has it he ratted out the guys that got busted because he owed them money and things were getting unpleasant."

"That's interesting," John said, thinking back to what Cynthia had said the night he took Maggie over to her trailer, "so he's on the run."

"Or dead. Doorway might be able to shed a little more light on it for you. Now, get me off this dock. I've got places to go and much more important people to talk to."

John and Harley watched Reeder disappear after lifting off from the lake, then turned toward the ATV's.

"You really think Kells is dead?" John asked.

"Nope. You can push scum down out of sight, but it always floats back up."

The weather continued cool and wet after the Johnsons' arrival. Frequent trips to dry off and warm up were made to the lodge, where Maggie kept a never-ending supply of snacks and hot drinks available. At the end of such a break, John found himself sitting alone with Maggie.

"They're a nice family, aren't they?" Maggie commented.

"They are, but those boys are a handful! God, no wonder Bill and Kayla are fit. The boys keep them running non-stop."

"You're good with them, though."

John chuckled to himself. "You didn't hear our first conversation on the dock."

"No, but I've watched you with them, and you're very patient. You'd make a good dad."

"I don't know about that," John said, uncomfortable with the compliment. "What about you? You want kids?"

"I've had kids." John's eyebrows shot up at the comment. "I called them boyfriends at the time."

John nodded, and decided to push his luck. "Kells one of those kids?"

"Yeah, maybe the worst."

"Why Kells? Why pick him?"

Maggie hung her head and sighed. "I don't know. Maybe to piss off Harley as much as anything else."

John felt his pulse quicken. He couldn't tell if she wanted to talk about their relationship, or if he was prying. "What do you think about Kells disappearing?" he finally asked to skirt the question he really wanted answered.

"I don't know. Really, it doesn't matter. I don't ever want to see him again. Our relationship was never going to be a permanent thing, and when he started using, well..." Maggie glanced up and saw John's quizzical look. "Sure, I knew he was using. But I thought I could help him. What can I say? Some shit from your childhood haunts you forever."

"I'm sorry. I really didn't mean to pry."

"No, it's okay. Really." Maggie reached out and touched John's cheek lightly. "You're a good guy, John."

Her touch was soft and gentle on his cheek. John felt the urge to blurt out what he'd been thinking for weeks, but instead, he listened to his inner warning, *"Don't do it! Don't even think about it!"*

John stood up and mumbled something about helping the Johnsons move their highbanker. He grabbed his rain slicker and stepped out of the lodge. Maggie watched John walk across the porch and down the stairs. She continued to stare out the window in the direction he had disappeared for several seconds. The realization she was feeling something she hadn't felt in a long time, prior to even meeting Mark Kells, broke her gaze.

CHAPTER 12

Things quieted down considerably when the Johnson family left. The couple immediately after the Johnsons were newly-weds, and spent little time out of their cabin. The next clients were two men from Illinois who were decidedly reserved. Following their initial instruction and getting set up on the first day, they wanted little, or nothing, to do with John, Harley, or Maggie. Harley quickly nicknamed them the "Sunshine Boys." They showed up for meals punctually, then immediately went back to their highbanker, saying little. The one time John offered to help out with the highbanking, his offer was bluntly declined.

"Those guys are a load of fun," John commented during a game of dominoes.

"They've got the fever."

"What?"

"Gold fever," Harley said, "they've found some gold, and think if they talk about it, we'll move them. I've seen it before."

"You're kidding," John replied incredulously. "They actually think we'd move them off their spot to get the gold?"

"Oh, yeah. Don't ask them how they're doing and expect an answer. I walked up on them while they were panning out their concentrates this afternoon, and they all but told me to leave."

"That's just nuts."

"That's gold fever. We had a couple who took turns watching their highbanker at night to make sure nobody else moved in on 'their claim.' We're lucky we don't have any other clients out here with these guys. We've actually had clients get into arguments over who got to highbank where. One guy got so belligerent, Hardrock refunded his money and called Reeder to come take him out."

John shook his head in disbelief. "Incredible. How do you think they're doing?"

"Well, they haven't asked to be moved, and there's plenty of black sand in the panning tubs when they're done. They also asked me for two more vials, so they're getting something. We'll find out as they leave."

"How so?"

"They won't be able to resist showing it off."

Harley had the Sunshine Boys pegged. At breakfast on the morning of their departure they were more than willing to show off their gold. The men voluntarily produced four of the plastic vials given to clients to store their gold. Each man proudly held out one full vial, along with a second vial containing a thin layer on the bottom. The vials held coarse flake gold, mixed liberally with black sand. Harley produced a small digital scale from a drawer in the desk by the wood stove, and offered to weigh the vials. The total weight of the vials was just under three ounces.

"How can you go wrong with a vacation that pays for itself?" one crowed, and both vowed to come back in the future.

While loading the Sunshine Boys' bags for the trip to the dock, John asked Harley if they had really paid for their vacations.

"Maybe one," Harley replied, "there's lots of black sand in those vials. They have less than three ounces of actual flake. Gold from here probably runs about seventy-five percent pure. It doesn't matter."

"Why not?"

"Do you really think either of those guys would part with any of it?"

John smiled at the thought of the Sunshine Boys anguishing over selling their precious gold.

The four clients Reeder brought in were boisterous and eager to get up to the lodge. They introduced themselves as Turk, Willie, Gomer and CJ. CJ was getting married the end of

June, and they were on an extended bachelor party. They referred to themselves as the "Wild Bunch." After instructing Harley to be very careful with their gear, they strutted off toward the lodge. Their dismissive manner visibly rankled Harley, and elicited a comment from Reeder.

"You're going to have your hands full with that group. They're primed for a good time, and brought enough booze for a month."

"Yeah," Harley agreed, "we've had clients like that before. They think they just bought a plantation with slaves. It's going to be a long week."

As Harley started offloading the plane, Reeder pulled John aside for a private conversation. "See the big fella, Turk?" he asked very quietly. "Big mouth, big ego, and I'm guessing big trouble. He's been bitching about no women on the adventure since he fell out of the cab at the airstrip. He's sure to hit on Maggie. Didn't want to mention it in front of Harley."

John nodded. He knew Turk's type well; someone who let the wrong organs run the show. He thanked Reeder for the warning. He found himself feeling more jealous about Maggie, than concerned for both of his employees. He reminded himself of his position in the situation, pushed the jealousy out of his mind, and went to work helping Harley.

The four new clients immediately set out to live up to their self-proclaimed title. They brusquely declined the tour of the claim and setup of mining gear. They opted, instead, to gather at the fire pit and pass around a bottle of expensive Scotch. John could see where they were headed, and asked Maggie to make sure plenty of snacks were available to them. By lunch, they were well into their cups and pronounced the order of the day was that meals were to be served at the fire pit.

The day wore on and more bottles of various types were worn out. By evening, it was far easier to carry dinner down to the clients, than the clients up to dinner. John and Harley served dinner, mainly to relieve Maggie of the duty. The group's comments to Maggie during her trips out to the fire pit had grown more suggestive as the day had progressed. She brushed them off, but her patience was wearing thin. It was clear that Reeder's warning had been prophetic.

Turk, in particular, was a source of abrasion. Staggering toward the outhouse after dinner, he called back to the lodge, "Hey, Maggie! I may need some help with this!"

Maggie's patience was exhausted. She stomped out on the deck and shot back, "Well, if it's too little to find, you can always sit down."

Her acerbic retort garnered bellows of laughter from everyone present, except Turk. When he returned from the outhouse he sullenly withstood the ribbing from his companions. Unable to outlast the daylight, the Wild Bunch finally took refuge in their cabin to escape the mosquitoes.

"I'll give them one thing," Harley observed as the last of the Wild Bunch staggered into the cabin, "they can sure put it away."

"They're going to feel it in the morning," John replied, then turned to Maggie. "As much as the guy deserved it, your little witticism earlier wasn't a good idea."

Maggie scowled at John. "You weren't doing anything."

"You're right, I should have stepped up."

"Hey, I thought it was damn funny," Harley interjected.

"Piss off, Harley," Maggie said without looking at him.

"But I know that kind of guy," John continued, "and believe me, he'll be looking for a way to get back at you."

"He won't even remember it tomorrow."

"But one of his buddies will, and they won't let it go."

"I won't apologize," Maggie stated firmly.

"I don't expect you to. In fact, you shouldn't bring it up at all. I would suggest, however, you avoid being around the guy as much as possible. And I'll be quicker to respond if he gets out of line. Deal?"

Maggie nodded in agreement.

The Wild Bunch showed residual effects from their previous day's excesses when three of them showed up in the lodge shortly after ten. Turk was not among them. Their breakfast requests were simple: coffee and toast. With breakfast ordered, Maggie went into the kitchen, as much to avoid the company as to make the toast.

"Looks like you boys had a good time, yesterday," John said cheerily.

"Maybe not so great right now," mumbled the one called Gomer, "although I think I'll survive."

"Surviving is what I'm afraid of," groaned CJ.

"I think it should be a simple funeral," Willie added.

"You're all a bunch of pussies!" boomed Turk as he strode into the lodge. "All you need is a little hair of the dog."

He stepped up to the table and poured a healthy dose of Irish Cream into each of his friends' mugs. He added an even larger dose to the coffee John set on the table for him.

"How about you?" Turk asked John, "You need a little starter fluid?"

"No thanks," John replied amiably, "I'm fine."

"Nonsense! It's rude to turn down a drink." He reached forward to pour some of the liqueur into John's mug, and John covered the mug with his hand.

"What I meant to say," John said firmly, "is that I don't drink."

"I thought miners were real men," Turk taunted. "Guess I was wrong."

John shrugged in response to Turk's verbal jab, and turned to the other men, "Speaking of miners, are you boys ready to find some gold today? Harley is setting up a couple of highbankers right now."

Mixed in with the mumbled responses were questions about what highbanking involved, so John provided a brief description of the equipment and the process. The initially low level of enthusiasm plummeted the moment he uttered the word "shovel."

"Hell," Turk said loudly, "I didn't come here to dig ditches. I came here to have some fun!"

"I don't know, Turk," Gomer said softly, "sounds like finding some gold would be a hoot. We can't do that back in Dallas. That's why I wanted us to come here."

"You want to find gold?" Turk asked in a derisive tone, "You are such a *fucking dweeb*, Gomer. I'll give you a bottle of Goldschlager to mine." Turk laughed hard and slapped Gomer on the back. He was still laughing at his own wit when Maggie came out with a stack of toast. "There she is! How ya doin' darlin'?"

Maggie set the plate on the table and asked Turk icily, "You want something?"

Turk slowly looked Maggie up and down for a moment, then drawled, "Oh... yeah."

John saw Maggie bristle, but she bit her lip and walked back into the kitchen. The Wild Bunch giggled and nudged each other when the door closed behind her. John could feel his pulse quicken in anger.

"Turk," John said in a calm voice belying what he was feeling, "you need to ease up on the comments."

"Hey, we're just having a little fun," Turk responded as he stepped around the table to John's side. "No harm in a little fun."

Turk put his arm around John's shoulders and squeezed tightly on the muscle at the base of his neck. The move was meant to produce enough pain for John to wince. Instead, John put his own arm around Turk's shoulders, gripping the same muscle on his antagonist.

"I know that," John said slowly, increasing the tension of his grip, "but your comments aren't appreciated by my staff."

The two men stood side by side, each shaking the other slightly, as if they were two old friends sharing a special moment. The other three members of the Wild Bunch watched intently. They had seen Turk pull this stunt before, he called it his "persuader" move. Unfortunately for Turk, John's years of dealing with dominating office bullies had made him very familiar with subtle physical intimidation games. He pressed his thumb deeply into the back of Turk's neck, and rolled his grip. He felt Turk stiffen slightly.

"Okay!" Turk almost squealed, dropping his arm off John's shoulders and spinning away from him. "What do you guys want to do?"

John forced a smile and looked at the other three men. Their faces were blank. They had never seen Turk beat at his own move.

"It's your call, gents, your week. You can do whatever you want. I have no problem with you leaving the gold for the next clients."

After a mumbled discussion, during which Turk remained silent, the Wild Bunch decided to give highbanking a try. John told them to meet him at the ATV's when they were ready.

"Turk!" John called out as the men were leaving, "Don't forget your Irish Cream." John held the bottle out as Turk walked back, but clung tightly to it when Turk grabbed it. "Do we have an understanding?" John asked quietly.

Turk snorted as he jerked the bottle from John's grasp, and stomped out of the lodge. He ignored Harley's greeting as they passed on the steps, and continued toward his cabin.

"What's with Turd... I mean Turk?" Harley asked as he walked into the lodge.

"I guess he's a little under the weather. We'll need to take them out, shortly. Everything set up?"

"I raked down some fresh dirt and ran a couple of test pans. It's good dirt, with chunky flakes, maybe even some jewelry nuggets."

"Good," John said rubbing his neck, "maybe it'll distract them from the fire pit."

"Maybe," Harley chuckled, "until they break a sweat."

Following a quick rundown on ATV safety, John and Harley took the Wild Bunch on a circuitous route around the claim. John took the lead in providing the history of the claim and pointing out the remnants of old equipment laying about. Harley explained how the mine had been operated, and answered what few questions came up. Gomer and CJ seemed to enjoy the tour, looking closely at the old relics and taking pictures along the way. Willie hung back with Turk, who remained silently on his ATV whenever the group stopped.

At the highbankers John split the Wild Bunch in two, pairing Gomer with CJ on one, and Willie with Turk on the other. He worked with Gomer and CJ to get them started, and they quickly grasped the idea. Harley wasn't having as much luck with his half of the Wild Bunch.

"You're doin' good with that shovel there, hired hand," Turk said.

Harley stopped feeding the header on the highbanker. "I'm highly trained and experienced," he said with a smile. Holding out the shovel out to Turk, he continued, "Your turn now."

"Not me," Turk replied, sitting down on a rock, "I'm management. That's more my style." He nodded at the backhoe.

"Sorry, that little gem is for John and me, only."

"Shame. Guess I'll just have to supervise, then." He produced a bottle from his daypack and held the bottle up, "Hey, Gomer! Got your gold right here!" He took a slug from the bottle and held it up to Willie, "Want some?"

Willie stood in a moment of indecision, then reached for the bottle and took a drink. He, in turn, offered the bottle to Harley.

"No thanks, not when I'm working."

"When do you get off?" asked Turk.

"The end of October." Harley paused for a moment, then continued, "Listen, if you guys are going to drink, I can't let you ride the ATV's back to camp. It's a liability thing."

Turk stood up. "Sounds like a good reason to head back to camp right now. C'mon Willie."

Willie looked at Harley, shrugged and fell in step behind Turk. Harley shut down the water pump to the highbanker and walked over to John to let him know what was going on. John suggested that he return to camp with Willie and Turk, and Harley stay with Gomer and CJ.

John followed his two charges back to the lodge. They backtracked the way they had come in, instead of taking the direct route John would have taken them. At the lodge John asked the men to leave the keys in the ATV's. When they went into their cabin, he pulled the keys and put them in his pocket. He worried they'd drink just enough to believe they were invincible, then want try their hands at boon docking.

John was at the top of the stairs to the lodge, petting Dawg, when Turk and Willie reappeared from their cabin. They both held a bottle and were headed toward the fire pit.

"Yo! How about something to eat?" Turk called out. "And we're getting low on firewood, too."

"I'll get you some lunch," John replied, "and you can help yourself to the wood, over there." He pointed to the large supply of split wood stacked less than twenty-five yards from the fire pit.

"I thought hauling wood was your job."

"I'm not the one burning it," John shot back as he disappeared into the lodge.

The front portion of the lodge was empty when John

entered, so he looked for Maggie in the kitchen. When he saw she wasn't there, he assumed she was in the back lean-to, doing laundry. He opened the door for the hallway to the living quarters and laundry area, and proceeded down the hall. He glanced left into the shower room as he passed it. There stood Maggie. Believing she had some time to herself, she had taken a shower. She was rubbing her hair dry with the towel, and totally unaware she had company.

John knew he should turn around and say something to announce his presence, or perhaps just leave, but he couldn't move, couldn't speak. What stood before him was flawless. The curve of waist to hip, the long legs, the smooth skin glistening, all held him frozen in appreciation. Her breasts were covered by the towel hanging down, but were exposed when the hand holding the towel dropped to one of the perfectly shaped hips. The breasts were in perfect proportion to the torso, gently rounded and swept slightly upward to nipples that stood out against the cool air. John thought they, like the rest of the figure, deserved to be immortalized in marble.

"Hey! My eyes are up here," a loud voice from the distance called. John jumped at the voice. "*Leave!*"

Snapped from his reverie, John saw Maggie standing with her hands on her hips, totally naked, shouting at him. He immediately looked down at his feet, and desperately willed them into life. "I'm... there's lunch... and..." he stammered, "Bye."

When John's feet finally cooperated, the door to the shower room slammed shut in his wake. He was half-way out of the lodge before remembering why he was there. He stopped, his pulse racing, and forced himself to calm down. It was silly, but he hadn't felt this way since he was twelve, camping with his parents, and had wandered upon a young woman skinny-dipping. That encounter had also not gone particularly well.

John took a few moments to collect himself, then went back into the kitchen and started gathering sandwich makings. As he organized things on the counter, his mind kept drifting back to the vision he had just seen. He couldn't shake it. For the second time in five minutes, Maggie's voice jerked him back into reality.

"Get out of my kitchen. I'll make lunch, and you drag it out. And you can stop staring at your feet," she added, "I'm dressed now."

John looked up and directly into Maggie's eyes. His immediate thought was that he wished he'd done it five minutes earlier. It would have made the vision in his head perfect.

"Yeah, that's good. I'm out. I mean, I'll *be* out. There. Waiting. You know." He turned to leave.

"How much?"

Again, John's heart jumped, making it hard to breathe, let alone speak. The vision of her standing, beautifully exposed, still hung in his mind.

"Um, all of you. I guess. Not your eyes."

"Jesus, John! How much *lunch*? How many people?"

Maggie broke into such uncontrollable laughter she had to grab the counter to steady herself. Tears trickled down her cheeks. Her laughter served to embarrass John even further, but broke the tension. When Maggie had finally recovered, he could answer her question without stammering.

John carried lunch to the fire pit, then returned to the deck and stared out over the lake. He didn't want to sit around and exchange barbs with Turk, but wasn't sure what kind of reception he'd receive inside. He scanned the shoreline around the lake. He tried to think about the beauty surrounding him, but his mind kept seeing Maggie standing before him. He turned around and saw she was leaning in the doorway, staring at him.

"Your lunch is on the table," she said with a little smirk before turning to go back inside.

John followed Maggie into the lodge and sat down in front of one of the two plates set opposite each other at the table. Maggie sat down at the other. They ate in silence for several minutes before John spoke.

"Sorry about earlier... I should have, I don't know. Something, I guess."

Maggie set what was left of her sandwich on her plate and looked at John with a steady gaze.

"Look, we're both adults." Her tone was matter-of-fact and wholly unabashed. "You aren't the first guy to see me 'au naturel' and I'm sure I'm not the first woman you've ever seen straight out of a shower."

"Well, no. But I'm supposed to be the boss, and you're an employee, sort of, and..." John's voice trailed off.

"And what? You're afraid of a harassment suit? Get real! Give me some credit, John."

"No. God, no! I know you'd never think about doing something like that."

"Well, what then?"

John paused before replying. He debated whether he should tell her what he was really thinking, or let it go. "It was embarrassing is all," he finally answered. "And you're so damn beautiful," was out before he could stop it. "Let's just forget it happened."

"Agreed," Maggie said quickly and stood up from the table. "I need to start on dinner."

John watched the door close behind Maggie as she walked into the kitchen. He kicked himself for having feet that lay dormant when they should move, and a tongue that ran when it shouldn't.

Maggie placed her hands on the island counter in the kitchen, leaned heavily, and took a very deep breath, letting it out slowly. *"You don't need this kind of complication,"* she thought, *"not now, not with him."*

The sound of ATV's and whooping caused John to abandon his thoughts and trot out to the deck. Gomer, CJ and Harley rode up to the lodge. Gomer was waving a vial in his hand screaming about finding gold. John walked down and stood near the fire pit, thoroughly enjoying Gomer's exuberance.

"Look at all this!" Gomer exclaimed as he flashed the vial around to Turk and Willie. "It's nuggets we picked out, and we haven't even panned the stuff from the sluice! You guys really screwed up, leaving."

In response, Turk held up a bottle of amber liquor and said, "Good for you, little buddy, but I've got a bigger bottle of gold right here."

"Bet we didn't sweat as much as you, either," Willie added.

Gomer looked crestfallen at the lack of excitement his friends exhibited, so John stepped up and asked to take a look. He rolled the vial to spread out the nuggets. Even in the overcast daylight, they glistened brightly.

"Oh, hell yeah, those are nice jewelry nuggets," John said honestly.

"Yeah," CJ agreed, "and Harley says jewelry nuggets are worth twice as much as flake gold."

"It is," Harley said as he walked up, "and they're sure to turn the head of any babe you show them to." He turned to John, "Can you handle the panning tubs? I'm so hungry the south end of a northbound bear sounds good."

John led CJ and Gomer to the panning tubs and showed them how to process the concentrates. The two clients became even more excited when gold appeared in their pans. They were slow, and Harley had time to eat and join them at the tubs before they were finished. After finishing up at the panning tubs the men went to the lodge and weighed the day's gold. It was a quarter of an ounce, all totaled.

The Wild Bunch spent the evening in camp celebrating Gomer and CJ's success. They were perfectly content to sit at the fire pit and drink while passing around the vial and planning the next day's adventure. Even Turk, after enough lubrication and the opportunity to examine what his friends had found, confessed a desire to try his hand at highbanking. The hot topic for discussion was speculating how much more gold they could accumulate before leaving. Gomer called Harley down to the fire pit and posed the question.

"I really don't know," Harley answered. "You're in a good spot, and I'll keep raking down new dirt until the pay runs out. The gold is found in pockets, so it could play out. If so, we'll move you."

"Sounds to me," Turk said skeptically, "you just salted the dirt for today."

"You tell me if that makes sense," Harley replied. "Why would we throw gold on the ground for you to find? We already have your money."

"Well, shit," Turk mumbled, "you've got me there."

Harley left the clients to their conversation and returned to the lodge. When he walked in, John was talking softly on his cell phone on the other side of the room, away from where Maggie sat.

"What's the deal?" Harley asked Maggie. "Kind of late for a social call."

"It's Cynthia. At first, it sounded like we'll have short trip clients next week, but after that, he started talking low and walked over there."

"Bad news?"

"Well, Harley, I wouldn't know," Maggie answered in a patronizing tone, "I'm not in on the conversation."

Harley scowled and walked toward the door, pausing just before he stepped out. "You know what? Just once, I'd like to have a conversation with you that didn't degenerate into an insult. Tell John I'm working on the generator."

John finished his conversation with Cynthia shortly after Harley left, and returned to the table.

"So, we have extra clients next week?" Maggie asked.

"Yeah, we do. Four of them. Where's Harley?"

"He's out sulking at the generator."

John paused for a moment of thought. He wished Harley was present, but decided to continue without him. "There's more news. They found Kells this evening."

Maggie's face paled and she caught her breath. "He's dead, isn't he?"

"I'm afraid so, Maggie. I'm sorry."

Maggie laid her hands on the table in front of her, and looked down. She rubbed the thumb of one hand across the back of the other, absentmindedly, as she stared at them blankly. After several minutes, she raised her head.

"You know, at one time Mark really was a very fun and charming man." Tears welled in her eyes as she continued, "But that man got lost in the drugs, and I couldn't help him find a way back. I tried. Really."

She lowered her head again, and a tear dropped onto her hand to be rubbed in by her thumb. John sat uncomfortably, not knowing exactly what to do, or say. He remembered Maggie telling him she never wanted to see Kells again, but knew reality often changes sentiment. He watched quietly as she sat, staring at her hands. No more tears fell.

"If you want, I can call Reeder right now," John finally offered, "and he can fly you back tomorrow."

Maggie looked up and wiped her eyes. "Thanks, but no. There's no point to it. What little there was between us died before he did. Besides, if I left, you and Harley would either starve, or kill a client with food poisoning." She forced a smile and stood up. "I'm going to go for a walk, I think."

John followed her out onto the porch and watched her walk past the fire pit, with Dawg at her side. He hoped there wouldn't be any catcalls from the Wild Bunch. As it turned out, his concern was unwarranted. Turk had fallen into a drunken sleep, and the rest of the gang were completely absorbed in taking turns having their pictures taken as they dangled a cigar from their flies, in front of Turk's face.

"It's always good to have friends," John thought as he walked to the back of the lodge to find Harley.

As John expected, Harley's initial reaction to the news of Kells' death was the polar opposite of Maggie's.

"Good! The son of a bitch deserved it. Just one more thing to check off my to-do list. How'd he die?"

"Car wreck, apparently."

"Oh, no," Harley gasped. His cavalier manner changed immediately, and he quickly asked, "Anyone else hurt?"

"No, he was by himself. He went off the road and rolled several times. Guess he was flying low when he lost control. You know the rumor mill though, Cynthia says there's speculation he was run off the road."

"Does Maggie know how he died?"

"No. She didn't ask, and I didn't see that it mattered."

"Well, unless she asks, she doesn't need to know. Okay?"

"Sure, but why is how he died important?"

"It just is," Harley replied. "It's a history thing, something best left alone." Harley turned, and without any further comment, walked away.

Fueled by their success at finding gold, the Wild Bunch got into a routine of getting up late, working the highbankers until the late afternoon, and then drinking away the evening. Harley let it be known that Maggie had lost a close friend, and no further off-color comments were heard from them. John decided Turk had some decency in him after all.

Whatever issues Maggie may have had about Kells and his

death, she seemed to have worked through them during her solitary walk. John didn't know where she'd gone, or how long she had walked. He waited in the lodge long after talking to Harley, finally falling asleep on the couch. When he awoke, she was in the kitchen, starting her day. She looked tired, but assured John that she was fine.

It was the day before the Wild Bunch was due to leave, and they were busily working the highbankers in an effort to increase their take. John sat in the warm sun and watched them washing dirt, ready to rake down more tailings, if needed. Harley was at the lodge working on the generator, which had been refusing to run. With the exception of the generator, things were finally going smoothly, John thought. He was thinking about the next day's trip back to Nikiski to attend the Grilling for God event when a float plane buzzed the camp, cruised over the valley, and turned back toward the lake. John thought about riding back to the lodge, but knew if he was needed, Harley would ride out to get him. Besides, it was almost time for the Wild Bunch to quit for the day.

Less than an hour after the plane had flown over, the Wild Bunch decided to call it quits. John shut down the pumps to the highbankers and walked over to join them while they checked the riffles for nuggets. There was a bet between the two pairs on who would find the biggest nugget.

"Ha! In your face, Gomer!" Willie shouted. "You won't never top this one."

"You losers get ready to pay up," Turk added.

John looked at the nugget Willie held in his palm. It was definitely the biggest they had found so far, but still worth less than the two-hundred dollar bet.

"I'll bet you scuzzballs pulled that one from our pile," CJ shot back. "It looks like one I dropped."

Trash talk flew the entire time the Wild Bunch cleaned their concentrates from the highbankers. As John lifted the two buckets containing the concentrates onto his ATV, the plane that had flown in an hour earlier flew back over the valley and turned back toward the inlet. He wondered, again, who it had been, then followed the Wild Bunch as they made their last ride to the panning tubs.

The Wild Bunch had become proficient with their panning technique, and John didn't feel it was necessary to stay. He was curious to find out who had flown in, and excused himself to head up to the lodge. Dawg stood at the screen door to the lodge, looking in. John had to push him aside to get in. The main room was empty, but he could hear a heated conversation in the kitchen. John quietly approached the window into the kitchen and stopped short. He didn't necessarily want to eavesdrop, but was tired of playing referee for his staff's spats. He thought if he let them hash things out, it might be for the best.

"Get out!" Maggie demanded.

"Come on, Mag," Harley pleaded, "it's been almost five years. When are you going to forgive me?"

"When you stay the hell out of my life! Get out!"

"I know it was my fault. Do you really think that thought doesn't haunt me every day? You know, I really do love you. I only want the best for you. I worry about you."

"Goddamn it! Don't touch me!" Maggie sounded almost hysterical.

"Just a hug because you're upset."

"*Get off me!*"

The urgency in Maggie's voice launched John from his spot. He slammed through the kitchen door and saw Harley holding Maggie from behind, his arms wrapped tightly around her. Maggie struggled to wrench free of his grip. A feeling of protective jealousy swept over John at the sight.

"Back off, Harley!" John ordered.

Harley looked at John with surprise and released his grip. When he did, Maggie spun around and slapped him hard enough to force him a step backward. John immediately jumped forward between them, facing Harley, and Harley took another step back.

"You're jumping into the middle of something that's none of your *goddamned business*," Harley growled.

"When it's out here, it *is* my business," John snapped. "Now, back off and get out."

The two men stood facing each other, each breathing deeply from the tension of the moment. Finally, after glancing past John at Maggie, Harley turned and punched the door to stomp out of the lodge. John turned around and laid his hand on Maggie's shoulder.

"Are you okay?" he asked, trying to look into her eyes.

Maggie responded by slapping his hand off her shoulder. "Harley's right about one thing," she said quietly, "you're meddling in something that's none of your business."

"You're crying. Did he hurt you?"

Maggie laughed bitterly, "No, I'm pissed. Just leave me alone."

"Are you sure?" John prodded gently. "You want to talk?"

"Oh, for God's sake, *stop hovering!* The both of you! Now, get out of my kitchen, and stay out!"

John turned and followed Harley's route out of the lodge. "Well that sucks," he grumbled loudly to himself on the way, "all my life I thought the hero at least got a kiss."

Harley didn't show up for dinner. Once the Wild Bunch was fed and happily ensconced at the fire pit, John decided to go looking for him. The rush of jealousy he'd felt when he saw Harley with his arms wrapped around Maggie had been replaced with a feeling of guilt. He needed Harley's help to make Last Chance work, that was true, but beyond that, Harley had become his friend. John told himself that friendship had to take a higher place than anything he might possibly feel for the feisty young woman. When he told Maggie where he was going, she put a leftover steak from dinner in a hoagie roll and wrapped it up.

"Take this," she said, planting the packet in John's hand, "Harley would rather eat than fight."

As he suspected, John found Harley working one of the highbankers the Wild Bunch had been using. He didn't look up from his work when John parked the ATV and turned it off. John surveyed the area. Harley had been very busy working off his anger. Not only was the pile left behind by the Wild Bunch gone, a large hole had been shoveled into the tailings.

"Hey!" John called out.

Harley turned, stabbed his shovel into the ground and leaned on it. "What?" he demanded.

"Who flew in this afternoon?"

"The Troopers. They wanted to talk to Maggie about Kells."

"About what?"

"I don't know. They told me to wait outside, and Maggie

didn't say anything except that in the process of asking their questions, they told her how Kells died."

John considered asking why Harley was so fixated on how Kells died, but decided if peace was to be made, it was best to avoid the subject. Instead, he waved the wrapped sandwich at his friend,

"This is for you. Maggie sent it." Harley pulled his shovel up and turned to go back to work. "It's steak on a hoagie," John persisted, holding the foil packet out. "The steak is really good."

"No shit? A steak sandwich?" Harley responded. He let the shovel drop and walked over to the ATV to take the offering. "Seasoned with arsenic?"

"I don't think so. I didn't keel over from mine, and she seems equally pissed at both of us."

"I'm glad to see someone else on her shit list," Harley said around a mouthful of bread and steak, "I could use the company."

"I'm not going to ask."

"Don't."

"Okay, but here's the deal: I'm going to Nikiski tomorrow, and I need to know things aren't going to get ugly while I'm gone. Things looked a little," John paused to find the right word, "shall we say, intense, earlier. I need your word you won't let things get of hand again."

Harley bit off and chewed another big bite before answering. "I can do that. But I want you to do something for me."

"What?"

"I want you to talk to Maggie for me."

"You just told me to stay the hell out of your business!"

Harley gulped down the bite of sandwich. "This is different. I want you to ask her royal highness not to spew venom on me every time I try to be pleasant. It hurts my feelings. Both of them."

"Pepperdine, you ask a lot."

Harley declined John's invitation to go back to the lodge for dominoes. He wished John luck in dealing with Maggie, and went back to washing dirt. John found Maggie sitting at the edge of the lake, by the dock.

"Mind if I sit a moment with you?"

"Yes," she answered coolly.

"Well, tough shit. I'm the boss," John replied, sitting down several feet away. Maggie started to get up. "Don't leave. Please." When she settled back down John continued. "I'm here with a request from Harley."

Maggie rolled her eyes. "A little high school, don't you think?"

"Lady," John said sharply, "I think your whole relationship is way high school. And I'm sick of playing referee to a couple of kids."

"Fine. What's the request?"

"He wants you to let up with your acid tongue. Frankly, I don't think that's so unreasonable."

"You want me to be nice to him?"

"Oh, hell no! I'm not looking for miracles here. Just don't spit in his eye every chance you get."

Maggie giggled. "Okay, but it's for you, not him."

John and Harley greeted the new clients at the dock the next morning and explained how John would be gone the first day of their visit. John settled into the co-pilot's seat after helping Harley pour the Wild Bunch into the Beaver. It had been a long last night of celebration for them. Reeder warned everyone there would be turbulence along the way and, after looking his passengers over, made sure each of them had a barf bag readily available. During the worst of the bouncing John glanced back to see how it was affecting the hung-over clients. The Wild Bunch were all asleep, or passed out, their heads jiggling in unison like four bobblehead dolls.

"You going to the Grilling for God thing?" John asked Reeder over the intercom.

"No, way! Last time I went, I had heartburn for a week. Besides, I've got a group of four going to Crescent Lake at two."

"You're a busy man, Reeder."

"Yup, the only time I get a chance for any shuteye this time of year is when I'm hauling you."

On the final approach to the strip at Nikiski a light flashed on the control panel. John turned to Reeder quickly, "What's that?"

"Just a safety reminder to put the wheels down on the floats."

Until Reeder mentioned it, John hadn't even thought about the fact the Beaver was on floats, and they were going to land on a paved strip. "I imagine landing on the strip with floats would be unpleasant."

"Not nearly as bad as landing on the water with the wheels down," Reeder replied seriously. "Floats on a hard surface slide, but wheels into water makes the bird flip. There's been a number of pilots that didn't walk away from the wheels on water thing. Lots of pilots won't use the amphib floats because of it."

When the Beaver touched down John noticed how much higher the plane sat off the runway. The extra height was even more apparent when it came time to unload. The hungover passengers slid gingerly from the top of the floats, groaning in the effort, instead of jumping to the ground.

There were two hours to kill before the barbecue contest started, so instead of leaving the Wild Bunch to wait on a cab back to Kenai, John offered to drive them in. It was not a Kodak moment at the airport. They were too busy struggling just to stay upright to offer anything more than a mumbled good-bye. John left them at the curb and felt sorry for whoever would be seated next to them.

John drove back to Nikiski after picking up spare fuel filters for the generator, which would fix the recent problems, according to Harley. A throng of people filled the parking lot from McCrane Mercantile to the Shuffle Inn and past, to the Chevron station beyond the bar. Amid the milling crowd were the volunteers running about and the contestants at their grills. The parking lots had been cordoned off, forcing John to park in a vacant lot down the highway.

John waded into the crowd and was greeted warmly by several people, some of which he didn't know. He pressed on toward the bar, hoping for a chance to see Doorway. Parents of youth group kids stopped him along the way, introduced themselves and thanked him profusely for his support. Since he didn't know any of the parents, John could only assume they were cuing off his hat with the Last Chance Adventures logo. Everyone he spoke with urged him to get his sampling tickets quickly. One father, obviously a veteran of many events, gave him strategy advice.

"When the tasting starts, you want to be in a line for brisket," he said quite seriously, "the briskets always run out first. After that, go for the ribs, then the pulled pork. Don't worry about the chicken, there's always plenty of time for the chicken."

John thanked the man for his advice and snaked his way toward the ticket tables set up in front of McCrane Mercantile. Billy McCrane was ramrodding the sales. Youth group members were swapping tickets for cash as fast as they could.

"Don't forget, folks," Billy said loudly, "one ticket will get you a taste of the competition, or one of the sides. You don't get both with one ticket. You can also buy a hotdog from the youth group grill for a ticket. Two bucks a ticket, or six for ten."

John picked a line to wait in and listened to the conversations around him. The atmosphere was like standing in the midway of a carnival, except the hawkers and the crowd knew each other. When the line moved forward far enough for Billy to catch sight of him, he pointed John out and asked everyone to give a round of applause for his sponsorship. The crowd enthusiastically complied. John raised his hand and waved, wishing he was standing anywhere else.

"How many?" Billy asked when John got to the table.

"I'll take six."

"There's fifteen in the competition, John. You've got to at least try them all!" Billy insisted.

"I don't think I can eat that much."

"Don't worry," the man behind John said sourly, "with the puny helpings they hand out, you might still starve."

The people standing in line had a good laugh at the remark.

"It's a fund raiser, Fred," Billy retorted. "You want a big meal? Try the Villa."

The same people who shared a laugh at Fred's comment, had another at his expense.

"Alright," John said, "you better give me eighteen tickets."

Fred nudged John, leaned close to him and said quietly, "You'll still have room for dessert."

With eighteen tickets in hand, John headed toward the shortest line he could see. His progress was interrupted by a younger man wearing a cap with "KPD" across the front of it. The man removed his arm from around the waist of the pretty blonde at his side and held it out.

"John Barstow? I'm Trevor Williams, Harley's brother."

"Oh, yeah, the cop that arrested him," John said smiling. "Good to finally meet you. Harley's told me a lot about you. I just haven't had much opportunity to get into Kenai."

Trevor introduced his girlfriend, Carole, to John then asked to have a private word with him. Carole wandered off to take a place in the shortest line for brisket, and Trevor pulled John over to a less crowded area.

"I've been trying to call Harley. He doesn't answer, and hasn't returned my calls."

"His cell phone is dead," John explained, "the generator crapped out several days ago, and he hasn't been able to recharge it. You can reach him on the radio, if it's important."

"It is, but not appropriate for the radio. I've got some information about Kells."

"Yeah, he's dead, we know."

"No, there's more to it than that. This won't be public for a few days, so don't mention it to anyone except Harley and Maggie. The rumors about Kells being run off the road are true. A vehicle with damage that would indicate a brushing collision with his car has been found."

"Anybody arrested?"

"Not yet, the Troopers are waiting on lab tests to confirm a paint match. But the suspect is associated with a gang out of Anchorage with ties to the meth lab that was busted on information Kells supplied."

John thought about the visit from the Troopers. He concluded their visit must have been strictly to gather information, not provide it. His heart pounded.

"Is Maggie in danger? The Troopers interviewed her yesterday."

"I wouldn't think so. The Troopers probably just wanted to ask about anything Kells may have mentioned to her."

Trevor's noncommittal answer didn't decrease John's concern for Maggie's safety. If the Troopers thought Maggie might know something, so might the dealers in Anchorage. John wanted to know what Maggie had discussed with the Troopers. He glanced at his watch and saw it was still before one o'clock. He handed his tickets to Trevor.

"Do me a favor, Trevor. Hold onto these, and if I'm not back in half an hour, give them to someone who looks hungry."

John left Trevor standing with two long strings of tickets and a puzzled look. At the airstrip he found Reeder stretched out on the couch in the flight shack, taking a nap.

"What the hell are you doing here?" Reeder demanded as he fished his glasses from his shirt pocket.

"Do you suppose I could hitch a ride back on your two o'clock?"

Reeder chuckled. "The eats were that bad?"

"Never got a chance to try anything."

"What's up, then?"

"I can't say. I'd just feel better if I got back to Last Chance. Can you haul me over with the two o'clocks?"

"It's fine with me. I'll sleep in an extra hour tomorrow morning if I don't have to drag your ass over. But the booked party has to agree to it, and you get dropped off last."

There was no objection from the scheduled group, and John was back at Last Chance three hours later. Maggie greeted the plane at the dock, and her surprise at seeing John was readily evident.

"I think that's pretty chicken," Maggie said after Reeder had taxied away from the dock.

"What?"

"You don't even trust us to get along for one day?"

"Well, I know it usually takes you two days to get really worked up," John said with a grin, "but I didn't want to risk it. Where's Harley? Oh, no! I'm too late, you killed him!"

"I'm serious, John. It's insulting."

"Okay, the truth is, I heard something from Trevor Williams that I wanted to let you and Harley know about."

Maggie looked at John skeptically. "And what could be so important that you came back a day early?"

"The Troopers are getting a case together to arrest someone for running Kells off the road." Maggie only nodded her head, so John continued, "But what I'm more interested in is your conversation with the Troopers."

"Why would that matter?"

"Maggie, the guy that ran Kells off the road is part of a gang out of Anchorage. He eliminated Kells because they apparently thought Kells was a threat. If they think you're a threat, you could be next!"

Maggie crossed her arms and gave John a little smile. "You're worried. That's sweet."

"Damn straight I'm worried! Aren't you?"

"No, I'm not," Maggie said calmly. "Mark never discussed what 'business' deals he had going. In fact, he didn't discuss meth with me at all, unless I brought up his use. And you saw how those conversations went. I was no help to the Troopers at all. They asked questions I couldn't answer, and showed me pictures of people I didn't recognize. I was a complete disappointment to them."

A long sigh of relief escaped John, but he covered it with, "To think of all that barbecue I missed. I'm starving. Isn't it about time for dinner?"

"Sorry, I didn't plan on you," Maggie said. She playfully grabbed John's arm as they headed to lodge and asked, "How's a Spam sandwich sound?"

"I'm sure Harley will love it."

The news about the pending arrest was not nearly as exciting to Harley as seeing the new fuel filters for the generator. John was glad Harley didn't inquire about the motive for his early return. The prospect of trying to explain the real reason for his irrational behavior, particularly to Harley, made him feel uncomfortable.

CHAPTER 13

The first short trip clients were talking about a return trip when they left. John called Cynthia to congratulate her on the success of her idea. The money expended to set up the local advertising campaign had been recouped with the first group. Still, even if every available week was filled out with short trip clients, the probability of showing a profit on the season was slim. The thought of losing Last Chance was bitter to John. He thought, perhaps, his initial impulse to pass on the agreement would have been the better choice. It would have been better to have never seen the life he was enjoying so much, than to know what he stood to lose.

Harley introduced John to the Burlingtons before leaving for Kenai to perform his community service. Sam and Polly were exactly as Harley had described. They were perfectly content to sit with a cup of coffee and visit, or go for walks. As Sam explained it, "I don't need to mine, anymore. I've washed enough dirt and moved enough rocks to satisfy me."

Having the Burlingtons for guests made for a relaxed pace. Aside from catching up on routine maintenance chores, there was little to do. Sam frequently accompanied John while he tended to camp business. When he did, Polly stayed with Maggie at the lodge, which was a pleasant change for Maggie from the regular all male company. In the evenings the four of them got together and visited. The conversations with Sam and Polly offered a chance for John to learn more about his uncle. Sam and Hardrock had been good friends from the time they met working as roustabouts during the construction of the Cook Inlet oil platforms in 1966.

"Neither one of us had any skills but a strong back," Sam related with a chuckle, "but we were willing to learn. There were five platforms under construction that year, and any warm body willing to work long hours in bad conditions could find a job. After three years things started to slow down, and by then we'd had enough of the oil patch."

"What did you do after that?" John asked. "When did you start mining?"

"Well, I worked as a welder, something I picked up while working on the platforms. Hardrock tried his hand at crabbing."

"You mean like the guys on that TV show, up in the Bering Sea?"

"Oh, good lord no. Used to be, there was a pretty good commercial fishery for king and Tanner crabs out of Homer and Seldovia, in the Kachemak Bay."

"I never thought of my uncle as a seagoing man."

"He wasn't," Sam said, shaking his head. "Got sick anytime the water got rough. He made it for two seasons before he gave up crabbing and went to working as a mechanic. Now that, he had a knack for."

Sam went on to explain that eventually he and Hardrock decided they needed more adventure. One day, Hardrock suggested they go north, around Fairbanks, to see what life offered. Between Sam's welding and Hardrock's mechanic skills, they found plenty of work with small commercial mining operations.

"And that's where the name 'Hardrock' came from," John said, remembering what Harley had told him.

"Yes, but we were working a placer operation, like this one."

"I don't get it. I thought the term hardrock is used for lode mining, mining solid rock."

Sam laughed loudly. "That's the beauty of it. Hardrock kept talking about finding the mother lode for the placers, and how rich we'd get if we did."

"So it was kind of a joke?"

"Definitely. Your uncle really didn't want a thing to do with lode mining."

"Why not?"

"He was claustrophobic." Sam laughed loudly again. "Once, at a mine north of Fairbanks, they were working a drift tunnel in the permafrost, and Hardrock went in to see what a drift looked like."

"Drift tunnel?" John interrupted.

"When you're placer mining in frozen ground, you can follow a pay streak by running a shaft down to the pay layer, then follow the pay layer digging a tunnel sideways, just like drifts in lode mining. It saves the effort of stripping away so much overburden." John nodded his understanding, and Sam continued. "Anyway, Hardrock didn't even make it to the drift. He only made it about ten feet down the shaft to the drift and started screaming to get out. That's when we all started calling him 'Hardrock.' I don't think he ever went underground again."

A smile crept across John's face thinking how he would have to share that information with Harley. Somehow, he'd imagined a much more exciting story behind his uncle's nick name.

"It was working at that mine," Sam continued, "that put the idea in our heads to have our own mine. Actually, it was Hardrock's idea."

"So, that's when he got Last Chance?"

"No, this place came later. No, we worked for several different operations before we decided to try getting into it for ourselves. It was kind of an apprentice program. We finally ended up working for a guy named Kettleson with a mine on Julian Creek, southwest of McGrath. He was an old codger who had been working the place since the twenties. He wanted to retire, so we bought him out. That was in 1976, the year before Polly and me got married."

"If I'd have only known," Polly interjected, "I thought I was marrying a rich miner! I didn't realize I'd be chief cook and bottle washer. Let that be a lesson to you, Maggie."

Polly followed her comment with a wink at Maggie. John glanced in Maggie's direction and thought he saw her blush.

"Anyway," Sam continued, ignoring the interruption, "when the price of gold started climbing, it sure enough turned out to be a smart move."

"Where'd you go in the winter?" John asked.

"Sam and I stayed in McGrath since my family was there," Polly answered. "Hardrock always went back to Nikiski."

"Hardrock never did warm up to McGrath," Sam added, "his heart was in Nikiski. So, it wasn't any great surprise to me when he told me about this place and asked me to buy him out of the Kettleson."

"So you bought him out of a successful mine, and he bought Last Chance." John shook his head.

"I told him it was a damn fool's errand, but he didn't listen. A few years back, we sold the Kettleson for more than anyone could have ever imagined. I offered Hardrock a portion of the money, it only seemed fair, but he said he was happy with the original deal."

John thought back to the single encounter with his uncle, and the way he had talked about Last Chance. There was no doubt in his mind that Hardrock had gone to his grave knowing what a good deal he'd made.

A perk to having the Burlingtons as guests was that they left the lodge each evening long before Maggie and John were accustomed to retiring. John relished the time alone with Maggie, talking quietly while they looked out over the lake in the dusk of the lingering Alaskan twilight. In the course of their conversations John learned quite a bit about her. He consciously avoided Harley as a subject, ostensibly to prevent Maggie from shutting down the conversations. The truth was, however, that deep inside he didn't want to face the guilt over his attraction to her. He told her about his failed marriage, his drinking, losing his job and his last girlfriend. She described growing up in Alaska, watching her father kill himself with drugs and alcohol, dealing with a step-father who worked on the North Slope while her mother ran around, and how Hardrock had been the only reliable adult in her childhood.

"What happens after the season is over?" John asked. They were standing at the railing of the deck, watching the lake shimmer in the twilight, listening to the haunting call of loons echo from the far shore.

Maggie nudged John with her shoulder. "I guess you'll be laying me off."

"Well, you haven't exactly been an exemplary employee. Lots of conflict with the rest of the staff." John leaned sideways into her gently, and felt her warmth. His pulse quickened with the touch. Maggie didn't move. Instead, she turned and smiled.

"Seriously, John, I want to thank you for everything you've done. You didn't have to help, but you did. You're a lot like Hardrock that way."

Not knowing what to say, John turned away to look out over the lake. Alarms and feelings of guilt ricocheted in his head. *"Don't do it! Think about Harley! You can't!"*

Just as his common sense was gaining the upper hand, Maggie put her arm around his neck and pressed her lips softly on his cheek.

"Sometimes, the hero *does* get a kiss," she whispered in his ear.

"Oh, you heard that the other day, did you?"

Maggie nodded slowly. John looked into her eyes, and for the first time, saw something other than fierce independence. He wrapped his arms around her and gave his best shot at what he thought a real hero's kiss should be. Nothing had ever seemed so sweet, until Maggie pushed him away.

"Mr. Barstow! That was entirely inappropriate!" Maggie gasped.

John stepped back, confused. "What the hell?"

"In view of the clients, anyway."

Maggie grabbed John's hand and pulled him into the lodge. Pausing only for a longer, sensual kiss, she led him down the hall to her room. John closed the door behind them while Maggie peeled off her shirt. She quickly wrapped herself around him and pressed eagerly for another kiss. John ran his hands gently over her warm, soft skin. They stayed intertwined, with John running his fingertips back and forth along her bra strap for moments lost in the passion until Maggie leaned back.

"John, it snaps in the front."

"Oh. Right. Let's see what happens if I do this."

Maggie giggled, then pulled John onto her bed.

Muffled conversation drifting through the partially opened door to Maggie's room woke John. Maggie was talking to the Burlingtons from the kitchen. John blinked from the light filling Maggie's room, and the previous night's passion rolled through his mind.

"*Oh, shit!*" John screamed inwardly. "*What have I done? What do I say to Harley?*"

It occurred to him the future could wait, it was the present he needed to deal with. He slipped from the bed and quietly closed the door before quickly pulling on his clothes. The door to the back lean-to offered a discreet escape out of the lodge. He walked along the outside of the lodge to the deck and entered through the front door. Empty plates sat before Sam and Polly, and they sat sipping what little remained of their coffee. John nodded to them as he sat down, too rattled to utter a greeting.

"Mornin', John," Sam said, "you're up late. Have a hard time sleeping last night?" Sam jumped at the end of his question. "Damn, woman, that hurt."

"Mind your P's and Q's, old man," Polly chided.

John glanced from face to face. Sam winked. Polly smiled sweetly. Maggie blushed. "What did you say?" he asked Maggie directly.

"Nothing!" she blurted, "I didn't say a..."

"C'mon, kids," Sam interrupted, "we're old, not stupid. Polly had the situation figured out the first night we were here." Sam turned to his wife, "Old woman, let's go for a walk. You kids just stay here and enjoy each other."

Sam and Polly waved as they stepped out of the lodge, and Polly admonish her husband as they walked down the stairs, "Don't you let those youngsters give you any ideas, you old fart."

John leaned on the table, face in hands, and groaned. He felt Maggie kiss the back of his neck.

"I don't think they have a problem with it," she giggled.

"But I do."

"What's that supposed to mean?" Maggie sounded hurt.

"You don't see a problem with this? Not a single problem?"

"Well, I didn't until about two seconds ago, when someone got a sudden attack of the bachelor regrets."

"What about Harley? You don't see a problem there?"

"Harley?" Maggie snorted in disgust. "What the *hell* does he have to do with anything?"

John studied Maggie closely and didn't want to believe she could be so cold. He thought about the first time he met her, and how she seemed to have multiple personalities that came and went with total unpredictability.

"Are you serious? What do you think he'll say? 'That's great John! You're the boss! Thanks for losing the mine, and by the way, why don't you take my ex-girl when you leave!' I don't think so."

"*Ex-girl?* Is that what you think?"

"My bad," John said sarcastically, "I guess it's ex-wife. I wouldn't know with the way you two avoid talking about your relationship."

"You are totally out of line, mister!" Maggie said in a raised voice.

"You know what?" John snapped back as he stood up, "I think we finally both see it the same way."

John turned toward the door, but pulled up short when Maggie shouted, "He's my brother, you idiot!" John stood rooted to his spot and Maggie corrected herself softly, "Well, half-brother, really."

Turning slowly to compensate for his spinning head, John walked back to the table and sank into a chair.

"Brother? Really? But I thought... how could..." his voice trailed off in confusion.

"Do you remember how I told you my real dad died?" John nodded dumbstruck. "And how my mom got remarried?" Again, John's head bobbed up and down. "That was Harley's dad, my step-father."

"So you're Harley and Trevor's half-sister," John mumbled.

"No, not Trevor's," Maggie corrected. "We're not related at all. In fact, we even dated. But it just seemed, I don't know, weird, so it didn't go far."

John rubbed his forehead trying to process the information, then asked, "Could you give me a brief description of the family forest, here?"

"Okay. My dad died, and Harley's mom and dad got a

divorce. My mom married Harley's dad, making us steps. Harley's mom married Trevor's dad, making Harley and Trevor steps, but Trevor and I aren't related at all."

John let her explanation soak in before letting out a long sigh, followed by, "I'm sorry, that's just plain fucked up."

"I don't know about that, but I guess it could be confusing the first time around."

"Why didn't you tell me all this before now?"

"I thought Harley already had."

"Oh, no," John said holding up his hands, "I learned early on not to ask either of you about the other. But now that things are out in the open, I do want to know what the issue is between you two. Since he's not an ex-anything, what could Harley have done to earn your everlasting spite?"

"It's complicated," Maggie replied. "Are you sure you want to hear it?"

"Lady, I just made it through your family tree, which, by the way, is more like a kudzu vine. I can take on anything."

Maggie took a deep breath before responding. "About five years ago, I was engaged to Harley's best friend, Mike Radner. To be brief, Mike died in a crash. He and Harley were racing each other on the highway when Mike lost control. He was probably dead before the truck even stopped rolling."

The importance Harley ascribed to the way Kells died was now clear to John. "And you blame Harley?" he asked.

Maggie shrugged noncommittally. "I did at first, but it was just as much Mike's fault. No, the issue is that Harley has never forgiven himself, and he's got some damned idea that he has to make it up to Mike, somehow."

"I don't get it. How could that offend you?"

"It wouldn't, except every time someone looks twice at me, Harley is there to point out they aren't good enough to replace Mike. Nobody has been able to measure up. Eventually, Harley creates enough bullshit, enough friction, to sour the relationship. In his mind, he's earning redemption. I've moved on, but Harley won't."

"I guess Kells was the exception."

"Yeah. Ironic, isn't it? Harley couldn't run Kells off, but Harley was finally right."

John stood up and wrapped his arms around Maggie. "So, where does that leave us?"

"I'm hoping," Maggie answered softly, "where we left off last night."

The morning of the last day of the Burlingtons' stay, Sam accompanied John when he rode out to rake down tailings for the next clients. John welcomed the opportunity to hear the old miner's opinion of the operation and wanted his input on an idea he had been rolling around for a few days.

"Sam, is there any way to work the tailings to make the mine pay?"

"You mean like a commercial mine? No. That's why I tried to talk Hardrock out of buying it. There's very little virgin dirt left on the claim, and getting the equipment you'd need to operate commercially wouldn't be cost effective."

"But we know there's gold in the tailings," John countered.

"Sure, there's gold in the tailings, maybe lots of it in certain pockets. The old methods weren't very efficient. Most of the small stuff was missed, and even some big stuff, but you'd still need to pay for the equipment to work the tailings, and transportation to get it here. Another thing, the claim may be patented, but it wouldn't be possible to run a commercial operation without impacting Gold Creek and the lake. You probably couldn't get the permits you'd need. No, this is strictly a recreational mine now. Hardrock knew that."

Sam's response wasn't unexpected. Even the Sunshine Boys, who had worked most of their waking hours, took out less in gold value than they had paid for the week's stay. With his last good idea squelched, John told himself he needed to realize he was grasping at straws, and to just make the best out of the season he could. He produced the map with the notes Hardrock had made and showed it to Sam.

"I was thinking about moving the highbankers from here, to this point," John said, pointing to a location at the far end of the tailings. "We haven't tried that spot yet, but there's a star by it. Harley says it means Hardrock thought it was better than average."

"The notes indicate fine gold, heavy with black sands," Sam said after studying the map.

"I know, it's strange. The current setups produced quite a bit of chunky flake, and a few jewelry nuggets, like the notes indicated, yet it didn't rate a star. Do you suppose Hardrock gave a star to the other location based on suspected potential?"

"It's possible. He may have been thinking the larger gold had settled deeper, below the fines, but that's not likely. Let me look at that map again."

John handed over the map, and Sam opened it fully to skim over all the notes. He then went back over the map and carefully read each of the notes marked with a star. Eventually, a grin appeared on Sam's face, and he pulled John over.

"Look at the notes again. Do you see anything in common with all those starred locations?"

John studied each of the notes before answering, "They are all noted as being heavy with black sands."

"Exactly. What do you do with your black sands?"

"Well, we separate them from the panning tubs and store them in the workshop. Harley insists on it because that's what Hardrock did."

Sam smiled broadly. "Your uncle was a crafty old buzzard."

"How so?"

"Any of your clients want the black sands?"

"Well, no." John paused, then corrected himself, "No, wait, the Johnsons did. They were the first clients of the season."

"I'll bet they were the only experienced miners you've had. Right?"

"As far as I know. Why?"

"Because black sands can easily contain more than twice the amount of free gold recovered. That's particularly true if the visible gold is fine. Some black sands run as high as thirty percent gold, by weight."

"So what you're telling me is that my uncle might have been getting two ounces of gold for every ounce of fine gold the clients took out?" Sam nodded in response. "Well, Wes did tell me my uncle had figured out how to mine the miners."

"Wes does have a way with words. That's a very good way to describe it."

The two men went over the map together. After some discussion, Sam suggested leaving the existing highbankers where they were located, and setting up two additional highbankers at locations marked with notes indicating the fine gold and heavy black sand. That way, Sam's logic went, John could move clients between the locations if they weren't happy with what they were finding. It would also ensure pre-positioned setups for any short trip clients, which were much more likely not to have any mining experience. He offered to help John retrieve the equipment and help him set it up.

At the workshop, while John loaded the highbanking equipment, Sam wandered around as if he were looking for something. When John finished loading everything onto the ATV trailer he joined Sam at the back of the workshop. Sam was going through the contents of a large trunk. John asked what the trunk held, explaining he hadn't taken the time to fully explore everything scattered about the large shop.

"Basically, it's a crude smelting kit," Sam replied. "This trunk has everything you need to extract gold from black sands."

"Really? We could do that out here?"

"Sure, no problem. It's not a complicated process. There's everything you need to do it right here: magnets, crucibles, a simple smelter, propane torch and most importantly, the flux. There's even a mortar and pestle to grind the sands. If Hardrock was as clever as I suspect, he checked the sands occasionally."

"Could you show me how to do it?"

Sam nodded, "I'll need to dry some out before we run them. You take care of the highbankers, and I'll get things set up here."

The very idea of smelting gold from the worthless looking black sands seemed implausible to John, but Sam seemed so confident he found himself imagining what they might find as he prepared the new highbankers. He tried to calculate how much gold would be in the material they had collected so far if it held the potential Sam had mentioned. After running the figures mentally, John decided he was missing something. The figure he came up with simply couldn't be right.

With the highbankers set up and the water pumps checked out, John anxiously returned to the workshop. In the hour John had been gone, Sam had set up the equipment and started drying a sample of the material. While the sample cooled down, Sam described the process to John. The first step was to remove as much of the iron as possible from the dried sample, using a magnet. The remaining material would be ground in the mortar and pestle to break down the larger pieces. A portion of the ground material would be measured out and mixed with twice that volume of the flux. The mixture of the flux and sample would then be put in a crucible and heated in the smelter with the torch until everything melted and glowed brightly. After that, the molten material would be allowed to cool down.

"Once the crucible is cooled off," Sam explained, "all the precious metals will be on the bottom as a button."

"What will be on the top?"

"Glass. You see, the flux is more than half silica sand. The silica sand absorbs the impurities, like iron and other worthless crap. The rest of the flux is a mixture of borax, salt peter and soda ash. The amounts of those can vary, but they serve to separate the precious metals from the other compounds. The melted gold is heavier, so it sinks to the bottom of the crucible. By weighing the raw sample and the smelted button, we can approximate the percentage of the gold by weight."

"So, the button on the bottom is pure gold?"

"No, it can have other precious metals, like silver, or even platinum. But to determine how much, you would need an actual assay. Like I said, this is used for a coarse estimation of what the black sands contain."

Under Sam's directions, John prepared the sample for smelting, and started the firing process. The anticipation of finding out what the black sands held made the firing process agonizingly slow for John. Finally, after what seemed to be more than an hour to John, Sam indicated it was time to turn off the torch. As the glow from the crucible began to dim, Sam suggested they go back to the lodge for lunch since it would take some time before the crucible was cool enough to handle.

"I think we should keep our little experiment under wraps," Sam said casually on the way back to the lodge.

"Why is that?" John asked with a grin. "You don't want to share in the disappointment?"

"There won't be any disappointment, I'm sure. No, it's obvious Hardrock didn't want the world to know what he was getting out of the sands. I suspected he might be doing some gold recovery, since a good miner wouldn't pass up on the opportunity, but we never discussed it."

John thought about it for a moment, and it struck him as odd that his uncle never mentioned it to Sam, his oldest friend. "Why would that be?"

"There's a number of reasons, particularly if the sands hold a high percentage of gold. If that's the case, and word got out, the clientele would change. Instead of clients looking for a good time, and maybe some gold, you'd get clients who were simply after the gold. To Hardrock, this operation wasn't about wanting gold. Like Robert Service wrote, 'it's not the gold that I'm wanting, so much as just finding the gold.' Your uncle was a big Robert Service fan."

"I've learned that about him. I'm beginning to realize it was an admiration of the spirit as much as an admiration for the writing."

"That would be a good way to put it."

In spite of his excitement over what information the smelting experiment might provide, John heeded Sam's advice and made no mention of it during lunch. When Maggie asked what the two men had been doing all morning, John simply replied that Sam was teaching him things Harley probably didn't know. He used the limited time left to learn even more from Sam to quickly escape back to the workshop after lunch.

"What about Wes?" John asked as he and Sam walked back to the workshop. "Do you think my uncle would have told him about the black sands, if they had any value?"

Sam thought the question over before answering, "I think so, yes. Wes was as much a business advisor to Hardrock as a friend. Why?"

"Just curious," John answered, and made a mental note to call the old lawyer.

The crucible was still warm to the touch when John pulled it from the stand. The exposed surface at the top of the crucible was black and frosted, giving no indication of what might lie below. As Sam directed, John flipped the crucible upside down on the bench. A distinct thump was heard as the contents in the crucible fell to the bench. John lifted the crucible away to reveal a solid cone with two distinct layers. The bottom layer of the cone was, by far, the largest. It was a glossy chunk of dark glass covered with iridescent streaks. The much smaller tip of the cone is what grabbed John's attention: a button of gold, as large as any nugget he had ever seen, glistened brightly. John picked the cone up and stared at it in awe.

"Fairly impressive paperweight, wouldn't you say?" Sam asked. "To get the button off, just tap it with this mallet."

John took the mallet from Sam and tapped the button lightly. It fell off and John held the gold in the palm of his hand. It was heavy for its size. He placed it on the scale.

"Just over a quarter of an ounce," Sam said, lifting the button from the scale, "less than I'd hoped."

"*Less?*"

"I was hoping for closer to half an ounce, which would have been about twenty percent by weight, since we used two ounces of sample. What we tested shows about ten percent by weight."

"That's still amazing," John exclaimed, "that bucket has to weigh at least twenty pounds! That's two pounds of gold!"

"Slow down, young fella, don't explode just yet. Close to half the weight in the bucket is water trapped in the sands, then more than half of the dried material is magnetic. Now, do the math."

John thought for a moment before answering. "Still, that's about eight ounces of gold."

"Not to put too fine a point on it," Sam replied, "but it would be closer to seven *Troy* ounces, which is how gold is traded."

"You're peeing all over my parade, Sam."

"Well, the good news is that the material we just tested probably has much less recoverable micro-gold than the material from the locations Hardrock marked with stars on the map."

"I guess the only way to find out is to run some material from those locations," John said slowly. His brow furrowed at a thought, and he asked, "Do you suppose Harley is aware of this?"

"I'm sure he's familiar with the principle, he's been around mining long enough to have heard about it. But as sharp as Harley is, he's prone to miss the bigger picture, and I doubt if Hardrock told him how rich the black sands are. Why do you ask?"

"It's just that I don't see how I'm going to be able to keep it from him. Hell, I don't know how Hardrock kept it a secret."

"That's easy, 'Harley, you stick with the clients. I've got things to do in camp this morning.' Four hours alone is all he would have needed."

"Maybe so, but I'm not Hardrock. Harley and I operate differently. I'm the boss in name only."

"Well, my boy," Sam slapped John on the shoulder, "just remember: the more who know, the more likely it is that even more will know. Now, if you don't mind putting up your toys by yourself, I'm going back up to the lodge."

Everything Sam had said made sense to John, but he just couldn't reconcile how he was going to keep the information from Harley. He finished putting everything back into the trunk, closed the lid and sat down on it to think. Pulling the gold bead out of his pocket, he rolled it around in his palm. As he pondered the value of the small chunk of gold, and how many just like it his uncle must have made over the years, the image of Cynthia's ledger came to mind. At that moment, the origin of the mystery deposits became obvious. Glancing at his watch, John stood up to go back to the lodge. He slid the gold button back into his pocket. He needed to call Wes.

John found Sam, Polly and Maggie sitting on the deck of the lodge, enjoying the sunshine playing down between the scudding clouds. Following a quick explanation that he needed to make a call, he stepped into the lodge and punched the number for Bartholomew Law. Doreen answered the phone with her usual cheery voice. After John had run the gamut of her social questions, she put him through to Wes, who was much more blunt.

"Hello, John. I'm busy, so we'll need to keep this quick."

Accustomed to the old lawyer's terse manner, John got straight to the point of the call. "What do you know about the black sands from Last Chance?"

A long silence ensued before Wes responded, "In what regard?"

"Come on, Wes," John said pleasantly, "don't play coy with me, you don't have the time. Remember?" There was a small amount of pleasure in dishing back some of Wes's own curtness. "Sam Burlington and I just ran a little black sand through a field smelting process."

"So, Sam's there," the old lawyer's tone softened noticeably. "How are he and Polly?"

"They're fine," John said irritably, "I'll let you talk to them when we're through. What do you know about the black sands my uncle used to take out of here?"

"As the trustee and executor of your uncle's estate, I can't tell you anything." After hearing John's exasperated sigh, Wes continued, "However, if you tell me what you *think* you know, I could confirm if you're right."

"You really enjoy this, don't you?"

"I'm just doing my job, John. Hardrock was the one with the sense of humor."

It was painfully apparent Wesley J. Bartholomew, Esquire, was not going to give an inch, so John proceeded with his speculation. "I think the fees from the clients have never entirely paid for the operation of Last Chance."

"You're wrong on that, there have been years in which they did."

"Okay, but for the most part, they don't pay all the bills. I think any deficits in revenue were made up by extracting gold from the black sands at the end of the season."

"What makes you think so?"

"I've seen the ledgers, Wes. Large deposits were made into the Last Chance account at the end of each year. Cynthia didn't know the source of the money, she said my uncle made the deposits. I think he sold the gold he extracted to keep Last Chance afloat."

"Bravo! You are correct."

John waited for Wes to offer some additional information, but nothing more was forthcoming. "Is that it," he demanded, "there isn't anything else to add?"

"Like what, John?"

"Like how much he had to run, and where he sold it, to start."

"Put Sam and Polly on."

John resisted the urge to hang up on the old goat, and asked,

"Does Harley know anything about this?"

"Ask him yourself."

"He's not here! Goddamn it, Wes!" John squelched the raging frustration he felt and explained calmly, "He's in town doing community service for his drunk on premises charge."

"Sounds like Harley could have used a better lawyer," Wes chuckled. "To answer your question, Harley doesn't know. Now, let me talk to Sam."

"One more question."

"Oh, for Chrissakes! What now?"

"Can I trust Harley?"

"You have to ask? Shit. Put Sam on."

Sam looked surprised when John handed him the phone and told him Wes Bartholomew wanted to talk to him. Judging from Sam's end of the conversation, Wes wasn't nearly as gruff with old friends as he was with new professional acquaintances. John walked across the deck and leaned against the railing, hanging his head with a sigh. Maggie walked up and stood next to him, pressing closely.

"Bad news?" she asked, slipping her arm around him.

"No, it's actually good news, but I don't know what to do with it."

"Tell me. I always know what to do with good news."

John looked at Maggie's smile and thought about what Sam had said: the more who know, the more likely it is that even more will know. He wasn't sure where to draw the line, who should know, and who should not. Instead of answering, he kissed her forehead, and whispered, "Not now, maybe later."

What had started off as a raucous conversation between Sam and Wes had grown softer, John realized. He turned around and saw that Sam had gone into the lodge to continue his conversation with Wes. After a few moments, Sam came back out onto the deck and handed the phone to Polly, who chatted merrily with Wes. Sam walked over to the railing and joined the younger couple.

"It doesn't make any sense," Sam began, "but Wes said to tell you not to let the bear bite you."

"What's that supposed to mean?" John asked.

Sam shrugged. "I have no idea, but that's what he told me to say, 'Don't let the bear bite you.' I thought it was some sort of inside joke between you two."

"Wes and I don't exactly share a lot of laughs together," John replied sourly.

Sam picked up on John's tone and said firmly, "Believe it, or not, Wes is in your corner."

CHAPTER 14

Even though it was the Fourth of July, the last evening with Sam and Polly passed no differently than the night of their arrival. It was what happened after the Burlingtons retired that had changed over the course of the week. John lay on his back in Maggie's bed, staring at the ceiling, with Maggie snuggled tightly against his side.

"You're awfully preoccupied. Hardly the kind of afterglow that wows a girl."

John hugged her gently and buried his face in her hair. Her scent was an intriguing fragrance of the sensual combined with the soothing. He wallowed in it before he responded.

"The other night I asked you what happens after the season is over. You never answered."

"As I recall, the conversation got interrupted," Maggie purred and kissed John's chest.

John loosened his grip and leaned back to look directly into her face.

"So, I'm asking again. What happens after the season is over?"

Maggie laid her head back on John's chest and closed her eyes. She didn't want to see his face.

"That depends on what you want to happen."

"Meaning what, exactly?"

"Meaning I don't expect anything."

John lay there quietly until he felt a drop of moisture hit his chest.

"Are you crying?"

"No."

"Liar. What's going on?"

John started to sit up, but Maggie hung onto him tightly until he laid back.

"John, I've screwed up so many times," she said softly without looking up. "I've jumped into relationships, I've been with men that I didn't really know. I've been run through it all so many times, I don't think I could do it again. Worst of all, I don't think I could live up to what you think you see in me."

"Is that all?" John wrapped his arms gently around the warm body next to him. "You're talking to a guy who spent years living at the bottom of a bottle, has two failed long-term relationships, and nothing in the way of promise for a living. I love you. If you won't expect perfection, neither will I."

"Okay."

"So I'm asking, *yet again*, what happens after the season is over?"

Maggie finally looked up from John's chest and wiped a tear from her cheek to look into his eyes.

"I guess we'll figure that out together."

"Good answer." John kissed her forehead and added, "Not to be indelicate, but you're dripping snot on me."

"Hey, I'm not perfect."

"That's okay," John said sliding from the bed, "I'll get you something."

He stepped over to where he'd dropped his jeans on the floor, pulled out a handkerchief and tossed it to Maggie. He dug back into the pocket a second time before sliding back into bed.

Maggie finished wiping her nose and sat up, facing John to ask, "What did you mean about good news that you didn't know what to do with, earlier? Did that have something to do with your call to Wes?"

John raised himself up on one elbow before answering.

"The news didn't have anything directly to do with Wes. Hold out your hand." John reached out to Maggie's open hand and set the gold bead into it. "It was that."

"You found a big nugget!"

"Look at it closely. It's not a nugget."

While Maggie examined the gold in her hand, John explained where it had come from and the smelting process Sam had shown him. He also recounted his conversation with Wes, and how Wes had confirmed that Hardrock had kept Last Chance financially viable with gold extracted from the black sands. While it all added up to good news, he admitted he was stumped on exactly what to do with it.

"What about Harley," Maggie asked, rolling the gold bead around in her palm, "does he know?"

"Wes says no. And Sam seemed to think I shouldn't tell anybody, not even Harley."

Maggie fixed a steady gaze on John. "But you told me."

"That should be self-explanatory," John said in such a matter-of-fact way that Maggie blushed. "Personally, I think Harley needs to know. I owe him at least that much." When Maggie didn't respond, John said, "You don't agree."

"It's not up to me."

Maggie held out the gold to John, but instead of taking it from her palm, he wrapped her fingers back around it. "I want you to keep it," he said. "Is this about the rancor between you two? I thought you said you'd forgiven him."

"You didn't listen, John. It's not me, it's Harley. I honestly don't know how he'll react when he finds out about our relationship. What if he thinks you don't measure up to the impossible Mike Radner standard?"

Her question was one that hadn't entered into John's mind, and it rattled him. He had been so relieved to find out there was no romantic link between Maggie and Harley, he never considered Harley's approval might not be anything other than a foregone conclusion.

"Do you see my concern?" Maggie finally asked after John had sat silent for too long.

"I do," John said with a wink, "so come here. We've only got one night before your big brother slaps a chastity belt on you."

John asked Sam to step outside for a private conversation when they had finished breakfast the next day. There were several questions in his mind that had kept him up a good portion of the night.

"Yesterday was like everything else about my life since the end of March. The more I learn, the less I seem to know."

"Wait until you're as old as me," Sam grumbled, "you'll realize you don't know shit."

"I've got questions about what to do now. I don't even know where to sell the black sands."

"You won't sell the sands unrefined. You won't have enough to make it worthwhile for a refiner to deal with."

"You're telling me I'll have to smelt it all myself?" John's question had the tone of disbelief.

"That's exactly what I'm telling you. But you saw how easy the process is, you just need to think on a larger scale. Hardrock didn't do it here, one tiny batch at a time. He must have cleaned up back at his place."

As soon as Sam's words were out, the image of the impenetrable steel door at the Quonset hut flashed through John's mind. The old miner's preoccupation with security suddenly made perfect sense. If his uncle had been processing material worth literally tens of thousands of dollars, particularly on the sly, he certainly wouldn't have wanted anyone to have access to the area.

"There's something else to consider," Sam continued, "if the material the black sands come from is producing very fine gold, the sands will contain additional free gold too small to separate effectively with simple panning. That gold can still be separated without smelting."

"How so?"

"It's a simple matter of running the material over a shaker, or vibrator, table. That's what most commercial operations do. They're noisy buggers, but do a good job of getting the really fine stuff out. If I was a gambling man, I'd bet heavily that Hardrock had both a shaker table and a way to smelt the material."

Again, John's mind went back to the Quonset hut. He kicked himself for not asking Wes about the key for the lock on the door when he had him on the phone the day before. Doreen had obviously forgotten to relay the question back in April. He decided there would be plenty of time to get the question answered.

"Okay, let's say I extract the gold, one way or another, what then? What do I do with it? It's not like I'm going to hold a garage sale."

"There are refiners that deal in bulk gold. They assay it and pay market value based on the results of the assay. Of course," Sam added quickly, "that's minus a percentage for refining it further and the cost of the assay."

"That sure sounds simple enough. Almost too simple. What's the percentage?"

"Now you sound like a miner!" Sam laughed. "But to answer your question, it varies from refiner to refiner. It also depends on volume purchased and the composition of the metals."

"I'm right back to square one," John muttered, "I got answers that lead to even more questions."

"Make it easy on yourself. Find out who Hardrock dealt with, and contact them."

"What about the flux for smelting? There's plenty for testing here, but I'll need to make more."

"John, you're sweating the small stuff," Sam said patiently. "There's as many flux recipes as there are miners. If you can't find the one Hardrock used, call me."

"I'm sorry for all the questions, Sam, but you don't know what all is riding on this."

"Yes, I do," Sam replied, "Wes told me all about it yesterday. For what it's worth, I think you'll be okay."

John appreciated the older man's vote of confidence, he only wished he shared it. He felt frustrated. It was as if he were playing in a game of blind man's bluff. He was groping around aimlessly, as everyone else watched silently, all the while seeing clearly which way he needed to turn.

John and Sam went back inside to wait for the plane. John walked over to the window and stared out at the heavy overcast and drizzle that had moved in overnight. He felt anxious about Harley's return, and how he might react to the news regarding John and Maggie's relationship. It made waiting difficult. When John had talked to Harley during the week, he purposely said nothing, feeling it was something best announced face to face. It would be far better, he thought, for all three of them to be present.

"You don't suppose they're socked in on the other side, do you?" John asked.

"It's not even ten. Quit fidgeting," Maggie replied.

"You're right," John said, turning toward the door, "I'm going to take the ATV's down to the dock."

Polly looked up from the magazine she was thumbing through as John left and asked Maggie, "What's with him?"

"I think it's prom night jitters," Sam offered with a grin. "Just like meeting the date's dad."

"What would you know about that, old man?" Polly asked. "You can't even remember back that far."

"Maybe not, but I *do* remember telling your dad I wanted to marry you. I can appreciate how John might feel."

"Whoa!" Maggie interjected. "Nobody is saying anything about marriage, here.".

"Situation's the same," Sam replied, waving her off, "only thing different is, Harley won't be skinning a wolf when John talks to him."

The image of a much younger Sam Burlington nervously announcing his intentions as Polly's father skinned a wolf made Maggie smile. She didn't want to admit it, but she was nervous, too.

"How did that talk go?" she asked.

"Not too bad. I'm here, and so's Polly."

The throaty rumble announcing Reeder's arrival interrupted the conversation. Maggie stepped out on the deck with the Burlingtons to say good-bye. Sam and Polly assured her they would be back next summer, and started toward the dock. Maggie watched them make their way down the path and hoped she and John would be the ones to host them.

Harley was first out of the Beaver and introduced John to the new clients as they each stepped onto the dock. They were Sheila and Clark Baker along with Nan and Tony Garcia, two middle-aged couples vacationing together. Clark and Tony ran an automotive supply store together. Anxious to see the lodge, the couples left immediately following the introductions. Just before climbing into the Beaver, Sam wished John good luck and reminded him he could call for advice anytime he needed it.

"Damn, it's good to be back here," Harley said after watching the Beaver lift off. "They worked my ass off in Kenai."

"I thought you were tight with the supervisor," John said grinning.

"So did I."

"I heard from Cynthia. We're going to have a full camp on Tuesday. Short trippers, a family of four, are coming in."

"So, I get a roommate, then. All I can say is that I hope you don't mind my snoring."

"I'm sure there won't be a problem with it. What do you know about the clients?" John asked to sidestep any further discussion on the sleeping arrangements.

"Seem nice enough. They're from California and have done some panning, but aren't very experienced."

"Good. I set up two new highbankers in spots marked with stars on the map. I'd like to start them out on those."

After the clients checked out their cabins, John and Harley took them for a tour of the claim, and showed them where they would be working. Following lunch they got their first taste of highbanking. Their enthusiasm level, which started out high, increased even further after a couple hours of running material. They cleaned out the sluice as soon as the top riffles contained visible black sands with gold. Harley walked them through the clean up process and offered tips on their panning technique. The results proved to be exactly what Hardrock had noted on the map. The gold was predominantly fine, with a smattering of larger flakes, but there was enough of it to look impressive in the bottom of the pans. John felt more comfortable with the idea of putting them on fine gold after seeing the positive reaction of the clients. Even more pleasing to John was the amount of black sand; more than double what the previous locations had produced.

Following the first clean up, Harley adjusted the angle of the highbanker and positioned a hand sluice to catch the runoff from the highbanker.

"What's the point of that?" Tony asked.

"Just a precaution to make sure we're not missing anything.

We could be losing some of the finer flake."

Clark looked at the set up and commented, "Anything that fine, I'm not worried about. Too much work for too little gold."

"Yeah, we'll leave the tiny stuff to the girls," Tony said with a wink, then grinned when Nan punched him in the shoulder.

At the clients' request, the second highbanker John had set up the previous day was relocated to a position where the two couples could work side by side. Harley raked down a large pile of tailings material, and John motioned him over to the ATV's.

"That's some pretty good dirt," John said.

"Not bad, but it's going to get tedious for them to pan out the concentrates. Lots of black crap."

"As long as they're happy, let's keep them there. If they start to act disappointed, or ask to move, we'll put them on the other highbankers."

"Sounds like you've got a plan of some sort, John."

"I do, and we need to talk more about it later."

Harley raised an eyebrow in question, but John had turned his attention back to the clients.

The sky continued to send a cold drizzle down throughout the afternoon, and by dinnertime everyone was more than eager to go back to the lodge, warm up and eat. The break and hot meal were not enough to revitalize Nan and Sheila, who opted to remain at the lodge sitting next to the woodstove while their husbands panned the concentrates.

During the clean ups, Harley ensured the material from the secondary sluices was kept separate from the highbanker concentrates. While Tony and Clark worked the majority of the concentrates, John and Harley panned the material from the secondary sluices. Harley had been right about the tedium of panning material so heavily laden with black sand, but Tony and Clark were thrilled with the end result. The distinct yellow lines along the edge of each pan the men worked were enough to keep them going strong. The occasional picker found with the finer gold increased their enthusiasm.

The material from the secondary sluices was not as impressive.

"Brings a whole new meaning to the term gold dust," Tony

commented as Harley finished up a pan.

"Yeah, it does, but it's still gold."

"As far as I'm concerned, that's not worth the effort. I'd rather be sitting where it's warm and dry than spend time cold and wet for such a puny amount."

"I'll tell you what," John said, dumping his pan's contents back into the bucket, "we'll hold onto what comes out of the secondary sluices for a more pleasant day. It's worth checking out, but it's obvious the highbankers are holding the majority of the gold."

"I'm good with that," Clark responded, holding up his vial of gold. He beamed after looking at the contents and added, "This is more than we've found, all totaled, in all the times we've gone out. This is incredible."

John watched Clark and Tony walk back to the lodge, joking about cutting their wives out of the take for not helping pan. When he turned around, Harley was staring at him intently.

"Seems like somebody was awfully anxious to get rid of the clients, *John*."

"Indeed. We need to talk. Really, it's more like I need to tell you something before I explode."

"This doesn't sound good."

"To the contrary, it could be very good. While you were gone, Sam gave me quite an education. Did my uncle ever tell you what he did with all the black sands you kept?" Harley shook his head, and John continued, "Didn't you ever wonder?"

"No. John, I'm not going to pass the test, just get to the point."

"The point is, the black sands are worth more than double whatever the clients are finding in gold. They are that rich."

Harley looked at his boss skeptically for a moment before replying, "I'm familiar with entrained gold and micro-gold, John, commercial operations make their money getting it. But it's a complicated chemical process to refine gold."

"That's just it! Hardrock didn't *refine* the gold from the black sands, he *extracted* it."

"Refine, extract, what's the difference? It's still a complicated chemical process. I'm no chemist, and neither are you. And as far as I could ever tell, neither was Hardrock."

"I'll say it again. He didn't *refine* the gold, he *extracted* the precious metals," John said patiently. "There's a big difference. Extraction isn't nearly as complicated. Tell me what's in the back of the Quonset hut? What's behind door number one?"

Harley rolled his eyes in response. "I don't know. You tell me."

"Sam thinks there's both a fine gold separator, and a smelter in there."

"Yeah, right," Harley replied sarcastically, "Hardrock was the Nikiski branch of Anglo American."

"Okay, try this on: I asked Wes if Hardrock kept Last Chance afloat by extracting gold from the black sands. He said yes."

Harley didn't have a snappy comeback for that. Instead, he looked down at his feet and thought for a long moment before speaking.

"Why are you telling me this? Hardrock never did."

"Sam thinks Hardrock was afraid word would get out, and the nature of the clientele would change. In fact, Sam suggested I keep just as tight a lid on it."

Harley looked up from his feet and straight into John's eyes. "Again, why are *you* telling me this?"

"I'll need your help." When Harley shifted his gaze back down to his feet, John added, "And I trust you."

"It still seems pretty far-fetched to me."

"I've had a hard time wrapping my mind around it, too. Look, I'll show you the extraction process just as soon as I can, but believe me when I say this may be the only way to hold onto Last Chance."

Harley nodded. "The thing is," he said softly, looking back down at his feet, "I'm disappointed to find out Hardrock didn't trust me."

"I don't think it was a matter of trust, Harley. He didn't say anything to Sam, either, and they were like brothers. The only other person he told, as far as I know, was Wes. And that was because Wes was his legal and business advisor."

Harley stood quietly looking down and kicked the toe of his boot into the dirt a few times before saying, "Hardrock was definitely old school. That's how he liked it, and how he wanted to keep it."

"Exactly. The only people he told were those who absolutely needed to know." Again, Harley nodded in response without looking up. John decided the mood needed to be lightened, and added, "Besides, if you weren't so damned clueless, you'd have figured it out."

Harley finally looked up and smiled. "Bite me. Let's get out of the drizzle."

The warmth of the lodge was a welcome relief from the cold and wet outside. John peeled off his rain slicker and wondered why he even bothered wearing one. He was as wet from condensation collecting inside the slicker as he would have been without wearing it. He stood next to the woodstove to drive off the damp and listened to the clients and Maggie chat. Maggie smiled and laughed as she bantered with the clients. John marveled again at how beautiful she was, and how good she was with people. He felt lucky. No, it was better than that. He felt blessed.

The conversation was continuous until Tony mentioned he was tired. Nan, Sheila and Clark agreed it was time for bed. Maggie asked if there were any requests for breakfast, and after offering several suggestions, the clients left the staff of Last Chance alone in the lodge, sitting at the table.

Out of the corner of his eye, John could see Maggie looking at him. He was obviously expected to take the lead in the conversation.

"Dominoes?" he asked.

"I don't think so," Harley replied. "I'm beat. Besides, I need to enjoy sleeping alone before you invade my space on Tuesday."

"Yeah, maybe we ought to talk about that."

"What's to talk about?" Harley looked at John. "Oh, no. *You* are on the couch, my friend. I am *not* giving up my bed."

"There are other options... other beds."

"What? Are you nuts? There isn't room in my cabin for another bed!"

John could see Maggie covering a smile, and shifted uneasily in his chair.

"Well, maybe a bed in another building, then."

Harley snorted. "You mean down at the old bunkhouse? Shit. We'd have to pull a bed out of one of the other cabins! Besides, that place isn't fit to stay in. We'd have to scrape away fifty years of dust just to make a hole for a bed."

"There's always the lodge," Maggie offered with a snicker.

"That's not a bad idea," Harley said slowly, "the couch in here is probably more comfortable than mine."

"And I wouldn't have to put up with your snoring," John added.

"Oh, for Pete's sake!" Maggie exclaimed. She jumped out of her chair, walked over to John, shoved him upright and plopped into his lap. She turned into John, put her arms around his neck and planted a firm kiss on his lips. John's arms hung limp at his sides. Maggie released her lip lock on John and turned to Harley, smiling sweetly.

"Harley, we have something to tell you."

Harley sat silent, swapping his gaze between Maggie and John. Maggie hugged John's neck again. John wrapped his arms around Maggie, and looked back at Harley sheepishly.

"I didn't know exactly how to tell you," John explained. "I didn't know how you'd take it."

"You're boinking the boss?" Harley asked incredulously. "That is *so party foul!*"

"And that is so crass!" Maggie snapped back.

"No! Wait!" Harley shouted. He jumped up and stomped over to the door leading to the kitchen and pounded on it. "All of this," he declared, spinning around, waving his arms wildly, "everything forward of this door, it's a no boinking zone. *All of it!* Outside, in here... No! Wait! I take that back! I don't want to have to worry about what you're doing in the kitchen! Everything forward of the..."

"*Harley!*" Maggie shouted, "*I am not* going to put up with this!"

John stood Maggie up off his lap and stepped forward. Maggie grabbed his hand and stopped him.

"Harley," John said in a firm, loud voice, "we need to talk about this, not scream about it. Now, calm down, and we'll *talk* about it."

Again, Harley's gaze shifted between his half-sister and his boss. He raised his hand and pointed a finger at the couple and winked. "Gotcha! See you guys in the morning."

Maggie and John stood dumbstruck as Harley strode out of the lodge. John watched Harley descend the steps, then asked, "What the hell was that?"

"He can be such an ass," Maggie giggled.

John darted for the door and dashed down the steps. He caught up with Harley halfway to his cabin.

"Are you okay with this?"

"Oh, hell yeah," Harley answered. "In fact, I was beginning to wonder what was wrong with you."

"You knew?"

"John, I may have missed what Hardrock was doing, but I'm not completely clueless. You've been eyeballing Maggie since that first bowl of oatmeal at the Shuffle."

"And you're okay with it? I mean, it won't be a problem?"

"You want my blessing? You've got it. It's time Maggie finally hooked up with someone worth a shit." Harley looked at John, who was obviously relieved, and at a loss for words. "Oh, don't get all touchy-feely on me," he said, "and there will definitely be no damn hugging. Save it for my sister."

CHAPTER 15

On Tuesday, Harley positioned the short trippers to work another spot marked with a star on the map to maximize the collection of rich black sands. That location was several hundred yards away from where the Bakers and Garcias were working. The distance between the two groups created a problem logistically. Not only did it require Harley and John to work separately with each group, much time was spent moving the backhoe between the two spots frequently. The extra time spent in such an arrangement resulted in the postponement of John's smelting demonstration until the following week, when only three clients were in camp.

The three clients had some previous experience mining recreationally, and were not impressed with finer gold. After two days, they asked to try another location. Although disappointed at losing the black sand production, John moved them to the vicinity where the Sunshine Boys and the Wild Bunch had done well. Once larger gold started showing, the clients were very happy and required little additional attention other than the occasional raking down of tailings with the backhoe.

On Thursday, after raking down a large pile of tailings for the clients, John and Harley returned to the camp to run a batch of black sands from the previous week. Following Sam's instructions to the letter, John prepared a sample for smelting while explaining to Harley everything Sam had passed along.

John noted the volume of magnetic material removed from the fine gold black sands was much greater than what he and Sam previously tested. With the firing complete, John shut off the fuel and the two men went to gather up the clients for lunch as the sample cooled down. Once lunch was out of the way and the clients were back at their highbanker, John and Harley eagerly returned to check on the sample.

"Should be interesting to see the difference in how much gold is in this sample versus the one Sam and I ran," John commented. "According to Sam, we could get close to an ounce of gold out of it."

"That, I want to see."

"Skeptic."

"Maybe," Harley shrugged, "but as much as I hope it's true, it's hard to believe."

"Well, it better be, or keeping Last Chance becomes a very iffy proposition."

Both men held their breath as John flipped the crucible and pulled it away from the contents. The exposed cone looked similar to the one Sam and John had smelted, except the golden button was noticeably larger. John quickly knocked the gold tip off the cone and held the warm metal in his hand. He handed it off to Harley, who whistled slightly when he hefted it.

"Just under nine-tenths of an ounce," Harley said in awe when he set the button on the digital scale.

"That's what, roughly eighteen percent gold in the final sample?"

"Yeah," Harley replied, looking at the button more closely, "but that's not all gold. See how bright the color is? It's not a deep yellow."

"What does that mean?"

"It means there's some other metal mixed in with the gold. Probably silver, but it might be platinum, too."

"I like the idea of platinum a lot better than silver. Sam said the only way to find out for sure is to have it assayed. You suppose we ought to send it out with Reeder?"

Harley looked askance at John. "And tell him what? We found this chunk of gold laying around and would appreciate it if he'd have it assayed for us? I doubt if Reeder would even know who does assays. What about Wes?"

"Out of the question," John replied quickly, "he can't, or won't, give me any information, or help, at all. He made that perfectly clear when I talked to him on the phone the other day. No, we're on our own." John thought for a moment then added, "I guess it really doesn't matter if we know what it assays out, we just need to get as much material to process as we can."

"And that means," Harley finished John's thought, "we need to keep somebody highbanking on the fine stuff."

"Why couldn't one of us work a highbanker while the other works with the clients?"

Harley fixed his eyes steadily on John as he replied, "Think about what you're suggesting. You're suggesting we short-change the service we give to our clients. Is that what you really want to do? You're getting gold fever."

The remark struck home, and John's cheeks burned in embarrassment. This year was not really any different than any other, John reminded himself. His uncle had faced the same situation every year, but kept the spirit behind Last Chance intact.

"You're right, sorry. It's just that *so much* is riding on the success of this year, I'm kind of losing it."

"No need to apologize. The stakes are high for both of us. I suggest we keep the clients on the fine stuff as much as possible, and as long as they're happy with what they're getting. As it stands now, there's no clients in September and we'll be able to work the highbankers ourselves. I really think we can pull this off."

John thought back to what Sam had said about not sweating the small stuff. It was good advice, but it also represented another nebulous line. What, exactly, was the small stuff? Getting all the black sands they needed was one thing, figuring out what to do afterwards sure seemed like big stuff.

"By the way," Harley said grinning, interrupting John's thoughts, "I think it's only fair that since you gave Maggie the first button, I get to keep this one."

"What the hell? You and your sister are going to ruin me financially."

"That's the plan," Harley said as he slapped John on the

back. "We're going to make you so broke you'll be dependent on her. You'll never escape Nikiski."

"Well, hang onto that thing. I may need it back to make ends meet."

Only the second week of August had a full camp. Another group of short-trippers rounded out the four regular clients, and they were more interested in fishing for silver salmon and rainbows than mining. While the short trip clients added to the bottom line for the season, it was apparent those bookings wouldn't be enough to make up for the overall reduced income. It was the week of the last regular clients who were more inclined to swing their metal detectors than shovel into highbankers. Nothing was scheduled beyond the sixth of September, and John resigned himself to the fact the tourist season was over.

Throughout August, John had kept in close contact with Cynthia. He called her after lunch on the Wednesday before the last clients were scheduled to fly back, and asked for a complete accounting of the revenue and expenditures for the current season.

"What I need," John explained, "is a way to see where we stand monetarily at the moment, and what we can expect to spend through the rest of the year. Can you do that?"

"Sure, that's simple. It just takes a search filter on the recorded debits for whatever period of time you want to cover."

"Okay, could you do that on September through December, along with any significant deposits? It would be good to make a guess on what the year's end is going to look like."

"Do you want Hardrock's draws listed?"

"Hardrock's draws?"

"Hardrock made monthly withdrawals from the Last Chance Adventures account for his own use after the season was over. I think it's what he used for living expenses between seasons."

John mulled it over for a few seconds before answering, "No, those would be the same as wages. And would you send me three copies of that with Reeder this Saturday?"

"Reeder will have it. How are things going?"

"Just great," John lied, "everything's fine."

"How is Harley?"

"Why, Harley is just fine," John said grinning. He looked across the table at the object of Cynthia's affections. Harley was waving his hands frantically and mouthing the word 'no.' John wanted to hand the phone to him, but had too much regard for his young bookkeeper to set her up for yet another disappointing conversation with Harley.

"Tell him I said hi."

"I will, but I'm sure it won't be the same, coming from me. Bye."

"That woman is *relentless*," Harley said.

"Why don't you just date her for awhile?" Maggie asked. "I'm sure she'd dump you as soon as she got to know you. Problem solved."

"Very funny, Mag."

"No, seriously, why not?" John asked. "She's attractive, intelligent and very sweet."

"I was her babysitter, for Pete's sake!"

John turned to Maggie. "How long ago was that?"

"Twenty years, I think."

"Officially," Harley said firmly, "that topic is closed. New topic. Why did you ask for all that financial stuff?"

"I don't know," John sighed, "maybe I'm hoping it will show that things aren't as desperate as I think they are."

The comment squelched any further conversation. The three of them sat at the table in silence until Maggie gathered up their plates, kissed John on the top of the head and disappeared into the kitchen. Harley stood up and nodded toward the door. John followed him without uttering a word.

The large envelope Reeder delivered Saturday wasn't as thick as John had expected, considering it was supposed to contain three copies of the requested spreadsheets. John immediately opened the flap on the envelope and peered inside. It contained three sets of folded legal-sized sheets, and a handwritten note.

"You look disappointed," Reeder commented when he saw John's reaction to the envelope's contents.

"No, just surprised. I thought there would be more in it."

"Like a love letter to Harley?"

"Ease up, Reeder," Harley shot back, "I don't need you on my case, too."

"There's a note enclosed, but I don't see any hearts or little smiley faces on it," John said, winking at Reeder. "Geez, Harley, you may have lost a girlfriend."

"Bite me. Both of you. I've got stuff to do."

Harley walked to his ATV and drove back to the lodge, taking the supplies Reeder had delivered.

"That was enjoyable," Reeder said as he stepped off the dock onto the Beaver's float, "but I've got stuff to do, too. Call if you need me to drop something off. I'm running back and forth almost every day, ferrying hunters."

After the Beaver disappeared from view, it occurred to John how strange it was to be standing on the dock without clients waiting for him at the lodge. It had been an amazing and busy summer. As the last of the ripples from the plane's departure dissipated, John looked at the smooth surface of the lake, taking in the reflection of the mountains. The days had grown noticeably shorter and cooler, and there were bright patches of yellow in the reflection. The sour odor of ripe highbush cranberries hung in the chill of the morning air. The smell was, at the same time, both repulsive and appealing. John took in a deep breath to absorb the heady scent fully, and wondered what he would do if he had to give it all up. He decided that he wouldn't *give* anything up. He might lose it all, but nothing would be *given*.

"I'll give you a penny."

John jumped slightly at the sound of Maggie's voice. He turned and saw she was standing at the edge of the dock.

"You got something larger? We might need it." Walking over to her, he put one arm around her shoulders, and Maggie slipped her arm around his waist. John held the envelope from Cynthia out in front of them. "This should give us an idea how many pennies we're going to need."

"You never mentioned your obsessive personality. I've got faith in you. Things will be fine. Hardrock made it work, so will you."

"He knew what he was doing."

"And you have it figured out."

"Not all of it. There are huge gaps in the puzzle, and I don't even know where to look for the pieces."

The first day without any clients in camp was dedicated to evaluating everything needed to be done. Along with the usual preparations for winterizing the camp and performing maintenance on the equipment, John and Harley needed to accumulate as much additional gold and black sand as possible.

"That's one advantage we have, compared to what Hardrock had to work with," John said as the three of them discussed strategy. "We'll have the free placers to sell."

"It will help," Harley agreed, "but I don't think we should count on it being a significant source of income."

"What about the jewelry nuggets?" Maggie offered. "They're worth twice the value of fine gold. Should you concentrate on them?"

Harley shook his head. "Not unless we have a buyer lined up. And I don't know any."

"Sam might," John said, "but I think time is going to be our biggest problem, and we need to go with the sure thing."

"Still, you should keep them separated, just in case," Maggie argued.

"You're just looking for the chance at a perfect set of earrings," Harley gibed.

"Oh, piss off, Harley."

John flashed Harley a thumbs-up and said, "I knew you could get it out of her! Seriously though, we need to get the most for our efforts. Panning the fine gold out of the black sands is a real time suck. Maybe we would do better to concentrate on the coarser gold."

"The difference in the amount of free gold is probably minimal between the fine and coarse material," Harley said, "but the fine stuff will be quicker to process."

"How so?"

"You said Sam thought Hardrock had a shaker table. That's what they do, separate fines from sands. All we'll need to do is run the concentrates through a classifier to clean them up a bit, then let the table do the work."

"And if there's no table?" Maggie asked.

"We'll find somebody that has one," Harley replied. "I can

think of two guys, right off the top of my head, that might."

John nodded his agreement with Harley's suggestion. He didn't like the idea of potentially compromising the secret his uncle had guarded so carefully by using someone else's shaker table, but it beat losing the Last Chance entirely.

With their strategy established, time progressed as a routine of maintenance chores and mining. The routine varied only as dictated by the weather conditions. Good weather dictated outdoor maintenance on the buildings. Inclement weather dictated maintenance indoors, either at the workshop on the equipment, or indoors on the buildings. Always, time was made for mining. Every work day came to an end at the panning tubs, cleaning up the concentrates from the highbankers. After two weeks, the days of the week had become nebulous. It didn't matter. All that mattered was continuing on with the routine until the camp was ready for winter, and enough valuable material had been separated from the dirt. It was that last item that vexed John. How much was enough?

The daily routine for John differed from Maggie and Harley's only slightly. Every night he pored over the ledger sheets Cynthia had sent. He knew if he just looked hard enough, the answer to 'how much' would appear.

"John, come to bed. It's late, and I'm cold."

John looked up from the desk in Maggie's direction. She was leaning on one elbow, with her head tipped to one side. Her hair outlined an exposed breast. One bare leg protruded from under the covers. She wiggled her toes playfully at him.

"You're a smart girl," he teased, "if you're cold, get all the way under the covers."

"Really, what are you going to find that you haven't already read a thousand times?"

John shrugged in resignation and stood up to shut the valve on the propane light. The light in the room was extinguished with a soft pop, and John undressed. The nights had grown increasingly cooler, and when he slid into bed against Maggie's warm body she shivered slightly.

"You're not much help," she said, pressing herself against John's side and pulling him tight. "Maybe I'm the one doing the warming."

Laying on his back, John ran his fingers up and down the curve of Maggie's waist. Her smooth skin held a never-ending, tactile fascination for him.

"I've been over those figures time and again," he thought aloud, "and I still can't figure out if we're going to get enough to make it."

"Does it matter?"

"Hell, *yes*, it matters! I don't want to lose this!" John stopped running his fingers over Maggie's skin.

"I know *that* matters," she replied, leaning back and looking up, "what I'm saying is, does it matter if you have it all calculated out? What we *have* to get, is all we *can* get. After that, we make it, or we don't."

Maggie laid her head back on John's chest and he resumed exploring the mystery of her skin. The last thought to pass through his mind that night wasn't about figures in a ledger, or how much black sand they needed. It was, *"Funny thing how the word 'we' has crept into all our conversations."*

The morning the skim ice completely covered the settling pond at the tailings, and the suction lines to the water pumps for the highbankers were frozen, Harley told John it was time to call it quits. It was the sixth of October.

"Things will thaw," John argued, "we can work in the afternoon."

"Today, sure, but it's over, John. The season is over." Harley pointed into the line of trees at the edge of the tailings and said, "What do you see in the shade? That's snow from two days ago. It didn't melt. The ground is freezing. And things sure as hell aren't going to get any warmer."

Tipping his head back, John took a deep breath and let out a long sigh. The cloud of vapor from his breath drifted away slowly in the cold, still morning air. It validated Harley's statement.

"Look," Harley pressed, "we got the camp winterized, most of the equipment cleaned up, plus almost two weeks of straight highbanking time. It's time to board up the lodge and haul ass."

John looked around. The only leaves not on the ground were those few that clung stubbornly to the alder growing on the tailings. Even the needles on the spruce trees had lost the vibrant green of the summer growing season. The landscape looked haggard and ready for sleep.

"How long to completely finish up?" John asked.

"We'll need today to clean up this equipment and run maintenance on the backhoe, and tomorrow to board up the lodge, pull the dock and pack whatever we're going to take out."

"Okay, I'll call Reeder and ask him to pick us up the day after."

The rocks along the edge of the lake glistened with a coat of ice when the Beaver touched down early in the afternoon two days later. The thin skim was the initial stage of the ice that would quickly grow to enclose the lake for the next six months. With the dock out, Reeder had to cut the engine and let the airplane drift gently up to shore where John and Harley were waiting in waders to turn the plane and guide it gently to the shoreline. While Maggie kept Dawg in place, the two men loaded everything into the plane, where Reeder stowed the cargo to balance the load.

"Now for the hard part," Harley said as he walked from the plane toward Maggie and Dawg, "time to load the furbag."

Dawg's lips curled slightly to show his teeth in his usual bluff of ferocity at Harley's approach.

"Oh, don't start, you worthless mutt!" Harley snapped.

"Let me try," Maggie offered.

Taking Dawg gently by the collar Maggie began talking sweetly to him and coaxing him toward the plane. There was a pause at the edge of the water, and Dawg looked back. Maggie bent over and whispered in his ear until he leapt from the edge of the water onto the float. With a little more coaxing, and some gentle tugging on his collar, she got the big dog into the plane. John and Harley stood slack-jawed in amazement.

"Not nearly as entertaining," Reeder dryly observed, "but it sure beats him pissing on everything. Can you do anything about airsickness?"

The Beaver skipped down the lake and Reeder expertly lifted one float off the surface, then the other. Once airborne, John called out to Reeder to circle Last Chance, but he and Maggie were sitting in the back of the plane and Reeder didn't hear him through his muffs.

CHAPTER 16

John suggested going to the Shuffle Inn when they had finished offloading the plane. He explained it by saying he wanted to buy Harley's first beer, but truthfully, he wasn't eager to go to the trailer. Since she no longer had a place to live, he and Maggie had agreed they would move into the trailer together. He felt some hesitation about going there. When he'd left for Last Chance in April, he thought he'd be moving in and facing the ghosts that resided there by himself. He wasn't sure how Maggie would react to moving into a place that looked more like a museum than a home.

"Are you going to give me a day off, boss?" Harley asked. "I plan on yours being just the first of many beers tonight. Drink late and sleep later, that's my motto for tomorrow."

"It's good to have goals," Maggie quipped. "I like the part about sleeping in, though."

"To answer your question," John said raising his hands dramatically, "I proclaim tomorrow an official Last Chance Adventures holiday! Let the roar of the crowd be heard!" To Maggie and Harley's whoops and high-fives John continued, "And to begin the celebration, I will buy dinner. Pizza sound good? It's the best I can do. The business is, as you both know, financially challenged at the moment."

"Anything I don't have to cook sounds good to me," Maggie said, clapping her hands.

"Beer and pizza is exactly what I've been dreaming about!" Harley exclaimed.

Although early in the afternoon, several people were in the bar when the Last Chance crew entered. The scene seemed so familiar that John felt as though they hadn't been gone for nearly six months. Doorway stood at his usual post, as if he hadn't moved since April, and boomed a hearty welcome. It was, John realized, like returning home. Doorway stepped out from the bar and lifted Maggie off the ground by enveloping her in a bear hug, then shook hands with both the men. He waved off John's order for Harley's first beer, insisting the first round was his to provide.

The conversation didn't lag for two hours, and Harley got a good start on his plan to put down numerous beers. Not wanting Harley too far gone before they had pizza, John suggested it was time for dinner. They stopped long enough for Harley to unload his belongings and feed Dawg, then went on to the Tuscan Villa. Harley attacked his pizza with gusto, Maggie relished being waited on, and John simply enjoyed watching them.

"Okay, you're off tomorrow," John said to Harley as they left, "but I need you to plan on coming by Friday. We've got things to figure out."

"Not a problem, ol' pal," Harley said slapping John on the back. He had enjoyed more beer with his pizza, and was definitely on his way to a serious headache in the morning. "What time do you wanna start crackin' the whip?"

John looked at his friend for a moment before answering with a smile, "Anytime you can show up with a clear head, or at least a head you can squeeze through the door."

"Noon it is! You're a slave driver."

As they stood at the Suburban and watched Harley make his way back to the Shuffle Inn, Dawg wandered over to Maggie and nuzzled against her hand.

"You want to go home with us?" she asked opening the back door of the Suburban. The big dog jumped in immediately.

"God help me," John sighed, "a house, a girlfriend, and now a dog. I'm doomed."

"He practically lived with Hardrock," came the reply, "he'd show up eventually, anyway. Besides, what makes you think you've got a girlfriend?"

The daylight was fading when John pulled up to the trailer. It appeared dark and uninviting. John looked around before getting out of the vehicle. It seemed different without snow piled up at the edges of the drive. The open area behind the trailer was thickly covered with fireweed stalks and other plants that had withered from the frosts of the onrushing winter. A cow moose with a calf disappeared into the line of alders bordering the far side of the opening.

"Well, are we going to sleep out here?" Maggie asked after a moment.

"I'm thinking," John replied. "I'm wondering if you expect me to carry you across the threshold."

"Not if you want help carrying the bags."

"Good point. We'll save that for later."

They each grabbed a pair of bags and walked up to the door of the lean-to. As it had been when John left, the door was unlocked. He opened it and felt for the light switch, flipping it on. Inside, the bare bulb overhead revealed a note taped to the door into the trailer. John pulled it off the door and read it.

"Welcome home! I turned up the heat and put some groceries in the fridge for you. – Cynthia"

John handed the note to Maggie, and said, "Now, there's a good employee."

Maggie scanned the note. "No, there's a good friend," she corrected.

The inside of the trailer was dark. Barely enough light came through the door from the lean-to for John to see well enough to carry his bags to the middle of the living room. Maggie followed him inside and turned on the overhead light for the living room. It seemed, to John, to be an absent-minded movement.

"That was quick," John observed, "you didn't even look around for it."

"John, I practically grew up here. I spent quite a few nights sleeping on that very couch." She nodded across the room and continued, "Whenever things were ugly at home, Harley and I came running to Hardrock's." She set her bags down, looked around the room and smiled. "It's been years, but it's exactly as I remember it."

"That's good. No surprises then," John said with relief. "I was worried you'd take one look and run off."

"Don't think there's not some changes I have in mind."

"Madam, mi casa es su casa. Literally. Do whatever you want to cheer the place up. You've seen the bedroom, then?"

"No, it's the one place we never went as kids. Hardrock always told us it was his 'sanctuary,' and kept the door closed."

John led the way down the hallway and paused at the bedroom door. "Sanctuary is one way to describe it," he said as he opened the door, "family museum would be more descriptive. There's quite a crowd in here."

The door swung open fully and John turned on the light. Maggie stepped into the room and swiveled her head to take in all the pictures on the walls. "Wow," she said softly.

"That's better than, 'holy shit,' I guess. It's a bit overwhelming, isn't it?"

Maggie nodded as she walked over to begin looking at the gallery hanging on the walls. When she got to the wall where the pictures of she, Harley and Hardrock had hung she and turned to John. "What was here?"

"That's where the pictures of you and Harley were hanging."

Maggie nodded and turned back to her inspection of the pictures. She stopped short when she got to the one of John and his first wife on their wedding day. "This one," she said pointing at it, "definitely goes."

"I think they all should go. I'd like to start a new collection."

Even before they unpacked, the pictures in the bedroom were taken down and stacked in the office.

When John called Cynthia the next morning to thank her, she told him all of Maggie's recovered belongings were at her office. Between retrieving Maggie's things and getting settled in at the trailer, it was noon before John remembered he needed to call Wes. As soon as there was a lull in the domestic action, he sat down at the kitchen table to make the call. Much to his disappointment, Doreen told him Wes had left for the day.

"I'll give him a message," she offered.

"I actually have a couple of questions for him," John said

somewhat irritated, "one of which is the same as I left with you in April."

"You mean the question about the key, right?"

The swiftness of Doreen's response caught John off guard. Surely, if she remembered a question so small, so many months later, she must have delivered it. "Well, yes," he stammered, embarrassed at the tone he had been using, "I thought you'd forgotten to give it to him."

"No, I did not forget to pass it along." She sounded hurt.

"I'm sorry, Doreen, my mistake. I should have known better. I guess your boss forgot about it."

There was a pause before Doreen answered in a cool, professional tone, "Mr. Bartholomew rarely forgets anything. He'll be in at nine, tomorrow morning." After another awkward pause she continued in a much more cordial tone, "John, it was a mistake lots of people make. Call first thing tomorrow. I'll make sure he takes it."

"Thanks, Doreen."

John hung up the phone feeling like a total ass. Recalling the first day he went to Wes' office, he mentally kicked himself. Doreen had been nothing but helpful and friendly. Rubbing his forehead, John told himself to lighten up. Sam's advice about sweating the small stuff went through his mind, again. His thoughts were interrupted when Maggie kissed his neck. He turned and looked up at her.

"You look stressed," she said, and rubbed his neck. "Whoa, you feel stressed. You know, I have the perfect cure for stress."

"And that would be?" John asked, raising his eyebrows suggestively.

"Shopping."

"What? I thought..."

"I know what you thought," Maggie said, pushing away John's groping hands. "I want to get some stuff to brighten this place up before it makes me suicidal."

"What did you have in mind?"

"Paint mostly, but I also want to replace those curtains and add some color. Besides, since I'm out of a job, I need something to do."

"There's no question the place could use it, but money is an issue right now."

"Maybe for you," Maggie replied with an airy wave of her hand, "but I have a little money of my own."

Late that night, John Barstow collapsed on the living room floor to sleep. It was the same living room in which he had hung new window blinds just hours earlier; the living room down the hall from the bedroom where the scent of drying paint was too heavy to be tolerated.

The smell of coffee woke John. He looked at his watch and saw it was shortly past six o'clock. He stood up, wrapped his blanket around him, and wandered toward the dim light in the kitchen. Maggie was leaning on the stove, flipping through the pages of a catalog by the light of the stove's exhaust hood. She was wearing John's shirt, which hung loosely on her and stopped high enough to afford a generous view of her legs and fanny. John took a moment to appreciate the view before speaking.

"Good lord, woman, don't you ever sleep?"

Maggie jumped at John's voice. "I'm sorry, I didn't mean to wake you. I woke up and got excited about fixing this place up. Couldn't go back to sleep."

"You made coffee. You're forgiven."

John shuffled over to the light switch and turned on the kitchen light before sitting down at the table. Maggie turned off the exhaust hood light and poured John a cup of coffee. She set it down in front of him before sitting lightly on his lap.

"What's the game plan for today?"

"Call Wes. See Cynthia. Tag up with Harley. Ravish my girlfriend. The usual, although not necessarily in that order. And you?"

"Let me see," Maggie said, with a giggle, "get ravished by my boyfriend, then work on this place. Definitely in that order."

Maggie's giggling grew louder when John reached for the light switch and returned the trailer to darkness.

John called the office of Bartholomew Law precisely at nine o'clock. Doreen answered immediately after the first ring. Still embarrassed about the manner in which he had spoken to her the day before, he apologized again before asking to speak to Wes. To John's relief, Doreen assured him she completely understood the situation. Wes picked up immediately after Doreen put John on hold.

"What can I do for you, John?"

"I'm hoping to get some answers from you."

"You should know by now, that I'm limited to what I can tell you. The trust is very specific about that."

"I *know*, Wes," John snapped. "I just have a couple of simple questions. First, I need you to clarify for me what, if anything, the trust stipulates as far as wages and bonuses go in determining whether a profit is shown this year for Last Chance Adventures."

Wes asked John to hold on for a moment while he retrieved the trust document from his files. John heard pages turning as the old lawyer skimmed through the document before he came back on the line.

"There is a line in the section describing determination of profit that states, 'wages and bonuses paid employees of Last Chance Adventures shall not be less than those paid in the previous year of operation.' So, yes, it is very specific: you must pay your help at least what they earned last year." When John didn't reply, Wes asked, "Why do you ask? Were you thinking about stiffing somebody?"

"I will give you the benefit of the doubt, and assume you are joking."

"Only partially. I know what you're thinking, and yes, *you* are considered an employee. Last Chance Adventures is a corporation, and as such, you have to pay yourself, too. And that would be the same amount Hardrock paid himself."

"Shit." John paused and mulled his plan B over before continuing, "I really don't want to do this, but all three of my employees have said they would be willing to forego some, or all, of their bonuses if it made the difference."

"It's not their choice, it's a stipulation of the trust."

"Damn, that's not good news," John sighed, "but at least I have an idea how far in the hole I'm buried. I have one more question. Do you know where the key to the lock on the door into the back of the Quonset hut is located?"

"Didn't Sam Burlington give you my message?"

"What message?" John asked, puzzled.

"When we spoke in July, I asked Sam to pass along a

message to you."

Much had happened in the three months since that conversation, and it took John a moment before he asked, "You mean the thing about the bear?"

"You need to remember exactly how it was phrased. It's critical."

"Goddamn it, Wes! Stop playing games. I'm running out of time!"

"I am as aware of that as you, John," Wes replied calmly. "So, tell me, what was the message?"

The image of Sam standing in front of him that warm day in July came back to John. "Don't let the bear bite you."

"Exactly. That phrase is the key to your success."

"Thanks for the help," John said sarcastically, and ended the call before Wes could respond.

John took several deep breaths to flush out his frustration and anger, then got up from the table and walked to the bathroom. Maggie stood on a stepladder, stretching to cut the corner at the top of the wall. John watched her and smiled. The tip of her tongue protruded from the corner of her mouth in the focused concentration of producing a straight line of paint in the corner.

"Does the tongue help?"

Her concentration broken, Maggie turned toward him and scowled. "A lot more than you. How did it go with Wes?"

"Like always with that old fart. It was neither pleasant, nor overly informative. I'm going over to Cynthia's before Harley gets here. You want to come?"

In answer, Maggie held up her hands to show the paint on them. When she did, a glob of paint dropped from her brush and splattered on the floor.

"Yeah, maybe not," John said slowly. "By the way, you might want to save some paint for the walls."

"Go away, smart ass. I have important work to do."

John grabbed the ledgers Cynthia had sent out to Last Chance as he left. He had gone over them so many times, making notes as he did, that the pages were dog-eared and practically limp. On the drive to Cynthia's he reflected on what Wes had said about the wages and bonuses. If his calculations were correct, paying full wages would mean they needed at least eighty-thousand from the recovered gold to have more than a hundred grand in the account at the end of the year. Could the five buckets of black sand they brought back really hold that much gold? Even though he told himself to believe they could, the situation felt hopeless.

Cynthia smiled as John walked into her office. "How's that painting going?"

"Don't ask. Let's just say if the headline in tomorrow's paper reads, 'Nikiski Couple Dies From Paint Fumes,' you won't need to check the names."

"Better now than in the dead of winter. At least you can crack the windows to help air things out."

John shrugged, then spread the ledgers out before his bookkeeper. He went down the columns of figures with her to verify his calculations. When Cynthia added the additional charges from Reeder Air, taxes on the property, and other items from a seemingly endless list, the final result was worse than John's estimate by several thousand dollars. John stared at the final figure grimly and slumped down in his chair.

"I'm sorry, I don't know what to say, John," Cynthia said softly. "My offer to pass on the bonus is still good. I can even take a little less for my services for the rest of the year, if it will help."

John looked at the pretty bookkeeper. The sadness in her eyes showed the sincerity of the offer. Maggie had been right, Cynthia wasn't as much an employee as a friend.

"You don't know how much that means to me," John replied, "but I can't do that. It sucks, but that's what it is. Nobody could have guessed the bookings would be so low this year."

"If there's anything I can do, let me know."

John winked as he stood up, and asked, "How good are you with a paint brush?"

Harley was sitting at the kitchen table when John got back to the trailer. He was teasing Maggie, and enjoying himself thoroughly.

"No, I really mean it, Magpie, it's a good look on you."

"Oh, piss off, Harley!" Maggie shot back from where she

stood at the sink. She was using a damp rag in an effort to remove a large streak of paint that ran from almost the top of her head to the end of her shoulder-length hair. "It's not funny. And stop calling me Magpie."

"How did that happen?" John asked, stifling his urge to laugh.

"I was putting the paint can on top of the ladder when jerk-boy scared the crap out of me. I jumped and a bunch of paint slopped out onto my head."

No longer able to contain himself, John burst out in laughter. Maggie quit pulling her hair through the rag and put her hands on her hips. When she did, her paint-matted hair hung straight down stiffly. Both men roared with laughter. Maggie shot a dagger look at Harley and then addressed John with angry, slitted eyes.

"I think maybe you and the hired help might want to leave."

Still laughing, both men made a hasty retreat out of the trailer.

"Thanks a bunch," John said when they were out of the lean-to. "Guess I'll be sharing the couch in the Quonset with Dawg tonight."

"Probably not," Harley replied, slapping John on the shoulder, "she'll let Dawg stay in the trailer."

John glanced back at the trailer and saw Maggie glowering at them from a window. He decided to change the subject. "You got here early."

Harley followed John's gaze and immediately quit laughing, but couldn't hide his grin. "You said to come when I had a clear head. Here I am."

The two men walked over to the Suburban, where John had left the buckets of black sands. John nodded at the buckets. "Do you suppose there's better than eighty thousand dollars worth of gold in those? Because that's what we need to keep Last Chance."

Harley's grin evaporated. "That is a butt-load of gold!"

"Did Hardrock have more than this?"

"I don't know. I never really paid attention. I thought he kept the black sands simply to piddle away the winter by panning a little."

"Well, how many buckets did he have out at Last Chance each year, would you say?"

"John, *I don't know*. Does it matter? It's too late to get more."

John glanced at the Quonset hut and took a deep breath. "You're right. I guess we need to figure out how to process what we've got."

"Did Wes tell you where the key was?"

John shook his head and related his conversation with Wes. Harley couldn't ascribe any significance to the phrase about a bear, and agreed that it seemed to be of little help to the situation. After talking it over, they decided that if nothing else, they would hire a welder to cut away the box and lock.

John backed the Suburban over to the Quonset and Harley climbed into the back of the vehicle to wrestle the heavy buckets to within easy reach from the tailgate. John hefted one of the buckets and grunted.

"I'm glad we didn't fill these all the way. I'll bet there's forty or fifty pounds in each one of them."

He pulled another bucket from the back of Suburban and started into the Quonset. Harley climbed out of the vehicle, grabbed two more and followed him. Making his way across the room, John set his heavy load down on the floor, near the wall, on the right side of the door. He was scooting one of the buckets tight against the wall when he heard Harley drop his buckets and tell him to look up. Harley's voice had the tone of shock. John complied, and found himself looking at the largest of the bear skulls hanging on the wall.

"Don't let the bear bite you," Harley said slowly.

"That's the key to our success," John added.

Slowly, almost as if he were afraid the skull really could bite, John reached up and removed it from the wall. The lower jaw was fastened in place, so he turned the skull over. A small hook was screwed into the inside of the lower jaw. Hanging on the hook was a key with the word "Master" stamped across it.

John removed the key from the hook and set the skull on the couch. His hands were trembling so badly from excitement, it took several tries before he got the key into the lock. When he turned the key, the lock opened easily. Removing the lock, he lifted the latch and slid it to the side. The large door swung open with little effort. Harley stood at John's side and the two of them peered through the open doorway. With no windows on that end of the building, the room was dark. However, even had there been light, the view would have been blocked by the wall facing them four feet inside the door.

"What the hell is that about?" Harley wondered aloud.

John took a tentative step forward, through the door and looked in both directions. "It's only about ten feet wide," he said. "I think it's a privacy wall, designed to keep anyone from seeing into the room when Hardrock had the door open."

"Did I ever mention that your uncle was a little paranoid?"

"Did you ever have to use the horn to get his attention?"

"Yeah, when I was a kid."

"Did he open the door?"

"Yeah."

"Did you ever see what was in the room?"

"Good point."

John stood just inside the door and let his eyes grow accustomed to the dimmer light. He examined the back of the wall separating the two ends of the Quonset hut and saw a bank of light switches a little farther down the wall to the left of the door. Flipping the first switch produced a faint hum then a flicker of light from a row of fluorescent lights directly overhead. John could see a desk and filing cabinet ahead of him. Harley stepped through the door as John continued to turn on the light switches. With each additional switch, another bank of lights lit up, until that entire end of the building was bright.

Harley stepped to the right and around the wall. He let out a low whistle. John continued around his end of the wall and looked around the room. Directly in the middle, roughly eight feet beyond the wall, stood a table with a collection of motors mounted underneath. Half-way down the left side of the room was a large metal box with a large, insulated flue rising up from the top and extending through the roof. A long workbench lined the opposite side of the room. At the far end of the room stood a collection of equipment arranged in a haphazard fashion.

"Look at this, John. Sam had it pegged. Welcome to Hardrock's little shop of secrets," Harley said as he walked toward the table. He walked around it, pointing out various items connected to it. "Driver for the shaker, levelers, that's the water pump. Sump for return water supply. This thing is nice, John, top of the line."

"So you've seen one before?"

"Not this exact one, but similar. I don't get these," Harley pointed to two flat bars suspended very near the surface of the table at one end. "It looks like a Hardrock modification."

John walked over to the table and asked, "Think we, and by that I really mean you, can figure out how to run it?"

"Sure, Hardrock probably had it optimized already. Should be just a matter of figuring out which switch does what, and how fast to feed it."

Leaving Harley to examine the shaker table, John walked to the left side of the room to check things out. He opened a locker located near the desk and filing cabinet to examine its contents. It contained a shiny metallic coat, a face shield and thick mitts. John guessed it was safety gear for use when smelting the black sands. Next down the wall was a bench with two shelves underneath where rows of crucibles were lined up. The crucibles were similar to the ones he had used at Last Chance, except much larger and not ceramic. They were made of a dark gray material, graphite, John guessed.

Farther down the wall John examined the smelting furnace. A blower was mounted on the side to draw air from outside the building. John saw a pipe with a valve that was connected at the air injection point. He followed the piping as it rose up and then traversed the shop to the wall on the other side and exited the building at a point where the propane tank would be located outside. He opened the door on the furnace, which looked much like a large oven door, and peered inside. The cavity was lined with ceramic brick, as was the door itself. It was obviously designed for intense heat, capable of melting metals, and John thought to himself it wasn't something one would casually fire up.

For more than three hours the two men explored the shop and its contents. With every new, interesting discovery, they would huddle and discuss that item's possible use and operation. John felt relieved when he found a stockpile of the ingredients used in making the flux necessary to smelt the gold from the black sands. Although no prepared flux was found, he did find an air-tight bucket labeled for it. Harley focused most of his attention on the shaker table and the utilities in the building. He pointed out to John that Hardrock must have kept the large space heater in the shop on all the time to prevent the possibility of freeze damage to the water lines.

"I'm pretty sure how to run this thing," Harley said after he had gone completely over the table, "but it wouldn't hurt if I could find the manual."

"What about the filing cabinet? Suppose there's a manual for it in there?"

Harley slapped his forehead. "Duh! That's why you're the boss."

The filing cabinet had four drawers, none of which were labeled. They quickly flipped through the folders in each drawer. The top two drawers contained assay results and shipping invoices from previous years. John made a mental note to examine them more thoroughly, later. The third drawer held various kinds of correspondence related to Last Chance Adventures, from tax appraisals to letters from clients.

"Bingo," Harley said when he opened the bottom drawer, "there's manuals for everything here. God bless Hardrock's compulsion to keep everything in its place."

"Let me see the manual for the furnace."

More time passed as each man went over their respective pieces of equipment with manuals in hand. When John finished going over the basics of the smelter, he checked his watch.

"It's almost four," he said. "I'm getting hungry, what about you?"

"I guess," came an absent-minded answer. Harley was engrossed in examining the two bars suspended over the surface of the table. "I've got these things figured out. They're magnets mounted on pivots. They strip the magnetite out of the black sands. Really clever. Hardrock was a genius at saving time and effort."

"So, what happens when so much magnetite builds up on them it blocks the flow?"

"That's the really neat part. Watch." Harley moved one of

the bars away from the table on its pivot. "The magnet actually sits in this plastic trough. When there's a build up, simply pivot the magnet and trough away from the table, and pull the magnet out of the trough. With the magnet gone, the magnetite will drop off the surface of the trough."

The concept was truly ingenious John admitted, but repeated that he was hungry. He suggested they carry in the buckets of black sand and call it a day. After moving the buckets and locking the shop back up, John returned the key to its hiding place.

"What are you doing for dinner tonight?" Harley asked as they left the Quonset.

"I'm not sure," John said, looking in the direction of the trailer. "Between the mood we left Maggie in, and her painting all day, I think we'll be going out."

"I forgot about pissing her off. Sucks to be you. Maybe I'll just dine alone."

"Thanks a lot, buddy. What time are you coming by tomorrow?"

"Whenever you want. I can't wait to get that table running."

"Good enough, see you around nine."

Harley nodded and continued on toward his truck. Just as John stepped up to the door on the lean-to he heard Harley screech.

"Goddamn it! *Magpie!*"

"What?" John called from the steps.

"She painted the seat in my truck!"

John looked quickly in the direction of the window Maggie had been glowering from earlier. He saw her reappear with a big smile and blow Harley a kiss.

CHAPTER 17

Harley's confidence about being able to run the shaker table was justified, although it took three full days of minor adjustments to the water flows to obtain acceptable performance. The process also proved to be much slower than either man had imagined. Instead of simply pouring the black sands into the hopper at the head of the table, they quickly discovered the feed had to be carefully added in very small amounts. Feeding too much material at one time disrupted the flow of water, resulting in poor separation. Feeding the table was tedium at its height.

"Before we tried to run this thing," Harley shouted over the loud thumping of the table, "I wondered how one man could possibly feed it and keep the magnets clear."

"It's still faster than panning."

"Maybe so, but it feels like we'll be here until breakup."

John shrugged and turned away from Harley, returning to his examination of the filing cabinet contents. The furnace had proven to be much less of a problem than the shaker. It's operation was simple: line up the gas, start the blower and set the controller. Ignition was electronic, and temperature control automatic. On testing, it performed flawlessly, so John had been spending his time going through the documents in the filing cabinet. There were folders for a number of assay and refining companies in the cabinet, but the most recent dates were on invoices to a company named Oxford, in Anchorage. John decided to call them as soon as he had a chance.

Done with the filing cabinet, John turned his attention to the desk. Nothing he had seen so far provided any information on the flux mixture his uncle had used. Although they were nowhere near the point to use it, he would feel more comfortable if he had the recipe. John started going through the drawers of the desk and was interrupted by two blasts on the horn, announcing Maggie was outside the door.

"Damn! I swear she comes out here just to scare the hell out of me," Harley groused loudly over the thumping of the table.

"Just be glad she doesn't amuse herself by repainting your truck," John shouted back.

When John unlatched the door and opened it, Maggie stood with a proud smile and held out a bound notebook. Her hand had a new shade of paint on it, indicating she had moved on to another room in the trailer. John laughed when he saw it.

"And how's the painting going today?"

"I'm done with the hall, and working on the living room, thank you very much. I found this while clearing off a bookshelf. At first, I thought it was a diary, but it's a notebook. Go to page seventy-nine."

John took the notebook and flipped through the pages. Some of the writing was barely legible, as if the writer were jotting things down just to make sure the information was recorded somewhere. On page seventy-nine, the words "flux tests" were underlined. On that page, and the subsequent six pages, were dated entries spanning a period of months. Under each date was a recipe listing the volumes of the ingredients for a different flux. Under each recipe comments on that flux's performance were entered. Some of the notes referenced problems with pouring the smelted material, others referred to differing assay results. Next to the flux dated November 30, 1986, were the words "best bet."

"This is it!" John gasped. "Sweet cheeks, you are a goddess!"

"I know," Maggie said, beaming, "and I think I deserve a kiss."

"Would you settle for something more?"

"We will negotiate that later," she replied while stepping

forward to steal a quick smooch.

John watched Maggie bounce across the parking area and disappear into the trailer, then returned to the shop. He walked over to Harley and held out the notebook.

"I think you can quit being pissed at your sister," he shouted. "She found the flux recipe."

"I don't know about that," Harley replied as he slowly added more material to the hopper, "it's kind of fun to be on the indignant side of things, for a change."

There was only one more item to nail down, and that was to call Oxford. The next morning John called to ask about shipping materials and how payment was made for the refined metals. It was a simple process, and with roughly a two week turnaround time, it wasn't as long as he had feared

"All we have to do now," John told Harley, "is get through separating the free gold and smelting the sands."

"Oh, is that all?" Harley laughed. "Bold words from someone who has yet to smelt a thing, and has over 150 pounds of black sand sitting in buckets."

"Oh, ye of little faith! While you've been spending your nights in debaucherous revelry at the Shuffle, I have been doing my homework on smelting."

"Do tell, professor."

"With the volumes we'll be smelting now," John said, suddenly serious, "it's a different animal. Even a small screw-up can be dangerous. We have to pour the smelted material, which will be over 1700 degrees, from the crucibles into cone molds. Spill that on cold cement, and I guess things get very exciting. The cone molds have to be heated to prevent the glass layer from shattering violently. If the pour cools down too quickly, the glass can explode and become shrapnel, like from a grenade."

"Okay. Kids, don't do this at home, John here is a paid professional."

"Yeah, something like that."

"Maybe you ought to practice your crucible handling before we actually put anything in the box."

John nodded in solemn agreement.

Work at the shaker table proceeded steadily for the next week, until enough clean black sands had been separated for the initial smelting. During that time John took Harley's suggestion and practiced using the long, heavy tongs to handle the crucibles. He tried various ways to grip them and practiced tipping them over the mold cones; first, with cold crucibles, then, after heating them up to full temperature in the smelter. It took some practice to get comfortable handling the tongs while wearing the thick mitts and heavy fireproof coat, but feeling the heat that penetrated his protective face shield proved to John they were necessary, even if nothing went awry.

Early in the morning on the day of the first smelting attempt, John went out to the shop and started the furnace. It would require more than four hours to reach operating temperature. He went over everything in his mind. The flux had been ready for three days, mixed according to the recipe in Hardrock's notebook. The separated black sands had been dried thoroughly and crushed in a ball mill. The crucibles had been lined up the day before. He checked the wheeled rack for the mold cones to make sure the heater on it had fuel. All that needed yet to be done was to fill and mix the crucibles. Everything was as ready as he could make it. Yet, he was nervous to the point of nausea. It wasn't just the inherent danger of the operation, but also worry over the results. Would they get enough?

As he left the shop and walked to the trailer, John thought about his uncle doing everything Harley and he were doing as a team, entirely by himself. The man must have had balls the size of watermelons, he decided.

John declined Maggie's offer to fix breakfast when he got back to the trailer. He sat down at the table and looked at his watch impatiently, tapping his foot nervously.

"What time did you tell Harley to be here?" Maggie asked.

"Around eight."

"Okay, six-thirty is not anywhere close to 'around eight.' Why don't you eat something to kill the time?"

John's face screwed up tightly. "The way I'm feeling, I'd just toss it up. I don't think that would be pretty behind the face shield."

"You need to calm down, John. This isn't a do or die situation. Things will be fine, even if we fall short."

John nodded in agreement, but kept tapping his foot. He stared out the kitchen window into the darkness of the morning as he replied, "I'm tired of failure."

"What, you think not overcoming the odds stacked against you would be a failure?"

"It's not just losing Last Chance I'm talking about."

"What else, then?"

John shifted his gaze from the window and fixed it firmly on Maggie. "What about us?"

Maggie brushed her hair back behind her ears, then crossed her arms in front of her before meeting John's gaze fully and answering, "I'm not in love with a gold mine, John. Beyond what it means to you, I don't give a damn about Last Chance."

John took a breath to reply, but was distracted by the flash of headlights out the window and the rumble of Harley's beater truck as he pulled up.

"Maybe we ought to finish this conversation later," Maggie continued. "Just know that I don't care about the profit clause. It doesn't matter to me."

The door to the trailer opened and Harley entered without knocking. "Am I interrupting something?" he asked, pulling off his coat. "By all means, continue. I love watching a good argument."

"Oh, piss off, Harley."

The tension broken, John laughed. "You're here a little early, aren't you? I said eight."

"Yeah, right, like you haven't been up since five," Harley replied, walking over to the coffee pot and playfully bumping Maggie out of the way. "Move, Magpie. If you won't be gracious enough to offer the help a cup of Joe, I'll grab it myself."

"It was more like three o'clock," Maggie grumbled as she slid out of Harley's way, "and if you want breakfast with your coffee, you'll have to fix that, too."

"No need for breakfast," came the cheerful reply, "grabbed a bite at the Shuffle. Doorway did good hiring Karla to replace you, Magpie. I haven't had heartburn once from *her* breakfasts. Must be the more congenial atmosphere. Better for digestion."

Maggie opened her mouth to sling something back at her

brother, but John interrupted. "Well then, maybe we ought to go out to the shop and get set up."

"You'll come and get me before you start pouring?" Maggie asked. "I really want to watch."

John assured her that he would, then kissed her lightly before following Harley out the door. At the shop, John went directly to the furnace and checked the pyrometer to gauge the preheating progress. From the times they had heated it up previously, he knew the last 500 degrees took the longest to achieve. He judged they had at least another hour before the oven was up to temperature, which was more time than needed to load the crucibles. John added the volumes of crushed black sand, and Harley followed, adding double that volume of flux. After they completed loading the crucibles Harley went over to the shaker table as John thoroughly stirred the contents of each crucible.

"How much is left to run through?" John asked when he was done mixing the contents of the crucibles.

"Just half-way through the third bucket. If this went any slower, I'd be tempted to hang myself."

"And we've gotten just over six ounces of free gold?"

"You weighed it yourself yesterday, you tell me," Harley replied peevishly. "You're driving me nuts, John! Stop obsessing! We can't make it any more than it is."

John was silent after Harley's rebuke, and split his time between watching the fine gold separated from the black sands collect in the thin lines on the table's surface, and clearing the magnets. He reflected on what Harley had said, realizing he was not only vexing Harley with his obsession over how much gold they might recover, but also Maggie. He walked over to the oven and saw the temperature was still low.

"You know what they say about watched pots," Harley shouted.

John nodded and started toward the door. "If you're okay here, I'm going to the trailer for a few minutes."

Harley waved John off with his free hand while continuing to slowly feed material into the hopper.

A light snow was falling when John stepped out of the Quonset and walked to the trailer. It wouldn't be daylight for almost another two hours; an hour later than when they had come back from Last Chance. The change from practically all daylight to almost all dark seemed as striking as the dramatic increase in daylight he'd experienced seven months earlier. Closing his eyes, he took a deep breath and thought about the first time Harley told him it was possible to smell snow. At the time he scoffed at the idea, but after experiencing the phenomenon firsthand, was convinced. They were just small things he had come to appreciate about life in Alaska. Just two small things in a long list of incredible things he would not give up, no matter what.

"Is it time already?" Maggie asked when John entered the trailer.

"No, far from it. The furnace isn't up to temperature, and it will be over an hour after I put in the crucibles. I came back to finish our conversation."

"Oh, that. I was just..."

"I heard what you said," John cut her off, "and I came to ask you what happens if I lose Last Chance."

"You won't."

"But if I *do*," John pressed, "what do you see in your future?"

"Absolutely nothing that I couldn't live with, happily. What about you?"

John held up his hands and turned around slowly, as if surveying the trailer. "I'd have a home and fifty grand in cash," he said, "but I've come to the conclusion that's not entirely it. I've seen what I want, and I simply won't give up on it."

Maggie let out a long sigh of exasperation. "It's just a stupid gold mine, John."

"It's not only about the gold mine. Look, no matter how things turn out, I'm staying here. For the first time since I can remember, I feel like I have family, a home, a place I belong. I worry about losing Last Chance, not just because I want it, but because in the process, I might lose everything else."

"Do you honestly think I won't stay if you don't have Last Chance?"

"It isn't simply not having the mine, it's not having any kind of future, no prospects. I'm sure you don't want that."

"First off, this state was built by people who came here without prospects. You heard Sam. He and Hardrock didn't have 'prospects' when they got here. You're just the next generation. Second, *you* don't get to decide what *I* want."

"And you're sure of what you want?"

"Unless you finally manage to talk me out of it."

"I've never been able to talk you into, or out of, anything yet."

"That's right. Now, don't you have some smelting to do?"

CHAPTER 18

The first smelting went slowly, but smoothly. The added weight of the black sands and flux made handling the crucibles more difficult than simply going through the motions with them empty. John was disappointed in the outcome, however, which came as no surprise to anyone. After weighing several sample scoops used to measure the volume of the processed black sands, John determined that approximately eight ounces of black sands went into each crucible for firing. The buttons produced varied from one and a quarter, to one and a half ounces.

"That's less than what we got out at the mine," John said after calculating the percentage. "At best, we're only getting seventeen percent gold by weight. I wonder if we're using the wrong flux recipe."

"It's not the flux, John," Harley replied irritably. He was growing tired of John's constant fretting. "We didn't completely separate the free gold out there. It will work out in the long run. Quit crunching numbers, and let's get the gold."

By the twenty-fifth of November, when the last of seventy-eight crucibles had been fired, they had accumulated just under 115 ounces of gold, including the twelve ounces of free gold from the shaker table.

"I don't care what you say," Harley said, surveying the results of their labor, "that is a helluva lot of gold."

"No doubt about it," John agreed. "But will it be enough?"

Maggie picked up one of the buttons and looked at it closely. "It sure is bright."

"Yeah, it is. Sam told me that could be bad news if the brightness is due to a high silver percentage."

"He also told you it could be from platinum," Harley quickly countered. "Quit borrowing trouble."

John shook his head. "The assay results in the cabinet indicate anything other than gold will be mostly silver. But you're right, and we'll find out soon enough. I want to take it all up to Oxford on Monday."

"Why not take it up tomorrow?" Maggie suggested.

"The day before Thanksgiving? No way," John replied. "We're going to take the weekend off, starting now. We deserve it."

Thanksgiving dinner was the first time anyone, other than Harley, had been to the trailer since returning from Last Chance. Doorway accepted their invitation readily, closing the Shuffle Inn for the first time in years.

"It's not what you'd call a high traffic day," he explained, "being a family-oriented day. I've always stayed open in the past, mostly for the chance to have some company while I chill out."

Doorway's question regarding what the three of them had been doing for almost two months provided an awkward moment.

"Look around," Maggie said to deflect the question, "you don't think this place looks better? It didn't fix itself up."

"No doubt about it," Doorway agreed, "it beats the hell out of how Hardrock kept it."

"John and I have been going over business plans for next year," Harley added.

"All I know," Doorway said with a laugh, "is that business has gone to hell in a handbag without you hanging around, Harley. John, show some mercy, give your help some time off. I'm going broke!"

"I can say with complete confidence you'll be seeing more of us after next week," John said.

Doorway's eyebrows raised in curiosity. "What's going on next week? Are you seeing Wes about finalizing things on Last

Chance?"

"No, that won't happen until after the first of the year. I promised these two a night on the town in Los Anchorage."

"A little early celebration never hurt anybody," Harley added.

The rest of Doorway's visit went by without any additional awkward moments. Doorway filled them in on the arrests made associated with Kells's murder, and asked how John's first season at Last Chance had gone. Everyone agreed that although the number of clients had been low, it had been extremely successful, and fun. Harley was particularly entertaining in describing Maggie's exchange with Turk. Even Maggie had to laugh. As he pulled on his coat, the big barkeep offered Harley a holiday nightcap, which was cheerfully accepted, and the two of them left. With the last of the feast cleaned up, and the dishes put away, John and Maggie collapsed on the couch.

"I can hardly breathe," John grunted as he sat down.

"Me too." Maggie sat with her legs curled under her and snuggled against John. "When are we leaving for Anchorage?"

"I was thinking we could drive up Sunday. That way we could go into Oxford early Monday morning, drop the gold off and have the rest of the day to play. If we wait until Monday to drive up, we could run into bad weather and not get into Oxford until Tuesday."

"Sounds good," Maggie said through a yawn.

"It will take about two weeks to get paid for it, so that would be the fifteenth. That would give us plenty of time to clear up the accounts and, hopefully, show a profit."

"Um-hmm..."

"What?"

No response came from Maggie other than her soft rhythmic breathing as she lay against his shoulder. He didn't say anything else, choosing to let her sleep as he worked the numbers over in his head for the millionth time. It was going to be close, so very close.

"Do you have an account with us, Mr. Barstow?" the Oxford agent behind the counter asked.

"It should be under Last Chance Adventures," John answered.

"Possibly under the name of Grant," Harley added.

The agent looked at them skeptically before typing on her keyboard. After a moment, she looked up and said, "I show both. I have a corporation named Last Chance Adventures, and an individual named Grant. For the individual account, I will need a first name, a social security number and photo identification."

"It's the corporation," John replied.

"And you are the agent for the corporation?"

John was taken aback at the question. "Agent? I don't understand."

"In order to conduct business for a corporation, you must be the registered agent. All our corporate gold transactions must be recorded and reported to regulatory agencies. There are state royalty taxes involved, as well as federal taxes."

Before John could say anything, a man stepped up behind the counter agent. "Hello, I'm Don VanGundt, the managing agent, is there a problem?"

John immediately recognized the name. "I'm John Barstow, with Last Chance Adventures, we spoke a few weeks ago about your services. Apparently, I didn't probe deeply enough."

VanGundt extended his hand to John. "I remember our conversation." John wondered how such a brief conversation could be so memorable, until VanGundt added, "Mr. Bartholomew called me shortly after you did, to find out if you had made contact. When I told him you had, Mr. Bartholomew set up the account for Last Chance Adventures, and arranged for you to act as agent."

"Wes set things up? I should have known that old fart would check up on me," John mumbled. "So you know him."

John's casual and irreverent reference to the lawyer made the counter agent sit up a little straighter, and look a little more attentive to what was going on.

"There aren't many people in the mining industry who don't know Mr. Bartholomew," VanGundt said respectfully. "I also knew your uncle. Please accept my belated condolences." John nodded, and VanGundt turned to the counter agent, "Sheri, Mr. Barstow is the agent on record for Last Chance Adventures. The usual identification check will be all that is required." He turned back to John and again offered his hand with, "Sheri will take

A. E. Poynor

care of everything from here. Thank you for your business."

The process of transferring the gold to the refiner took longer than either John, or Harley, had expected. The transfer was carefully documented, as was the total weight. It was no surprise the gold they were turning in was weighed, but the final figure came as a shock.

"That's more than ten ounces less than we came up with at our shop," John said when Sheri presented the final figures for his review.

"That figure is in Troy ounces," came the response. "You probably weighed in avoirdupois. It's a common mistake."

John felt like a fool. Sam had mentioned the very same thing. Making the situation even more embarrassing, John knew the scale at the shop had a setting for Troy ounces. In his excitement to get the final number, he forgot to set the scale correctly. It was a sloppy mistake; more than a ten-thousand dollar mistake in the figures he had been counting on.

"Don't sweat it, buddy," Harley said softly, "it's still enough."

"It will have to be, won't it?"

Neither of the men mentioned the weight discrepancy to Maggie when they returned to the hotel. The three of them spent the rest of the day enjoying the holiday season in the city. Harley made arrangements to go out on the town with a friend in the evening, while John and Maggie went to Club Paris for the best steak John had ever experienced. The next morning the three of them drove back to Nikiski to wait.

The days passed slowly. Harley bided his time helping Derrick Smythe with a sheetrock job he had contracted. Sheetrock work was right down there with picking worms out of halibut filets on a slime line, in Harley's estimation, but it beat just sitting. Maggie continued working on the trailer, deciding the bathroom needed updating. She enlisted John's help to keep him busy and prevent him from brooding. However, by the eighteenth, all three were edgy.

John jumped out of the bathtub, where he and Maggie were gluing new tile to the walls, and dashed for the phone. Cynthia's voice sounded excited when he answered. He had told her to watch the business account for a deposit.

298

"This is huge," she said. "I checked on line, and it was deposited last night."

John's heart pounded in his ears. "How much?"

"Just over eighty-six thousand. It's going to be very close, John, but I think this will do it!"

"I'll be right there." In his excitement, John slammed down the phone harder than he intended. The thought of deafening his bookkeeper in one ear flitted through his mind.

"Maggie! Grab your shoes!" he shouted. "The money's in the bank. We need to run over to Cynthia's. *Now!*"

"I can't go like this," Maggie protested, "give me a minute to clean up."

"You're fine! You're beautiful! Let's go!"

Ignoring Maggie's continuing protests, John grabbed her by the arm and dragged her toward the lean-to.

"Wait! I need socks!"

"We aren't walking, just put on some shoes."

The Suburban had barely slid to a stop at Cynthia's when John was out of the vehicle and headed for the office entrance. Maggie followed closely behind him. Snow fell into her shoes at each step, a cold reminder of her absent socks. When they burst into Cynthia's office, out of breath from their mad dash, Cynthia looked at them and laughed.

"If I only had a camera right now. *This* is definitely going to be a topic the next time we're all in public together."

Maggie blew an errant strand of hair out of her face and pulled first one shoe off to dump snow out of it, then the other. Cynthia continued laughing and clapped her hands in delight.

"You're sworn to secrecy," Maggie said. "I was kidnapped by a madman."

"Hey, every family has skeletons."

"When you two are done yukking it up," John interrupted, "I'd like to see what we've got."

"What you've got is an angel," Cynthia responded. "Where did this come from? Who is Oxford?"

John's first reaction to Cynthia's question was regret at choosing a direct deposit to the business account. He glanced at Maggie before answering, "It's a source of operating capital that has to remain confidential. All I can say is that it is from the same source Hardrock used for his large deposits. We just put it all in at one time. Can you live with that, and keep it between us?"

Cynthia nodded, then turned her attention back to her computer. "Okay, the deposit was $86,568. Added to the existing balance, that gives you $119,843. Property taxes, wages, and other charges have been accounted for, so that leaves just the bonuses." Cynthia switched to a calculator on her desk and tapped in some numbers before continuing, "Using last year's bonuses to the employees leaves you a *profit* of $343."

Maggie let out an ear-splitting shriek and jumped out of her chair. She threw herself at John so enthusiastically his chair tipped over backwards, sending them both to the floor. "You did it! You did it!" she shouted over and over as they lay in a tangle.

John couldn't stop laughing.

CHAPTER 19

Other than offering a brief congratulation, Wes showed little more than lukewarm enthusiasm when John called. John couldn't tell if Wes was disappointed, or surprised, at his success.

"I believe we could schedule the final disposition of the estate for the eighth of January," Wes said matter-of-factly. "It shouldn't take the auditor more than three days to check the books."

"What auditor?"

"We have to verify the numbers with an independent auditor."

"You don't trust Cynthia? That's absurd!"

"It's not a matter of trust, John. I *know* Cynthia is honest, but in matters of this nature an independent, certified auditor has to confirm the numbers. It's a matter of legal protocol."

"I see. And you have someone, I suppose?"

"I do, they are an established accounting firm I use frequently, McGrath and Cottal. It's short notice, but I'm sure they will accommodate us. I'll have them contact Cynthia."

"Do I need to do anything?"

"No, it's all between Cynthia and the auditor at this point. Relax and enjoy your Christmas, John. You've earned it, and again, congratulations."

John hung up the phone, leaned back in his chair and let out a long sigh. "It's going to be another three weeks to finalize it."

Maggie sat across the table with a puzzled look on her face. "What was that about an auditor?"

"Some sort of legal bullshit. Wes has to have an independent audit performed. The good news is that he knows somebody who can get it done soon. Everything should be finalized on the eighth of January."

"It's just a formality, right?"

"According to Wes, but you know the auditor is going to ask about the deposit from Oxford."

"Maybe, but we can explain it, if necessary, and Wes can confirm it. If you're worried about the source of the deposit going public, I'm sure there's some sort of confidentiality requirement on the part of the auditor." Maggie stood up and walked around the table, behind John. She wrapped her arms around his neck and whispered in his ear, "Don't sweat the small stuff, enjoy the holidays."

That Christmas reminded John of the ones he had as a little kid. The local spruce were gangly and sparsely limbed, but the fun of cutting one himself made it something incredibly special, even if it did border on being homely. Billy McCrane insisted John and Maggie attend the Christmas pageant the youth group put on, and invitations for other gatherings carrying into the new year were generated from that event. It was almost a relief to take a break from the socializing when the new year finally arrived.

The call from Wes on the seventh was entirely unexpected. It was shortly after one in the afternoon.

"The auditor is done," Wes said in his usual curt fashion. "Can you be at Cynthia's at four, sharp?"

"Sure, but where are you? What's the hurry?"

"I'm on my way to Merrill Field. Reeder is going to pick me up. I'm as anxious to get this over with as you."

"I'll be there. By the way, Harley asked to be there, can I bring him?"

"Yes. I was going to call him anyway. Bring Maggie, too, if you'd like."

John was going to say good-bye, but the line was already dead. Instead, he turned to Maggie. "The auditor is done, and

Wes is flying in. We need to be at Cynthia's at four o'clock."

"That's weird. I wonder why the big hurry."

"Wes probably has a court date tomorrow," John said as he punched the number for Harley's cell, "and just wants to get this out of the way."

Harley was sitting in his truck at Cynthia's when John and Maggie pulled up. The weather had turned cold, and the windows on the battered pickup were frosted on the inside from his breath.

"Why are you waiting out here?" John asked. "It's got to be twenty below!"

"Wes told me to wait out here. We're supposed to go in together. Go figure."

As the three of them stepped through the door into the office, John had the feeling he was entering a tribunal. Three chairs had been placed in front of Cynthia's desk, where Wes sat. The auditor, a matronly looking woman sat behind him, as did Cynthia. Cynthia's eyes looked puffy, and her makeup appeared smudged.

"Come on in, and sit down, please," Wes said in a solemn manner. John, Harley and Maggie each took a chair. Wes stood up and motioned toward the matronly woman, "This is Eleanor Cottal, of McGrath and Cottal," the auditor smiled and nodded before Wes continued, "she served as the independent auditor in review of Ms. Smythe's books." He turned to the bookkeeper and auditor, "Maybe you ladies would like to wait in Cynthia's home while I wrap this up."

Eleanor Cottal quietly got up and walked around to the door into Cynthia's trailer. Cynthia stood up and sniffled. Two large tears made their way down her cheeks when she looked directly at John.

"I'm so sorry, John. So sorry," she said, then dashed through the door Eleanor Cottal had opened.

"What the hell was that all about?" John asked when the door had closed.

"It seems Eleanor found a discrepancy in the books," Wes said softly.

"Discrepancy? Like embezzlement?" Harley asked in disbelief.

"Oh, nothing illegal," Wes assured, "but something careless. It seems Cynthia missed a debit that has significant bearing on the disposition of the trust."

"Like what?" John demanded. "I went through everything with her. We double-checked. We triple-checked! She didn't miss a thing!"

"No, not for this year," Wes agreed. He turned the computer screen around so it was visible to the other three people in the room and walked around the desk and sat on the edge so he could point to the screen.

"This is the ledger for December of last year. You will see a debit against the Last Chance Adventures account on the thirty-first for fifteen hundred dollars. On that line is the annotation, 'Draw for Grant.'"

"So, what's the big deal?" Harley asked.

"There is nothing else noted for that draw," Wes said, "and no receipts to indicate it was anything other than a wage."

"Wait a minute," John interrupted, "Hardrock took his draws the middle of the month."

"He did. There was a draw the fifteenth of December, and for whatever reason, he took another one on the last day of December. He did not take a draw on the fifteenth of January. I suspect he wanted to leave money in his checking account for automatic payments while he was out at Last Chance in January."

John slumped back in his chair, closed his eyes, and tipped his head back. "What's the bottom line, Wes?"

"I'm sorry, John, but that fifteen hundred was, for want of any other evidence to the contrary, a wage. You owe yourself fifteen hundred dollars more in wages for the year, which will put the final balance for Last Chance Adventures slightly more than eleven hundred short of the required amount. That being the case, the trust must default to the secondary."

"That is such *bullshit!*" Harley roared, jumping up and pointing his finger at Wes. "You can't *do* that! It's not fair! It's fucking chickenshit lawyer stuff! It's..." Harley's words choked off in his rage.

Without moving, or opening his eyes, John said quietly, "Sit down, Harley. Please." Harley looked at John and slowly sat down. John sat up and looked at Wes. "So, I've lost the Last Chance."

"I'm sorry, yes."

"May I ask who the secondary is?"

Wes got up from the edge of the desk and returned to the chair behind it. He placed his hands on a binder laying on the desk, and shifted his gaze between the three people in front of him as he spoke.

"Harley, you and Maggie already knew how Hardrock felt about Last Chance. John, I think you have come to realize how much it meant to him, and why, over the past few months. When Hardrock came to me three years ago to make this trust, his primary concern was to preserve the intent, his dream, behind Last Chance. He wanted, first and foremost, for it to become a family legacy, which is why you were named primary beneficiary, John. Barring that, he wanted to ensure it stayed under the control of someone who saw it as he did, and would continue to run it as he had."

"Oh, get to the point," Harley growled.

Wes fixed a cold stare on the rash younger man until Harley shifted uncomfortably in his chair, then continued, "For whatever reason, and I sure as hell can't explain it, Hardrock felt that person should be Harley Pepperdine."

"No fucking way!" Harley gasped.

"Those were my exact sentiments," Wes said dryly, "but Hardrock was set on the idea."

"I own Last Chance?" Harley paused a moment, then jumped up and changed the question to a declaration. "*I* own Last Chance!" he shouted. "*Me!*"

"There is more to it than that," Wes continued in an even tone. "Hardrock directed the one existing share of Last Chance Adventures be split into two equal shares if the primary beneficiary did not succeed. Having seen enough twists in his life to expect the unexpected, Hardrock wanted an insurance policy, as it were, in case John made an honest effort, but failed."

"I don't understand," John said. "Last Chance Adventures is now Harley's, but the corporation is to be split into two shares?"

"Two equal shares, that's correct," Wes answered, "and I am to suggest to Mr. Pepperdine that he sell you one of those shares for any sum that is agreeable between the two of you."

"Hold on, hold on," Harley said waving his hands. "*I* own Last Chance now! Two shares, or not. I've put in nine years, busting my ass to keep Last Chance going! John's only put in one. Hell, six months ago he didn't even know what end of the highbanker to dump the dirt into! And now I'm supposed to make him an equal partner? *I don't think so!* Wes, I don't want to sell."

"Legally, that is your prerogative," Wes answered, scowling.

"*Harley*!" Maggie gasped in disbelief. "How could you do that?"

Harley looked at Maggie and John, pointed his finger and said with a smile, "Gotcha!"

A WORD FROM THE AUTHOR

First, I would like to thank you for reading this book. I have been living, working and raising my family in Alaska for over thirty years. For the majority of those years, I recorded my misadventures and observations about Alaskan life in an award-winning, weekly newspaper humor column.

A prodigious liar from an early age, I was forced to start writing things down as a means of keeping my stories straight. My writing has become the ultimate in irony: I used to be punished for lying, now I make a living at it. It's not all wonderful, however. When I tell people I make my living by lying, they immediately think I'm a politician.

When not writing I spend as much spare time as possible outdoors, with my wife. A fishaholic, recreational miner and gun crank, I can usually be found on the water's edge, or at the shooting range, when not tapping on the keyboard.

In addition to this novel, I have put together two collections of short humor pieces: *Of Moose and Men: A Skewed Look at Life In Alaska*, and *Of Moose and Men II: Home is Where the Harm Is.*

As with any author, reviews of this book would be appreciated greatly. And you can continue following my Alaskan ramblings by going to my blog at www.ommwriting.com.

There are strange things done in the midnight sun
By the men who moil for gold;
The Arctic trails have their secret tales
That would make your blood run cold...

From "The Cremation of Sam McGee"
by Robert Service